PETER McLEISH

To Emma

From one creative writer to
another — I hope it gives you
as much pleasure as it does me

Deborah Hatton

PETER McLEISH

DEBORAH LATHAM

SilverWood

Published in 2014 by SilverWood Books

SilverWood Books Ltd
30 Queen Charlotte Street, Bristol, BS1 4HJ
www.silverwoodbooks.co.uk

ISBN 978-1-78132-294-9 (paperback)
ISBN 978-1-78132-295-6 (ebook)

British Library Cataloguing in Publication Data
A CIP catalogue record for this book is available from
the British Library

Set in Bembo by SilverWood Books
Printed on responsibly sourced paper

For David John McDonald and Christopher John Davison, neither of whom I have met in person, but whose exercise of their respective professional talents has, for me, ranged from alleviating the consequences of life to reminding me of what can be most wonderful about it.

I would like to express my appreciation for the contributions (intended or otherwise) of Laurence Latham, Pamela Wentworth, Patti Taylor, Rebecca Martin, David ("I am that man!") Hayward, Nabeeh Marar, and last – but not least! – the actor Anton Lesser, for quite unknowingly, but always, from the very outset, 'being' Richard Taylor in this book.

Chapter 1

He assessed the conditions yet again. He'd done so several times already, but in his line of business, it paid to check and re-check. In spite of the grim, enclosing blanket of drizzling cloud above, the visibility to the target area was still good. He retrained the crosshairs of the rifle's sights onto it. That bend in the road, there, about a hundred yards away. That was the direction they'd be coming from. When they came into view around that curve, he'd have perhaps as much as five seconds to select his target and fire. Ample time, for someone of his skill.

He glanced over to his right, down the slope on the other side of the narrow, almost single-track road. A good steep slope, dotted with boulders, levelling out to the edge of a plantation of firs. Potentially extremely helpful, if things developed the way he expected them to. The road was already treacherously wet. And the camber after the bend would encourage descent in the desired direction. He'd had a fair bit of experience of the way a car with a suddenly dead driver behaved in certain types of terrain.

His head turned back to face in its original direction, and he stiffened to the alert as his eyes picked out the point in the distance where the road first came into view, about a mile away, winding around the shoulder of one of the several hill slopes between there and his own hidden vantage point. A small moving dot had appeared. Featureless at that distance, but as it drew nearer, he nodded with satisfaction. An anonymous silver saloon car. Two occupants. It was them.

He nestled down, settling into position, cradling the stock against his shoulder and lining up on the undefined area, about four feet above the road, where he estimated the driver's head and shoulders would be when the car finally traversed the bend. It was near, now. Just another few yards…

He sighted the crosshairs again, as the car emerged from around the shoulder of the hill. The head of the driver was framed in them within a second, momentarily imprinting like a still photograph on his brain. He'd wondered which of them would be driving; now he knew. Without hesitation, he squeezed the trigger. A small red dot sprang into being on the targeted forehead, which jerked violently backwards. The fingers on the steering wheel spasmed, then slid limply off as both hands fell away.

The effect on the trajectory of the car was instant. The man in the passenger seat had no time to react as it swerved sharply across the wet tarmac to its left, away from the gunman, and over the edge of the slope. That edge was steep enough to tip it sideways as its momentum carried it forward, sending it rolling over and over down the long hillside with an occasional crashing sound as it encountered a boulder, until at last it came to rest, on its wheels, down near the trees, sideways on to him, as neatly as if it had been parked there deliberately.

The gunman put down his rifle and reached for his field glasses. A streamer of smoke was starting to rise from under the wrecked and distorted bonnet. That was hopeful.

Yes! There was a flicker of flame. And again. Growing bigger. Another one, in a different place. The man in the driver's seat was just visible, only held upright by his seatbelt, shattered head fallen forward. The airbag had triggered, uselessly, obscuring any view of the other front seat, but the gunman was in no doubt that the other man – the real target of his attack – whether unconscious or dead, must also be pinned in place. There was no detectable movement in or around the vehicle other than from the dancing flames.

And if the other man wasn't already dead, he soon would be. The interior of the car was filling with smoke. Tongues of flame were licking the exterior of the driver's door from underneath the bodywork. He caught a flicker of orange from the area of the dashboard, curving around the side of the visibly deflating airbag. There'd be no explosion – it was just a petrol fire – but it had definitely penetrated the interior of the car. Suffocation, or immolation. Either way, they were both dead.

Satisfied, the gunman – a tall, powerfully built man with short-cropped fair hair and hooded blue eyes – got to his feet, resting the barrel of the rifle casually on his shoulder. For a few more moments he watched the coppery glow growing in intensity, the smoke billowing ever more energetically. Then he shrugged, slung the rifle over his other shoulder by its carrying strap, and strolled away. Job done.

He made his way unhurriedly up the hill to the crest, then down the other side, whistling between his teeth. Though, in a way, he regretted the fact that the long duel was over. It had given an edge, a particular stimulation to his life that he was going to miss. Still, there it was. These things couldn't last forever.

A few minutes later he'd reached his own car. Just in time; it was coming on to rain more heavily. He popped the boot, disassembled his rifle, and carefully stowed it into its customized case. Then he got in, putting the field glasses on the passenger seat. A large paper bag was already there; he picked it up, pulled the folded lips apart, and thrust his hand inside, extracting a thick brown bread sandwich, into which he bit with satisfaction. He sat chewing, looking absently at what could be seen of the view through the streams of rainwater pouring down the windscreen, until the sandwich was gone. He took a few pulls from a bottle of water, then yawned, and considered.

This was a sparsely populated area; the chances that another vehicle would be passing for quite some time were minimal. And, in any case, he was the other side of the hill from where the stricken car had crashed. Therefore, clearly nothing to do with him. He could afford a short nap, before heading for his next destination.

He reached down for the lever that allowed him to change the angle of the seat, reset it, and sank back, snuggling into position, making himself comfortable. He closed his eyes. He slept.

What he had not seen before he turned away, could not have seen at the angle of view from where he had been standing looking down at his handiwork, was that the passenger side door had been sprung open by one of the many impacts on its journey down the hill. When the abused vehicle finally came to rest, the man in the passenger seat was nearly insensible – but not quite.

Coughing weakly as the acrid smoke was inhaled into his lungs, he fought to open his eyes. His left hand wandered instinctively to the clip of his seatbelt. He hardly had the strength to push down the button to release the clasp, but in spite of the battering the car had taken it sprang out easily.

Every cell in his body felt raw and bruised, but he tried to force his limbs to move, aware, despite his receding consciousness, that it was imperative that he get out of the car. His head hurt; it must have made contact with something. His left shoulder hurt, too. He felt sick and dizzy, but his innate instinct to survive was urgently telling him to *move, move, get out*. He grunted with pain as he forced his body to swivel in the seat, weakly reaching for the edges of the door to pull himself out with his failing strength, pushing at the door itself with his foot to force it further open. It was only tenuously attached by its top hinge; the slight extra pressure sent it skewing away from the vehicle with a shriek of abused metal, stubbornly clinging on by the lower hinge.

He managed to make it to a standing position, even managed a few swaying steps away from the burning car, before outraged nature took its course and, like a discarded coat, he folded to the ground. He lay sprawled on his stomach, motionless under the drizzling sky, as the car went on smoking and flaming only a few feet away. Even when the rain began in earnest, striking the visible side of his face with heavy drops, soaking him as thoroughly as if he'd been submerged in a lake, he never moved.

The first I knew about any of this was when I saw the smoke.

I'd better make something clear; not everything I'm going to put on record here is my personal experience. It couldn't be – there were so many occasions when I wasn't personally present – but some of it I've been told by others; some of it I've had to extrapolate from subsequent events and outcomes. But this moment, when I first became conscious of that darker shadow swelling against the grey of the cloud-covered sky – this was the moment where I got involved.

Occasional visitor though I was, I knew the sight of smoke in the more remote parts of the Scottish Highlands isn't that unusual. But not so often on such a damp day as this was. And I strongly suspected that it shouldn't have been coming from anywhere near the fir plantation. Whatever its source, it probably couldn't take sufficient hold in the moisture-laden air to do any major damage, but maybe I ought to check it out. I wasn't comfortable with the image of explaining to Fergus – Fergus Riach, the owner – that I'd spotted his property on fire and ignored it.

So I changed direction towards the column of drifting smoke, cursing the way the rain had picked up since I'd embarked on my walk – the one that had started slightly south-east, then turned north in an arc that brought me back to the Lodge from the north-west. It had been one of my favourite walks ever since I was a little girl, and I often chose it. Because of the weather I'd almost turned back several times, but once I was past where it was as far back as it was forward, there was no point. And of course if you're not prepared to walk in the rain in the Highlands, you'd never walk there at all.

As I made my way through the soaking, shin-high clumps of heather, I couldn't help noticing the smoke wasn't the customary colour of an ordinary heath fire; it was a thick, ugly black. I began to feel unaccountably uneasy. What could be on fire, to be making smoke that colour? And it must have a fairly good hold after all, to be persisting in such a downpour. Though, happily, it looked as if the rain was going to let up shortly; the approaching clouds were becoming an encouragingly paler shade, rather than the dark grey they had been for the last half-hour or so.

By now I'd reached the edge of the plantation – Douglas firs, old enough to give a clearance of around ten feet to the lowest branches. Under them the ground was clearer, too – moss and fallen fir needles – so it was easier to make speed between the trunks toward where I estimated the source of the fire to be.

I felt tense. I supposed it was because 'fire' implies 'danger', and you never approach danger without that knot of apprehension creating itself in the pit of your stomach. Not if you're normal. I like to think I'm pragmatic; I'd vigorously deny that I'm particularly brave. Not when I'm anticipating danger, anyway. But I felt sure I'd be able to assess the level of any threat before I ended up in really serious trouble.

Famous last words.

The picture began to compile itself, the more I could see through the trees as I approached the further edge of the plantation, near the road. As all the elements fitted themselves into a coherent whole, I slowed, then stopped to stare for a few seconds, before forcing myself to go closer. My eyes flicked from each component of the scene to the next with growing horror.

The wrecked, smouldering car. The man lying crumpled on the soaked ground. The starred hole in the windscreen. The diminishing billows of black smoke. The passenger door hanging from one hinge, allowing a clear view of the interior. The tiny, sinking flames. The scorched car furnishings. The deployed airbags hanging flaccid, penetrated by the fire. The partially burned body in the driver's seat. The bullet hole in the skull. The smell of petrol and burnt car and burnt flesh.

I stared. Then I turned, bent double, and vomited violently. Once, then again. The third time, the only result was stomach acid, leaving a stinging sensation in my throat and mouth. For a while I continued to retch, even though there was nothing left to bring up. Then my knees gave out, and I collapsed sideways into a sort of sitting position, my weight supported on one hand. The other was over my mouth; whether because it was an instinctive physical reaction to shock or because I was automatically trying to muffle my panicked panting, I wasn't sure.

After a while I felt marginally better. Very marginally. Trying to ignore the foul taste in my mouth, I climbed reluctantly to my feet, and stood wavering for a moment. There was nothing to be done for the man in the car. But the other one might still be alive; he certainly didn't show any signs of having been burned. Though he, too, might have been shot, and the wound just wasn't visible from here. I had no choice but to go to see.

Slowly, I forced myself to approach. He was so still, he might very well be dead. I looked down at him, subliminally noticing the black jeans and black leather jacket, and the longish dark hair and neatly trimmed beard plastered to his head by the ministrations of the rain. Nervously, I crouched down next to him, and tried to remember the principles of the first aid course I'd done way back when, in my late teens. I pressed two fingers against the side of his throat under his jaw, to see if I could feel a pulse.

I could. He was alive! That was something, anyway.

The best thing I could do was to summon an ambulance, even though it might take quite a while for it to arrive. Maybe they'd send a helicopter. I rummaged in the usual pocket for my phone.

It wasn't there. It wasn't in any of my pockets. It couldn't have fallen out – they were all zipped or velcroed shut.

Damn, damn, *damn*! Of all the times! I must have left it in the Lodge. For once, forgotten to pick it up from the bedside table where I put it every night. Frustrating beyond measure, because it was something I almost never did. But, of course, the one time I really needed it…!

I'd have to fall back on that half-forgotten first aid course, after all.

He was lying on his stomach, his head turned to one side so that only the right side of his face was visible. His arms and legs were sprawled any which way, but didn't appear to be broken, unless there were any hairline fractures my hands were unable to detect. I wondered how safe it was to turn him over, but I really didn't have much choice. Wincing as much as if it was my own injured body that I was trying to turn, I carefully rolled him over onto his back, trying to protect his head as much as possible, wondering if he was concussed.

I was pretty certain on that point almost immediately. The left side of his face was an alarming sight, covered with blood diluted to various degrees by the water on the soaked ground it had been pressed against, and the hair was wet not just with rain but with blood. There was a darkening bruise on the temple, level with the eyebrow, and when I explored further I found a patch of lacerations on the scalp that would account for the bleeding. I know scalp wounds always look much more dramatic than they really are, but that bruise looked quite a brute; concussion must be a virtual certainty. There didn't appear to be any other head wounds, not that I could see.

It was only then that it occurred to me that *he* was probably carrying a phone. Most likely in one of the breast pockets of his jacket. I pressed my palm down onto the right breast, but there was nothing in there. I could feel something in the left pocket, though. I lifted the left side of his jacket, intending to see what it was. And froze, staring.

Not just because the left breast of the T-shirt he was wearing underneath was drenched in blood.

There was something else.

He was wearing a shoulder holster. A gun.

I stared at it as if it was a snake. By the shape of the butt, it was some sort of automatic pistol, not a revolver.

A gun…

Who *was* this man?

Slowly, as if afraid he'd suddenly spring into life and attack me, I reached into the pocket I'd been targeting, and pulled out – with no little difficulty, since both it and the pocket were soaking wet – his wallet. With my eyes repeatedly flicking nervously back to his face for any signs of awareness, I opened it.

An ordinary sort of wallet; cash, credit cards, that sort of thing. But with it was another, smaller, flap-type wallet, about two inches by three. I opened the flap. From behind a protective plastic covering, his photograph stared glassily back at me from a warrant card that identified him as Peter Blair McLeish, an officer with the London Metropolitan Police.

A police officer. Surely that wouldn't account for the pistol? The average UK copper doesn't carry. But if he was with one of the specialist teams, or an undercover man, maybe it would. Either way – police. When I'd been fearing some kind of criminal. I felt a surge of relief. Though what a London Met officer would be doing in Scotland was beyond me.

But that blood…! Aware that I was trembling slightly, I shoved his wallet into my own pocket and looked more closely. I saw that something, presumably during that violent tumble down the hill, had sliced deeply into his trapezius muscle, halfway between his neck and the point of his shoulder. It was still bleeding quite freely, and clearly had been for some time. Between that and his head wound, he must have lost a fair bit of blood. Not a dangerous amount, but probably enough to significantly weaken him.

I bit my lip, thinking. I had a couple of spare handkerchiefs in one of my pockets, but how could I strap them on so as to apply sufficient pressure? The bald truth was that, beyond a certain point, I couldn't. But by dint of a fairly inventive combination involving the nylon scarf that I keep as a standby in one of my jacket pockets and the thin leather belt that I tugged free of his jeans, I managed to improvise a makeshift arrangement which I hoped would be robust enough to hold the handkerchiefs in place. There was nothing else I could do. My hands were slippery with blood at the end of the process, but hopefully the bleeding should be staunched, or at least reduced, for now.

Then I remembered I was trying to find his phone. Gingerly I turned him again onto his back, wiped my bloody hands on the soaking grass, and went through the rest of his pockets. No joy. Had he dropped it somewhere? Had it fallen out of his pocket during the crash? No way of knowing.

So – apart from the fact that he was soaked through, possibly concussed, most likely in shock, a prime candidate for hypothermia, bleeding like a stuck pig, totally unconscious, and there was no way of getting help – he was doing just fine, then.

Although – maybe not totally unconscious. Under the pale lids, I could see his eyeballs rolling about, as if he were trying to find his way back from wherever he now was. The rhythm of his breathing was picking up, too. I hesitated, then put a hand on his uninjured shoulder and gave it a gentle shake.

"Hello?" I prompted. "Can you hear me?"

He groaned. I winced, but gave him another gentle shake.

"Can you hear me?" I repeated.

This time, his eyelids began to flicker open. The eyes eventually revealed were dark brown and dazed, the pupils slightly dilated. He stared at me vacantly for several seconds; I could see the exact moment when intelligence returned and he became properly focused on my face.

"Peter," I said to him. He continued to stare at me. "Peter," I said again. "Listen to me. Can you hear me?"

His lips worked.

"What…?" he husked, at last.

"My name," I said, carefully and distinctly, "is Jenny. Peter, listen to me. You've been in an accident." Liar. No way had that been an accident. "I need to ring for an ambulance, but I don't have my phone, and I can't find yours. Have you got one?"

His right hand wandered weakly over the area of his chest, but he clearly wasn't capable of finding it himself.

"Can I look for it?" I asked him. As if I hadn't already. Though a double-check wouldn't come amiss; the state I was in, I could easily have overlooked a pocket somewhere.

He closed his eyes; I took that for assent. But with no more luck than before; if he'd had a phone, he'd definitely become separated from it in the course of the crash. I cast a despairing glance at the area between us and the car, but there was nothing visible there. It might even have fallen through the open side window and be lying somewhere on the hillside above. And if it was in the car, there was little hope it had remained undamaged by the fire. I wasn't sure my stomach was strong enough to contemplate going to look, in any case. The stink of the scorched carcase inside was sickening.

There was only one thing for it. I had to get him back to the Lodge, as quickly as possible, and phone from there. It never occurred to me to leave him and make better speed by myself. I simply couldn't abandon him.

"Peter, I don't think you've broken anything, but can you find out? Carefully!" I added hastily.

He began to move, slowly, and flinched as the pain of his injured shoulder bit. He cried out, and I winced; the sound of true agony isn't comfortable hearing. I reached out a hand in protest, but he brushed it away, and slowly, painfully, hoisted himself into a sitting position. He stayed still for a few moments, his head hanging. Then, with an effort, he raised it.

"Nothing broken," he whispered.

I breathed a sigh of relief.

"Can you stand? We need to get to my house. It's about a mile." I looked at him doubtfully. Was he really in good enough shape to even make the attempt? But what other choice was there? "I'll help you – if you can stand?"

He nodded, slowly. I reached down and he took hold of my upper arm; I supported him as best I could as he climbed laboriously to his feet and stood, swaying slightly, still clutching me. Then, as I'd done earlier, he abruptly doubled over and vomited. I thought he was going to collapse again, but he managed to stay on his feet, albeit lurching somewhat alarmingly once or twice. I helped him upright once more.

"All right now?" Stupid question. Whatever he was, 'all right' was just about the last phrase on the list to describe him, and between the concussion and the blood loss, let alone anything else, he was in a pretty poor way. Nevertheless he nodded, gasping slightly. I looked at him carefully, assessing his physical state.

"Come on, then," I said. Mindful of the shoulder holster, I positioned myself on his right, took his right arm and put it across my shoulders, grasping his wrist with one hand, and putting the other around his waist. He was taller than me by about eight or nine inches; supporting him wasn't going to be easy. Already his weight bore down on me heavily.

I had a premonition this was going to be one of the hardest miles I'd ever travel in my life.

On the other side of the hill the gunman had roused, and seen that the rain had let up. He glanced at his wristwatch. He'd been asleep for over an hour. That was about right; enough rest to see him back on his way south to London. A long drive. He pulled himself up, reset the angle of the car seat to its normal driving position, and gunned the engine.

When he came to the first T-junction, he considered his route. Avoiding the scene of the hit would send him many miles to the west before he could pick up the next road south. Did he really need to bother? The chances of encountering another car anywhere on this tiny backwater road were minimal at best; the chances of doing so at the crash site were vanishingly small. No, he'd go east. It would save time.

But as he neared the scene, his eyes automatically going across the intervening distance to the foot of the hill where smoke still rose from the burning car, he saw movement. He stamped on the brake, leaving the engine running, and grabbed for the field glasses.

Two tiny figures sprang toward him through the lenses. He muttered an imprecation under his breath. He'd been careless. Assumed, when he should have checked. That tall, bearded, staggering figure was McLeish. Still alive.

He turned his attention to the person trying to support the injured man as they slowly made their way into the plantation of firs. A woman with rain-darkened, brownish-fair hair. Ah, yes; he knew who she must be, given the direction they were heading. When he'd reconnoitred the area a couple of days ago, he'd checked out the house where she was based, as the only habitation within ten miles of the spot. It was a single-storey building, situated on the edge of a pine forest – hence its name, Giuthas Lodge – and lay at the end of a small dirt track about a mile south of the position he'd chosen for his attack; the turn-off was about half a mile to the east. It belonged to her parents, so the population of the local pub had helpfully informed him when he'd engaged them in apparently casual conversation. They were English – name of Taylor – based on the outskirts of London, but apparently the mother's side of the family were Scots, and they'd inherited the lodge when the grandmother had died. They mostly let it out to holidaymakers, but sometimes used it themselves. He'd established that at the moment only the daughter was staying there, had been for a week or more; her name, he'd been told, was Jenny Gregory.

He'd always been good at getting people to tell him more than they realized.

He lowered the glasses and thought, concisely and swiftly, as the two in the distance made their painful way among the trees, out of sight. If they were on the move, it meant that, for whatever reason, if they'd called for help, it certainly wasn't coming here. So maybe, for some reason, they hadn't been able to. And McLeish couldn't be in good shape after the beating such a violent crash must have administered, which implied moving was his only option. So perhaps the only way to get help was for that woman to take him to the lodge and summon it from there.

He grinned, buoyed by the knowledge that the duel wasn't over, after all. That there were still things he could do to hurt McLeish.

The next turning on the right in this direction was the track to Giuthas Lodge. At the speed they were moving, he had plenty of time to get there ahead of them.

He put the field glasses back onto the passenger seat, and purposefully set the car in motion.

Chapter 2

How we managed that journey astonishes me even to this day.

We had no breath to spare for talking, and we both kept catching our feet in the wet heather; him because he could hardly lift each foot from the ground to put it in front of the other, me because I was so concentrated on trying to support his weight that I hadn't much attention to spare for watching where I was putting my feet.

What would have taken me about fifteen minutes to walk by myself took the two of us closer to three-quarters of an hour. He was so weak that we had to keep stopping for him to gather himself for the next stretch, and I dared not let him go down, in case he couldn't be got up again, either by himself or by me. So we'd stand there, him swaying, me braced under him and against him, both of us panting; after a few moments I'd say something like, "All right?", and he'd nod without speaking and make the next effort. Despite my attempts at bandaging, his exertions were making the blood continue to flow from his wounded shoulder; every now and again, beneath the leather jacket, I could see the red stain on his T-shirt spreading, slowly but surely.

Even when the lodge was in sight, nestling in its hollow in the landscape, it felt as if it was taking forever to get there. As if for every step we moved toward it, it moved away. But gradually, tortuously, we closed in on it.

It wasn't until we got close to the doorstep that I noticed that something about the door wasn't right.

Peter McLeish was clearly close to crossing the borderline of consciousness, and his weight was bearing down on me more and more heavily; I was desperately hoping he'd hold up until we got inside, but my confidence on that front was rapidly dwindling towards zero. And when I saw the door, I instinctively halted; inevitably, he went down then, and I couldn't hold him, only try to stop him falling too heavily. I hastily knelt and checked, but he'd merely lapsed into unconsciousness. Which was in itself a matter of urgent concern. However, my real attention at that moment was on the door. I rose to my feet and stared at it.

When I'd left earlier, to take my walk, I'd shut and locked that door.

I know there are some people living out in remote rural areas like this one who still feel able to leave their doors unlocked, though they're probably a dying breed, the way the world's gone. But it was something I'd never done, even here. I'm from the south-east of England; I always lock a house, any house, when I leave it. And that's what I'd done earlier. I'd even checked the front door with a hefty push, the way my husband, who'd verged on obsessive about things like that, had trained me into doing. So I knew there was no possibility that I'd been negligent, left it ajar by accident.

Now, it was open. Only just. But open.

Somebody had broken in. Had to have done.

I felt a surge of nervous adrenalin. What should I do? Having struggled so hard to get here, now I was afraid to go in – but I couldn't stay out here, either. And the man sprawled in an ungainly tangle of limbs at my feet certainly couldn't afford to stay out here; he was wet and cold and in shock, and he desperately needed to be dry and warm and inside.

But what if whoever had broken in was still in there? What would I do? How would I cope? Would it be dangerous to go in? I was a jumble of emotions: not only afraid, but also angry with myself for being so indecisive in a crisis. But I knew and was forced to accept one thing.

Doing nothing wasn't an option.

And neither was carting my man off anywhere else. Because there was nowhere else. Not for many miles.

I thought of his automatic, cradled in the shoulder holster. But I knew nothing about guns. I wouldn't know a safety catch if I saw one, and certainly not whether it was on or off. A gun I didn't know how to operate and couldn't be sure would fire was no use to me.

I swallowed nervously, crept up to the right-hand window – as if *I* were the intruder! – and very, very cautiously moved my head past the brickwork to where I could see inside. No movement in the living room. Bent double to stay out of sight, I scrambled with an undignified gait past the door to the other window; again, within, all was still. I hesitated, fighting the instincts still screaming at me to flee, then forced myself to make a circuit of the whole building, the same surge of fear churning in my stomach at every window I approached.

Nothing. No sign of anyone.

I let out a long, shuddering breath of relief, but my heart was still pounding wildly. Just because whoever it had been was no longer there, didn't mean they weren't still around somewhere nearby.

Or that they wouldn't decide to come back.

There was nothing I could do about those possibilities. What I needed to do now was go inside and make absolutely sure there was no one there, then get back to the unconscious Peter and get him inside. Somehow.

I fearfully pushed open the door and made a tentative survey of the interior, ready at every instant to take to my heels if need be. Thankfully, no need. I went back outside.

I quickly established that, slightly built as my new acquaintance was, I was only going to be able to move him by dint of some inappropriately robust handling for someone in his state; I simply wasn't strong enough to treat him with the care he needed. As I struggled to haul him up over the single step that led into the lodge, I could tell that, as I had feared, his shoulder was bleeding again, with renewed vigour. I could feel the warm flow running over the hand with which I was gripping him under his left armpit.

The living room was as far as he was going; I was nearing the limit of my strength, such as it was, and I'd never lift him up onto either of the beds in any case. But first, panting heavily, I laid him down on the tiled floor of the hallway, awkwardly trying both to lower him gently and at the same time support his lolling head so it didn't smack against the floor as he went down; despite what you've seen, unconscious people don't helpfully keep their heads up and forward, the way stricken heroines so often used to do in films. Then, with anxious glances back at him, I hurried to the kitchen, absently wiping the fresh blood on my hand onto my jeans, and swept the vinyl tablecloth off the large, square table. I took it into the living room and laid it out in the area between the two sofas and the fireplace; the floor rugs in front of the sofas were hastily pushed aside, out of the way, sliding easily over the ancient, polished pine floorboards.

Ever since, I've always thought how very strange that behaviour was. We never know how we're going to react in an emergency, do we? Why on earth, in the circumstances, was my subconscious insisting I protect the floor from bloodstains, the way I did? To this day, I don't understand it. Here was a badly injured man, and all I could think about was keeping the floor clean – how irrational was *that*?

Except that I wasn't consciously thinking any such thing, of course. It just felt like the necessary thing to do, so I did it. Simple as that.

I went back into the hall, and with an effort that I thought for a few moments was going to be beyond me, I lifted him again by the shoulders and dragged him into the living room, manhandling him onto the tablecloth. In purely practical terms, it had been a sound decision, that tablecloth – it was already smeared with juicy, dark red trails of blood in the area of his left shoulder.

"Woh. For someone who wouldn't make a decent windbreak, you – are – heavy, pal," I told him, panting, as I straightened up.

It got no reaction, of course. I wondered if it would have, even had he been conscious. Anyway, I wasn't criticizing his build; I wasn't exactly a heavyweight myself, not with all the walking I did. Though the comfort eating after my marriage ended had bequeathed me a few extra pounds in one or two places that had proved more than durable in spite of my best efforts. Ah, well; you can't abuse your body – even for a reason like that – and not expect consequences.

I glanced longingly at the sofas. I was sorely tempted to collapse onto one of them, but knew I mustn't. There were things he needed me to do. Like phone for help.

I puffed out an exhausted sigh, and tried to remember where I'd left my mobile. On my bedside table, of course. Must be. Where else would I have left it? I was certain of that because at some point the previous night it had somehow been nudged right to the edge of the table – presumably when I'd put it down, last thing – and I distinctly remembered that when I'd picked up my wristwatch while dressing this morning I'd managed to catch the phone and knock it onto the floor. I'd promptly picked it up to check it was all right before putting it back on the table so as to finish doing up my watch strap. That memory was clear. That had definitely happened today. So, even though I was still cursing the fact that I'd managed to forget to take it out with me for once, at least I knew, without any doubt, where it was.

A few moments later, I knew, without any doubt, that it was no longer there.

Not on the table, not on the floor, not even under the bed. There *was* nowhere else. Nowhere else it could be. Not if it had simply fallen off the table again.

I rose to my feet and stared at the place on the tabletop where it had been, as if, by doing so, I could somehow summon it into existence.

Then, as my eyes swept round the room, looking for it in places where it couldn't possibly be, I realized there was something else that should have been there that now wasn't.

My laptop was gone. It should have been where I'd left it last night, at the right hand end of the dressing table. It wasn't there. I felt punch-drunk.

Of course, in these circumstances, your mind for some reason wants to insist that there must be some other explanation, wants to make you doubt that you've remembered accurately, tries to insist you must have done something other than what you know you did do. Why does it behave like that? On this occasion, probably because the logical explanation, the obvious one, was one I didn't want to contemplate, I suppose.

That whoever had broken in had taken my phone and my laptop.

That made me feel very, very vulnerable.

I forced myself to table that problem for the moment. I still needed to phone for help, and there was still the landline. I went back into the living room, casting an anxious glance at my patient; he was motionless, but apparently breathing regularly. I went across to the window sill where the phone lived, and picked up the receiver.

Completely dead.

I stared at it in denial, panic starting to rise inside me. Then I began to follow the cable around to the junction box, which was hidden from view behind the easy chair in the corner of the room between the window and the fireplace. When I pulled the chair aside, I couldn't prevent a sharp intake of breath.

The junction box had been ripped out of the wall. The wires leading into it had been cut. I had no way of contacting the outside world.

The car. Somehow, I'd have to get him into the car. Drive him to a hospital myself. Though how I was going to get him back outside and into the car was something I didn't want to contemplate. It was parked in the usual place, in the slot on the west side of the lodge, which made it just visible to the left when in this room. Given my preoccupations at the time, I'd not even given it a glance when I'd approached with my living burden. Now I looked out of the window at it, as if that would shore up my courage.

It didn't.

I stared in disbelief for a moment, then ran out of the room, out of the front door, jerking to a halt about six feet away from my vehicle, my eyes flicking frenetically from one tyre to the other. Then, although already sure what I'd see, I went round to the other side, and looked at the other two tyres.

Exactly the same. All completely and utterly flat, and all with a small, jagged hole in the tyre wall.

The boot wasn't quite closed. Someone had jemmied it open. I looked inside. The spare tyre had one of those same holes in it.

I reached down to touch tentatively at the edges of the incision, and was more afraid than ever. I'd never seen a real bullet hole before today, but I was pretty certain what had been used to make those punctures.

I'd heard that fear makes your mouth dry, but I'd never experienced it myself. Until now. I looked back at the living room window. Who was it that I'd undertaken to help? Because I couldn't believe that this persecution was directed at me. It *must* be him.

Someone had shot at the car he was in, killing his companion, and leaving him for dead. Someone had broken into the lodge, taken my mobile, taken my laptop, vandalized the other phone, and shot holes in all the tyres on my car. Not just the two that would have rendered it immobile. All five, even the spare. Not so much making, as hammering home, a point. Systematically and thoroughly removing every way I might have had of summoning help for him.

Not short of a ten mile hike to the next nearest habitation, anyway.

And I didn't have the time for that. Nor the inclination. It would mean leaving him unconscious and alone, at the mercy of his persecutor. And that, though I was scared, I was not prepared to do, knowing what I knew. So, even if I'd had the courage to do it, which I didn't feel sure of, at that moment – I simply couldn't do it. The man in that room needed me. Needed me now. I was all he had.

I stared round without really seeing what I was looking at, not really helped by the fact that my eyes were blurring with tears of fright. My mind was too filled with the image of whoever was doing this being somewhere nearby, monitoring his victim – perhaps watching me, at this very moment.

I shivered, and hurried back inside, slamming the front door behind me. The lock was now useless, irretrievably damaged by the break-in, but there were still a couple of hefty bolts, which I swiftly threw across. I leaned back against the door for some moments, breathing hard. And thinking hard. Then I went back into the living room and stood looking down to the motionless body on the floor.

We live in a world where it's very hard to tell who's on the side of the angels these days. Bad people do bad things, certainly; but very often so-called good people do bad things, too, as if the end does justify the means. Who was this man? What scenario was being played out here? In the terms I was using, was he a bad man, or a good man?

I had no real way to make a judgement, no body of evidence, no basis on which to reach a conclusion. Except the fact that he was a police officer, albeit one who carried a gun – and I harbour doubts how much angels value the kind of assistance offered them via the barrel of a gun.

I could only do what my nature dictated, stick to my own rules of engagement with life, and hope they led to the right outcome. And my nature was to want to help. I just hoped I was helping someone who met my definition of a good man.

I took a deep breath, making a conscious effort to ignore my fears, since it was clear they weren't going to helpfully go away by themselves. Now I needed to prioritize, settle on what to do first.

Wet and cold. He needed to be dry. He needed warmth.

I took the box of matches from its customary hiding place behind the vase on the mantelpiece and, dropping to my knees, lit the fire. I'd never been so thankful for Mother's insistence that we always laid a new fire immediately after clearing the ashes of the previous one, ready to light when needed. The scent of pine was soon stealing out into the room as the flames took hold. By then I'd gone out and raided the linen cupboard and the bedrooms, assembling what I needed to make him an improvised bed. I made it up on the floor beside where he lay, hoping that, when the time came, I'd be able to get him onto it without too much risk to his shoulder; but I wasn't overly hopeful, given how heavy an inert adult body can be to move.

I returned to the linen cupboard and got out a couple of thick towels, ready to dry him once I'd got his soaking clothes off him – something that was becoming top priority, if he wasn't to contract pneumonia on top of everything else.

I stood for a moment, looking down at his body sprawled helpless at my feet. Really looking at him, for the first time. Initially – as no man or woman can stop themselves doing when they first encounter someone of the opposite sex – I must have subconsciously assessed his appearance. But whatever agenda my subconscious had been following then, that hadn't been the time to analyze its conclusions. His looks hadn't been the first priority of my conscious mind; I'd been more focused on his long-term survival than his physical characteristics. Now I could catalogue them: tall, lean, and of the dark-eyed, dark-haired type I've always favoured. I estimated him to be in his late thirties.

I went on studying him for several seconds. Then I knelt beside him.

Sounds sexy, does it? Stripping an unconscious, attractive man?

Well, let me tell you, it's damned hard work! Especially if you've not been trained to do it, as a medical professional would be. And wet clothes are hard enough to take off your own body, let alone when the body in question is someone else's and out of its senses; the material drags and resists being separated from the equally damp skin it's clinging to. I had to keep rolling him onto one side or the other, tugging the wet fabrics off his uncooperative limbs – and he was long-shanked, this one – all the time trying not to exacerbate any of the damage he'd already suffered, and especially not to make his shoulder bleed any worse. I didn't entirely succeed on that front; the vinyl tablecloth was definitely turning out to be an inspired decision. I just hoped he'd been correct with that self-assessment that he hadn't any broken bones. Maybe he hadn't, before I started heaving him around so unceremoniously; he might not have been so convinced now, had he been in a fit state to monitor his current condition.

And the process doesn't exactly do anything for the subject's dignity, either. Just as well he was out of his senses. Mind you, by the time I'd tugged his underpants down his legs and free of his ankles and tossed them who knows where, I was in no condition to appreciate him even had he been Michelangelo's David. I was worn out! Today's big discovery about myself: manhandling a clammy, comatose, injured man does nothing to arouse my baser instincts. Other than my protective one, maybe.

My handling must have been causing him pain because, despite being unconscious, from time to time he uttered low moans. I flinched every time he did that, but I had to get him dry, and I had to clean and rebandage that shoulder of his. I was aware of the risks of unbandaging a wound, but since there was no way of knowing how soon I could get him into the hands of medical professionals, and the makeshift bandage I'd improvised out by the fir plantation was by now no longer fit for purpose, I was more worried about the risk of infection than I was of more bleeding. By being meticulously careful, I managed to keep the fresh blood flow to a minimum. But I'd never learned how to do stitches, so the best I could do, once I'd cleaned it with some diluted antiseptic, was use a few strip plasters from our first aid kit to try to ensure the edges of the sliced skin were kept together before I bandaged a thick pad of lint over the wound, hopefully thoroughly enough to ensure it wouldn't move, even if he did. The rest of the antiseptic solution dealt with the lacerations on his scalp; they were still oozing tiny trickles of blood, but nothing like as much. They'd soon seal themselves over.

At last, with a great deal of difficulty, I managed to heft him onto the improvised bed and cover him with a duvet, ensuring his head was propped in a comfortable position, so he wouldn't end up with a cricked neck to add to his woes. He had more than his fair share of those, at the moment, it seemed to me. He might not have broken bones, but he was certainly developing a fine crop of bruises in various places. He'd probably feel as if he'd been put through a washing machine on the spin cycle by the time he came round again.

I got wearily to my feet, checked the fire, and put a couple more logs on it. Finally, I draped his wet clothes over the fireguard and stood it a safe distance away from the emanating, pine-scented heat. The holster and gun I put on the seat of the sofa by his feet.

After that I was simply too exhausted to think about anything else. I went to the other sofa, collapsed wearily down on it full-length, and within moments I was as completely out of it as he was.

The gunman peered cautiously over the top edge of the depression, ringed on three sides by a combination of larches and pines, in which Giuthas Lodge nestled. He was scanning the windows for signs of movement. None were visible.

He'd hidden his car off the track, deep in the trees, and waited; he'd have been virtually impossible to see, but he'd had a pretty clear view of the approach to the lodge. It had taken an encouragingly long time for the two struggling figures to come into view. That must mean that McLeish was in a pretty poor state. He'd watched their painful journey with satisfaction until they passed from his sight into the enclosing arms of the bowl in which the lodge stood. Then he'd waited for another hour, to be on the safe side – and to allow for the results of his attentions to the house and car to register their full emotional impact – before making his approach.

The bedroom windows were on the far side of the building from where he now was, so he carefully circled round the back. There was no hint of anyone moving inside the kitchen, at least. Safe enough to approach from this angle, then. He topped the slope and scrambled down into the small back garden, then, bending low, ran across the rough lawn, until he was by the back door. From there, he carefully edged his way to the window of the back bedroom. The curtains were pulled back; there was no one in there.

He progressed to the other bedroom window and cautiously peered through. Here the curtains were partially drawn, but he had a clear enough view to establish that there was no one visible there, either. They must be in one of the front rooms.

He made his way to the front corner of the lodge, sparing a brief moment to appreciate the efficiency of his handiwork on the immobilized car. Then he crouched down, edging slowly to the living room window. Moving slowly enough not to alert anyone's peripheral vision, he moved his head upward far enough for his eyes to get a clear view of the interior.

There they were. The woman – she was in her early or mid-thirties, he estimated – stretched out on her stomach on a sofa, facing the window. Asleep, apparently. Her head turned to one side, one hand flat under her cheek, strands of her brownish-fair hair still clinging damply to her face; had her eyes been open, she'd have been looking straight at him. On the floor at a right angle to her, sideways on to the merrily burning fire in the hearth, McLeish, in makeshift bedding. Whether asleep or unconscious, it was impossible to say; only the top of his head was visible from where the gunman stood.

He straightened up, slowly, and looked at them for a while. Then he grinned, briefly.

"Sweet dreams, Jenny Gregory," he said under his breath, in a tone that promised anything but.

When I woke, for a moment I was disoriented. Then I took in the sight of the man on the floor, and recollection hit like the proverbial pile driver. I jerked upright and hastily looked around, but everything seemed to be normal, despite the panicky thudding of my heartbeats. Had anything happened while I was asleep?

I crept to the door and listened, but all was silent. I nervously checked the other rooms, but they were as empty as before. I breathed a sigh of relief, and went back into the living room.

The colour of the light outside indicated the day was drawing near to dusk. I must have been asleep for something close to three hours. I glanced at the fire, which was sinking. Better put another couple of logs on, to keep the temperature up.

I did that, then turned to look at my patient, dusting my hands on my jeans. His breathing was shallow and regular; maybe his blackout had transmuted into ordinary sleep. But if it had, he might wake up at any moment. I wanted to be ready when he did. The ensuing conversation had the potential to be extremely – what would be the most apt description? – interesting? As a euphemism, it would do. Until we got to the bit about the dead man still sitting in the burned-out car on the hillside, of course. 'Intense' might be a more appropriate word then.

I couldn't help wondering why he hadn't reacted to those things at the time. He'd been only a few yards from the still smouldering car when I'd been urging him to his feet. How could he not have seen it? Or smelled the horrific smell coming from it? I could only conclude that he'd been so dazed, so disoriented, so distracted by my presence and what I had been urging him to do, that those things had simply failed to register. He'd only been half-conscious at best, concussed, and in shock; maybe that combination had conspired to blank out everything else. If that was true, I could only be grateful. It would have been too complicated to try to deal with that as well, on top of dealing with a shocked and injured man. It was going to be hard enough when I did have to. And it was inevitable that I was going to have to, at some point. I tried to put it out of my mind for now.

I went out again and used the bathroom, then realized I was both thirsty and hungry – physically hungry, that is, though, perversely, I didn't feel much like eating. I went to the kitchen and drank a couple of glasses of water. Doing so made me wish I could get some liquid into my patient. He'd lost a fair bit of blood, though I still didn't consider it a dangerous amount, and there was the possibility of dehydration. But unless he came round, I didn't know how I could do it; I didn't want to risk pouring water down his throat while he was unconscious only for him to end up choking on it. I bit my lip, trying to decide which was the lesser of two evils. In the end, I opted for waiting for him to come round before I tried it. But I wished I could know if it was the right decision.

Rifling through the refrigerator produced some kind of savoury pastry slice. I took it back into the living room and forced myself to eat it, watching Peter McLeish sleep, thinking about the events of the day, and speculating on what a London-based police officer was doing up here in Scotland. Besides being shot at and half-killed.

I looked out of the window at the falling dusk with sudden nervousness. What if his attacker hadn't gone, but was still around? The break-in, the damage, showed he'd obviously known this was a potential refuge for his victim. What if he was out there, planning a further attack, waiting for darkness to fall?

What should I do? What could I do?

Make sure everything we might need was in this room, and barricade us in, as far as I could. What might we need? The first aid kit was already here. Food. Drink. More logs. Some proper bedding for me – assuming I could manage to sleep, in the circumstances. A change of clothes? No, I could do that before shutting us in. A torch. Candles, in case something happened to the electricity supply...?

At that point I did a mental double-take. Was this getting ridiculous? Had I watched too many fictional thrillers on television? Was I letting my imagination run stupidly wild? Overreacting?

I glanced again at the mute warning of the wrecked telephone junction box and decided I didn't care if I was. That damage was real, and deliberate, not imagined. If someone had done that to the phone, he might be equally prepared to sabotage the electrics. I could see nothing against it being a perfectly valid possibility – other than my wishing it was not. So, better safe than sorry – and right now I felt anything but safe, and definitely pretty sorry for myself.

Despite the fact that they'd be worried when I didn't reply, I hoped my parents were trying to reach me. I didn't want them distressed, but if they couldn't contact me, they might alert someone. Cherishing that hope, I set about collecting the items on my mental list, bringing them into the living room as quietly as I could, so as not to disturb the sleeper.

I needn't have worried; he never so much as stirred. I was glad about that. Sleeping was the best thing he could possibly do at the moment. The great restorative. In a way, I envied him. I wished I, too, was unaware of mental distress, physical pain, tension, anxiety, the knowledge of the dead man in the burned-out car, the dread that we were the targets of the man out there, whoever he was...

I changed my clothes and used the bathroom once more. Then I collected one of the kitchen chairs, to wedge under the handle of the living room door, and took up the stout oak walking stick that had belonged to my grandfather and that my mother had kept here after he died, as a potential means of defence.

There was nothing more I could think of to do.

Except what I did do, which was to spend most of what seemed an endless night on alert, too tense to sleep properly. Instead, dozing only fitfully, starting nervously at every slight sound, putting more logs on the fire when needed, and generally watching over the sleep of Peter McLeish.

I hoped he'd appreciate it.

Chapter 3

It was close to six o'clock the next morning when he finally stirred.

At times it had felt as if the night was never going to end, but at last it had. Thankfully without incident, despite my fears. I pushed aside my duvet, rose from the sofa, and went to the window to scan the surroundings. An unbroken blanket of light grey cloud still covered the ever lightening sky – this being Scotland in early summer, it had never truly got dark, of course – but there didn't seem to have been any more rain overnight. There was no sign of anyone, no hint of movement, other than the tree tops gently moving in the morning breeze.

The pile of logs I'd laid in had been much reduced in the course of the night, but there were still a few left. I knelt down by the fire and put on a couple more. Their predecessors had done their job; the room was beautifully warm.

I was crouched, waiting for the new logs to catch the flames, when I heard a faint stir behind me. I swivelled round, sharply. He was rousing. I turned to kneel beside him.

Even before his eyes opened, his forehead was drawn into a frown. He must be in pain. When he saw me, the frown deepened. Due to the concussion, he might not even remember me from the day before, or what had happened to him. I tentatively tried a welcoming smile.

"Hello," I said.

"Who are you?" he returned, ignoring the greeting. His voice was husky, as if stiff from disuse. "Where is this?" He had a Scots accent, which was no great surprise, given his name; a lowland Scot, if my untrained Sassenach ear was reporting accurately.

"My name's Jenny," I said, just as I had yesterday. "This is my parents' house. I brought you here."

He stared at me, confused, visibly trying to remember.

"Why? What—?" he stumbled.

"You were in a car accident." I gave him the half-truth again. "You've hurt your head and your shoulder, and you've lost quite a bit of blood. Are you thirsty?"

He nodded.

"Okay – hold on a minute." I got to my feet and retrieved a bottle of water from the stash of supplies, unscrewed the cap, knelt back down and held it out to him. He automatically started to slide his left hand out from under the duvet, that being the one nearest to me, but quickly arrested the movement, hissing through his teeth as the pain of his wounded shoulder made itself felt. I hastily held the bottle nearer to him, where he could more easily reach it with his right hand.

He must have been pretty dehydrated; he nearly emptied it before his hand sank back to the duvet. I relieved him of the bottle and put it aside.

He was watching me, trying to place me.

"Do I know you?" he asked, frowning.

"No. We met yesterday. Sort of," I amended awkwardly. I looked at him anxiously. "There're some things I've got to tell you. Some of them aren't... They aren't going to make good hearing. But you need to know. All right?"

He didn't entirely understand yet, but he nodded.

"I found you yesterday afternoon. You'd been in a car accident," I repeated. "You were concussed, and wet through, and you'd lost some blood. I helped you get here. Do you remember?"

He thought, and nodded slowly. It was starting to come back to him. I wondered how long it would be before the thing I was dreading he'd remember would come back, too.

"I remember," he said. "My head was swimming, but – I leant on you. I remember that."

"Well, I got you here, but you passed out. I couldn't get you into a proper bed. So I had to do the best I could."

He looked down, evidently realizing the makeshift nature of the bed for the first time. Then he seemed to realize he was naked under the duvet.

"Did you—?" he started, then broke off. I felt embarrassed, and flushed.

"Sorry," I apologized. "I had to. You were wet through. You'd have gone down with pneumonia or something if I hadn't."

"Don't be sorry," he reproved me, with the first glint of humour I'd seen in those dark eyes. The left one really was going to be dark; he was developing quite a black eye, thanks to whatever had struck the side of his face. "Did you do this, too?" He gestured at his bandaged shoulder.

I nodded.

"Don't be sorry," he said again. "Sounds as if you've saved my life. I—"

And that was the moment he remembered. His face froze, and his eyes stabbed at me.

"Mike!" he exclaimed. "Where's Mike? What's happened to him?" He started to try to raise himself, but dropped back down with another grunt of pain. He grimaced, then sought my eyes again, demanding an answer.

I didn't know how to say it, but then, I didn't need to. He could see the look on my face, and he knew. He covered his eyes with his right hand. There was a brief silence.

"What happened?" he asked in a low voice.

I told him how I'd found him, about the wrecked car, the bullet hole through the windscreen, the corresponding hole in the head of the man in the driver's seat, the fire burning and scorching everything. Even about my throwing up. Everything.

"I went through your pockets," I went on. "That's how I know your name." I got up and retrieved his wallet from the mantelpiece, where I'd put it the previous evening, resumed my kneeling position at his side, and gave it to him. He took it, gazing at it as if he'd never seen it before, then let it and his hand drop to the duvet again. "And I found that."

His gaze followed the direction of my pointing finger to where his holster was bundled at the far end of the sofa, then came back to me.

"And if you're wondering why I haven't called for an ambulance, or the police, or anything – it's because I couldn't." Then I told him about my being alone here, about the break-in, the taking or destroying of any of the means by which I might have summoned help. "That's why I tried to barricade us in here," I explained, gesturing at the chair still wedged under the door handle. "I was afraid he might still be around. Try to get in during the night. But he didn't. I – I didn't know how to use your gun." I felt irrationally ashamed of that last admission, as if it was some kind of failure on my part, some gaping flaw in my education, not to know how to fire a handgun.

He lay silent for what seemed like a long time, just staring at me.

"I'm sorry," I said at last, feeling driven to break the silence. "I didn't know what else to do."

Unexpectedly, he smiled at me, briefly. It changed his face entirely for a few moments. I felt a momentary surge of something in response – oh, I don't know how to describe it! – but whatever it was, it took me by surprise. I quashed it, hurriedly, even while I was somewhat tentatively returning the smile.

"You've no business being sorry," he said.

For some reason, despite the brusqueness of his words, I blushed.

"What should I do now? What about you? Are you hungry?" I asked.

"What I need most is a pee," he announced bluntly.

"Oh. Right. I'll get you a dressing gown," I said hastily. "Don't go anywhere!"

"Is it likely?" he asked with a brief hint of amusement, suddenly sounding very Scottish indeed.

I muffled a quick breath of laughter as I got to my feet, unwedged the chair, and went to find my father's dressing gown.

"Here," I said, bringing it back and dropping it on the sofa next to him. "Can you get up by yourself, or do you need help?"

He tried, but he was still too weak, and the pain of his shoulder hindered him. So in the end I had to help him up and into the dressing gown, and he leaned on me as I supported him for the short journey across the hall to the bathroom.

"Don't lock the door," I told him. I didn't want him collapsing in there with me not able to get in. He didn't reply as I pulled the door to.

He was in there for quite a few minutes, and when he called me to help him back to the living room he had gone even paler than before. His eyes had become dark holes looking out of grey pits in a parchment-white face, and I could feel him trembling. He slumped down onto the sofa while I moved the pillows from the floor to the end where the gun was, scooping it out of the way. Then I lifted his legs up for him as he tiredly swivelled to lie back on the pillows, and covered him with the duvet again. I made him drink some more water.

"Do you want anything to eat?" I asked him.

He shook his head, his eyes closed.

"Tired," he murmured.

"Okay," I said. "I'll keep watch."

"You've already been watching over me," he said in such a low voice it was almost as if he were speaking to himself rather than to me. He opened his eyes as a thought visibly struck him. "Where's my gun?"

I picked up the holster and handed it to him. He awkwardly pulled the pistol out with one hand, shifted his grip to the barrel, and waved it in my direction. I hesitated, then took it from him, my fingers curling gingerly around the grip.

"It's a Glock," he said weakly, as if he expected that to mean something to me. "Integrated trigger safety system. It's on safety unless you squeeze both parts of the trigger. If you need to, do that. It'll fire." The last words came out as little more than a whisper. His eyes closed again.

I held the pistol up, looking at the trigger mechanism more closely. I hoped to high heaven I wouldn't need to know what he'd just told me.

An hour or so later he woke again.

"Still watching over me," he murmured, wincing as he incautiously moved his shoulder.

"Not for the entertainment value," I retorted. Something resembling a smile briefly touched his face.

"Look, you ought to eat something," I told him. "And you're probably still pretty dehydrated." I handed him a fresh bottle of water. He obeyed the implicit instruction and gradually, pausing to take breaths between swallows, emptied it.

"You should eat something, too," I persisted. He pulled an unenthusiastic face.

"Not hungry," he muttered.

"Even so. I really do think you should put something in your stomach. You emptied it pretty thoroughly yesterday. What about some soup?"

He gave in, and indicated the pistol. I handed it over without comment, and went out to the kitchen. A few minutes later I returned with a large mug of steaming liquid, which I proffered.

"You okay with that? Or should I start spooning it into you, like they do in the old Westerns?"

He smiled faintly. "Think I can manage."

While he was somewhat laboriously downing his soup I gathered up the constituents of the makeshift bed where he'd spent the night. Despite my best efforts with the bandaging, blood had soaked into the sheet and the duvets. The sheet joined the bloodied towels in the linen bin in the bathroom, the tablecloth was restored to the kitchen, to be wiped clean later; the duvets I just bundled up and dumped in a corner of my bedroom, to be dealt with another time.

Then I went back into the living room and checked his clothes. They'd spent the night on the fireguard, and seemed to be dry now, even his trainers. But I doubted the T-shirt was wearable. It was stiff with dried blood.

"You won't be wearing that again," I told him, holding it up for him to inspect. "You can borrow one of my father's."

But that could wait. I came across and sat carefully on the end of the sofa he was lying on; he shifted his feet slightly to make room for me. He put the empty mug down onto the floor, and we looked at each other.

"Peter, what do I do now?" I asked him abruptly. "What *can* I do? We can't stay here forever. You ought to be in a hospital." He shrugged dismissively, then winced as his wounded shoulder reacted to the careless movement. "But the only way I can see of making that happen is" – I swallowed, nervously – "is for me to leave you here and walk to Fergus' place. That's about ten miles away. I'd be gone for hours. You'd be on your own, and – so would I." I bit my lip. "I'm sorry, but – I'd be afraid."

He accepted that with a slight nod.

"My people'll be on the alert by now," he said quietly. "We" – a shadow passed over his face – "haven't reported in. They know more or less where we were going. Someone'll be looking. But it might take them a while to find us. The best thing is probably—"

He broke off, like a pointer on the alert.

I started to speak, but he cut me off with an abrupt gesture, not even looking at me. He was totally focused on some sound not yet discernible to me. Swiftly, he picked up the pistol. With his disordered hair and intense dark eyes and the gun in his hand, he suddenly looked incredibly dangerous. I stared at him with widened eyes.

"What is it?" I whispered.

"Car," he snapped in a low, tense voice. "Someone's coming."

I listened. He was right. Outside, the sound of an approaching engine was gradually rising in volume.

He swept the duvet aside, unable to repress a hiss of pain between his teeth, and made for the window, dropping to his knees on front of it. I did likewise, intensely aware, as I looked out, of the pistol in his hand, hovering in my peripheral vision.

A battered Land Rover was pulling in off the track. It drew to a halt, and a tall, spare man in his late fifties, with whitening hair that had once been sand-blond in colour, opened the driver's door and got out.

I felt weak with relief. "It's all right," I said. "It's Fergus."

Peter McLeish looked at me. "Who's Fergus?"

"He's our nearest neighbour. He owns most of the local area. The hill where I found you – that's his."

"You're sure of him?"

"Yes."

He accepted it. As I rose to my feet, I could see Fergus looking over at my car. Unlike me, he'd evidently seen straight away that something was wrong, and was clearly about to take a closer look. I banged on the window to get his attention. He immediately turned and saw me. I gestured vigorously in the direction of the front door, hurried to it, and unbolted it.

"Jenny?" He came towards me, clearly confused. "What's going on? What's happened to your car?"

"Fergus! Come inside! Quick!" I was filled with anxiety that the man who had tried to kill Peter might be somewhere close, watching. With his rifle.

Fergus looked at me oddly, but obeyed. When he got to the doorstep, I reached out and hauled him almost bodily into the hallway, slamming the door shut behind him.

"Jenny! What's wrong?"

"Fergus!" My voice quavered slightly. *What's wrong? Where do I start...?* "How did you know to come here?"

"Your father rang me this morning," he explained in his soft Highland burr. "He's been trying to get hold of you since about midday yesterday, but he couldn't get you on either phone or email all day. I think he'd got a bit anxious by this morning, so he rang first thing and asked me to come over and check that you're all right. *Are* you all right?" He looked at me more closely, concerned. "You're very pale, lassie. What's going on?"

Lassie. One of his few concessions to the common preconception of Scots vocabulary. It made me feel like a little girl of ten, instead of a grown woman of thirty-five.

"Fergus, I'll tell you everything, I promise, but right now I need to use your phone," I said, sounding rather desperate even to myself. "We need an ambulance, and we need the police."

He frowned.

"Who's 'we'?"

"Please, Fergus! I'll explain it all, I promise you, but, please – I've got to ring for help *now*! It's important!" I was angry with myself for being on the verge of tears again.

He saw my desperation, and wordlessly handed over his phone. When I got through, he listened with increasing incredulity as I outlined my reasons for needing both ambulance and police emergency services. A car crash. A dead man. An injured one, needing to be hospitalized. I couldn't stop the tears of relief that I'd finally been able to get help rolling down my cheeks as I spoke, but beyond that I held myself together fairly well.

"Jenny!" he protested, when I'd ended the call. "What on earth is this all about?"

"I'm not even very sure about that myself, yet," I admitted, choking back another sob. "Come inside. You should meet Peter."

"This is the man who needs the ambulance?" he asked, as he followed me in.

"Yes. He's in here. Peter..." I opened the living room door, hastily scrubbing at my wet cheeks.

He was sitting on the sofa again, his elbows resting on his knees, the hand with the pistol hanging limply from his wrist. Somehow, goodness knew how, he'd managed to get his jeans on, though his feet were still bare. But the bloody bandage on his shoulder and the bruises on his face and naked upper body were striking testament to my desire for urgency. His face was still very pale as he looked up at us.

Fergus uttered a muffled exclamation at the sight of him.

"Fergus, this is Peter McLeish," I said, ignoring it. "He's a police officer. Someone shot at his car. It's down at the foot of Craigie Hill, by the fir plantation..."

Together, we gave him a précis of what had happened. He listened with growing astonishment.

"Then, those flat tyres—?" he began.

"Bullets through every one," said Peter flatly. "He didn't want her getting help for me. Perhaps he was hoping I'd die overnight." He clearly wasn't joking. Fergus was silenced.

After that brusque summary, we sat him down and gave him a more extensive account. His eyebrows spent more time closer to his hairline than his eyes for much of the time, and he expelled a long breath when we'd finally finished.

"That's quite a tale," he observed. "But at least you've both lived through it. And you" – he eyed Peter significantly – "largely thanks to Jenny, it seems."

Peter looked at me with those dark eyes.

"I know," he said.

"But who—?" Fergus began, only for Peter to cut across the question abruptly.

"Shouldn't Jenny phone her father?" he suggested brusquely. Fergus awarded him a thoughtful look before turning to me.

"Aye, that's a good idea," he agreed, proffering his phone. "Take your time. You'll need to." For the first time, his eyes gleamed with a tinge of humour. "It's a long story, isn't it?"

"Thank you, Fergus," I said, my eyes filling again. I wiped the corner of my eye angrily. "Sorry to keep dissolving like this."

"You're reacting," said Peter. "It's quite natural. Don't be sorry."

"You keep telling me that!"

"You keep taking no notice of me," he pointed out calmly, with the merest hint of a smile. "Go on. Go and make your phone call."

I thought about going into the kitchen, but I felt a greater illusion of safety from staying in the hall, where there were no windows. I sat down on the cold tiled floor, my back supported against the wall, and keyed in my parents' number.

"Richard Taylor," came the swift response.

"It's me, Dad."

"Jenny! Thank goodness! What's going on? Why couldn't we reach you?" Then he latched on to my tremulous voice. "Are you all right?"

"That's a relative term at the moment, Dad. Look, I'm on Fergus' phone, so I'll try to be brief for now, but—"

"Why are you on his phone? Where's yours? Why haven't we been able to get hold of you?" He could tell there was something really wrong;

we've always shared the same wavelength, my father and I.

"Look – just listen, Dad…" I said, rather desperately.

It was, despite my intentions, an understandably long phone call. When I'd told him as much as I was going to at that point, he said flatly, "I'll come up. Today. Now."

"No! No, don't do that," I told him quickly. "Let me ring you back later, when I know what's going on. I don't know much about how these things go, but the police are bound to want statements and all sorts of stuff, and I don't know how long all that'll take. And I'm not staying here. Not after this. When they say I can go, I'll come home again. I'll get a flight. I'll be all right, I promise."

"Are you sure, darling?" He didn't sound convinced.

"Very sure, Dad. You wouldn't achieve all that much. You'll be much more useful staying there and getting your shoulder ready to be cried on, truly." The idea of being held in my father's comforting embrace was suddenly very attractive indeed. I brushed at the sudden excess of moisture that had risen in my eyes at the image, and sniffed inelegantly.

"I'll be ready," he assured me. "And you'll ring me as soon as you know anything more?"

"I promise. Try not to worry too much, either of you. I love you, Dad…" I couldn't prevent my voice breaking slightly on the last word. "Love to Mum. Talk to you later." I hurriedly ended the call before he could say any more.

I stood up and went into the bathroom to wash my face and try to get myself into better order. Then I went back into the living room. Peter had slumped back on the sofa, but his dark eyes sought mine immediately. Fergus, too, looked at me anxiously.

"Thank you, Fergus," I said, holding the phone out to him.

"You got through all right?" he asked, taking it.

"Yes, thanks. Dad was all for coming straight up here, but I told him to hold fire. There'll be a lot of questions to answer, and I told him I didn't know how long that'd take, and I'd let him know what was happening after that."

"You'll be coming to Mary and me, that's what," Fergus said flatly.

I shook my head. "I'll go home," I said. "I can—"

Peter interrupted me. "Fergus, can I use your phone? Sorry if it's taking a bit of a beating, but there's someone I need to talk to, as well."

Fergus looked at him steadily, with a touch of reserve. Then he nodded, and handed it over. "You'd like to be in private?" he suggested.

Peter shook his head. "Doesn't matter. I won't be saying anything you haven't already heard."

"Aye, well…" Fergus eyed us both. "Even so, I think I'll go and fix Jenny a hot drink. In fact, for both of you. She's looking near as pale as you, and you're no oil painting at the moment, laddie," he added, with a slight lift to one corner of his mouth.

Peter nodded. I sat down on the other sofa as Fergus left the room, and watched Peter's profile as he thumbed in the number. Like my call, it was answered within seconds.

"Alan, it's me…" He paused for the other man to speak. "Yeh, I know… I couldn't, before. Listen. He was on to us. Laid an ambush. Alan" – he paused, and his voice was heavy – "Mike's dead…" A long pause. "Yeh… I would've been, too, if someone hadn't found me." His eyes flicked across to me as he spoke. "Jenny…" He hesitated as he realized he didn't know my full name.

"Gregory," I said quickly.

"Jenny Gregory," he went on, with a nod of acknowledgement to me. "I'm at her place now. And the local boys are on their way… No, I'm fine." He glanced across at me as his peripheral vision caught the expression on my face at the voicing of this blatant lie, and half-smiled. "Well, maybe not entirely fine, but I'll live, thanks to her… You'll want to talk to her, too. When can you get here?" Another pause. "Which flight? Right… Either the local station or the local hospital, probably… No, I promise you, I'm fine! Ask at the station, when you get here – they'll know where I am. I've lost my phone… I'll fill you in when you get here… Yeh, you, too… See you."

He lowered the phone.

"A colleague, I take it?" I suggested. He nodded.

"He'll be here sometime this afternoon. He'll want to talk to you." He lifted his eyes to mine. "You'll have to make a statement to the local police first." One corner of his mouth lifted slightly. "You'll have to tell your story a fair few times, I'm afraid."

"As many times as you need me to," I assured him.

He leaned back and closed his eyes again. I wondered if it was still physical weakness, or whether he was thinking about his dead colleague. I decided not to ask. After a few moments, though, I realized there was something I did need to ask.

"Peter – do you think he's gone?"

He turned his head, carefully, because of his shoulder, to look at me. He didn't need to ask to whom I was referring.

"I think so," he said, after a few moments. "Could be he's decided to watch the fun from a safe distance. It's the kind of thing he'd do. But I doubt it, this time. Fergus got here without interference, so he's probably gone. He knows there'll be police all over the place before long. He's too clever to get caught that way."

"But" – I struggled to understand – "if he was going to do that anyway, why go to all that trouble to stop me getting help in the first place?"

"Because it's what he likes to do." Suddenly Peter's voice, though low, was as grim as any I'd ever heard, and I had to suppress a shiver. "Play games. Send messages. Keep you guessing. Show you how vulnerable you are. Let you know he could've taken you when he chose, but by the fact that he didn't, letting you know he still might at any time. He's a sadistic—" He bit off the next word, and stared with almost manic eyes at the dying fire in the hearth.

I didn't ask anything else.

Not even who 'he' was.

Chapter 4

The next few hours were busy. The ambulance and the police turned up within minutes of each other. After a brief, grudging wait by the paramedics to allow him to answer initial questions, Peter was swiftly taken away, leaving me to recount my experiences almost as an anticlimax. The police listened to my story, then took me briefly to Craigie Hill, now swarming with uniforms and forensics officers, to confirm where exactly I'd found him. Though I thought to myself afterwards they could just as well have got their confirmation from the splatters of vomit – mine under the trees, his near the car. Then, while they continued to swarm over the Lodge and the scene of the crash, I was allowed to pack what things I wanted to take with me and was put in the charge of a female constable to be driven to Inverness to give my statement. Fergus, bent on accompanying me, followed in his own car.

Once there, a doctor was called in to look me over as a precaution, but, apart from shock – or, to use the proper terminology, 'acute stress reaction', as he informed me with professional relish – he pronounced me well enough.

"It'll pass," he told me. "But you might find yourself having feelings of anxiety or anger for a little while. Maybe feel a bit depressed, or withdrawn. But once you're out of the environment that caused the stress in the first place, the feelings don't tend to last long. If you find they're still persisting after about three days, you'll need to consult your own doctor. All right?"

I told him it was, and thanked him.

"Don't mention it. And don't let these mannerless thugs give you a rough time," he added cheerfully as he rose to go, throwing a meaningful glance at the young constable who was in charge of me. "Not a shred of empathy between the lot of 'em!" The constable grinned back; clearly it was a standing accusation. And, equally clearly, an expression of reciprocal professional regard.

After a brief interlude for refreshment – I still couldn't face food, though I was glad of a hot drink – there was the giving of the statement. It took quite a long time, and I found it tiring, despite the professional solicitude of the constable. Fergus, likewise, was asked to give a statement.

At last, come mid-afternoon, having been told that a senior officer from the London Met was on his way to interview me, we found ourselves installed in an otherwise unoccupied office, waiting until he – or someone – decided to come along and take further notice of us.

"Are you all right, Jenny?" Fergus asked. "That's been quite a performance."

I let out a breath of amusement.

"Rigmarole's the word I would've used... Don't worry. Just a bit tired," I assured him. "I'll be all right."

"If there's anything you need me to do, just say so," he said. "Doesn't matter how small or how big. I'll take care of it."

"Bless you, Fergus," I said gratefully. "I promise I will. I – I shan't go back to the lodge at the moment. Will you look it over, once the police are done with it? Dad's given you a key, hasn't he? Not that they won't be careful, of course, but to reassure Mum...?"

"Of course I will. And I suppose there'll be your car to sort out, once they've finished with that. I'll ring to tell you when it's all all right. Once I'm sure of that myself, of course," he added, with a twinkle in his eye.

I murmured my thanks, grateful for such kindness. Then I leant my head back against the wall and closed my eyes for a few moments.

Only to realize, when I next opened them – with something of a start – that I must have gone to sleep for a while. Because now there was another man in the room, looking down at me, conducting a low-voiced conversation with Fergus.

I felt stupefied, disorganized, as I pulled myself erect in the chair.

"I'm sorry," I muttered, rubbing my hand across my eyes.

"Please, don't be," said the other man. He looked briefly at Fergus, who nodded.

"Aye, well, I'll leave you to talk," he said, getting up. "I'll be outside when you need me, Jenny." He went out and closed the door behind him.

This new stranger was tall and spare, built along the same lines as Peter. The bone structure of his face was quite similar, too, though his colouring was blander, with mid-brown hair rather than dark, blue eyes rather than brown. He looked at me with a rather penetrating expression as he held out his hand for me to shake.

"Hello, Mrs Gregory," he said. "I'm Detective Chief Inspector Alan McLeish."

"McLeish?" I blurted, surprised, before I could stop myself.

"Cousin," he said succinctly, with the air of a man who's had to say the same thing many times before.

No wonder they were so physically similar. Though Alan McLeish sounded thoroughly English – a touch of some form of Midlands accent, if anything – not Scots at all. I wondered why that was.

"Ah," I said, trying to sound intelligent. "Cousins *and* colleagues. Didn't see that one coming!"

He smiled, and instantly I felt better. He had a very nice smile, once he chose to use it, though I had the feeling that professionally he might not do it that often. He pulled a chair round so he could sit facing me, and I realized that, among other papers, he was holding a copy of my statement.

"The first thing I want to do is to thank you," he said. "I think Peter's life would have been in great danger without your help."

"I think Peter's life was in great danger anyway – nothing to do with me," I retorted. Then I realized how abrupt I must have sounded. "Sorry. I didn't mean it to come out like that." He waved my apology away. "But someone tried to kill him, didn't they? Or was it his friend they were after?"

Alan McLeish looked at me sombrely, and even though he didn't say anything, I could read the answer in his eyes. I nodded. So it was Peter the attacker had been targeting. I thought back.

"He said – he kept talking about '*he*' and '*him*'. '*Perhaps he was hoping I'd die overnight.*' And he talked about him '*playing games*'. '*Sending messages*', and being sadistic. He knows who it is." I saw the look on his face. "And you know who it is, too, don't you?" I realized how accusatory I sounded. "I'm sorry, Chief Inspector – I had no business saying that."

He shrugged, dismissing it.

"Call me Alan, please…" I wondered if he was always so informal, or if it was a concession to my newly acquired acquaintance with his cousin. "Now, I'm sure you've been through this as thoroughly as you can," he said, with an air of deliberately deflecting any further questions I might have had on the subject, "but I need to double-check some of the things you've said." He gestured with the statement. "Do you mind?"

"Of course not," I assured him. "Not if it'll help…"

"One thing that struck me," he said, flipping through the pages until he found the right place. "You suggest the attacker had two weapons. Why did you think that?"

I frowned, trying to concentrate.

"I'm probably talking rubbish," I apologized. "But I thought that it must've been a rifle that shot through the windscreen of the car. I mean, I don't really know anything about guns – firearms…" I looked at him uncertainly, but he nodded encouragingly, so I went on. "But I just thought it would have to be a largish weapon to do that. Because of the size of the bullet hole. And the range. I mean, if he'd been close enough to use a handgun, they'd've seen him, wouldn't they? And then, the holes in the tyres were quite small. A different calibre – that's how it looked to me. So I thought it must be a different gun. A handgun, I mean, not a rifle. *Am* I talking rubbish?"

"Not at all," he said. He even sounded a little impressed. He consulted another piece of paper that he had in front of him, not part of my statement. "Forensics have retrieved all the bullets that were used on your tyres, but they're not likely to be much help."

"I thought these days you could tell which gun a bullet's been fired from?" I queried. "By the rifling, isn't it?"

He cocked an eyebrow at me. "I thought you said you didn't know anything about firearms?"

"I don't. I just remember seeing a documentary once that mentioned it, that's all. I watch a fair number of documentaries," I added, with a faint smile. "It's my version of adult education."

"I see..." One corner of his mouth rose in momentary response. "Well, you're right, but the problem is finding the matching gun. Which we haven't, and probably won't. Or not in time to help us with this case, anyway. A lot of weapons do the rounds of the criminal small arms dealers, but by the time we get hold of them, the chances of tying them to a particular individual months or years before is—" He broke off, and shrugged.

I waited, while he referred back to the forensics report.

"Tell me," he continued, "did either Mr Riach, or Peter, at any point stand up close to the front right-hand window?"

"No. I did, when I was first checking whether there was anyone inside," I offered helpfully, a little puzzled.

"But that was at the side of the window nearest to the front door, yes?" he queried, consulting my statement.

"Yes," I agreed, wonderingly.

He pursed his lips.

"The forensics team found a set of clearly defined footprints in the earth at the other side of the window, the one nearest the car," he said thoughtfully. "Not yours. A man's, from the size of them. Someone stood at the window, facing in. Could that have been on some other occasion?"

I swallowed, and shook my head.

"No. The rain was very heavy for a while. And it was coming from the north. The lodge faces that way. Anything from before that would've been washed completely away." I looked at him uneasily. "If someone stood there, it had to be after the rain stopped."

And I knew it hadn't been either Peter or Fergus.

Alan exchanged a grim glance with me, without comment. Then he looked back down at my statement, and went on with his next question. He covered every aspect of my statement, referring to maps, photographs, and other papers. He was considerate in his manner, but by the time he'd finished I had some inkling of what the phrase 'a thorough investigation' really means.

At last he seemed to feel he'd gleaned everything from me he usefully could.

"Thank you, Mrs Gregory," he said. "You've been extremely helpful."

"If I'm to call you Alan, you might at least call me Jenny," I told him. He accepted the rebuke with a smile. "Er – what happens next? What do I do now?"

"Whatever you like. It's possible we might need to speak to you again, but for the moment, you're free to go. Have you got any plans?"

I hesitated. "Well, I was wondering – do you know where they've taken Peter? I'd – well, I'd like to know how he is. Then I think I'll go home."

"Peter's been taken to one of the hospitals here in Inverness, so I'm told," he said, regarding me with a somewhat summing look. "I'll be going there myself as soon as I'm done here. Perhaps I could offer you a lift?"

I let out a breath of relief.

"Yes, please," I said. "I'd be very grateful..."

"Don't mention it," he assured me. "After all you've done, it's the very least I can do. And – where's home, again?"

"Croydon," I said.

"Croydon?" he echoed, as if astonished. I couldn't see why. Maybe he'd been so focused on the rest of the information I'd supplied, he'd overlooked that bit, but even so – why so surprised? I looked at him enquiringly. "Croydon!" he repeated. "That's where *I* live!"

After we'd worked through the whole 'fancy-that-isn't-it-a-small-world' thing, he looked at me, consideringly. "How were you planning to get there? Your car being out of commission, that is? Not to mention Forensics crawling all over it, of course," he added lightly.

"I was going to see if I could catch a flight."

"If Peter's fit to travel, we'll be flying back down ourselves, either today or tomorrow," he said. "If you want to come with us, I'd be happy to offer my services as escort, in the circumstances. If you'd like."

I looked at him, astonished.

"Bit beyond the bounds of professional duty, isn't it?" I couldn't help asking.

"Not exactly. You could think of it as witness protection, if you like," he suggested, with a momentary glimmer of amusement. "But the offer was more out of personal gratitude. He's my cousin, and you did a pretty spectacular job of looking after him, in the circumstances. I'm grateful, and I'd like to show it."

I hesitated; I was afraid he might simply be feeling constrained to be polite. But, looking at his face, I decided the offer was a genuine one.

"In that case, thank you," I said quietly. "Yes, I'd appreciate that. I'm the one who's grateful. I just wish I could have done more than I did."

He shook his head, firmly. "You handled it really well," he said.

"Is that what you think?" I asked, and promptly burst into tears.

He waited patiently for the reaction and the stress to vent themselves. He was silent, but it was a supportive, comforting silence, and in a strange way it helped that he didn't make any verbal attempt to calm me. Gradually I regained my composure, enough to retrieve a handkerchief from my handbag and use it to soak up the excess moisture from my eyes and face. Then I sat clutching it in my hand, taking deep breaths, until I was fit to speak again.

"Thank you," I said.

"For what?" he asked, his forehead creased in bemusement.

"For taking that so calmly. It's reaction, I think." Peculiarly, I didn't feel at all embarrassed about having wept so violently in front of a virtual stranger. I found Alan McLeish a very comforting presence.

"I think so, too, and hardly surprising," he commented. "Anyway, I've got a wife and a newly teenage daughter. I therefore have some experience with unexpectedly weeping women."

I laughed, dabbing again at my eyes with the damp handkerchief.

"You poor man! Be sure to thank them for me, won't you? I'm grateful for the benefit of their training."

He laughed, too. "Don't worry. I've also got a teenage son to balance things out. Who vents his feelings in other ways entirely, but he's always ready to roll his eyes at me in male sympathy when the situation merits it."

I gave my eyes one last wipe, crumpled the soaked square of cotton into a ball to thrust it deep into my handbag, and got to my feet.

"I mustn't hold you up," I said, trying to sound brisk and businesslike. "I'll go and tell Fergus what's happening, and then you tell me where you want me to wait for you until you're ready to go. I'll try to keep out of your way."

He rose too, and smiled at me.

"You've not yet once been in it," he assured me.

Some while later, Alan McLeish was at the wheel of a car that had been provided by his local colleagues, driving me to the hospital where Peter was being treated. For the most part I kept silent – he was a comfortable person to be silent with – but there was one thing I very much wanted to know.

"Don't answer this if it isn't appropriate," I began uncertainly, "but can I ask you something?"

"You can always ask," he agreed.

"Well, it's just – Peter's with the London Met, so – presumably – so are you. So, I realize it's a bit out of the ordinary for you even to be here. In Scotland, I mean. But, as well, he was carrying a gun. Does that mean you're not – I don't know how to phrase this – not ordinary officers? Are you with some sort of specialist unit?"

"You might say that," he concurred, with a touch of reserve in his tone, perhaps wary of what else I might ask.

"I thought you must be," I said, satisfied.

There was a pause, as if he was expecting me to pursue it. But I'd simply wanted confirmation of my theory.

"That it?" he enquired.

"Don't worry," I told him. "I had no intention of asking you to tell me something you shouldn't. I just wanted to be sure I'd got that bit right."

He gave me a look that was part amused, part puzzled. I wondered what he was thinking.

But I wasn't going to ask that, either.

Before we got in to see Peter, Alan buttonholed the doctor who'd been treating him. Privately, I thought that was a wise move. I remembered how Peter had shrugged when I'd told him he needed to be in hospital. A not uncommon male reaction in matters of healthcare – and I'm not saying that in a derogatory way; it's a factual recognition of how the majority of men behave.

But it meant that if Alan didn't find out direct from the doctor – Doctor Forbes – what Peter's actual condition was, he wasn't likely to learn it from Peter himself. The most he'd probably get would be another shrug and a muttered "All right". That much I'd already deduced about Peter McLeish.

Besides, I'd got previous form with a man who steadfastly disregarded the need for medical help, so I was familiar with the attitude.

"…Mainly shock and blood loss, and a touch of dehydration," Forbes was saying. "He's also running a few degrees of fever. Shouldn't be a problem, but I'd be happier keeping him in overnight. Considering the severity of the accident and the subsequent time he spent being wet and cold, he's in remarkably good shape."

"This is the lady you can thank for that," Alan said, gesturing at me. Taken by surprise, I coloured as Forbes looked at me with approval.

"Oh! It was you that looked after him? You did very well, in the circumstances, er—" He looked at me, suddenly at a loss.

"Jenny," I said, supplying the missing information. "Jenny Gregory. Mrs."

I noticed Alan looking at my left hand as if for the first time he'd realized the discrepancy between my title and my ringless ring finger. This wasn't the moment to enlighten him; in my mind I tabled the matter for a more suitable occasion.

"I take it you've done a first aid course at some point?" Forbes asked.

"Getting close to twenty years ago," I disclaimed. "I blush to admit I haven't done a refresher lately."

"Well, you seem to have retained the bits that mattered in this case. He'll end up with no worse than a scar on his shoulder, and that'll fade with time. You dealt with that very sensibly."

"I don't suppose I did anything anyone else wouldn't have done," I said, pleased but embarrassed.

"Oh, you'd be surprised! The number of people who bandage a wound and then take it off again just to see if the bleeding's stopped would probably make you weep. It does me!" He smiled at me; guiltily, I decided – since he seemed quite happy about the outcome – not to mention that in fact I had taken the first bandage off, even though I hadn't done it lightly. "Anyway, he's just along the corridor there. In a private room. Somebody made quite a point of asking for that, I gather." He cocked an eyebrow enquiringly at Alan, who nodded.

"That was me," he agreed, blandly. "Thank you, Doctor Forbes. I'm very grateful."

"You're welcome, Chief Inspector," said Forbes. "Mrs Gregory," he added to me by way of farewell, and, with a polite smile, left us to our own devices.

The room Peter was in had a window into the corridor built into its interior wall; a row of three chairs were lined up with their backs against it. A slatted blind had been installed for when privacy was needed, but at this moment the slats had been left horizontal, so we could see him lying in the bed, parallel to us as we came along the corridor. His face was turned toward us, but his eyes were closed. He wore no pyjama jacket, so the neat, professional bandaging of his shoulder and chest was clear to view. His left arm was cradled in a sling. Altogether better than that first mess of bloody rags I'd been able to provide for him.

"Is he asleep, d'you think?" I asked in a low voice.

"I'll see," he said, and discreetly opened the door.

Through the slats of the blind, I saw Peter's eyes fly open as he detected the presence of an intruder. I even saw the flash of alarm in them. But then he relaxed, as he realized who it was that was standing in the doorway.

"Alan," I heard him say. Alan went swiftly over to the bed, and I saw the way their knuckles paled with the strength of their grip as they clasped each other's hand. Not just cousins, then, but friends. Close friends, if the whiteness of those knuckles was anything to go by.

"I've brought you a visitor," said Alan. He raised his voice. "Come on in, Jenny."

Feeling like an interloper, I sidled round the jamb of the door. Just in time to see a second flash of feeling in Peter's eyes as they flew to my face. I couldn't identify it, exactly, but it felt, somehow, significant.

"Hello, Peter," I said shyly. "I hope you're feeling better?"

"Yeh, thanks," he agreed. His face wasn't showing much, but I had a distinct feeling he was pleased to see me.

"Someone's done a much better job of bandaging your shoulder than I did. Stitches, I suppose?"

"Yeh. I'm trying to remember not to shrug. Too sore."

"Even so, sounds as if they're going to let you go tomorrow," Alan said. "So we'll pick up the first flight we can. And Jenny'll be coming with us." Peter looked at me again, quickly. "I offered to see her home, given what she did for you. Her car, you'll remember, isn't functional at the moment," Alan concluded, with a touch of dry humour.

Peter looked at me for several seconds without speaking, his dark eyes roaming over my face. I wondered what was going on in his mind. But the corners of his mouth lifted in a slight smile, and he nodded again.

"Good," he said briefly, and I felt that he meant it. I didn't know quite what to say.

What I came up with, somewhat awkwardly, was: "Look, you two'll have lots to talk over. I'll sit outside and wait for you. And it doesn't matter how long you take. Whatever this is about, I know it's important. I'm happy to wait. As long as you need."

Alan smiled at me, and touched my shoulder briefly.

"Thank you, Jenny," he said, and ushered me politely to and through the door.

"Now, then—" he began, as he pushed it to.

He probably meant to shut it entirely, but the catch failed to engage, so there was a generous hairline of space between the door and the jamb. A gap through which, I realized, as I sat down in the nearest chair in the corridor, I could – just about – hear what they were saying.

And though the knowledge that I was eavesdropping on a conversation I probably shouldn't have been made me slightly uncomfortable, yet I did it. I'd been drawn, through no doing of mine, into something that was clearly dangerous. Nevertheless, besides feeling unsettled by the whole thing, I felt a strong compulsion to find out what it was about. And I was honest with myself on one point – perhaps the main point, as far as I was concerned. I wanted to find out about Peter McLeish, and why someone wanted to persecute him. To kill him.

Occasionally people went by, varying examples of the catholic range of individuals that are to be found roaming hospital corridors. But luckily for me, it seemed that this particular corridor wasn't on the way to anywhere important, because such interruptions were relatively few. So I was able to hear quite a lot of what was being said in the room behind me.

"…We got an anonymous tip-off," I heard Peter saying. "Must've been him. Or else he used someone else as cover. Setting us up. And we fell for it. Went haring off. Right into his rifle sights." He sounded disgusted with himself. There was a pause, then he said, in a voice so low I could hardly catch the words, "Does Sally know?"

"The Laird's told her himself," said Alan. I wondered who 'the Laird' was. A real laird? Or just someone he referred to in that way? A senior colleague, perhaps? There was a definite implication of authority in the way he'd used the title.

"How did she take it?"

"As you'd expect," said Alan heavily. "Even though she knew the score. Doesn't make it any easier to take when it happens. He was a good professional, and a good man."

"Doesn't make it any easier when it happens the other way round," muttered Peter grimly. I wondered what he meant by that.

There was another short silence. While it lasted, I had a feeling there was much that was not being said, yet totally understood.

"If there's a positive to be got out of this at all, it means you must've been getting close again," said Alan at last. "Too close for comfort. Why else would he go to all this trouble? Drag you all the way up here to set you up? Usually he's happy enough just making your life a misery from time to time. What made it different now? You must be on to something worthwhile enough for him to bother."

Peter's silence managed to convey a sense of reluctant agreement.

"I wish I'd come alone," he said, suddenly savage. "It wouldn't have made any difference to me. And Mike'd still be alive. It's my fault he's dead."

"Don't talk such damn rubbish," Alan said quickly. "You know the Laird'd never send you out without someone to cover your back. Not against Lesser! He's pushing the boundaries letting you even work on this at all, and you know it. You know how many people think you shouldn't even be in the team anymore. They'd never stand for him letting you work alone. You'd be straight out. He's doing what he needs to, what he *can* do, to let you see this through to the end. But there are some things he can't let by. So whosever fault it is, *it's not yours*."

This time the silence was expressive of a concession that Alan was right.

And I'd been right, too; whoever 'the Laird' was, he must be someone high up in the London Met, senior to Alan and Peter, and evidently in operational charge of them.

"So what now?" Peter asked at last.

"Now? You behave yourself, get some rest and do exactly whatever else they tell you to do, so they don't have any excuse not to let you out of here tomorrow," said Alan firmly. "I'll take care of Jenny, and we'll be back for you in the morning. I'll brief the Laird tonight."

"Is she all right?" Peter asked, in a different voice. "Jenny, I mean?"

"Bit shocked by it all, but I think she'll be okay," said Alan reassuringly. "You were lucky she was around."

"Yeh," Peter agreed pensively. "I was." Another pause. "I thought she lived here. Why's she coming with us?"

"Parents' holiday home," said Alan succinctly. "So they tell me. Apparently she lives in Croydon, believe it or not. Yes, I know…" That must have been a comment on Peter's expression. "So, feeling a bit shaken up by everything that's happened, quite understandably she wants to go home. So I offered my services as escort. You know, she did one hell of a job, considering she's a civilian."

"Yeh," said Peter again, slowly.

"Well, you be sure to thank her properly," Alan said sternly. It sounded as if he was getting to his feet. "At risk of sounding a touch melodramatic, you might just owe her your life. And even if you're not that attached to it, the rest of us would still prefer you here and alive. Okay?"

"Okay," Peter agreed.

"Right – we'll be going, then," Alan said, his voice getting louder as he neared the door. I stared straight ahead of me as he pulled it open and leaned around the jamb.

"Time we were off," he announced, as I looked up at him. "Want to say goodbye?"

"Yes, thanks," I said, with a faint smile. I stood up and followed him back in, stopping just inside the door.

"I'm glad you're feeling better, Peter," I said tritely. "I hope you'll feel even better tomorrow. Have a good night."

"Hey," he said, and gestured imperatively with his right hand. "C'mere."

I blinked, and obeyed, following his beckoning fingers until I was standing by the edge of the bed, looking down at him. It hadn't struck me before just how long his fringe was; it almost trailed in his eyes, but he didn't seem to notice it. He studied my face for a few seconds, then put his hand out and took hold of mine. Not to shake it, just to hold it.

"Thank you, Jenny," he said quietly, but with deep feeling. "I'm sorry you got dragged into this. But I'm grateful."

"I'm not," I said bluntly. "Sorry, I mean. I'm very, very glad I could be of help. And I'd do it again. As many times as you needed. And, anyway, I'm grateful to *you*."

He couldn't have doubted my sincerity, given the fervour with which I made this declaration, but looked understandably perplexed. "What for?"

"Because I learned something about myself. You don't know how you'll be in a crisis, until one comes along. Even though this wasn't really my crisis! But now I know something about how I react. That's worth knowing." I smiled. "Even if it is that I cry a lot!"

One corner of his mouth curved upward; the pressure of his fingers around mine increased momentarily.

"You did a lot more than that," he told me. "You go and get a good night's sleep."

"I will if you will!" I retorted brightly, withdrawing my hand from his grasp and retreating back toward Alan, who had been watching this with evident interest. "See you tomorrow!"

"Yeh," Peter said. "See you tomorrow."

Alan nodded to him and ushered me out. But as we walked back along the corridor, Peter's eyes met mine through the slats of the blind, and stayed locked on them until I was lost to his sight.

Alan booked us into adjoining rooms in a small hotel. I tried to pay for mine, but he wouldn't have it.

"Don't worry about it," he assured me. "This is me, being grateful. Besides, by keeping Peter from dying you've rescued a hefty investment in a very able public servant on the part of the British taxpayer. They'd be very grateful, too, if only they knew! Now, I hope you'll have dinner with me?"

"Mr McLeish!" I pretended to bridle. "What *would* your wife say?"

"She'd thank you for saving her cousin-in-law's life and tell you to accept," said Alan firmly. "But after that I'll have to leave you to your own devices. I'll have more work to do. Phone calls to make, that sort of thing."

"Of course." *Briefing the Laird, for one*, I thought to myself. "I did tell you I'd try not to be in your way. But you're still being very kind, you know."

"You deserve it," he said, matter-of-factly.

Over dinner, he did a bit of explaining. In my ignorance of normal police procedure, I hadn't realized that under ordinary circumstances a DCI would never be involved in interviewing a witness, as Alan had me. But with Peter being family as well as professional subordinate, he'd elected to combine both responsibilities in his visit.

"It's been a while since I did anything of the sort," he admitted, with a wry smile. "A DCI is pretty well desk-bound, as a rule."

"Desk-bound, or meeting table-bound?" I amended.

"Both," he agreed.

There was one question I couldn't stop myself asking him.

"Alan – you sound so English, not like Peter. Why's that?"

He smiled.

"Ah. Well, my father decamped to England when he was young. Set up a small restaurant in Manchester. Ended up running half a dozen of them. Meanwhile, married a girl from Bolton. Had me, then my sister. Then they decided to move down to London, and downsize. They now happily run a small but popular eatery in Haringey. So, with the exception of my father, all the influences on my accent have been exerted south of the border."

"But Peter evidently was brought up in Scotland?"

"My uncle and aunt lived in Wishaw their entire lives," Alan confirmed.

"The implication being, they're now dead?" I enquired tentatively.

Alan nodded. "Some years ago now."

"So how did you and Peter both come to end up in London? And not only both working for the Met, but apparently for the same unit as well? That's got to be fairly unusual, hasn't it?"

"I suppose so. Not that we planned it that way. I'm older than him by about four years. I" – for the first time, he looked slightly abashed – "I think Peter saw me as a bit of a role model. When I opted for the police, he did the same when he was old enough. He started out in Glasgow, then came down to London, where I already was. We seem to have a talent for the same sort of things. So now I'm his senior officer and team leader." He smiled, briefly. "Theoretically makes it easier for me to tell him what to do."

"And you find that works, do you?" I enquired with tongue-in-cheek scepticism.

"Not always," he admitted, slightly ruefully. He glanced at his watch. "Look, sorry to abandon you, but I really ought to get on with those calls now. Do you want to stay down here?" He glanced around the sparsely populated dining room. I shook my head.

"No, I'd rather come up. If I'm going to be on my own, I'd rather be in my room," I said. He nodded, accepting this, and escorted me up the stairs. I was in the room next to his, which shouldn't have made any difference, but somehow it did. I felt as if there'd be someone within call, if...

If what? Nothing was going to happen. Whoever was after Peter wouldn't have any interest in me. Why should he?

Nevertheless, I was grateful for the knowledge of Alan McLeish's reassuring proximity.

Chapter 5

Mid-morning next day found me in the car, waiting in the hospital car park for Alan's return with Peter. When I caught sight of them, I promptly got out.

As Peter neared − walking rather stiffly, as was understandable in the circumstances, his arm still in the sling − I found my attention irresistibly drawn to his black eye. No longer entirely black.

"Hello," I said cheerfully. "Goodness, that's going to be an impressive range of colours! How many shades of the rainbow are you trying for, exactly?"

"All of them," he said promptly. "Nothing by halves."

"That's certainly not been my experience of you so far," I agreed.

He let out a muffled snort of amusement, and Alan smiled, too. I had a feeling he was enjoying listening to Peter engaging in this banter. From which I deduced that perhaps it wasn't all that common an occurrence. With relative strangers, anyway.

"Anyway," I said, "good morning! They've decided you're fit to travel, then?"

"Doctor Forbes had a whole list of do's and don'ts for him when he gets home, but apart from that, yes, he's being released back into the wild," Alan confirmed.

"Good-oh," I said. "Here, you're in the front, Peter."

"No, no, you stay where you are," he protested.

"Be practical," I told him. "Your legs are longer than mine."

He couldn't argue that one.

"Alan," I said, as we headed along the road to the airport, "when we get back − what happens then? Will you need me for anything more?"

"Probably not," he said, concentrating on the traffic. "Not as far as this business is concerned, anyway." Which later struck me as a rather odd comment, but passed me by at the time. "We've got your contact details if we do. And don't forget he's got your phone and your laptop." He still avoided being explicit about who the mysterious 'he' was, I noticed. The man I now knew − though Alan didn't know that I knew − was called Lesser. "We'll be monitoring the phone and your email account for a while, just in case he tries to use either of them. You might want to consider replacing both of them," he advised, as an afterthought.

"I will," I said fervently. I hesitated, then added, slightly nervously,

"Will you tell me if he does? Use them, I mean?"

"If we need to," he agreed.

I wondered what constituted 'need' – and who would be defining it in this context. Alan glanced in the rear view mirror and caught my expression.

"Don't worry," he said. "If we think there's any risk to you, we will tell you. I promise you that."

I believed him, and felt better.

"Thanks," I said. "Though – I suppose, in a way, it'd help you if he did?"

"Yes, it would," he agreed. "But I'm not sure he'd make that kind of mistake."

I wanted so much to ask who 'he' – Lesser – was! But, since Alan hadn't volunteered the information, I didn't quite dare. I certainly didn't want to admit I'd deliberately listened in on a private conversation.

Peter McLeish sat motionless and silent in the passenger seat in front of me.

I found myself staring at the back of his head, remembering something else Alan had said to him yesterday.

"*...You might just owe her your life. And even if you're not that attached to it, the rest of us would still prefer you here and alive...*"

I wondered what he'd meant by that.

At the airport I had time to make a brief call from a public phone, advising my father what flight we would be on and when, approximately, we should be landing at Gatwick. We made some provisional arrangements on where to meet, and then I rang off, vowing to myself to make getting a replacement mobile a priority.

During the flight Alan made sure the conversation was kept light. He told me a bit more about his family; his wife Jane, the children, Craig and Sophie. In turn I gave him a sketch of my own – my father Richard, an English teacher and head of department in a comprehensive school, on the point of retiring; my mother, Beth, now working part-time as a proof-reader for an education publisher; my brother David, married and living in Wales; and lastly me, a library assistant, four mornings a week only. Peter mostly sat silent, listening to us, and – I realized – spending a lot of his time watching me.

It occurred to me that there was something Alan was probably still speculating about, but hadn't asked. That matter I'd mentally tabled yesterday. I felt I owed it to him to explain.

"By the way," I said. "You've been much too polite to ask, but I thought you might still be wondering."

He raised his eyebrows in polite enquiry. I waved my left hand at him, the back of my hand turned toward him, the fingers spread wide.

"The wedding-ringless Mrs Gregory thing," I said.

"Ah!" he said, his face clearing. "Yes, I admit, I did wonder about that."

Peter stirred for an instant, then sank back into stillness. Even though I wasn't looking directly at him, I was aware of his eyes fixed on my face.

"It's just that I'm a widow," I explained, still – ostensibly – addressing Alan. "Of about two years' standing. So I don't wear the ring anymore. But I was proud to take his name when I married him, so I've kept that."

"I'm sorry," said Alan. "What happened?"

I felt the familiar twinge of grief in my chest.

"The official verdict at the inquest was death by misadventure," I said briefly. Briefly, because I could feel the familiar tightening of my throat muscles that still occasionally afflicted me when on this subject.

Peter had picked up on my phrasing.

"What do you mean by 'official'?"

I meant to answer him; I even opened my mouth to speak. But, unexpectedly, I found I couldn't. It was as if everything that had happened in the last couple of days had welled up and combined with the memories of bereavement, and it was too much. Which took me by surprise, because I was perfectly willing to tell him. But I could tell that if I tried, all I'd do would be to start crying; I was familiar with that tight sensation in my throat. The anguish on my face as I looked at him in apology was directed at myself, at the way grief and stress were unexpectedly crippling me when I least wanted them to, but, naturally enough, he misinterpreted it as being my reaction to his asking the question in the first place.

"Okay," he said quickly. "It's okay. Don't worry about it. Forget I asked. I'm sorry."

I shook my head.

"It's all right," I managed, forcing the words past the lump in my throat. "I don't mind. I *want* to tell you. It's just… I don't think… Not right now…"

"I'm sorry," he said again.

"Another time," I promised him, nodding urgently, fighting to impart my willingness, as opposed to my current inability, to do so. "Promise…"

"Okay," he agreed. "Don't worry about it now."

I smiled at him tremulously, and looked away, out of the window, at the cloud-shrouded expanse of England's green and pleasant land passing underneath us, to give myself time to recover my self-possession.

And for Peter's sake, and Alan's. They were probably feeling highly embarrassed by my sudden emotionality. Just as I was. Poor things.

Eventually the plane touched down at Gatwick, and the procedures for exiting the plane and the airport itself inexorably carried us through and out into the concourse. Alan and I had both retrieved our minimal luggage, but Peter, of course, had nothing but what he stood up in. Everything he'd had with him had been in the burnt-out car. I wondered what had become of his pistol after it had been borne away by the police to Inverness. He obviously couldn't have had it on the plane. I guessed it would probably be couriered down by road, or by some other equally efficient and covert means.

We carefully threaded our way through the other people milling about in the immense thoroughfare; as we neared the main exit, by unspoken mutual consent we slowed to a halt. I put my bags down, and looked at Alan and Peter.

"I suppose this is goodbye, then," I said, surprising myself by the degree of reluctance I felt about the concept. "Thank you for seeing me home, so to speak."

"Your father's collecting you from here, is he?" Alan asked. The sort of superfluous thing people say in these situations, even when they already know the answer. I nodded.

"I told him I'd wait just inside till he turned up." I held out my hand, and he accepted it and shook it. "Thank you, Alan. You've been immensely kind," I told him.

"Well, you may not have seen the last of me yet," he said. "I might be getting in touch again."

"I hope you do," I said. "I'd hate to be left on a cliffhanger. And I'd like to know how" – I glanced momentarily in Peter's direction – "things go. If you're able to tell me."

Alan had caught that brief movement of my eyes, and understood.

"I will," he promised.

I looked at Peter.

"Bye, Peter," I said, as casually as I could. "Look after yourself, won't you?"

"I'll make sure he does," said Alan firmly. "I'm not having all your hard work go to waste."

I continued to look at Peter.

"Whatever happens, I hope" – I wasn't sure quite how to express what I wanted to say – "I hope everything works out all right in the end."

He raked my face with those huge, dark eyes of his. Then, with a swift movement that took me by surprise, he stepped forward and clasped his sound arm round me in a fierce embrace. Instinctively I responded, putting both my arms around him, and stood motionless while he held me close. I heard the hiss of breath being expelled between his teeth as his grip briefly tightened. Then, equally swiftly, he almost thrust me away in an abrupt gesture of separation, and strode toward the exit doors without a word or even a backward glance.

I looked at Alan, and he at me; he seemed as perplexed by Peter's behaviour as I was.

"Go on," I said. "Get after him. Don't worry about me."

He nodded, already on the move. But he turned back briefly, to say "I *will* be in touch, Jenny," before he hurried after the rapidly distancing figure of his cousin.

I watched him go, saw him catch up with Peter just as he got to the doors. Then I lost them in the shifting crowd of other travellers exiting the terminal.

I was still thinking about Peter's strange behaviour when I realized my father was there. A slim man of medium height, brown hair beginning to thread with silver, his face lighting up at the sight of me. He came straight up to me and I threw my arms around his neck, burying my face in his shoulder and inhaling the familiar, comforting scent of his aftershave.

"Oh, Dad," I said, my voice muffled against his jacket.

"Come on, darling," he said. "Let's get you home."

It's not so far in distance from Gatwick to Croydon, but the volume of traffic can make it a moveable feast in terms of the time it takes to drive from one to the other. On this occasion, I had plenty of time to tell Dad about everything that had happened, in full detail. Sometimes I found my throat tightening up with remembered tension, sometimes I dissolved into entirely characteristic tears; I can be very emotional at times, but of course Dad was used to that.

I told him everything; he's a good listener, my father. Both my parents are, in fact, but I've always taken pride in the fact that our relationship is such that there's never been anything I haven't been able to tell my father. Not everyone is so lucky.

When I finally fell silent, he mulled over what he'd heard for some seconds.

"What are you thinking?" I asked at last, somehow unable to wait for him to tell me in his own time. He smiled.

"I was thinking how very proud I am of you," he observed calmly. I swallowed as a sudden lump appeared in my throat. Then he glanced at me with a glint of his customary dry humour, and went on, "Plus, I'm wondering how long it'll take to organize a new set of tyres for the car. How much it'll cost. Whether the Bank of Mum and Dad will need to take a hand. That sort of thing."

I pretended to punch him, gently, on his upper arm.

"Well, at least you've got your priorities right," I said happily.

"Of course," he agreed. "I'll give Fergus a ring later on."

"He was so kind, Dad."

"Quite a lot of people still are, despite the evidence of social trends. Of course, you do realize you're going to have to go through the whole story again for your mother, don't you?"

I smiled.

"No problem. She'll listen to it all, ask penetrating and insightful questions about anything she thinks I've left out, and promptly ask me what I want for tea. She's the practical one of the family."

"Oh, I've got my uses, too," my father disputed amiably. "Besides, from what you've been telling me, you've been pretty practical yourself over all this."

"I suppose so," I said, looking out of the window.

"And do you think you'll be hearing any more from either of them? These McLeishes of yours, I mean?"

I considered for a moment.

"I – think so," I said at last. "I don't think Alan was fobbing me off. I think he meant it. When – no idea. But – yes, I think so."

"Then we shall await developments with interest," said my father.

After that, it was only a few more minutes before we were pulling into the driveway of the house.

Someone in Dad's family, back in the early years of Victoria's reign, had evidently had a bit of money – enough to acquire the medium-sized detached villa which had made its way, unsold, down the family tree to him. It had been my home until I married, and now it was my home again. When David and I had been very small, our paternal grandmother had lived with us as well, and Dad had had the back rooms of the second floor converted into a self-contained annexe flat, with the half of the loft over that part of the house made into a couple of extra rooms, one of which was the main bedroom. That done, he'd had an external brick staircase built on the side of the house to give the flat a separate entrance from the main house. After Gran had succumbed with merciful suddenness to a heart attack, David had lived in the flat for a bit, to give him a measure of independence, until he met Bronwyn, got married, and moved away. Now it was my home, the place where I lived. With my parents, yet not with them. Independent, but close. Ideal for all of us.

Mother must have had an ear cocked for our arrival, because as soon as we drove in she appeared at the living room window for a moment, confirmed it was us, and disappeared again. Moments later she had the front door open, waiting for us. For me.

"Darling," she said, her arms spreading in welcome like a flower opening to the sun. We shared a fervent hug.

"Sorry if you've been worrying," I apologized. She smiled dismissively.

"You're here, you're safe," she said. "That's the important thing. I expect you're tired, aren't you? I gather a lot's been happening to you."

"I am, a bit," I admitted.

"Well, have dinner with us. Then you can go and have an early night. Come on – get yourself inside. I want to hear all about it, you know!"

"Who'd have thought?" I commented demurely, preceding her into the house, while my father enacted the role of rearguard with a quiet smile.

Life went back to its customary routine after that. More or less. That doctor at the police station had been quite right; I did feel a bit low for a few days, but it passed, and I seemed to be all right after that. I acquired a replacement mobile and opened a new email account, as Alan McLeish had advised, after deleting all the emails and contacts in my previous one. Uselessly bolting the stable door, as one does.

When Fergus phoned to say that both the lodge and my car had been released from police custody, so to speak, I made the necessary arrangements for the local garage we usually dealt with when we were up there to fit a replacement set of tyres for me, and repair the broken lock on the boot. We also needed to organize a telephone engineer to repair the damaged junction box; Mary Riach helpfully volunteered to be present when he came, to let him in, and so on.

We got the notification from the Riachs on a Thursday evening that all had been done, so on the Saturday Dad and I flew up to Scotland together to check on the lodge, and before that, to collect my car.

"Good as new," Dad observed, as I slid into the driver's seat beside him, gave a last wave of thanks to Robbie, who'd done the work for me, and drove out of the garage.

"Let's hope we can say the same about the lodge," I said dryly. "I don't want Mother on my case. *'What would your grandmother say if she saw the place in this state…?'*"

He chuckled.

Unlike the last time I'd been there, it was a beautiful day; the sun was pouring down honeyed light out of a cloudless blue sky as I pulled off the track and into the parking slot. I switched off the engine and sat for a moment, looking at the familiar frontage, thinking about what had happened.

My father leaned forward slightly to catch my eye.

"All right, Jenny?"

I smiled at him.

"Yeh," I said. "Just remembering, that's all. Don't worry." I got out and led the way over to the front door. The ghost of Peter, being dragged in with lolling head, followed me up the step and into the hall.

"I'll start us a coffee," said my father, heading directly for the kitchen.

My first priority, though, was to divert into the living room and scan the flooring, rugs and sofas minutely for any traces of blood. I did find what I thought were a couple, but they were hard to detect.

"Think I might have got away with it," I said, joining Dad in the kitchen. He was spooning coffee and sugar into a couple of mugs while the kettle rumbled towards boiling point. "Oh – we won't have any milk, will we?" I said, momentarily diverted from what I was saying.

He pointed at a plastic half-litre container on the table.

"Got that while you were sorting things out in the garage. I know you don't like it black."

"You're the most wonderful man in the world," I told him, giving him a peck on the cheek.

"Probably not, in reality, but I don't mind if you tell me so from time to time," he said equably. "And what is it you might have got away with?"

"Mother not seeing a flock of bloodstains when she's next here. I could spot a few little traces, but that's only because I knew where to look. Next time she has the rug cleaned, that'll sort it, I should think."

"Such relief," said Dad tranquilly. He handed me my mug, and took a sip from his own. "No *bean nighe*, then? No Washer at the Ford?"

"I always thought she materialized before the event, not after. Now, if she'd turned up a few weeks ago, that might have been a warning worth having." *Would have been for Mike, anyway. And for Peter.*

I didn't want to tell Dad what had just crossed my mind, so I lifted my eyebrows at him and took a mouthful of coffee.

"Still, there is some bloody linen to be washed," I went on. "I doubt the police clean-up went that far. Might as well take it home and do it. Mind you, some of it might be beyond saving."

"I'm sure your mother will forgive you, in the circumstances," Dad assured me. "Now, I'd better give Fergus a ring and see if he's about. I've got a bottle of Highland Park in the car by way of a thank you for him. And a large box of suitably expensive chocolates for Mary, for being so helpful with the telephone engineer."

The outcome of the call to Fergus was an invitation from himself and Mary to come to dinner, which I was relieved for Dad to accept on behalf of both of us; it meant I wouldn't have to cook, and we were only staying overnight in any case. A few hours later I was able to assure Mary she'd outdone herself in the culinary stakes, and both her and Fergus that I was perfectly all right and quite recovered from my experiences.

"Glad to hear it," said Fergus with feeling. "That young man definitely owes you a debt of thanks."

I couldn't help smiling inwardly at his definition of a 'young' man – my own estimate was that Peter was within a very loud shout of forty – but didn't say anything.

"Talking of thanks…" said my father, producing his gifts. "That's to thank you for all your help. Much appreciated, both of you."

Mary exclaimed over the chocolates, and at the sight of the bottle Fergus's eyes positively glowed. I hadn't yet come across a single malt he didn't like, but Highland Park was one of his particular favourites; he'd acquired a taste for it on a holiday he and Mary had taken on the Orkney Islands many years back, and never lost it since, despite the competition available.

"Well, that's one of the best 'thanks' I've had in a long time," he said warmly. "I think I should break it open now and we should all have a dram to celebrate Jenny's – well…" He obviously couldn't think of the right word, but as it was only an excuse anyway, I didn't mind.

"Heroic achievements? Outstanding courage? Phenomenal personal beauty?" I suggested, primping ostentatiously. Mary laughed out loud.

"What about your incredible modesty?" suggested my father, his tongue firmly in his cheek.

"That'll do," I agreed, accepting a tumbler from Fergus, who was also laughing. He raised his own glass.

"Here's to the English sense of humour," he said.

"And here's to the kindness of the Scots to their friends," returned my father, his eyes meeting mine, glowing with laughter and love.

And that, I thought, was that.

Three weeks went by, and I began to assume that if there'd been anything further the police needed from me, I'd have heard about it by now. I found, however, that the memories from that day, far from sinking into latency, seemed never to be very far from the surface of my mind, and were ready to replay themselves in my mind's eye with great frequency. Perhaps I hadn't told Fergus and Mary the truth after all; perhaps I wasn't completely recovered. Though it was no great surprise that something so – disturbing, I supposed, was the right word? – still had its hooks in my psyche. I'd just have to be patient, and let time do its work. I did hope, though, that Alan McLeish would keep his word, and let me know how Peter was doing; that was a bit more difficult to be patient about.

Then, at last, I got the call.

It came through on my parents' landline. All the extensions for that are in their part of the house, so when there's a call for me, Dad rings my mobile.

"Jenny, call for you," he said. "Are you free, or shall I give him your mobile number? I don't think he's got your new one."

"Who?"

"DCI McLeish."

My heart gave a little jump of anticipation.

"I'll come," I said quickly. "Tell him I'll be there in a minute."

I hurried to the 'back door' – the door from my hallway that opens into the main part of the house, but that I never use except on occasions such as this, or when my parents expressly invite me – and downstairs to the hall, where my father was waiting, holding the receiver out to me. I took it from him, mouthing my thanks to him silently; he smiled and vanished into the living room.

"Hello?" I said, slightly breathless.

"Hello – Jenny? Alan McLeish here," came his voice. "How are you?"

"Oh, fine, thanks. Got my car back safely, and all that. So, what can I do for you?"

"Well, on an official level, nothing. Although, I imagine you've got another mobile by now? It might be handy if you could let me have your new number. In case I need to get hold of you for any reason?"

"Of course." I gave it to him. "Sorry I didn't do that before."

"No problem. There haven't been any developments to tell you about, so far. But thanks. However" – his voice changed to a more casual tone – "this isn't really an official call. I promised you an update on how Peter was doing. So I wondered if you'd care to have dinner with us? Myself and Jane, that is. She'd like to meet you, very much."

I was taken by surprise. The most I'd expected was a phone call, not a social invitation to his home. That put things on a different footing entirely.

"Well, that's – I'm…" I stammered. Then I pulled myself together. "Sorry – not being very coherent, am I?"

"I'll forgive you," he said. From the tone of his voice, I could easily picture the smile on his face. "Provided the answer is yes."

"Yes! Yes, it is. And thank you. Very much! Where and when?"

He gave me his address, and we fixed up for the coming Friday evening.

"By the way, you won't mind if the kids are there, I hope? I'm pretty certain they'd like to meet you, too."

"Well, provided they want to be there – yes, I'd be delighted." Again, he'd managed to surprise me. If I'd given the subject any thought at all, I would have assumed two teenagers would have had other ways in mind to spend their Friday evening. "You do know you're making me feel like some sort of celebrity, don't you?" I accused.

"I promise you, no autographs will be requested," he chuckled. "See you on Friday, Jenny. Thanks."

"Thank you," I told him.

I put the receiver into its cradle and stood there, staring into space, mulling over this unexpected development. Then I went to the living room door and knocked lightly before opening it.

My parents, both seated on the main sofa, looked up at me enquiringly.

"Everything all right?" Mother asked.

I let out a little breath of wry amusement.

"Yes. Quite all right. I just thought you'd like to know Alan McLeish and his wife have invited me to dinner on Friday. Apparently she wants to meet me."

Mother nodded, quite without surprise.

"I'm sure she does," she agreed. "I would, if I were her."

"Yes, but – he's a DCI," I said, still slightly incredulous about the whole thing. "I mean, he can't go round inviting everyone he meets in the course of an investigation back for dinner!"

"It's nothing to do with that, silly girl," said my father with fond amusement. "It's because of what you did for his cousin. That pulls it out of the realms of the official and into the realms of the personal. They're grateful. They want to show it. This is how." He shrugged, clearly comfortable with the whole concept.

"Don't undersell yourself, Jenny, darling," my mother advised. "Or what you did. Alan McLeish clearly doesn't."

"Okay," I said, putting my hands up in a gesture of surrender. "I'll go quietly, promise."

But I still thought Alan was going above and beyond.

However pleased I was about it.

Chapter 6

A few minutes before the appointed hour on Friday evening, I approached the door of the McLeish home – a good, stout piece of workmanship in gloss-painted oak – and rang the bell. After only a few moments Alan answered.

"Jenny," he said, smiling a welcome. "Thanks for coming."

"I'm a little early," I apologized. "I tend to err on the side of too punctual. Hope that's all right?"

"Of course! Here, let me take your coat. Okay? The lounge is the first door on the right. Jane'll be with us in just a moment. She's at a particularly crucial point with a sauce, I gather." He smiled again, and ushered me in. "Please, sit down."

"Thank you, but before I do – this is a thank you for this evening," I said, proffering the bag he'd so far politely been ignoring in my hand.

"Before it's even happened?" he teased, accepting it. He peered inside, and his eyebrows raised briefly in appreciation.

At that moment the door was pushed further open as Jane McLeish came in. She was a tall woman of medium build and a good figure; she had a graceful and elegant air about her. She wore her dark hair shoulder-length, and her eyes sparkled with intelligence and good nature. She came across to me, holding out her hand, which I shook.

"Hello, Jenny. It's lovely to meet you. Thank you for coming," she said. Her manner was easy and genuine. I liked her immediately.

"It was very kind of you to ask me," I said.

"Given what you did for Peter, it was the very least we could do," she said, and her tone made it clear that what could have been a mere bromide was sincerely meant.

"Jenny's brought us a present," said Alan, thrusting his hand into the bag and withdrawing a bottle of white wine. "More than one, actually."

Jane looked impressed as he followed it with the bottle of red and then the large tin of Belgian chocolate-covered biscuits.

"Goodness!" she said, laughing.

"Well, I thought I'd hedge my bets with the wine," I excused myself. "And sometimes I think biscuits are more generally useful than chocolates. I hope I got that right?"

"With two teenagers in the house? Absolutely," she assured me cheerfully. "Dinner should be ready in about ten minutes. Would you like a drink of some sort in the meanwhile?"

"No, I'm fine, thanks."

She looked at me more closely, with the sort of vaguely puzzled look people wear when something is jogging their memory.

"We haven't met before, have we?" Then she smiled, laughing at herself. "Sorry! That's a terrible cliché, isn't it? But you do look a bit familiar…"

"Clichés were invented for a perfectly valid reason," I said, smiling back. "Maybe I look a bit like someone you do know?"

"Perhaps that's it. Oh, well, not to worry," she agreed equably. "Anyway, time I returned to the scene of the crime!" She exchanged a brief glance with Alan before she left the room; the sort of look a husband and wife share when they're on the same wavelength, laughing at the same thing.

"Family in-joke," Alan explained. "They mostly tend to be on the same theme."

"I can imagine," I smiled.

"Right, so – Peter. Update report," he said, dropping into one of the armchairs and indicating I should do likewise. "Clean bill of health impending. The cut in his shoulder was a pretty nasty one, very deep, but it's okay now. He's due for his medical on Monday. If the doctor gives him the all clear, he'll be back at work Tuesday."

"I'm glad to hear it. But" – I hesitated – "what about – well, Mike? How is he about that?" I put the question carefully, aware that it would be a sensitive subject with Alan, too.

The corners of his mouth went down slightly.

"We all went to the funeral," he said, the memory making him momentarily dour. Then he met my eyes. "But it's an occupational hazard in the areas in which we operate. So, unfortunately, you have to deal with it from time to time. Peter knows that. He's doing it, gradually. It's just that he feels more than normally responsible, because—" He broke off.

"Because he was the real target." I completed his sentence; he nodded, briefly.

"That's got to be so hard…" I said slowly.

He nodded again, but before either of us could say anything more, we heard Jane's voice out in the hall, calling upstairs.

"Come on, you two! We're just about ready!"

"Coming!" replied a girl's voice from somewhere above.

"Well, make sure Craig's coming, too," her mother instructed. A moment later, she put her head round the door.

"Come on through," she invited me.

"Thank you," I said with a smile, and got up. Alan did likewise, and guided me further along the hall to the dining room. He indicated my place, on the far side of the immaculately set table, but I'd not got as far as taking my seat when two young people entered the room.

"Ah, there you are," said Alan. "This is Jenny. Jenny, meet Sophie and Craig."

"Hello," I said.

"Hi," they said, almost together. Sophie was about thirteen, I estimated, and both facially and in colouring favoured her mother, though she'd clearly got her eyes from her father. Craig, on the other hand, was very much like Alan, though he, too, was dark-haired, like Jane. Though at about fifteen years of age or so he probably still hadn't reached his full height, he was clearly going to be tall and slim, like Alan and Peter; indeed, because of his colouring, I suspected that when he had finished outgrowing his teenage tendency to be all knees and elbows, he was probably going to resemble Peter quite a lot. As we sat down and the meal got underway, it was obvious Sophie was the more outgoing of the two, though Craig, while he didn't comment as much as she did, was merely quieter, not shy; in fact, he revealed a remarkable degree of self-possession for a boy of his age. After only a few minutes all of us seemed to have overcome the initial struggle to seem at home with complete strangers, and the conversation became more relaxed.

"Of course," Jane observed, as she passed me one of the dishes from which to help myself, "what we're really dying to hear about is how you rescued Peter. Alan's told us a bit, but we were hoping for the gorier details." She smiled conspiratorially at me.

"Yeh – did you really have to take all Peter's clothes off?" Sophie asked mischievously, with a giggle. She promptly covered her mouth with her hand, but her eyes sparkled with laughter.

"Indeed I did," I confirmed amiably. "But I'm afraid it's no substitute for a formal introduction."

Craig couldn't muffle his snort of amusement, and there were smiles all round.

"Although I would like to point out, in my defence, it wasn't a social occasion," I reminded them, euphemistically. "I was trying to prevent him contracting pneumonia, otherwise I might not have been so – precipitate..."

"Good thing you were," said Jane, briskly. "And we're all very grateful." She raised her wine glass in my direction, and Alan echoed the gesture.

"To Jenny, and her impromptu, if brief, career as a nurse," he said, encompassing all his family with a sweep of his eyes as he did so.

"Thank you," I said, and winked at Craig and Sophie, both of whom were doing a very bad job of suppressing their amusement.

Of course, I gave them the full account, as they wanted. And the fact that they wanted it, and their parents permitted it, was a revelation of its own. Because I realized that whatever the history was that had led up to someone trying to kill Peter, they must all be aware of it, the children included, or Jane would never have issued an invitation for the whole story. Which was – interesting. Even at thirteen, Sophie, aware that her – well, I suppose technically Peter was her second cousin, but the relationship came across more as that of a favourite uncle – but aware that he was under such a threat, and yet apparently regarding that as normal? And her parents endorsing that degree of openness? I very much hoped that at some point I'd be favoured with the explanation behind it all.

But for the time being I simply gave them my story, deliberately editing out mention of the wrecked car and its grisly occupant, and, while not omitting it, playing down the fear I'd felt at the Lodge; instead, taking a more factual, 'this is what happened' witness-statement approach. I detected approval in Alan's expression; even if the background was well known within the family, I sensed he was grateful I wasn't trying to sensationalize anything.

"Now let's talk about something more cheerful," he said decisively, when I'd finished. "What about you, Jenny? Tell us about yourself."

"Oh," I said, not very intelligently, and pulled a face to indicate that the answer wasn't going to be very exciting. "Well, the 'in a nutshell' description is that I'm thirty-five, and I work part-time as a library assistant."

"That's a bit bald," Jane reproved me, as she rose and started to collect the used dinner plates. "I'm sure there's more to you than—" She broke off, and treated me once again to that puzzled look she'd worn earlier when she'd asked me if we'd met. "Wait a minute! Library assistant? Do you work in the local library, by any chance?"

"Yes. Four mornings a week," I said.

"That's where I've seen you! Oh, I'm so glad I've remembered! It was going to keep nagging at me that I'd seen you before somewhere. I'm not surprised you don't remember me, though," she added, with an unnecessary tinge of apology, resuming her collection of crockery and cutlery. "I don't go in there that often, and you must have hundreds of people going through every day."

"Happily, yes," I agreed. "Sorry my memory isn't as good as yours."

"I expect it is, really," she demurred. "Now, what about pudding? Then you can tell us about your interests, and we can tell you about ours." She rose and headed for the kitchen.

"So, what are yours?" I said, turning to the rest of the family.

"Haven't got time for any," Alan disclaimed.

"What, none at all?" I frowned at him in mock disapproval.

"Well, I do try to keep track of what Bolton Wanderers are doing, but I don't get the chance very often," he admitted.

"And you draw, Dad," Sophie reminded him.

"You're an artist?" I followed up swiftly, raising my eyebrows at him.

He snorted. "Hardly! Can't paint, to save my life! But I do a bit of pencil doodling sometimes, when I get the chance to unwind. Again, not something that happens very often, sadly."

"Doodling," I repeated, sceptically. "You must be better than that, or Sophie wouldn't be advertising."

"You should show her some of your stuff, Dad," Craig chipped in, unexpectedly. Alan gave him a quick *Et tu, Brute?* look, and gave in.

"Maybe another time," he agreed.

"And what about you, Sophie? What do you do for fun?"

"Apart from playing music much too loud in her bedroom, and spending half her life either texting or online, you mean?" said her father dryly. Sophie pulled a face at him.

"That's not fair, Dad!" she protested, and turned back to me. "I like swimming and tennis, as well – I do those after school with my friends, sometimes. And Mum takes me to dance classes every Thursday."

"Goodness! I'm exhausted, just listening to you!" I laughed.

"Well, what about you?" she returned promptly. "What do you like doing?"

"Ah! That's the bit I'm interested in," said her mother genially, returning from the kitchen with a tray laden with dessert dishes and a huge and spectacular-looking meringue pavlova, heavy with fruit and cream.

"I'm not talented in any kind of stand-out way, but I like photography, and filming with my camcorder. And I'm interested in television and films. Not just watching them, but knowing how they're made, and who makes them. I like all sorts of drama series, and I like history and science documentaries, that sort of thing – I watch quite a lot of them. I suppose I listen to Radio 4 quite a lot. Plus quite a few sports I like watching on TV."

"Which ones?" Alan enquired.

I shrugged. "Oh – golf, sailing, cycling, winter sports, WRC rallying. That sort of thing. Wouldn't be any good at any of them, but I enjoy watching them. Not like Sophie! I'm definitely an armchair athlete. Oh, and I like reading, of course. Better not forget that one, given the nature of my job!" I added lightly.

Jane smiled and glanced at her son, then back at me.

"You'll get on all right with Craig, then," she observed briskly, starting to section the pavlova and transfer it into the dishes. "The TV and film thing – he's mad keen on all that."

"Have you got an enormous DVD library, like him?" Sophie enquired.

"Quite a few," I admitted. "Maybe we should compare notes sometime, Craig."

He looked surprisingly accepting of the suggestion; I'd thought he'd have been less enthusiastic, but in fact he seemed quite keen.

"I'll show you my DVD collection after dinner," he said calmly. "If you like."

"If you go in his room, watch out for the rats," said Sophie unexpectedly, and somewhat dramatically.

"Rats?" I'll freely admit I was slightly taken aback by the warning.

"Yeh, he's got two pet rats," she enlarged, screwing up her nose. "I hate them. Don't you hate rats?"

"Er – no, actually," I admitted. "I think the poor things get an undeservedly bad press. Like wolves." I turned to Craig. "What colour are they?"

His eyes gleamed at me approvingly from under the long dark fringe. "One's albino, the other's a sort of chocolate brown," he said.

"What do you call them?"

"I know what *I* call them," said Sophie, with emphasis.

"Shut up, you," Craig said with big-brotherly, tolerant scorn. He looked back at me. "The albino's Ruby, because of the eyes. And the brown one's called Chocky."

"Chocky as in chocolate? Or Chocky as in the John Wyndham novel?" I enquired.

"Chocolate," he confirmed. His slightly quizzical expression made me wonder if he'd ever heard of either book or author before. Ah, well...

"Sounds very appropriate," I commented. "I look forward to being introduced to them."

After the meal Sophie accompanied me up to Craig's room, where I duly met the rats; Sophie squealed in an overdramatic fashion when I consented to have them loaded onto me – one on my shoulders, the other into my hands, from both of which locations they inevitably scuttled all over me. I didn't mind; actually, I thought it was rather fun. After they'd been restored to their cage, Craig and I started discussing his DVD collection, diverging onto a wide range of topics touching on film-making. He showed me his camcorder, which was a much more sophisticated one than mine.

Sophie gamely hung round for a while for politeness' sake, but then went back downstairs, where her parents were clearing the table and loading the dishwasher.

"Hello – where are Craig and Jenny?" asked Jane, straightening up from slotting the last of the plates into the rack.

"Oh, they're up there talking about editing software," Sophie shrugged. "Or something like that, anyway. Honestly, she's as mad about film-making as he is! And they both like a lot of the same TV programmes, sounds like. You know, some of those old series he likes so much. I get bored with all that."

"What did she make of the rats?" Alan enquired.

Sophie's eyes widened.

"She liked them!" she blurted, almost accusingly. "She had them running all over her! Yuck! I don't know how she could stand them. They're horrible!"

"Not to everyone," Alan observed calmly. "Luckily for the rats."

"Well, I think they are," she declared emphatically.

"And what do you think of her?" Jane asked, drying her hands, and turning to look at her daughter with interest. "Do you like her?"

Sophie considered, then shrugged.

"She's all right," she allowed. Then she grinned. "I still think it's funny, her taking all Peter's clothes off!"

"You," said Alan disapprovingly, "have a one-track mind."

"Of course I do, Dad," she agreed. "It's my age. All those seething hormones! Didn't you know?" She screwed her nose up at him, laughing as he pulled a face at her. She looked at Jane. "Is it all right if I go up to my room now? Even though she's still here?"

"Provided you promise to come down again to say goodbye, later," Jane agreed.

"Thanks, Mum!" Sophie waved a little gesture of appreciation, and bolted back up the stairs.

"And what about you?" Alan asked, turning to his wife. "What do you think of her?"

"I like her," said Jane promptly. "She's so" – she sought the right adjective – "up front. Unpretentious. She meets your eyes when she's talking to you. And when she's listening to you. And she's nice. Considerate." She looked at him. "You took to her straight away, didn't you?"

"I thought she showed a lot of common sense in a situation outside of her experience," he agreed, putting some of the bottles and jars whose contents had contributed to the meal back into their cupboards. "I noticed the eye contact thing, too, when I interviewed her. I think she genuinely cared about Peter's welfare, too. Still does." He looked up, and caught Jane's eye. "Now, now," he chided her. "Don't start getting ideas."

"It's hard not to," she complained, making a brief moue with her mouth. "He can't stay as he is forever."

"Maybe not, but let's let things take their own course, shall we?" he advised. "I've told him the least he owes her is a dinner, and he didn't argue. So let's see what happens, eh?"

Jane smiled at him fondly.

"Okay," she said. "But I don't promise not to hope!"

"I wouldn't dare suggest it," Alan said, a teasing gleam in his eye.

Jane pulled a face at him, and went out into the hallway. Putting one hand on the newel post of the staircase, she called up, "Jenny! Craig! When you come down, we'll be in the lounge…"

"Be down in just a moment," came my response from above.

"It's all right; no need to hurry," Jane assured us.

A few minutes later Craig and I appeared in the doorway of the lounge.

"Sorry to be so long," I apologized. "We got talking…"

The remainder of the evening went on in the same vein; easy, light conversation that touched on a range of subjects. Often seeking my thoughts and views. Of course, they were trying to find out about me. I'd done something they valued for someone they valued; it was only to be expected. I didn't mind. I liked them. And when it came time to go, and Jane offered the usual commonplace about doing it again sometime, she wasn't just mouthing a platitude; I could tell she meant it. Which was flattering and gratifying, and I could honestly assure her that I felt the same. And could therefore take heart from Alan's promise to get in touch again.

As I drove home, mulling pleasurably over the evening, I found there was one particular exchange that kept coming to the surface of my mind. It had been when I'd been up in Craig's room. He'd unexpectedly come out with something that had both surprised me and given me a rather inordinate degree of pleasure.

"Jenny," he'd said with what was meant to sound like casualness, not looking directly at me.

"What?" I'd enquired.

"D'you mind if I say something?" His eyes were still averted.

"Of course not," I'd assured him gently. Whatever he was about to come out with, it evidently wasn't something he could express all that easily, and I hadn't wanted to frighten him out of saying it.

"I just wanted" – he'd paused, then gone on quickly, his voice cracking in its earnestness – "I just wanted to say – I think you were very brave. When you helped Peter." Then, at last, he'd glanced at me; almost nervously, as though afraid I might scoff, or otherwise reject his approval for some reason.

As if! I'd been too touched by his being prepared to venture such a comment to a woman he'd barely met.

"I didn't feel brave while it was happening," I'd told him honestly

"But thank you for thinking so. And for saying so. Thank you."

Then Jane had called up the stairs, and we'd gone down.

But I couldn't help replaying his words over and over in my head. Or feeling quite disproportionately pleased and proud about what he'd said. That that was what he thought.

That's the kind of compliment – and source – you don't forget.

A week or so went by after that, without anything of note happening. Until the evening when Dad and Mum had gone up to London to see a couple they'd been close to early in their married lives, but who had relocated to Canada about thirty years ago. Despite the distance and the time, they'd kept in touch, sporadically, and now they were visiting England for a while they'd booked my parents in for a couple of days at the hotel where they were staying, for a reunion.

"We'll be back the day after tomorrow," Mother assured me as they left. They were making an early start; it wasn't even time for me to leave for work yet.

"You make sure you have a wonderful carouse, the lot of you," I told her with a grin. She smiled and got into the car.

"Bye, darling," Dad called from beside her, just managing to get the words out before she shut the door. They both waved, and the car pulled away.

The day went normally after that. It must have been about seven o'clock that evening when I became aware of a faint noise rising through the deserted house. Downstairs in the hall, the telephone was shrilling out its insistent demand for attention. And went on doing it. My parents must have forgotten to put the answer phone on before they left.

I opened my 'back door' and hurried down the stairs, fully expecting the ringing to stop before I got there, in that irritating way that telephones have. But, no – it was still going by the time I picked up the receiver.

"Hello?" I said, non-committally.

"Hello? Jenny? That you?" asked a man's voice. I instantly recognized the Lowland Scots accent.

"Peter!" I exclaimed, hoping he couldn't tell, as I could, that my heart had executed a small leap of excitement at the sound of his voice. "How's the shoulder?"

"Fine, thanks. Just a scar now, but the doctor says that'll fade, with time."

"So has Alan let you go back to work, then?"

"Yeh. I, uh, hear he and Jane had you round to their place?"

"They did! Wasn't that kind of them? And I had a really wonderful time.

You've know you've got a brilliant family, don't you? I'm afraid I rather fell for Craig! Turns out we're both TV buffs, so we got on like a house on fire."

"Yeh, he was telling me. From what I hear, he thinks you're pretty cool." Peter sounded quietly amused.

"Really? Wow! I'm flattered! If a fifteen-year-old boy thinks a strange woman twenty years his senior is 'cool', that *is* cool!"

Peter laughed.

"Oh, Craig's all right," he said indulgently, clearly not trying to sound like a proud uncle. Then his voice changed, became more diffident. "Thing is, Jenny – you see… Well, what I rang up to ask you was – have you got a free evening sometime this week?"

Hope sprang.

"Yes. All of them, as it happens. Why?" I tried to ask that as if I had no idea he might say what he was clearly about to.

"Well" – he sounded oddly hesitant, now he'd come to it – "I wondered if you'd be free for dinner, maybe? I thought – well, I owe you that, at the very least."

"You don't owe me one single, solitary thing, Peter McLeish," I contradicted him cheerfully. "But if you're really asking, then – yes, I accept with pleasure. Where and when? And do you want to pick me up, or shall I meet you there? Wherever 'there' is?"

There was a noticeable hesitation before he answered.

"Maybe you could meet me, if that's all right?" he said, with what sounded to me like slightly forced casualness. I wasn't sure if anyone else would even have noticed it, but, for some reason, I seemed to have been attuned to the nuances of his voice right from our first encounter, and apparently I still was. He went on to name time and place, and we finalized details.

"Right – I'll see you there," I announced happily. "Thank you, Peter. I'll look forward to it."

I think he could tell how sincerely the trite phrase was meant.

"Me, too," he assured me. "See you, then."

"See you," I agreed. "Thanks for ringing. Bye…"

I put the receiver down and stood there, my fingertips still resting on the phone, analyzing the sensation of rising excitement and delight I was experiencing. Still cherishing it, I went back upstairs and into my flat. The rest of the evening was going to seem distinctly anticlimactic after that phone call, somehow.

But even though I was filled with pleasure at the prospect, I found myself wondering quite how it would go when I did see him again.

After all, what *do* you say to a virtual stranger who you stripped naked without his knowledge the first time you met…?

Chapter 7

I don't know why, but I didn't tell anyone. Not even my parents. I wasn't thinking in terms of it being a secret, or anything of that sort – after all, why would it be? But what I did feel was that something quite tenuous, fragile even, shouldn't be exposed to analysis unless it was going to turn out to be something more substantial. After all, it wasn't as if we'd met under any kind of normal circumstances. The fact that I now felt some sort of emotional investment in the wellbeing of a virtual stranger because of the manner in which we'd become acquainted might in no way be validated by his own feelings in the matter. So I felt perhaps a little more trepidation in the anticipation with which I looked forward to that Friday evening than might be normal for a first date. If that was how it could be classed, and wasn't merely the discharge of an obligation.

Thankfully, it wasn't. I could tell that by the look on his face as I walked into the foyer of the restaurant where we were to rendezvous and we made eye contact; he didn't exactly smile, but I could tell he was honestly pleased to see me again.

"I hope I haven't kept you waiting?" I said a little anxiously, glancing at my watch.

"I was early," he said, with a shake of his head. "But I wasn't worried. Alan said you'd be on time. He said you were an unusual girl. Punctual." There was a brief glimmer of humour in the dark eyes.

"Thank him for the character reference," I replied lightly. *Not to mention calling me a girl, at my age…*

He steered me in the direction of the bar, and I watched him covertly as he bought the drinks, comparing him with my memory of when I'd seen him last. Unsurprisingly, he looked a lot healthier. His colour was better, though it seemed that he was naturally quite pale-skinned, and his hair, which he evidently habitually wore quite long, looked in much better condition than I remembered it. His beard was tidily trimmed, the under edges of it shaved to a neat outline under his chin.

"Thanks," I said, as he handed me my glass, hoping I'd have the skill to handle the evening successfully. It would be only too easy to put a foot wrong if certain subjects were touched on. I wasn't sure if he'd remember the promise I'd made him, but if he had, it was a promise I intended to keep. Though maybe not yet. *Wait to see how it goes. Pick the right moment. If it comes.*

As we found seats, I decided I'd go in feet first and clear the air.

"Look, Peter, before we start – can I say something?"

He looked at me enquiringly.

"We – met under rather intense circumstances," I began carefully. "And I'm glad that you wanted to meet up like this now. But do we talk about what happened? Or would you rather not? Because we won't, if you don't want to."

He studied me for a few moments. Then he shook his head, but not in dissent.

"No, it's okay," he said, taking a swallow from his glass. After a pause, he went on, "Went to Mike's funeral."

"Yes. Alan told me."

"Did he?" His eyes flicked up to mine for a moment, then returned to the glass in his hand.

"I asked him how you were."

"It wasn't great." He stared at his drink without really seeing it. "I kept looking at the coffin and thinking, *That should've been me.*"

There was something about the way he said it that made me frown in momentary puzzlement. As if there was something more to it than being due to luck, good or bad, respectively. *Why? Why* should *it have been you…?*

"It could've been you," I agreed. "But it wasn't. Someone tossed a coin and it came down on your side, this time, that's all. But I don't suppose there's any point in trying to convince you not to feel guilty about it. I expect you're as prone to irrational guilt as the rest of us."

He glanced at me, in a way that made me wonder what he was thinking.

"Yeh," he agreed. "Anyway, sooner or later, the coin'll come down the other way."

That was a more difficult one to field.

"Is your job always so very dangerous?" I enquired, carefully.

"Can be," he said flatly.

I took a sip of my drink, and said nothing.

"What about you?" he asked.

"I've thought about it a lot," I said. "What happened, that is. I've never experienced anything remotely like that before. I won't say it's preyed on my mind, exactly, it does keep coming to the surface. No nightmares, or anything like that; it just – persists, if that's the right word? It – made an impression, I suppose is the best way to put it."

"It did," he agreed, but didn't enlarge on that.

"And is your shoulder really all right?"

One corner of his mouth quirked slightly. "Got a nice dramatic scar line, still, but – yeh, it's all right."

"Glad to hear it. By the way, I've been wondering. Did they ever find your phone?"

"Oh, that! Yeh. Halfway up the hill somewhere. Must've fallen out through the window as we were rolling down." He looked at me from under levelled eyebrows. "I keep thinking – if it hadn't, you wouldn't've had to go through what you did."

"I didn't exactly go through it on my own, remember?"

"You wouldn't've had to be scared like you were."

"Maybe not. And I didn't enjoy that side of it," I said frankly. "But, like I told you – because it happened, I found things out about myself that maybe I wouldn't have done otherwise. How I react in a crisis. Obviously I'd far rather your friend was still alive, and you'd never been hurt. In that sense, I wish none of it had ever happened. But since it did – well, I've been trying to concentrate on what positives there are in it. And that's one of them. For me, anyway."

His mouth twisted in a half-smile.

"You're – sort of strange," he commented quizzically. "You look at things differently, don't you?"

I blinked, absorbing this perception of myself. What I'd said seemed quite normal and obvious to me. But then, it would, I supposed.

"That depends who you're comparing me with," I said lightly.

He smiled briefly, but didn't comment, and swallowed the last of his drink.

"Ready to eat now?" he asked.

"Yes, please," I said.

We were shown to our table, and menus were presented. I let Peter choose the wine.

"I'm not really much of a wine drinker," I admitted, when the waitress had left. "I don't tend to have it at home. Just when I come out to posh places like this. Which isn't very often, so this is a real treat – thank you."

"Do you not go out much?" The phrasing, like the voice, was beautifully Scots.

"Can't afford to," I said frankly. "Let's face it, you don't become a local government employee for the pay, do you? Not even if you're full-time. But then, you're a government employee, too – of a sort – aren't you? So I daresay you know what I mean!"

He expelled a quick breath of amusement, but didn't pursue it as a conversational gambit.

"Are you not full-time?"

"No. Mornings only, till one. Monday to Thursday. I'm a library assistant."

"Yeh, Jane said." He looked at me with that sort of remote concern one shows for people one hardly knows when they describe their personal complications to you. "How do you manage on a part-time wage?"

"With difficulty," I grinned. Then, more seriously, "Luckily, it's not my only source of income. I've got a – that is, I own a cottage in Hampshire. It was where I lived when I got married. It belonged to Alex's grandparents, and they rented it to us to start with, though eventually it came to Alex as a legacy anyway." I didn't feel the need to explain Alex was – had been – my husband; I felt sure Peter would make the correct deduction unassisted. "After he died, Dad suggested I come back to Croydon, so I wouldn't be entirely on my own. But I didn't want to get rid of the cottage, so I decided to rent it out. Long term lets. So I get a bit of income from that, as well. None of it adds up to very much, but even though I'm renting myself, I've got a *very* understanding landlord!" I grinned again, and described my flat and its location in my parents' house.

Peter nodded.

"You were lucky," he said seriously. "You had somewhere to go. Someone to go to."

"Yes," I agreed carefully, struck by the sombreness of his tone.

At that point we were interrupted by the arrival of the food; the conversation hung awkwardly suspended in the atmosphere until the waitress had left, accompanied by our smiles and thanks. When we picked up again, I deliberately turned the talk to other subjects.

Usually, one of the best ways to put a man at ease is to get him to talk about himself, though I was instinctively cautious about what questions I prompted him with. I certainly didn't think asking too deeply about his job would be a good idea. I'd already gathered from Alan that Peter's parents were dead; Alan and Jane and the children were his only remaining family, it seemed. In turn, I told him about my own family, enlarging on the thumbnail sketch I'd already given on the flight back from Scotland.

"Dad's the head of English at one of the biggest secondary schools in the area. He's going to retire at Christmas, which is making his Head complain furiously about the loss to the profession." I smiled. "But he and Mum've got plans – they want to do a bit of travelling and suchlike before they get too old to enjoy it, as he says. Mum doesn't work full-time – she wouldn't have time to fit everything else she wants to do into her life if she did! But she works part-time for a publishing company as a proof-reader, so she can do that from home."

"Proof-reading? How did she get into that?" Peter enquired.

"Ah, well – that was Dad's doing, in a way. He wrote a book – sort of a textbook for professionals, that kind of thing. Mum helped him proof it before it went to the publishers. They picked up on how good she was at it, and offered her the occasional job. Then it got to where she does it for about half the week. And then there's David. He's younger than me. Married a Welsh girl – Bronwyn – and moved to Pembrokeshire. They've got a couple of boys. He's an architect in Haverfordwest; small-scale stuff, mostly. And that's us, really."

He nodded.

"And did you always want to join the police?" I enquired lightly. "Or did you have other career plans when you were – oh, I don't know – five, say?"

He smiled.

"There were loads of things I wanted to do when I was five," he agreed. "None of which included joining the police. Not the kind of thing you'd admit to, growing up in a Glasgow suburb!" A brief glint of amusement. "But somehow that was the way it worked out. I turned out to be quite good at it." A momentarily poignant expression crossed his face as he made this admission. I wondered why.

Quite unbidden, it came to me that it might be something to do with the mysterious Lesser. *"Usually he's happy enough just making your life a misery from time to time,"* Alan had said to him. That word, 'misery' – it described almost perfectly the look that had briefly touched his features.

"But it wasn't your original intention?" I persisted.

"No."

"Then I think I should thank you," I said.

He cast a look of surprise at me.

"What for?"

"For being prepared to stand between people like me and the chaos. What I mean is" – I thought carefully about how to express what I wanted to say – "well, it's obvious you're not a standard sort of officer. Plain clothes and – well, other things. You know." Although there was nobody particularly close to us, I didn't intend the word 'gun' to be overheard by anyone, even by accident. Peter knew what I meant, though. "I don't know much about how your lot are organized, but, to me, that adds up to a team working out on the edge somewhere. In fact, Alan as good as told me so."

He looked at me unblinkingly, his face expressionless, neither confirming nor denying. But I ploughed on, because I wanted to get across to him the importance of what I was trying to articulate.

"So – assuming that's right – you probably have to deal with some pretty unpleasant people, don't you? I mean, by my standards, the average bobby on the beat does that just in the ordinary run of things. But I think you have to face a lot worse, in a way, don't you? If what I saw was anything to go by, anyway." His eyelids flickered, briefly. "But don't you see?" I leaned forward, earnestly. "It's people like you who keep that world and my sort of world from overlapping, as often as possible. I don't know what you deal with – drugs, violence, extortion? Blackmail? Murders? All sorts of nastiness and viciousness that I've never had to face. Not directly, anyway. I mean, I know those things happen, and they must be happening all around me, all the time, but they've never touched me personally before. Partly through sheer luck, but mostly it'll be because of people like you. Who *are* prepared to face them, on behalf of people like me. So that's why I want to thank you. And that's why I'm glad I was able to help you."

I suddenly realized how far toward him I had leaned in an unconscious attempt to convince him of my sincerity; I could feel myself flush as I pulled back.

"Sorry," I apologized. "I'll get off my soapbox now, if you like."

"No! No, it's – it's all right," he said quickly. "It's just – not something many people think to say."

"Well, I don't suppose you go round telling them that you're someone they ought to be saying it to," I said, striving to sound casual. "I only found that out by accident myself, let's face it!" I threw him a quick smile. "Gosh, this is heavy going for a dinner date, isn't it? Let's talk about something else, quick!"

He went on looking at me; then he smiled back, briefly. So we discussed other things. I told him about my childhood, and learned something of his; told him about my hobbies, and discussed where Craig's taste in entertainment overlapped with mine. Peter didn't tell me that much about his own interests, but I gathered when he'd been a boy he'd learned how to sail, though when I asked him whether he still did, he just shook his head.

In fact, he didn't seem disposed to tell me much about himself at all, though I didn't get the feeling he thought I was prying; he just seemed to be naturally reticent on that subject. Fair enough, I supposed; not everyone is as open about themselves as I am. Besides, I got the feeling he didn't have much to say about hobbies and interests, but not because his work was his life and crowded other things out; more because the other things simply weren't there to be crowded out. Which, if true, was extremely sad. I wondered why it had become that way, but I didn't pursue it.

It was only after we'd finished eating, and the dessert dishes had been cleared away, that I decided to keep my promise. After all, I couldn't be sure I was going to get another opportunity.

"Peter…" I said, tentatively.

He looked at me enquiringly.

"On the plane, I promised I'd tell you about Alex," I said. "I'll do it now, if you like – if you still want me to?"

He looked at me quickly, then down at his wineglass, his long, elegant fingers playing with the stem. "Only if you want to. I don't want you to get upset again."

His tone was level, but I had the feeling that he did want to know. And I didn't mind. In fact, I found it quite interesting to discover just how much I wanted him to know.

"Don't worry, I won't," I said with deliberate nonchalance, to try to put him at ease about it, make it clear I didn't mind in the least talking about it. "That is, I don't think I will. I don't often get like that about it anymore. Though I suppose it wasn't that long ago. Only a couple of years. On the plane, it was just... I don't really know why that happened. Unless it was because I was in a rather emotional state generally? I'd just been through quite an experience, you'll recall..."

I detected the slight twitch of his mouth with which he responded to my tone. Satisfied, I went on.

"Anyway, it went like this. Boy, twenty-seven, meets girl, closing in on eighteen. They become friends, fall in love and get married within the year. And set about living happily ever after. Except they can't, entirely. Because girl gradually realizes boy has a problem. A long-term, fundamental illness."

Peter looked at me intently with those dark eyes of his.

"What kind of illness?"

"Depression. Clinical depression. Which needn't have been a problem, of course. Except for one thing."

"What?"

"That he never admitted it. It wasn't until much later on I realized he was already ill when I married him, but I had no idea what was going on at first. And while I had picked up on the fact that he could be a bit down on himself, what I hadn't realized was just how fundamental his lack of self-esteem was, and how much it was tied in with the depression. When I did realize, and I read up on it, out of a list of about sixteen symptoms, he had all but a couple. *All* the time. And official advice is that if you've got more than two of them for more than two weeks, you should talk to your doctor!" I expelled a rueful snort. "But he wouldn't. Just came to the best accommodation with himself that he could. It wasn't a bad one, on the whole. Inasmuch as other people usually couldn't tell there was anything wrong. I mean, in social situations – assuming you could get him into one – you wouldn't have had a clue he had a problem! But if you'd seen us at home, sometimes... *I* knew. And so did our doctor. So of course he found it rather frustrating."

"Why?"

"Because there wasn't a thing he could do about it! Alex just wouldn't recognize he had a problem. No" – I caught myself – "that's not fair, actually. I think he really did believe it was all his own failing, that his problems were his own doing, that he was the one at fault. The self-esteem thing again… But it meant he refused to talk to the doctor about it. Or let him try to do anything about it. So it was never treated. Because it couldn't be. Alex was able to function at a level which meant it wasn't something the doctor could order him – if that's the right word – to sort out. But it crippled him in so many ways…"

I smiled; a rather crooked smile, I could tell. Peter's face remained the same, but his eyes were a giveaway. I felt sorry for him, trying to encompass what I was telling him. People who've never been in that kind of relationship usually don't really get it; often, they don't get it at all. What it's like for the other person, the one who doesn't have the illness, but has to live with the person who does. The accommodations you have to make, the strange set of rules you have to live by to make it all work. But at least he wasn't breaking in on the narrative, was allowing me to tell it my own way.

"It's a funny thing, you know," I went on, reflectively. "If he'd had a broken leg, there'd've been no question about what would have happened. He wouldn't've been allowed to try to function without it being treated. The doctor would've said what needed to be done, and he'd've had to do it. But if you've got a broken mind, seems it's not always as clear-cut as that. You're allowed to use that same mind to decide that you don't want anything done about it. And it's something that's equally, if not more, serious in the way it affects not just you, but those around you, too. And it was such a shame, such a waste! Because he had so many good qualities, so many potential abilities that he never believed in because of it. He was actually a very clever and intelligent man. But there it was." I shrugged. "It was his decision, so I had to honour that, accept it, and make my own accommodations to it. Which wasn't always easy. Because I knew things could have been so much easier for him, if things had been different. If he'd let them be different."

I paused to take a sip from the diminishing puddle of wine at the bottom of my glass. Peter was watching me intently, but still didn't interrupt.

"What you mustn't do," I went on, "is think it was all bad. Because it wasn't. There was a lot of good, a lot of laughter. People think depressives are only miserable all the time, and it doesn't work like that. But what it does mean is that underneath, their fundamental view of themselves is a negative one, and without help that doesn't change, it doesn't get better, it just gets worse. And it affects the way they look at everything. Absolutely *everything*. So if you're going to be with someone like that, you can't afford to dwell on the negatives, like they do. I couldn't, anyway. So I ended up spending most of my time contradicting him."

"What d'you mean?" He hadn't been expecting that.

"Well," I said decisively, "every time he said something bad about himself, I'd contradict him, and tell him what was good about him instead. Which I happened to think was rather a lot. I was never going to convince him, of course," I commented a little sadly. "By the time I got a handle on what to do, I was fighting over thirty years of negative self-image. But I was flippin' well going to let him know how *I* saw him, every chance I got! I don't regret marrying him – not for a moment. And I never will. Because he was a wonderful man, no matter what he thought."

There was a pause, while I took another sip of wine.

"What happened? In the end, I mean? How did he die?"

"Accident," I said. "At least, I hope so."

He frowned.

"He…" I swallowed. Despite everything, this was still hard to talk about. But I managed to keep my voice under control as I went on. "It seems he stepped out in front of a van without seeing it." I stared at the dregs of wine in my glass without seeing them. "It was the poor driver I felt sorry for. He was so cut up about it – of course he was – but there wasn't a thing he could've done about it. He just didn't have the time to react. The only good thing about it is that Alex was killed instantly."

Even in my self-absorption, I was startled by the glitter in his eyes as he looked at me.

"You're right," he said flatly. "Instant is good. It's good."

I wondered what lay behind that, and the intensity with which it was said. It wasn't the reaction I'd been expecting.

"I think so," I agreed, after a slightly awkward pause. "For Alex's sake. All his problems solved at a single stroke. He'd found just living, just having to be alive, more and more of a burden as time went on. In a strange way" – I glanced at Peter uncertainly – "this is going to sound a really weird thing to say, but – in a strange way, I was glad for him, you know?" For the first time, my voice trembled a little. "I wanted so much to make him happy, but I couldn't do that. All I could do was – was to alleviate life for him. A little. So I couldn't be sad for *him*. Because now he wouldn't be unhappy anymore."

"But you were," Peter said quietly.

I nodded, dumbly, then let out a long, shaky breath, and met his eyes again.

"I loved him," I said simply, with a small, helpless shrug.

He nodded, once, and a short silence fell. Then he looked at me again, his eyes slightly narrowed.

"What did you mean – you *hoped* it was an accident?"

I sighed again.

"Most of the time, I know it was. But when I'm feeling down, it's hard not to wonder if – well, if…"

"Ah," he said, and nodded again. Then, after another short silence, he said decisively, "Well, I don't think you should. Because I don't believe it's true."

I was surprised by the conviction of his tone.

"Why?" I blurted.

"Because he had you," he said.

I let out a quick, tremulous breath.

"Now you *are* going to make me cry," I said, blinking furiously.

"If paying you compliments is gonnae make you cry every time, I'd better start carrying a spare handkerchief," he observed, suddenly sounding very Scottish indeed, and once again there was a glimmer of humour in the dark eyes.

The implications of that remark passed me by at the time, but when the evening finally ended, and we had gone out on to the street, ready to return to our respective vehicles, naturally I was wondering if he was contemplating seeing me again. I hoped so. In spite of the serious turn the conversation had sometimes – and perhaps inevitably – taken, I had enjoyed the evening; I wanted it to happen again. But there was that nagging worry about the 'obligation' problem… Characteristically, I decided to lay it on the line.

"Peter," I said, stopping and turning to face him. "Can I say something?"

"Again?" he teased gently. "Is this how you top and tail an evening? '*Can I say something?*'"

I half-smiled, then ploughed on.

"Well – like I said before, we met under pretty intense circumstances. It would be easy to… Look, I'm probably not saying this very well," I apologized. "But I've enjoyed this evening very much. And if you wanted to meet up again, I'd be happy to. But I wouldn't want you to feel obliged."

"I don't," he stated bluntly.

"Right…" I said, uncertainly. I thought I had detected a hint of amusement in his voice, but I couldn't be sure.

There followed a long pause. He was staring at me with an unreadable expression, his eyes fixed unblinkingly on my face, his whole body almost unnaturally still. It wasn't an entirely comfortable experience, being subjected to such a strange examination. Not for the first time, I wondered what he was thinking; it was as if there was more at stake than a simple 'yes or no' choice. Then his eyelashes flickered. A decision had been reached.

"What's your mobile number?" he said abruptly. He held out his phone, implicitly requesting me to put the information in for him; I did so, then handed it back to him.

"On the understanding that I'm under no obligation to use it, of course," he said dryly as he restored the phone to his jacket pocket.

"I should hope not!" I assured him fervently.

There was a pregnant pause.

"But I will," he said then, and turned away. I felt a strange little lurch in my chest.

"Good night, then," I called after him. "And thank you!"

"G'night," he replied, without looking back.

Chapter 8

And so it went on. A week later he rang me and we fixed up to meet again. Then, after another eight days. Then, four days. Then another week. Never the same day of the week, and sometimes not even an evening; knowing that I left work at one o'clock, sometimes he met me for lunch.

At first I thought it must just be his working hours that were dictating this sporadic timetable. In fact, I even spoke to him about it.

"By the way – something I've been meaning to say," I said over a late afternoon coffee in some obscure little café he'd chosen. "If you ever make any of these arrangements and you have to cancel at the last minute, I just want you to know it's all right. I know something could turn up at any hour of the day or night, and take priority over your personal life. And I just wanted to tell you that if that happens, I shan't mind. We can always rearrange. But I don't want you on any guilt trips because you've made an arrangement and had to pull out of it. For *any* reason. Okay?"

He looked at me quizzically, his mouth pulled slightly to one side by a wry half-smile.

"Sure?"

"Or I wouldn't have said it," I agreed. "I try never to say things I don't mean. Saves confusion. See, I've been thinking about what you do. Or what I assume you do, because obviously I don't know much about it, and I don't intend to ask. But it seems to me that, in your job, you've undertaken to try to look after society. If that doesn't sound too pretentious! And society's a big thing. Takes a lot of looking after. And quite often doesn't want to be looked after! So I reckon smaller things like your Saturday evenings or your dentist appointments or whatever are bound to take a lot of hits because of that. Sounds as if a lot of policemen don't get their work–life balance right. Because the job's too big for it. So I wanted you to know that – as far as an outsider can – I think I might understand that. In principle, at least. I can't promise I shan't ever feel disappointed, but I do hope I can behave as if I understand why."

He went on regarding me with that strange half-amused, half-sad expression on his face. Then he nodded.

"Thanks, Jenny," he said. "Thanks."

But in the end, I realized it wasn't that. Or, rather, not just that. I didn't figure it out straight away, of course; it was only after it had been going on for close to three months that I'd amassed enough data to start meaningfully analyzing things. When I did, I found I was somewhat bemused by my conclusions.

Because when I thought it over, I realized that not only was there no pattern to the days and times we met, there was something else a bit strange. Because he never – *never* – met me in the same place twice. It was always somewhere different, sometime different. It was as if he was living the phrase '*it's harder to hit a moving target*'.

I found myself thinking again about the man who'd been responsible for our meeting in the first place – by trying to kill Peter. The man Alan had described as making Peter's life a misery. Lesser. Was there some connection between that and the fact that Peter was behaving as he was? I wished to heaven I could ask him. Or Alan. Or someone. Anyone! But I knew I had to wait until he told me himself. If he ever did.

And when I looked back, I realized something else.

The first few times, when it had come to the point of deciding whether we were meeting again, there had been a strange sort of pause before he'd suggest the next time and place – but not because he was reluctant to see me again. It never felt like that. If it had been, he could have packed it in, at any time. But he never did. It was, I came to think, more as if he was making very sure he'd taken something else into consideration – whatever it was. As if, every time, he was asking himself, "*Am I doing the right thing...?*" But I had no idea why.

What I did notice was that gradually, with every fresh encounter, he seemed to be relaxing more and more in my company. We never talked about anything really serious – by which I mean that I never asked him about his work, and he never volunteered anything – but, just the same, I really enjoyed his company, and it seemed that he did mine.

So for the time being, I decided to be grateful that he wanted to see me at all, wanted to go on seeing me, even in this staccato way. Because, when it came down to it, I was. Very much so.

At last there came the next significant landmark. When I invited him to my flat for a meal, rather than going out somewhere.

Somehow I wasn't surprised when he didn't accept instantly, but hesitated. I felt a little pang of fear that perhaps, despite everything, he didn't really want to, and didn't know how to break it to me. But it wasn't that. It was simply the same caution he applied to all of our meetings. It was almost as if – was I being silly here? – as if he was trying to decide if it was *safe* to accept.

But at last he nodded.

"Yeh, I'd like that," he said. "Thanks."

"With the usual caveat that if something turns up to stop you coming, don't worry about it," I assured him, fighting down the urge to smile with sheer relief, as well as pleasure.

"Okay," he agreed. "What time should I come?"

"You tell me," I suggested.

"Seven-thirty?"

I loved the way his Scots accent made that 'thirty' come out as 'thairty', and smiled to myself.

"Yep, fine. And do you need my address? Or can you look that up at work?" I teased.

He looked at me with a touch of reproof, but a faint smile, too.

"Remind me," he said, diplomatically.

It was after that that I came to the conclusion it was time I told my father what was going on.

I intended to tell both my parents, but as it turned out, Mother was out when I got home from work the next day. Dad, however, was out in the back garden, kneeling by one of the flowered borders. He looked up as I approached.

"Thought I ought to do some weeding before the holiday gets too far in," he said, gesturing at his handiwork with the trowel he was holding. "I don't know where the time goes! I always think I'm going to have time to do all the things I want to do before term starts up again, and I end up doing virtually none of it!"

"Well, you'll have lots of time to do it soon," I comforted him. "Only another four months, remember?"

"True," he agreed, wiping his forehead with his forearm. "Sadly, that doesn't get the weeds out now."

He looked up at me, squinting into the afternoon sunlight, and cocked his head slightly to one side.

"Everything all right?" he enquired.

"I can't get anything past you, can I?" I said, simulating rue.

"So what is it?"

I sat down on the grass beside him. "I thought it was about time you knew," I said. "I've been seeing Peter McLeish for the last couple of months or so."

He looked at me for an instant, then merely cocked his eyebrow and contented himself with an interrogative "Oh?" while he went on weeding, waiting for me to expand on that one, bald announcement.

"He rang me up, not long after I went to Alan and Jane's," I said, and went on to give him an overview of how things had progressed since then – or as much of an overview as I felt he had a right to know.

"And why are you telling me this now?" my father asked, wrestling a long-rooted dandelion out of the earth. "Is some new development imminent?"

"Yes, sort of. I've invited him here for dinner. So I thought I ought to tell you he was coming. I know you've always told me my private life is private, even to you, but I thought it was time you knew. What I shan't do" – I wanted to make this very clear – "is bring him down to meet you. Not this time, anyway. But you know how these things go… You might have decided to go out just as he was arriving, and then there'd have to be awkward explanations in the middle of the driveway, and – I didn't want it to be like that, when you do meet him."

He expelled a breath of laughter.

"Life is, indeed, like that," he agreed. "If you'd said nothing, that's probably exactly what would have happened. Now you've told me, I don't suppose I shall lay eyes on him. Until you want me to, of course." He glanced at me. "I take it I can tell your mother about this?"

"Of course! If she hadn't picked this afternoon to go out, I'd've been telling both of you. But you can tell her for me, of course you can."

"Then, of course, I will," he said comfortably.

I paused for a moment or two. Then I said, "He's nice, Dad. You'll like him."

"Oh, I'm quite certain of that," he agreed. There was a confidence in his tone that slightly surprised me.

"Why?" I asked, intrigued. "You haven't even met him yet."

"Because, my darling, you've always shown impeccable judgement in your selection of friends. Even as a teenager, when your choice in such matters might have been expected to be somewhat skewed, heaven help us. And even Alex, for all his problems, was, and right to the end remained, your best and closest friend. So I'm sure that if you like Peter as much as you evidently do, so will I. And so will your mother. What's he like?"

I expelled a long breath as I considered that, and found it surprisingly hard to answer.

"I trust he's handsome, at least?" my father teased, gently.

"I can't quite make up my mind on that one," I admitted. "He's certainly tall and dark. And he's quite – what's the right word? – 'spare' is probably the best way to put it. And he's got a beard, which I must say I do rather like. Handsome, though…" I tried to contemplate the concept objectively. "He's got an interesting face. Speaking as a girl – of course! – think I'd class it as downright fascinating, actually." I grinned at Dad. "Definitely attractive! But *handsome*…?" I wrinkled my nose. "Not sure. Not by my definition of it, anyway. Lovely dark eyes, though!" I concluded, with another grin.

He chuckled.

"A most thorough analysis. I can see you've been giving the subject prolonged and serious consideration," he remarked, gently poking fun at me.

"You know me – over-analytical, to a fault!"

"Well, I hope it goes well, darling," he said, sincerely. "And if it does, no doubt we'll meet your Peter, in the fullness of time."

"Don't think it's really accurate to refer to him as *my* Peter," I demurred.

"You never know," said my father tranquilly, rooting out yet another mislocated dandelion.

Peter was prompt to his time; it was only a minute after seven-thirty when I heard the car pulling into the driveway. I'd left my front door open, in the hope that it would help me detect his arrival, and when I heard the faint sound of the engine swell and then cut off, I knew he had come. I went to the front door and stood at the top of the steps. He was just locking the car, and I expected him to come straight up.

Instead, he walked back to the end of the drive and stood there for a few moments, looking up and down the road, as if he was checking for something. I wondered what, and why.

Then he turned and came back; as he did so, he looked up and saw me. I waved, and he waved back, then made light work of the steps, taking them two at a time with those long legs of his.

"Hello," he said.

"Hello," I smiled back. "Come on in."

I ushered him along the passage to the living room, which is the most decently sized room in the flat, being twice the size of the kitchen, although the latter is just about big enough to include, by the large window overlooking the back garden, a table at which four people can, at a pinch, be seated. The equivalent window in the living room is even larger; Dad had made good and sure, when designing the flat, that even though the hallway perforce has little in the way of natural light, the main rooms have as much of that as possible.

Peter looked round, taking in the cream and pale green themed décor, the deep, comfortable three-seater sofa and matching easy chair dutifully facing the television, the cushioned window seat running the length of the window, the neatly stacked shelves of books, DVDs and CDs, the print of *Phares dans la Tempête – La Jument* by Jean Guichard hanging above the mantelpiece and the one of *Evening Splendor* by Hong Leung on the opposite wall, the door that opened next to the fireplace onto the adjoining kitchen.

"Nice," he said with approval. His eyes scanned the shelves. "Is this the famous DVD collection that Craig was on about?"

"Some of it. I keep the rest up in the spare bedroom," I said. "Haven't got room for them all down here."

He lifted his head slightly, and inhaled the scents filtering through from the kitchen.

"Don't know what you're cooking, but it smells good," he said. "Hope this'll go with it." He held out the tissue paper-encased bottle of wine that he'd been carrying but that I had politely failed to acknowledge until now. It was a good quality red.

"Thank you. Ravioli, among other things," I said. "You're the wine expert – will this work with that?"

"Yeh. Smells good," he said again.

"It should be about ready for you to test whether it tastes good, too," I said, glancing at my watch. "I'll just go and check…"

When I came back in, I found him by the little cabinet that stands in one corner of the room. The framed photograph that usually stood on it was in his hand, and he was looking down at it. He looked up as I came in, and gestured with the frame in my direction.

"Alex?" he asked.

"Yes. That was taken not long before he died. About two and a half, three years ago?" I went over and took it from him, looking down at the well-loved face. "I didn't use to have it out like this. And when I did, it was a long time before I could look at it without dissolving into tears. Now I just get frustrated, more than anything. Thinking what a waste it was, when he could've been so much, if that wretched illness hadn't got in the way!" I smiled sadly, and put it back. Then I squared my shoulders, and gave Peter a real smile.

"Still, the good news is, dinner's ready. Don't have a dining room, I'm afraid, so – the kitchen's this way…"

He dealt with the wine for me while I served up the first course, a cauliflower and broccoli cream soup – tinned, but a good quality make, I assured him.

"I'm afraid I'm not one of those people who regard cooking as an art form," I apologized. "It's more of an exercise in logistics, with me."

He chuckled, and spooned up another mouthful.

"Don't be sorry," he said. "This is good. Haven't had this combination before."

As he'd predicted, the wine did complement the ravioli and salad, and it was all going quite well, until he had his mishap.

He'd put his fork down on the edge of his plate in order to take a sip from his wineglass. I don't know how he then managed to hit the heel of the fork hard enough for it to launch the fragment of soft, mushy tomato resting on its tines at himself with such force, but somehow he did. He exclaimed something – probably fortunately, I didn't catch what – and grabbed for his serviette to scoop the offending item of food from his lap, whence it had slid after hitting his shirt.

It suddenly struck me how much – and how disturbingly – the uneven splatter of red over his left ribcage, with sluggish red trails dripping down the clean white cotton, resembled a bullet hole, as if he'd been shot through the lung.

"Sorry," he muttered, looking in dismay at the mess the tomato sauce had made on his shirt.

"Don't worry about it," I assured him quickly. "But you might want to wash that off before it stains. You know where the bathroom is."

"Yeh. Thanks," he agreed, and left the table, still clutching the serviette.

When he'd gone I wiped up the rest of the spill and restored the table to proper order. Then, as he hadn't reappeared, I headed for the bathroom. I stopped in the open doorway; he was standing at the hand basin, his back to me.

"How's it going?" I asked, but instantly saw it wasn't going very efficiently. He was still wearing the shirt, and was dabbing at it rather ineffectively with the now damp serviette.

"You won't get it out like that," I said bluntly, and held out my hand imperatively. "Come on, give it here. I'll do it."

He regarded me for a moment. Then he said "Thanks," pulled his shirt off over his head without unbuttoning it, and handed it to me.

He watched me silently as I soaped and rinsed the stained area, then rubbed it with a clean towel to soak up as much of the residual dampness as possible.

"There – that should do it, until you can give it a proper wash," I said, holding it up for his inspection. "It might be a bit wet for comfort, still."

"Don't worry about that," he said quickly. "A bit of damp won't hurt me."

Just for a fraction of a second, our eyes met, and I knew that in both our minds was the image of him lying soaked to the skin under that downpour on Craigie Hill.

"If you're sure," I agreed, and handed it back to him. Aware, as I did so, of experiencing a frisson of pleasure, a thrill of physical sensation, directly attributable to the fact that he was attractive, and close, and wasn't wearing his shirt.

Time for a strategic withdrawal! While recording the sensation for future playback, perhaps...?

But then something distracted me. As he prepared to put the shirt back on, I saw the faint, thin red line, as if drawn by a biro, which lay across the trapezius of his left shoulder. He caught the direction of my arrested gaze and made an abortive attempt to glance down at the scar, though of course it wasn't physically possible for him to see it without a mirror. He met my eye, hesitating; then, conceding my rights in him on this, deliberately dipped his shoulder down toward me, so I could see more clearly.

"They made a neat job of it," he observed. "A couple more weeks and you'll never know it was there."

"Yes, I will," I contradicted him, almost absently, as I peered at the fading traces of the wound. "However" – I smiled at him briefly – "you're right; nobody else will. Come on. I don't know how eatable the rest of the dinner'll be by now, but there's always pudding."

As I left the bathroom, his eyes and the gleam of humour I'd detected in them as I turned away felt like a tangible – and pleasurable – pressure between my shoulderblades as he followed me, pulling the partially damp shirt over his head and shrugging it back into place.

Chapter 9

"So how did it go, darling?" Mother enquired the next day.

"Okay, I think," I shrugged, deprecatingly. Then I laughed. "Though I think he's still coming to terms with just how much of my music collection is allocated to Chris de Burgh!"

She laughed, too. Dad, his eyes on the book on his lap but evidently listening nevertheless, also smiled.

"Did you tell him that was my fault?" Mother asked. "Brainwashing you with my musical tastes?"

"As if I was going to tell him it was a fault, you heretic!" I contradicted her. "But when I maintained that Mr de Burgh is one of the best singer-songwriters of his generation, he definitely blinked – as you can imagine! They always do, don't they? So I gave him my usual line of '*if you've only ever heard* Lady in Red *and* A Spaceman Came Travelling *you simply haven't* got *him at all*.' And showed him the full range of the studio albums as evidence."

"And then I suppose you made him listen to some of them?" my father conjectured, still not lifting his eyes from his book.

"I did," I confirmed, with a mischievous grin.

"Did he put up a fight about it?" Mother enquired tranquilly.

"He tried," I admitted. "But by the time I'd played him a few tracks as evidence, he was forced to concede I might have a point. He was like a lot of people who take a pop at our Chris, of course – he hadn't actually listened to any of his music. He'd just accepted the myth, like most people."

I paused, mentally replaying what I'd said to Peter after that. "You know what I think Chris de Burgh's problem is?" I'd challenged.

"Looks like you're going to tell me," he'd said dryly.

"He knows the difference between the way women want their men to interact with them, and the way they actually do," I said, ignoring his tone, perhaps even slightly fired up because of it, since this was something about which I happened to feel quite strongly; perceived injustices do that to people, no matter what they happen to be about. "Some of his lyrics are pretty straightforward about describing a man's desire for a woman, but he's also up front about a man expressing tenderness in a relationship. And why he should! But that's what a lot of women just don't get from their men, and I think that's why so many of his songs resonate with women. That's why they did with me." Even though Alex had loved me, and I him. I wasn't going to articulate that to Peter, but if he worked it out for himself, fair enough. "Why do you think he's got such a huge worldwide following, in the teeth of all the critics being so dismissive of him? But I reckon there are a lot of people who don't like to be reminded that they're failing in that particular department. So they shoot the messenger. Let's face it, the one thing nobody ever forgives you for is the truth!"

"No," Peter had said. "They don't."

The grimness of his response had taken me by surprise. I'd meant that comment as a witticism, but clearly I'd inadvertently touched a nerve of some sort. What I didn't know then – though I learned it later – was that the one thing someone hadn't forgiven *him* for was the truth. All I knew was that somehow I'd said the wrong thing, and I felt horribly uncomfortable about it. The sensation was almost identical to the one I'd felt after I'd talked about Alex being killed instantly, when Peter had immediately said, *"You're right. Instant is good. It's good,"* with such intensity. A sensation of discomfort, knowing something was off-key. But what, and why?

But then he'd looked at me with a slight upward curve on one corner of his mouth. "Okay, then, I'll give Mr de Burgh the benefit of the doubt from now on." And the moment had passed.

"Anyway," I continued, not bothering to recount that part of the conversation to my parents, "I'm going to continue to press my case, every chance I get!"

My father emitted a snort of amusement. "If you haven't driven him away for good, with that tactic," he commented.

"I don't think so. In fact, he said something rather nice. He said the flat's got a good ambience. The kind of place you could immediately feel at home in. Feel relaxed in."

"Then perhaps he will come again," said Dad, deliberately bland.

"In spite of the other man in my life," I agreed, equally blandly. He raised his eyebrows enquiringly.

"Chris de Burgh, of course," I clarified, with a grin.

It wasn't long after Peter's first visit to my flat that Alan, too, learned about us. He told me himself, later; it had been one of those rare occasions when Peter had come round to see him at a time when both Jane and the children happened to be out.

They were in the lounge, talking sporadically about nothing in particular, when Alan became aware of a muffled sound coming from his cousin's direction. He looked across. Peter was slumped untidily in his seat, one long leg dangling over the arm of the sofa, his half-empty beer can held poised in mid-air in front of his face. His eyes had the slightly unfocused look of someone replaying a memory; from the broad smile he was wearing, the sound had evidently been him laughing to himself.

"What's so funny?" Alan enquired. It wasn't as often as all that that Peter was to be seen smiling, let alone laughing.

"Oh, I was just thinking," said Peter, slightly dreamily, still with the smile on his face. "D'you remember Kelly?"

"Kelly?" Alan said blankly.

"You know," said Peter, focusing on the here and now. "Tall brunette, with fantastic legs. A couple of girlfriends before Laura."

"Kelly... Oh, yes! I remember. What about her?"

"I was just thinking," said Peter again. "About how glam she always was. All that lip gloss and mascara and stuff she used to use. Never saw her less than spectacular."

"Okay... So?" Alan couldn't see where this was heading.

"I was just thinking about how different Jenny is."

Alan looked at him, quickly. That use of the present tense – *Jenny is...*

"Jenny?" he said interrogatively, briefly raising his eyebrows in an expression of what he hoped looked like no more than natural interest.

"The other day I pitched up at her place early," Peter went on, taking another pull at his beer can. Whether it was a deliberate strategy on his part to imply that Alan already knew that he was seeing Jenny Gregory – and evidently on a regular basis – or whether he had honestly overlooked the fact that this was in reality something of a bombshell, his cousin could not for the life of him work out. "About half an hour before she was expecting me. She was right in the middle of washing her hair. She came to let me in with it all sudsed-up. Then when she'd finished washing it, she came in with me and set the hairdryer up in the sitting room, and she was wearing the most ancient, battered old dressing gown you could imagine. One of those old Father-Christmassy red ones with the red and white twisted belts – remember them?"

"I do," Alan agreed, with a smile.

"Used to be her gran's, apparently, and she still uses it. But I was thinking... Kelly would've *died* before she let anyone see her like that, let alone me. And Jenny didn't give a damn. She was blowing her hair all over the place and I told her she looked like a mad dandelion. She just laughed. No fuss. No affectation. '*What you see is what you get.*' It's – good." Peter delivered the precise adjective with due deliberation, and took another mouthful of beer.

Alan regarded him with a carefully expressionless face, but he could hardly have articulated how encouraged he was by what he was hearing. It was a long time since Peter had voluntarily discussed his relationship with *anyone*. A long time since he'd even considered one. Given his history, it was something of a surprise that he was prepared to do so. Yet what he had just confided implied that he was seeing Jenny Gregory quite often, and felt comfortable enough in her company to say the sort of thing he'd just said. Perhaps not to anyone else, yet, but at least to him, Alan.

"Can't say I'm surprised," he said casually. "One of the very first things Jane said about Jenny was that she liked her because she was – what was the word she used?" He looked up at the ceiling for inspiration, then remembered. "Oh, yeh – '*unpretentious*'. That was it. And '*up front*'."

"Yeh," mused Peter. "She is." He sank the last of his beer, and put the can down on the coffee table.

"Want another one?" Alan offered, deliberately changing the subject. He would have liked to ask further, but he was a little afraid that if he pursued the subject too avidly, Peter might withdraw any further confidences. Let him volunteer them, if he wanted.

"Yeh," said Peter, flicking his thanks with a quick glance. And even before Alan had left the room, he noticed that Peter's eyes had that unfocused look again, the same faint smile once again hovering on his lips. Whether he realized it or not, maybe?

The occasion when I found out that this exchange had taken place was when Alan and Jane invited me for a drink one Saturday lunchtime in a local pub.

"A rare circumstance!" Jane informed me, with emphasis. "It's not often he gets any free time on a Saturday! But since we were around, we thought we'd try our luck. I'm glad you could make it."

"So'm I," I assured her, raising my glass in her direction.

"I did mean to have you round for dinner again, but everything's just been mad, lately," she apologized. "And we will do it, sometime, promise. But I hope this'll do, for the time being."

"Beautifully," I agreed. "How are Craig and Sophie? What've they been doing with themselves lately?"

Alan leant back and let Jane fill me in, and we chatted on happily until she decided she needed to go to make use of the toilet. When she'd gone, Alan took a pull at his half pint, and eyed me over the rim.

"I hear you and Peter have been seeing each other from time to time," he announced.

I was slightly taken aback, though I didn't know why I should have been. If Peter was going to tell anyone, it was sure to be Alan.

"I'm also told you look like a mad dandelion when you're drying your hair," Alan went on, teasing gently. I remembered, and laughed.

"So he's told you, has he?" I said. "I wasn't sure whether he'd said anything – yet."

"To me, he has," said Alan. "Not Jane. And I haven't told her. Not for the time being."

"Ah," I said, puzzled as to why, but understanding now why he hadn't said anything until she'd gone. "So I shouldn't tell her, either?"

"Not just yet," Alan agreed. He smiled at my mystified expression. "There is a reason for that, Jenny, but it's nothing you need worry about. It's just that Jane can get a bit" – he searched for the right diplomatic description – "excited about that sort of thing, especially where Peter's concerned…"

He let the sentence trail off, but I'd got the picture. He didn't want Peter under any sort of pressure from his wife, no matter how well-meant.

"Okay," I agreed, and he could tell I'd grasped the situation. "You'd better tip me the wink if the situation changes, then."

"I will," he promised.

"I just keep worrying that he's doing it out of some misplaced sense of obligation," I confided. "You don't think he is, do you?" I looked at him a little anxiously.

"Absolutely not! He wouldn't do that, believe me." Despite the lively twinkle in his eyes, there was a serious edge to the words. "No, he thinks very highly of you, trust me. He says you've got the gift of silence at the right times."

"*Does* he?" I raised my eyebrows. "Very poetic! And quite a recommendation. I bet there aren't many women get *that* accolade from their men friends," I added dryly.

Alan chuckled, and took another pull of his beer. He put the glass down and regarded me.

"You're good for him," he announced. "He's a lot more relaxed. Laughs more. More like he used to be."

"I don't know why, particularly," I disclaimed, though I was delighted to hear it. "We don't really do anything much. We go out for a drink, sometimes. Or if he comes to me, we usually just watch TV. Films, or sport, if there is any – football, golf, whatever. I even make him watch documentaries with me, hard cruel woman that I am."

Alan laughed. "Ah, yes – documentaries. I remember… What kind?"

"Science ones are my favourites. But anything, really. History – any time period. Mathematics. I can't even cope with arithmetic, let alone mathematics! But I'm still interested. Geography. Geology. Natural history. Anything that came out of the Industrial Revolution. Oh, I don't know – everything!"

Alan was amused by the hyperbole. "And he watches them all with you, does he?"

"He seems happy to," I agreed. "In fact, we've ended up having some really interesting conversations after some of them. But then, sometimes we listen to music. Or just talk. Just hanging-out-with-your-mates type of stuff. Nothing to write home about." I pulled a face. "I'm making it sound really boring, aren't I?"

"Well, nothing else's changed, so it's got to be you. Can't account for it otherwise." He smiled at me, as if that last comment was a friendly tease.

I was charmed, but also pleased; elated, even. Not just that I might be helping Peter, as I so much wanted to do, but also that Alan apparently approved me. That felt important.

"Let's hope you're right, then," I said earnestly, but returning his smile.

He nodded.

"Sometimes, though..." I began, then stopped.

"What?"

"Well," I started again, slowly, "it's just that sometimes I get the feeling that there's something holding him back. As if he wants to be friends, but – well, as if he's *afraid* of something."

Alan considered me gravely for some seconds before replying, as if he was debating with himself.

"He is," he said at last. He met my eyes. "For good reason. But bear with him, Jenny." There was something close to a plea in his voice, as if he was begging a favour. "I can't tell you why. That's for him to say. But be patient, please. Keep things on the footing they are now. It's doing him so much good. Maybe it can get even better. If you're patient."

I looked at him for a couple of seconds, then nodded, aware that I was promising him something more important than I knew.

Then Jane came back, and we started to talk about something else. I found it quite – what would the word be? – endearing? – that Alan felt so protective of Peter that, much as he loved his wife, he felt it incumbent upon him to shield Peter from the degree of enthusiasm she would apparently express when she learned that he was seeing me on a regular basis. I could imagine where he was coming from on that one. Some women, no matter how lovely their nature is, can't suppress that matchmaking gleam in their eye where their friends and relatives are concerned. It looked as if Jane was one of them, bless her.

Well, fair enough. I was content to abide by his judgement. No doubt he'd let me know when reporting restrictions were lifted.

A few minutes later, we were interrupted by the ringing of Alan's mobile. Jane looked at her husband quickly as he answered the call, clearly already suspecting what the outcome would be.

"…Okay… Yes… I'll be there as quick as I can," was his concluding sentence. He glanced at us apologetically. "Sorry, something's come up. Got to go."

"Of course you have," Jane agreed calmly. "Don't worry. It'll give us plenty of opportunity to talk about you, once you're out of the way." She smiled impishly at him.

"I'm sure you'll make the most of it," he said dryly. He looked at me. "Sorry to abandon you like this, Jenny."

"Don't worry," I assured him. "Trust me, I have picked up from various sources that it goes with the territory."

His eyelids flickered; he understood me.

"I'll make sure Jane gives you that dinner invitation as soon as possible, then. But for now" – he got to his feet and drained the last of his beer – "got to go. See you later, love." He stooped to give his wife a brief kiss on the forehead, then left.

We both grinned at him encouragingly until the pub door closed behind him; then we looked at each other with the same rueful smile.

"I suppose that happens a lot?" I suggested, sympathetically.

She groaned humorously.

"You have *no* idea," she said, flopping back in her chair.

I studied her for a moment.

"I don't know if it's true, because you can't always trust the media," I said carefully, "but if what generally gets portrayed is true, policemen seem to have a high failure rate in their marriages. You seem to be very lucky with yours."

Jane nodded slowly, with a hint of sadness.

"I'm afraid it often is true. The job can be very hard on personal relationships. Too much time away from home and family. But you're right. I am lucky. You know," she said thoughtfully, "I've never forgotten my mum telling me my best chance of having a lasting marriage was to find a man who *wants* to be married. That's where I'm lucky. Because Alan does want to be married, in spite of how difficult his job makes it. But I'm not just lucky. I was prepared. My father was a policeman, too. A Superintendent. So I knew what it was going to be like."

"What do you mean – be like?"

Jane looked at me with a rather wry smile.

"I knew how often he wasn't going to be around. How prepared you have to be to make arrangements and then have them broken, because '*something's come up*' and he can't make it. Or else go by yourself, or with just the children. Having to explain to them why he wasn't able to be there for their birthday party or their sports day or their school play. How much time you have to spend on your own, waiting for him to turn up. Getting woken up in the small hours because he's only just come home to bed. Or else because the phone goes and he's got to get up and go, right away."

I didn't know what to say. Or, rather, how to say it right. But one thing was clear.

"He's worth it, though." I made it a statement, because it was so obviously true, for her.

She nodded, very definitely.

"He is worth it," she confirmed. "The twenty percent of his life that I get to share is still worth more than the whole hundred percent of some other marriages. I know that. He tries so hard not to let the job affect us, or the children, and of course sometimes he can't help it. But he's been terrific. They're used to him not being around so much, but they know he does try to be with us as often as he can. They know he loves them. I know he loves me. But so many people haven't been as lucky as us. I've seen so many others trying to dissolve their problems in alcohol, or one or the other ending up having affairs because they don't see enough of their partners. Feeling they're in second place to the job and ending up tearing each other to pieces. None of that's happened to us, thank heaven. So you're right, Jenny. I am lucky. And he is worth it. To me."

"I think that deserves another drink," I said, gesturing with my empty glass. "My round, yes?"

Jane still hadn't got round to the promised dinner invitation when Dad and Mum pre-empted her. I don't know which of them came up with the idea, but they suggested to me that it might be nice if they set up a barbecue for the last weekend of the summer holidays, and that besides a few of our friends it might be a logical step to invite the McLeishes. All of them.

"They've been very kind to you, and it would be a way of our meeting Peter without the pressure of anything especially formal, from his point of view," Mother explained. "A group situation, not one to one. What do you think?"

I thought about it, then nodded with increasing enthusiasm.

"I think it's a good idea. A very good idea. Though you'll have to remember that even if they say they can come, Peter or Alan – or both – might suddenly get called into work. From personal experience I can assure you it does happen, from time to time," I added wryly.

"But would you like to issue the invitations on our behalf?" Mother suggested.

"Do my best," I said agreeably. "At least I can assure them that Dad's one of the few men who doesn't just think he can barbecue – he really can."

"You're right about that, darling, but tell them we'll have a finger buffet as well, just in case they don't like to risk it," Mum said comfortably. And when I caught the mischievous gleam in her eye, we both laughed.

I was half right with my caveat, as it turned out.

Fortunately, it was a beautifully warm day, quite sunny, and little breeze; just the sort of afternoon you'd want for a barbecue. The trestle tables on one side of the back lawn were ready laden with all the necessary paraphernalia, and the barbecue was, under Dad's expert supervision, producing delicious smells from the various foods being disgorged from it onto the waiting plates. The Martins, neighbours from a little way down the road, were already there, and so were the Corricks and the Weavers. I was glad to see that the Corrick teenagers had come; that would mean Craig and Sophie would have peers of their own age group they could resort to if the adult elements of the gathering failed them. When they turned up, that was.

At last, behind the already healthy buzz of conversation, I detected the sound of another car engine out at the front. I apologized quickly to Chris Corrick, to whom I was talking. "I think that's our last guests arriving. I ought to just go and, er..." I gestured vaguely in the direction of the driveway. He waved me away cheerfully, and I headed across the garden toward the drive. My peripheral vision picked up both Mum and Dad watching me as I went.

With our own two cars and those of the others already jammed into the limited space available, there wasn't much room left for Peter to slot into, though he was managing it. Because it was Peter's car, not Alan's, though I could see Jane in the front seat beside him, Craig and Sophie in the back. No Alan, then.

"I'm so sorry, Jenny!" Jane was apologizing before she was even out of her seat. "He got called in at the last minute. He says to tell you he's very disappointed!"

"You can tell him the same from me, if you like," I retorted ruefully. "Never mind – at least the rest of you made it." I was looking at Peter as I spoke, and his head dipped briefly in acknowledgement. "Hi, you two!" I went on, addressing Sophie and Craig. "All right?"

"Yeh, thanks," said Craig.

"Okay, then – this way," I said, and ushered them to the back garden.

Dad came forward to greet them, with Mother closing in discreetly as he did so. I needn't have worried that they were going to make a production out of it.

"Richard Taylor," said Dad smoothly, offering a handshake. "Peter, how nice to meet you. I'm glad you could come; I know your time isn't always your own in your job. This is Beth." He indicated Mother, who also shook Peter's hand.

"I expect Jenny's already told you all about us?" Mother twinkled briefly in my direction. "So we needn't retread that ground at the moment! But thank you for coming. I'm so pleased you could," she said. "And this would be Jane? And Craig, and Sophie? But – no Alan...?"

I stepped back and let them engage on their own terms; Jane explaining Alan's absence, and Mum commiserating with her, while Dad greeted the youngsters, swiftly putting them at their ease with that personal, conversational quality that made him such a good teacher. Peter, characteristically, didn't say much; if he was, as I assumed, assessing this initial encounter with my parents, the expression on his face seemed to imply he was coming to some fairly positive conclusions. I would've been surprised had it been otherwise; I'm very proud of my parents and the kind of people they are, so I'd had no real fears that he wouldn't like them when he met them. Now he had. Box ticked.

"...But I'm afraid you'll have to excuse me now," said Dad. "I'm on barbecue duty. KP – kitchen patrol, as they used to say in the army. I'm not sure whether they still do...? Anyway, forgive me, but I do think I should give it some attention..."

"Jenny, why don't you see what Craig and Sophie want to drink?" Mother suggested. "And I'll take Jane and Peter and introduce them to everyone else."

"Okay," I agreed. I looked at the kids and jerked my head in the direction of the relevant table with a wink before leading the way.

And it all went beautifully thereafter. Jane happily transferred from conversation to conversation; Peter had more of a tendency to observe than talk, even if ostensibly part of a group, but I did see him having a long conversation with Dad at one point. Even Craig and Sophie seemed to be getting on well with the Corrick children, the oldest of whom was about Craig's age, and the others not far behind. I circulated, just as Mum and Dad did, happy that the McLeishes were there, gratified that they seemed to be enjoying themselves so well, and deliberately not making any attempt to monopolize Peter, or even particularly approach him at this stage of the proceedings. It wasn't as if I didn't see him on other occasions, after all.

After a while, Craig came over to me, his hands stuck in his jeans pockets with the same gesture that Peter used; he really did look very like him.

"How's it going?" I greeted him. "Looking for an escape route yet?"

"Not yet," he said, responding to my tone. "But I was wondering – you said about your DVD collection. Can I see it while I'm here?"

"Of course! This way," I said. As I did, I caught Peter's eye and made a tiny movement of invitation with my head. I was sure Jane wouldn't object, but I preferred the security of a chaperone, just to be on the safe side. He picked up on it straight away, said something briefly to Jane, whom he happened to be sitting next to at that moment, then got up and followed us across the lawn.

"Can I use your bathroom, Jenny?" he asked as he caught us up, providing a credible reason for his presence.

"Of course. You know where it is," I said incautiously. I saw Craig's head move slightly as he caught that, but he didn't say anything. I wondered if I'd blown the gaff before Alan – or Peter – was ready for me to do so. Peter nodded reassuringly.

"Should do by now," he agreed. "I was telling Jane on the way here how I knew the route so well."

Ah – so now she knew. And so did Craig and Sophie. At least I needn't worry about that from now on.

"Was she surprised?"

"I don't think so."

"*We* weren't," Craig interjected.

"Don't sound so smug. It doesn't suit you," I grinned, and he laughed as he followed me up the steps.

When Peter came to find us – it seemed he really had wanted to use the bathroom – he followed the sound of our voices up the stairs and found us in my spare bedroom. One entire wall – the one opposite the head of the big double bed that had used to be mine and Alex's, and that I'd retained for the use of visitors – was given over to white-glossed shelves; every one of them, save a couple near the floor that were lined with books, was stacked with DVDs. I was sitting on the bed, watching Craig scan the collection. Peter brought up short in the doorway, eyeing the display.

"Whenever do you get the time to watch all these?" he asked incredulously.

"I don't," I told him. "But somehow I'm comforted by knowing that they're there if I do want to."

"What's your favourite film?" Craig asked, throwing a glance over his shoulder at me.

"Ah, well, that depends on mood, doesn't it? Unless I'm feeling particularly girly, it would probably be *The Hunt for Red October*, I think. Tight, tense, exciting, and no gratuitous insertion of superfluous females into the story by the screenwriter!"

"And what is it if you are feeling girly?" Peter enquired.

"Oh, definitely *A Matter Of Life And Death*," I said immediately.

"Haven't heard of that one," said Craig, frowning slightly.

"Released in 1946 – a bit before your time, young man," I told him.

"Bit before yours, as well, then!" he retorted.

"Yeh, but it's always been one of Mum's favourites. I like it for slightly different reasons. She goes all gooey over the love story, but what I like about it is the sheer imagination of the concepts, and the way they put them onto screen with the technology they had then. It's absolutely brilliant! Tell you what, Craig – why don't you borrow it?" I got up from the bed, reached out a forefinger and tipped the plastic case forward from between its companions to where I could get a proper grip on it. "I'd really love to know what you think of the concepts in it. And the way they used special effects to get them across, given when it was made. Would you mind?"

He took the case when I offered it to him, turned it over and began to read the information on the back, then shrugged.

"Okay," he said. "I'll give it a try."

"I shall look forward to finding out what you think of it," I smiled. "At worst, it'll only be about an hour and a half out of your life."

He smiled.

"I can probably spare that," he agreed.

"And now it's about time we went back," Peter opined. "Your mother's probably wondering where we've got to."

"No problem," said Craig, preceding me down the stairs. "I'll just tell her you were stupid and got locked in the loo."

"Yeh," Peter muttered sardonically. "Thanks for that, Craig. Appreciate it."

The McLeishes were the last to leave, Jane insisting that they would help us clear up. Sophie was a bit reluctant – being a teenager, clearing up was not 'fun', of course – but pitched in anyway, helping the rest of us gather up the detritus and carry it into the kitchen. Peter and Craig took down the tables for us, and, at Dad's request, re-stacked them in their normal place in the brick outhouse that stands in the far back corner of the garden.

When it came time for them to go, Jane said, "Thank you so much for inviting us. It's been lovely! I do wish Alan could've come, though!"

"Perhaps next time," said my mother comfortingly. "We'd love you to come again, sometime – we've really enjoyed meeting you. All of you," she enlarged, glancing round at Peter and the children, too.

"We have, indeed," Dad confirmed, offering handshakes to everyone. "So we'll make sure it happens again."

While the reciprocal chorus of farewells was going on, I caught Peter's eye. "*Thanks*," I mouthed at him silently.

"*You, too*," he replied in like manner. Out of the corner of my eye I could see that Dad had noticed the exchange, but he didn't comment, not then.

However, when we'd finally waved the car out of the driveway and had turned back toward the house, he put his arm round my shoulders as we walked.

"I like him, Jenny," he said quietly. Mother didn't say anything, just smiled.

And that was all. But it was enough.

Chapter 10

Peter and I went on after that in the same pattern; regular meetings, but at irregular intervals. Sometimes, when he turned up, I could tell it had been a difficult day, and then I had to work a bit harder to make sure that, before too long had passed, he would start to unwind, relax, progress from initial monosyllabic responses to normal conversation. But, whether he arrived in a good frame of mind or not, generally that was the way he left, and that pleased me. I felt a fundamental desire to be of help to him, and this was a way I could do it. Which made me happy.

And despite that strange wariness over each decision to do so, Peter kept coming.

Surprisingly often, I thought, given the sporadic nature of our appointments up until then. Sometimes we'd still meet out at some pub or café or whatever, but after that first time he seemed quite content to mostly just come to the flat and – well, hang out, basically; the way he might with a male friend. As I'd told Alan, sometimes we'd talk, but sometimes we didn't seem to feel the need to talk at all; just listened to music, or watched television, or whatever else we felt like doing, in companionable silence.

The one time I never forget is when I got him listening to the rain.

It was one of those days when there was no wind, but it rained ceaselessly, a steadily drumming downpour. I let him in, and left him shaking the water off his jacket in the hallway while I resumed my favoured position at the right-hand end of the window seat.

A few moments later he came in, and halted, gazing at me curiously. Something in my bearing as I gazed out of the open window evidently struck him as unusual.

"What are you doing?" he enquired, looking at me quizzically.

"Listening to the rain," I said, a little dreamily.

"To the *rain*?"

"Haven't you ever done that? Just sat and listened to rain fall?"

"No." He was regarding me with a look on his face as if he didn't know whether to laugh or to summon the men in white coats.

"Well, you should," I declared. "It's one of the most relaxing sounds I know. Come and try it. Come here." I pointed at the other side of the window, indicating he should sit alongside me.

He shook his head tolerantly at my eccentricity. Then he shrugged, came forward, and took up the seat I'd indicated, copying my pose of resting one elbow on the inner window ledge with his chin cupped in his hand.

"Now listen," I said. "Don't say anything. Just listen."

The rain fell heavy and steady, with no wind to trouble it. It made a continuous background pattering as it hit the grass, the soil, the leaves, the slates of the roof just above our heads. Its gentle, hypnotic drumming was enhanced by the quiet gurgling of water flowing along the gutter, punctuated by the individual beats of drops that collected on the edge of the pipework and, when they had become too heavy to sustain themselves in suspension any longer, splashed down as huge drips onto the outer edge of the window ledge.

We sat there in silence, not even looking at each other, just out into the mass of falling silver lines. And gradually, the longer we sat there, the more I could feel him relaxing as he became attuned to the sound, really beginning to listen to it, starting to appreciate its lulling beauty. Starting to understand. Without a word between us, I felt as if we were coming together, really doing something *together*, even though it would have seemed to an onlooker that we were doing nothing at all.

I don't know how long it was before he finally stirred, and turned his head to look at me. For a few moments his face was expressionless. Then, slowly, he smiled. He had such a wonderful smile, when he chose to use it. I wondered briefly, and a little sadly, why it took so much to make him do it. But at least he was doing it now.

"You're right," he said.

And that was all he said. But we looked at each other, and were satisfied.

And I know it took, because one evening a few weeks later, when it was raining again, I got a text from him.

Listening to the rain. It really works.

For some reason I couldn't stop smiling about that for quite some time.

When I thought things over – not, in reality, that one ever thinks these things through in a structured way, in words and sentences in your head – but if I'd been asked to articulate it aloud, I'd have said that the overall sense I got of our relationship was that what he liked about it was that it was simply a friendship. No demands, no questions, no complications; just an easy companionship that made no demands of him and, as far as I could see, actively helped him to wind down when things in the rest of his life – meaning work, basically – were stressing him particularly. He still never volunteered information about his job, so I continued my policy of not asking. I think he liked that, and appreciated it. That was, it seemed, the way he wanted things to be.

I was only too aware that I was on the periphery of his life, but at least I was there, a part of it, however far out on the rim. It had only been a few months, but already I was acutely aware that if anything happened to put a stop to it, it would now create a horrible, gaping space in my life. I didn't want that; I'd already had one of those torn into my world, and the rawness of the emotions was still, even after more than two years, distressing. I didn't want anything like it happening again.

Because I knew that if for any reason it did, I would miss him. Really miss him. Perhaps too much.

But there was nothing I could do about it now. It was already too late. Our friendship, important as it seemed to be to him, might not be central to his life, but – whether he was aware of it or not – it was already pretty central to mine. And that was all there was to it.

So – carry on…

And then he told me the thing about himself that I didn't know.

He'd taken me out to a pub – another one, of course, that we hadn't been to before, on the outskirts of New Addington. We'd eaten, and now we were talking about Craig and Sophie.

"Sounds like Craig was quite impressed with *A Matter of Life and Death*," I commented. "I thought he might be. And even Sophie watched it, I hear."

"Yeh," said Peter with reservation. "Not sure I'm very grateful to you for that." He saw my grin. "Oh, you know about that, do you?"

"'Fraid so. A little bird told me she keeps calling you 'Peet-aire', now, *à la* Conductor 71!" I had a momentary vision of Marius Goring in his powdered wig, and my smile widened.

"Yeh, well, I hope she gets over that little habit before too long," said Peter, pretending disgruntlement. He suddenly smiled, evidently at some memory or another. "She's usually into teen romance films. I remember her coming back from one of them – can't remember which one – and then announcing, really grandly, '*I want to find a really gorgeous, fit bloke, loaded, so I can live happily ever after!*' It was the way she said it! She was only twelve at the time. You should've seen Jane and Alan trying not to laugh!"

It had been an effective piece of mimicry, and I laughed.

"I hope somebody told her living happily ever after's got nothing to do with that," I commented dryly. "Or not for long, anyway. Real life's doing the ironing and the food shopping and stuff like that. If she really wants to live happily ever after, tell her to find someone she's happy to clean the toilet for every week, for the rest of her life! If she can get that one cracked, *then* she's got chances of living happily ever after. But sometimes, they take some finding, those people," I added, with resignation.

"Sometimes," said Peter non-committally. "But then, sometimes you get lucky when you least expect it."

After a slight pause, during which I instinctively decided not to follow up that remark, I went on, "I just hope she doesn't end up going through a number of relationships and getting her life in a mess before she achieves it. People can get themselves into such tangles that way," I ended sadly.

"Speaking from experience?" he asked, raising an eyebrow at me.

"Good grief, no!" I let out a snort of amusement. "I only ever sleep with men I'm married to."

He blinked at me, clearly not sure if I was being serious.

"So – how many of those have there been, exactly?" he enquired carefully, after a pause.

"Just the one," I said succinctly. I think that was the moment when he realized I wasn't joking.

"You mean—?" He broke off, having trouble believing what I was apparently telling him.

"Oh, yes," I said, confirming it with a nod. "Just Alex. And then only after the wedding, too."

He stared at me, and I couldn't help smiling.

"Very out of step with the times, I know," I agreed, as if he'd spoken his incredulity aloud. "But I decided quite early on that was going to be my policy. When I was only twelve or thirteen, I remember there were at least half a dozen girls in my year at school who ended up pregnant. Becoming mothers at that age. Or else having abortions... I was pretty analytical about things, even as a hormonal teenager. And I saw the emotional messes those girls got themselves into. Not to mention the STIs some of them ended up with. No, I gave it some thought, and I decided I didn't want that happening to me. Prevention was always going to be better than cure. And there's only one really sure way to prevent that particular problem. Don't sleep with people you're not married to. Not fashionable, but effective. And something I intend to stick to."

"Haven't you found that" – he sought diplomatically for an appropriate adjective – "difficult, sometimes?"

I shrugged lightly.

"Disappointing people's social expectations, you mean? Not really. And there wasn't that much – how shall I put it? – that much interest... I think I'm too straightforward. The '*say what I mean and mean what I say*' thing. Doesn't seem to be what most boys go for, despite what they might say. I did go out with a few, but it was positively disheartening how quickly they vanished once they realized I meant it. I'm not overly impressed if all someone wants are the privileges of a relationship without the responsibilities. Plus I was still quite young when I married Alex, so I didn't really get the chance to feel I'd missed out on anything worthwhile. Or anyone, come to that. And, in case you were wondering, there hasn't been anyone since him, either. But even if there had been – that's the way it is." I shrugged again.

He didn't say anything, but I caught his expression, and one corner of my mouth lifted in a half-smile.

"Look, don't worry!" I assured him. "What other people do, or have done, is their business. I'm not telling anyone else what to do. I'm just saying what works for me, that's all. All I care about – all I wish – is that everyone could live happily ever after, the way Sophie wants to. Whatever works for them, fine! As long as it makes them happy. It's just that so often, it doesn't seem to. I want better than that." I leaned forward in my earnestness. "I'm the product of a lifelong, committed, monogamous marriage based on affection and respect and love. So I know it's possible. It can happen, it does happen. They've set my bar pretty high, Mum and Dad. Selfishly, I want what they've got. Or as close to it as I can get. And I nearly had it. I so nearly had it with Alex! So, who knows? Maybe lightning can strike twice. Someday." I felt a twinge of doubt, and eyed Peter with a touch of anxiety. "I haven't – disappointed you, or anything?"

"No!" he denied, sharply. "No, not at all!" His response was clearly genuine, and I relaxed, as he struggled to articulate his thoughts. "I was just – surprised, I suppose. But I think it's – well, it's just – unusual, these days," he concluded, slowly.

"I'm perfectly sure most people would classify it as downright eccentric, at the very least," I agreed, with a touch of self-derisive humour. "Not to say stupid. We live in an age where instant self-gratification is generally regarded as both right and normal." I shrugged. "But I just wasn't brought up to sleep around. Any more than I was brought up to be crude or blasphemous. Like I said, way out of step with the modern world! Just have to face it, Peter – you're keeping company with an anachronism. Sorry, but there it is!" I grinned at him impishly, and was relieved to see him smile back.

Just then we had to break off our conversation as a largish group of young men, perhaps some fifteen of so, came surging out of some other area of the pub, heading for the door. They were moderately drunk, most of them, but boisterously, not aggressively. They were all talking over each other quite loudly, but as they passed us I heard one of them declaiming, above the voices of his fellows, "*I've* got a Mazda MX-5 *and* a girlfriend…!"

I caught Peter's eye. For a moment both of us were visibly fighting the same fight. Then we couldn't manage to suppress our reactions one moment longer, and burst out laughing at the same instant.

"If that's the kind of thing he feels the need to announce publicly, I'm forced to wonder in which order he acquired them," I commented, wiping one eye, when I was finally able to speak.

Peter chuckled again. "I know where my money'd be on that one," he agreed.

There was a pause. Then I remembered something I'd been wanting to ask him; now seemed as good a moment as any.

"Look," I began, more seriously. "You may not be able to answer this, and I shall quite understand if you can't. But something's puzzling me."

He eyed me with a touch of reserve.

"See, I was looking at the Met's website. When – when we met, you had that shoulder holster. But the website says that firearms are only carried by Armed Response officers?" I ended the sentence on an upward note of enquiry.

He said nothing, simply eyed me steadily. Was that a very faint glimmer of amusement at the back of the dark eyes?

"Ah. I take it that's your *'you shouldn't believe everything you read on the Internet'* face?" I suggested.

He dropped his eyes and stared into the bottom of his glass, as if fatally fascinated by something he could see there.

"Perhaps you shouldn't believe *me*," he said in a low voice. "Perhaps *I'm* deceiving you. Lying to you."

There was a small, slightly constrained silence between us. I regarded his averted profile, wondering about what he'd said. The way he'd said it. What he might mean by it.

"Peter," I said at last, to make him look at me; he did. "I want you to understand something." This was not something I was about to say lightly, and I wanted him to listen to me. Not just hear me, but listen to me. "I'll always believe you. I'll always behave as if I believe you. Because I think that over things that really matter, if you choose to speak about them at all, you'll tell me the truth." His eyelids flickered momentarily in response. "And if you do lie to me – either by commission or omission – I'll assume there's a very sound and valid reason for it. Because I trust your judgement. I trust *you*. So I do believe you. And I always will. Okay?"

Some strong emotion seemed to overtake him; his eyes positively flashed, and he shot to his feet, the empty glass clattering noisily as he thrust it down onto the tabletop.

"Be right back," he said abruptly, and headed for the door.

I watched him go, and waited, wondering if what I'd intended to be a gesture of faith had somehow upset him. Through the window nearest the door, I saw him come to an abrupt halt outside, standing in the gathering gloom of evening, hands deep in his pockets, shoulders hunched, his body language tense. At first his head was bowed; then he threw it back, squared his shoulders, and stared up at the sky for a long time. He looked as if he was thinking hard, very hard. When he returned a few minutes later, he clearly had something on his mind. Something important. Serious.

"Let's go for a walk," he said briefly.

"Okay," I agreed. I downed the last dregs of my drink, waited while he paid for the meal, then followed him outside.

Almost absently, he chose a direction, and I walked alongside him. We were on a fairly minor road close to the edge of the built-up area, along which, if one went far enough, the front gardens ceased, to be replaced by field hedges. But there was still a pavement wide enough for two to walk abreast, and the stream of passing cars hardly impinged on our consciousness.

For a long time he was silent, so I just walked with him, to be there when he was ready to speak. At last he did, in a low voice, without looking at me. No preface, just launching into what he wanted to say.

"I went undercover once. About twelve years ago. There was some serious stuff going on, and we needed to break up the gang doing it. Though" – he corrected himself – "saying 'gang' gives the wrong impression. Makes it sound like some bunch of kids. It was bigger than that, better organized. Professional. But we could never pin anything on the people behind it, just pick up the odd small fry. So we needed to get someone on the inside. Took me a year to get to where I needed to be. But we got them. Big bust, and all that. Some serious people went down for some serious time. Made the national news."

He paused. I didn't say anything. I felt as if the thread of will by which he was delivering this to me was so fragile even a whisper might break it.

"One of the people we targeted was a kind of – well, let's say a lieutenant for the real bosses. A fixer. The man they'd give the orders to and know he'd see them carried out. In his way, an honest politician. And I got close to him. His name" – he broke off, drew a deep breath, then continued – "his name is Matthew Lesser."

He stopped walking, and did look at me, then.

Lesser, I was thinking to myself. *At last. He's finally going to tell me about Lesser...*

"Jenny – there's something you've got to understand. Sometimes undercover means... Look, I had to do some things that weren't... I had to get him to trust me, you see," he said disjointedly, in an even lower voice.

Some of the implications translated themselves into scenarios in my brain as I took in what he was trying to tell me. And I had the feeling he was afraid I would be repulsed by it. By him, for having done it. But I stood by my conviction that Peter McLeish was a good man. So I still said

111

nothing, just reached up and touched his shoulder for a moment.

He let out a shuddering, almost soundless sigh, and began to walk again. I kept pace with him.

"When it was over, I swore I'd never do undercover again. But it took another couple of years before all the trials were over. By then" – he hesitated momentarily – "I'd met Laura. We'd got married."

He threw me a quick glance, to see how I was taking this new development in the story. I suppose that, although I wouldn't have thought to predict that was what he would say, I wasn't really surprised. Even on the relatively little I knew about him, it wasn't exactly a startling concept that some girl had recognized his quality and put an accurate value on the kind of man he was. I nodded, accepting the revelation. I had an impression of almost physical relaxation from him at my reaction.

"She wanted children," he went on. "We'd been married a couple of years. Then she fell pregnant." He looked at me with eyes momentarily lit by remembered happiness. But the happiness turned visibly to ashes, and his voice changed. "She was six months gone when Lesser appealed his conviction. And got out. On a technicality."

His voice was now so grim I was afraid. For him. Because I was beginning to get an inkling of where this might be going.

"Peter," I said urgently, reaching out to grasp his upper arm, so that he had to stop and face me. "Peter, you don't have to tell me this, if you don't want to."

"I do want to," he said quickly, his face turned toward me but his eyes hidden in the shadow of his fringe cast by the street light above us. "I want you to know."

He began walking again. "I want you to know," he repeated. He sounded almost desperate to confide in me. "He got out," he went on, picking up the thread of his narrative again. "And he came after me. I'd been too good at my job, see? Suckered him completely. He didn't like that. He *really* didn't like that. He had a score to settle."

Neither of us had been taking much note of our surroundings, but by now we'd walked beyond the built-up area; at that moment we were about to cross a small turning off the main road that became a short, rough trackway leading into a small field on our right. Peter abruptly left the pavement and strode over to the gate, out of the reach of the street lights; he put out both hands and gripped the top bar as if he was about to wrest the whole thing off its hinges, his head ducking down and then rearing up again in a gesture of profound distress. I followed him, and stood beside him in the dark.

"What happened?" I asked. I hadn't wanted to break into his story, but now I couldn't help myself. I knew it wasn't going to make good listening, but he'd stimulated a compulsion in me to know the rest, however terrible.

Peter let out an ugly snort of distorted laughter.

"Oh, he didn't waste any time! Started following me. Finding all sorts of small ways to harass me. Stalking me. I could have taken it if it had just been me. But it was Laura. He started on her, as well. She was all right at first, but then… And he was so clever! There was nothing I could do to stop him getting at her. It went on for nearly three months. She was getting so frightened! I was worried sick the stress was gonnae harm the baby." He almost choked over that sentence. "And in the end…"

He leaned his forearms on the gate; his head dropped. He was just a silhouette in the gloom, but his entire body language spoke of grief and loss. I waited, tensely. Just how far had Matthew Lesser gone in his campaign of revenge? I knew instinctively I was about to hear something horrific.

"There was a fire," he said dully, at last. "At the back of the house, ground floor. She'd been gagged and tied to the banisters at the top of the stairs. Not much in the way of flame, but lots of smoke. They said it had been deliberately rigged that way. They could never prove who did it. But I knew. We all knew." He threw his head up and back, his face angled toward the sky. "She didn't burn. She suffocated. And our baby with her…"

His voice had been growing more and more tremulous, and now it gave up the ghost altogether. He turned toward me and reached out blindly for me in the darkness, and I spread my arms and accepted him into them, instinctively desperate to convey all the comfort I could in their grip, while he choked and gasped his torment into the hollow of my neck. Tears were coursing down my own face, but I hardly noticed them.

"Our little girl…! It was gonnae be a girl…!" The sobbing wail contained more distress than I'd ever encountered in my life – and, having lived with Alex, I'd encountered a fair bit of that, in my time. But nothing on this scale, of this intensity. Hearing that hoarse cry of pain was like a punch in the gut.

This, then, explained that comment of Alan's in the hospital up in Inverness. *You might just owe her your life. And even if you're not that attached to it, the rest of us would still prefer you here and alive.* Who could be surprised if his life had lost its value to him after his wife and unborn child had been so brutally, horribly taken from him? Maybe he *had* stopped caring if he lived or died after that. For a while. Maybe a long while.

The worst thing was knowing there was absolutely nothing I could say that would be of any good whatever, no words that hadn't already been offered to him by others. No conceivable words could cover it in any case, whoever said them. The only way I could speak my feelings to him, for him, was the way I was doing it now, holding him close. Conveying to him through the simple human act of physical contact the degree of my distress for him, the strength of my desire to comfort him.

We stood like that for what seemed a long time. Eventually he became still and quiet, and with one last sharply indrawn breath straightened up, releasing me. I let him go, and stood in front of him, waiting for him, without speaking.

"Let's go back," he said heavily, wiping his face with the palms of his hands before it became visible in the glare of the street lights and the traffic.

We walked back to the pub car park in silence. But not a constrained silence, this; a sad and sombre one, to be sure – but also an accepting silence, tinged with the relief of the unspeakable having been spoken. The silence of two companions who have understood one another.

It lasted throughout the homeward journey, until he pulled up outside our house and switched the engine off. Then he looked at me.

"I'm sorry if you're upset," he said quietly. "But – I wanted you to know. I really wanted you to know."

"I'm – honoured – that you wanted to tell me," I said, trying for a similar tone. And I meant it. What he'd told me was quite a thing to confide in anyone, let alone someone he'd only known for a relatively short time.

"I've never told anyone until now." His voice contained a tinge of puzzlement, as if he'd surprised himself with his own revelations. "Not about the baby being a girl. I've never been able to bring myself to tell anyone else. Only Alan and Jane. No one else."

"Then that's the way it'll stay," I said, making it a promise.

He looked at me strangely – as much as to say, *I already know that.*

I released my seat belt, opened the door, and got out. Then I bent down and looked back into the car at him, my hand on the top of the door, ready to close it.

"Thank you, Peter," I said clearly. "Truly. Thank you. Get in touch when you want to see me again. I'll be here."

He nodded.

I closed the door, and the car pulled away. I watched it go the length of the road. Only when it had turned out of sight did I walk in, up the steps, and into my home.

I didn't sleep well that night. Too much going on in my head. And no 'off' switch for it.

Chapter 11

I must have looked particularly tired the next day. They commented on it at the library in the morning, and when Dad caught sight of me, half-way through the afternoon – I was sitting on the garden bench when he came out to put a kitchen waste bag into the dustbin – he came straight over.

"What's the matter?" he demanded, sliding into place next to me.

"How did you know anything was the matter?" I parried, unconvincingly. "I had my back to you."

"Jenny, darling, how many times have I told you you'll never make a poker player? The set of your shoulders told me. So what is it? Anything I can help with?"

I shook my head, and looked down at my hands, loosely clasped in my lap. To my dismay, my eyes suddenly filled with tears.

"Jenny!" my father persisted, his arm suddenly a warm and comforting pressure around my shaking shoulders. "What is it?"

I wept silently for a while, then started to fumble in my pockets for my handkerchief, only to find his being presented to me. I produced a reasonable facsimile of a smile, albeit a watery one, and dried my eyes with the soft, white cotton. Then I sat up straighter under the reassuring weight of his arm, gusted a sigh, and hoped my voice wasn't going to tremble too much.

"I – found something out last night," I began, hesitantly. "About Peter."

"Something that means something's wrong between you?" For a moment his arm tensed around me.

"No! No! Nothing like that," I denied hastily. He recognized that instantly for the truth; I felt him relax slightly.

"Thing is, Dad," I went on, "he told me something last night. Something upsetting. A very terrible thing happened to him. A long time ago. I think I knew, because – I've sometimes seen it on his face. Like a sort of shadow. It's just that I never knew what it was until now. But now he's told me. Something really terrible." I shifted in my seat, almost sharply. "You know, we've lost the meaning of that word. Diluted it. Something very small or very unimportant happens, and we warble, *Oh, that's terrible*, without thinking about it. When it isn't terrible at all. Not horrendous, or monstrous, or harrowing, or appalling, or any of the other things that 'terrible' really means. What happened to Peter – that was terrible."

"What did happen?" My father tightened the grip of his arm, intent, responding to my tone.

I hesitated. I wanted so much to tell him! But I shook my head.

"It's not my place to tell anyone else. He told me in confidence… Can we see if he decides to tell you himself, sometime? See how it goes? But," I added swiftly, "I'm glad you know. That there is something. Because – well, I thought you'd probably pick up on it yourself anyway, at some point. Something being wrong, I mean."

"Because I'm a very astute chap," my father agreed. "Of course. You're absolutely right. Let's see how it goes. But are you really sure you're all right?"

I put my hand up to lay it over his where it rested on the point of my left shoulder, and pressed it reassuringly.

"I will be," I said. "I was just so – well, upset for *him*. Having to live with this – this *thing* in the background all the time. For years! It explains a lot of things about him."

"I'll take your word for it." He gave my shoulders another squeeze. "But whatever it is, it sounds as if it was a great thing that he should have confided in you. A quite formidable expression of trust, I suspect. And do you know something? It makes me feel more proud, even than usual, that you are my daughter." He leaned over and kissed me on the cheek, then let go of me.

"Brute," I said, dabbing hastily with the borrowed handkerchief. "Now look what you've done – made me cry all over again!"

"I'm suitably penitent," he assured me, rising from the bench. "And now, what about a coffee? Your mother's head down at the moment, but I'll see if she can be lured out. I expect we could all do with one."

I smiled up at him. "Don't you ever get tired of always being right?" I teased, my eyes still overbright.

"Never," he assured me serenely. "Come on."

And his arm went around my shoulders once again as he walked me back to the house.

It was a slightly anxious experience, this time, waiting for Peter to get in touch. I thought several times about making the approach myself. I even got out my phone to do it, once. But I hesitated, then put it away again. After what he'd told me, it had to be him who made the next contact. I'd vowed to myself I was never going to put pressure on him, and I wasn't about to start now.

So it was an enormous relief when the call came through, three days later. It was getting on for late afternoon, and I was busy loading the washing machine when my ringtone started demanding attention. My heart beat a little faster when I saw who the call was from. I made myself be calm as I activated the phone.

"Hello," I said neutrally.

"Hello," came the response.

There was a pause.

"Well, thank you for sharing that with me… Was that it, or was there something particular you wanted?" I enquired at last, with caricatured casualness. I heard him stifle a laugh. Which heartened me. I'd obviously struck the right tone.

"Doing anything at the moment?"

"Oh, my word, yes. My laundry. You can come over and watch my smalls revolving in the washing drum, if you're up for that much excitement."

"An irresistible offer," he commented, dry as sometimes only a Scot can be, and rang off.

I made a fist, and muttered, "Yes!" through clenched teeth, even though there was no one there to hear me. It was all right. He was coming back. He wanted to come back.

And since he hadn't deigned to tell me how long he'd be, or what he was intending we should do when he arrived, I started the washing cycle going, then started inspecting the contents of the fridge, in case we were eating in.

I was down in the garden, hanging the completed wash on the line, when I heard his car pulling in. With a damp T-shirt in one hand and a couple of pegs in the other, I walked to the end of the drive and waved at him, to show him where I was. He flung up a hand in acknowledgement, and headed toward me.

"I missed all the fun, then," he said, coming to a halt, hands in pockets.

I sighed with mock regret.

"I'm afraid so," I agreed. "Never mind. Better luck next time. Give me a minute or two to get this lot up, then we'll think of some alternative entertainment, okay?" I pegged the T-shirt up and pulled another from the basket.

"D'you want a hand with that?" he offered, coming forward to delve helpfully into the heap of garments. I shrugged in a gesture of amused acquiescence.

"If you like. Never let it be said I don't know how to show a man a good time!"

He straightened up, holding an item of clothing dangling from his upheld hand. One of my bras.

"No, indeed," he said dryly.

I met his eye, and we both burst into laughter.

When the last item had been pegged to the line, he carried the empty basket up for me, and I offered – and he accepted – coffee.

"So what do you want to do?" I enquired, spooning the dark brown granules into mugs. "Go out, or stay in?"

"Stay in. If that's all right?"

"'Course it is, you idiot," I said cheerfully. "I haven't got a lot in – I was going to go shopping tomorrow. But I can offer you a macaroni cheese, if that'd do?"

"Yeh, sounds good," he said, but a little absently, as if he had something else on his mind.

"Okay, I'll do that a bit later. And I went all domestic and baked a cake yesterday, so I can even offer you a sweet course! Of a sort." I picked up the mugs and carried them through into the living room. When he'd plumped himself down into the armchair, I handed his coffee over, then sat down in the centre of the sofa, cradling my own mug in my hands.

We looked at each other.

"Did you mind about the other night?" he asked, at last.

"Of course not!" I said, truthfully. "Why ever would I?"

"Because it was pretty disturbing stuff. I've been worrying ever since that I upset you. Did I?" His eyes, large and luminous, peered uneasily at me from under the long dark fringe.

"Of course I was upset," I agreed flatly. Anxiety flared on his face. "But for you, not by you."

He drew a deep breath, then let it go, slowly, and looked down at the floor for a moment before raising his eyes again to me. There was an expression of faint but genuine puzzlement on his face.

"I can't work out why I wanted you to know so much," he said slowly. "I kept wanting to tell you. I've been wanting to tell you for weeks. But it never seemed like the right moment. And then – it just came out. It was only after I'd done it I started to worry about what you might've felt about it."

"How do *you* feel about it? You don't" – I strove to keep my tone level – "you don't wish you hadn't told me?"

His headshake of denial was instant and genuine.

"No. No," he said. "It felt" – he hesitated, looking a bit puzzled by his own words – "right. Better. Like I'd shifted some sort of load off me." His head jerked back as he uttered a sudden snort of half-angry laughter. "Selfish, right? But – I'm sorry – it's true." He looked at me warily, gauging my reaction.

"Then I'm very, very glad you told me," I said firmly. "Someone came up with the phrase '*a problem shared is a problem halved*' for a reason, you know! Even if the other person can't do anything about it, it's still true, it's still worth doing. Trust me, Peter, I know just how true it is! I lived with a man with chronic depression. If I hadn't been able to unload onto my parents sometimes, I don't know how I would've managed. Sometimes, half the battle is just telling someone."

"I know," he muttered, dropping his eyes to the floor. "It's just – not the sort of thing you talk about to everyone."

"Alan and Jane," I said reflectively. "And Craig and Sophie know, I'm guessing? And your colleagues?"

"Some of them. Not all of them."

"Anyone else?"

He raised his head and looked at me. "Just you."

I was silent for a moment. Then I said, "Thank you for your trust."

"It's your own fault," he said. "You're too good a listener." He took a swallow of his coffee, then put the mug down on the floor beside his chair.

"If it's helped, then I'm glad. And if it helps in the future…" I left the offer lying. I hoped he'd take it up, if he needed to. And I had a strong feeling he did need to. Not that I welcomed the prospect of any more revelations of the same nature; I simply had an almost overwhelming desire to be of help to him. I didn't analyze why – which wasn't like me. I just knew I had it, and I hoped he'd make use of it.

"Don't tempt me," he advised, and there was no smile on his face now. "You don't know what you might get unloaded on you."

"I don't care. If you want to say something, you say it. Get it out, and get it said."

"Dangerous territory, Jenny," he said grimly. "Sometimes I get angry. Very angry."

"Even so," I persisted, though I was wondering if I was being wise. Even the thought of talking about it had put an expression into his eyes that I didn't much like the look of. But I'd made the offer now, and I'd stand by it. "Do you talk about it much?"

He shook his head, not looking at me.

"Not anymore. And only to Alan. It's enough that Jane and the kids know. But I can't tell *them* how it makes me feel. They're just kids! And Jane probably gets Alan unloading his own stuff onto her. Sometimes the job can be—" He broke off, paused, then went on, "It's just sometimes, when something makes it all come welling up again… Then I have to talk to *someone*. So it's him."

"I suppose they offered you counselling, did they?"

He snorted.

"Yeh. Didn't solve anything. Not their fault. Maybe I wasn't ready, or something. I don't know…" He paused, staring at nothing. I waited.

"I tried diving into a bottle for a while," he went on, reflectively. A very honest admission. "But it turned out not to be a very good fit… You blur your problems that way, but you don't solve them. Lucky I realized that before the habit got a hold." His eyes were sombre. "I've known too many guys who didn't. Maybe they didn't have the same things to anchor them that I did."

Alan, of course. And the family. I gave silent thanks for that, at least. Clearly Peter could have gone right off the rails without them – and without Alan in particular. I remembered that handclasp between them at the hospital in Inverness, and the volumes it had spoken about their relationship.

"I wish there was something I could do," I said sadly.

He looked up quickly at that.

"But you do," he said. "Just by being you." There was no flattery intended; he was clearly simply stating what, to him, was obvious. I coloured slightly, hoped he wouldn't notice, and changed the subject, slightly at random.

"What about your boss? Whoever he is. Or was, then. He didn't try to get you to resign, or anything like that?"

Peter leaned back, sprawling in the capacious armchair. A different look had come onto his face; the corners of his mouth curved upward slightly.

"The Laird? Never even considered it."

"The Laird?" Another name from that overheard conversation in Inverness…

"Robert Laird. Now Commander Robert Laird, no less. But known throughout the force as just 'the Laird'. He was in charge of the team when I joined. He's an Edinburgh man – started in the force there – but he made his way down to London eventually. Like we did. Alan took over when he got promotion. He's close to the top of the tree now. Is the top of our particular branch of it. The Laird and the McLeishes," he said, musingly. "They used to call us the Black Watch back then. Maybe they still do. It's a standing office joke that we put the 'Scotland' into Scotland Yard."

"But you're all three Lowland Scots, then. Don't they know the Black Watch is a Highland regiment?" I enquired.

"Well done you, for being someone who does know it! Most English don't even know the difference between a Highlander and a Lowlander," Peter observed caustically. "They just lump us all together and call us Scotch instead of Scots, as if we were a brand of whisky."

"Ah, well, we English are good at that," I observed. "Invade a country, impose our ways on it, and either suppress or ignore the indigenous culture unless it happens to suit us. Ask any Welshman you like."

He laughed. I was glad to see it, but I was trying to steer the conversation back to what I wanted to know.

"So he was in charge of you, back then?"

"It was him who asked me to go undercover." Peter looked out of the window. "So I suppose he felt responsible, in a way. Not that he should've. He couldn't've known. Though" – his voice was sober – "I don't know if it would've stopped him, even if he had. The job always comes first, with him." He threw me a slightly wry glance. "That's what his wife said when they divorced, anyway." More evidence that Jane was indeed, as she had admitted to me, lucky to have an enduring marriage to a senior police officer.

"So he let you stay on. Why?"

"There were a lot of others who wouldn't have," Peter acknowledged. "But he stuck by me, insisted he wanted me still in the team. Maybe a touch of guilt – who knows? I often think it might be because he thought it would motivate me. He wants Lesser, you see. He thought we'd got him, and then he slipped through the net. He's still out there, still thumbing his nose at us. So the Laird wants him. Professional pride, I suppose. Wants to see the job finished properly. And the way he puts it is that I've got *incentive*." He uttered the word bitterly. "So he thinks I can still be useful. Not that it's done him much good so far. Close to ten years, and we still haven't been able to lay a glove on him." The 'him', this time, being Lesser.

I regarded him for a few moments. Then I said, "Do you know what I think?"

He looked at me, brushing his fringe out of his eyes. "What?"

"I think the Laird's right. I think you'll get him. In the end."

"And what makes you think that?" he demanded in a tone that was half irritated, half amused. "In the face of the evidence to date?"

"I don't know. I just do. I suppose you can say I've got faith in you, if you want to put it that way. The Laird must have, mustn't he? So, so have I. I think you'll do it," I ended flatly.

It would have been easy for you to blame Robert Laird, I was thinking to myself. *But somehow you don't. Instead, he's got your respect, and your loyalty. He must be quite a man for that to have happened. So I think I'll trust his judgement on this, even though I've never met him. He thinks you'll make a difference. So maybe you will.*

I saw Peter's eyes on my face, and wondered if he knew what I was thinking. If he did, he wasn't saying so.

"Now," I said decisively, standing up. "What about that macaroni cheese? I'm getting hungry, even if you're not."

"Yeh, I am," he agreed.

"Does that mean you've got sufficient *incentive* to come and grate the cheese for me, then?"

The black humour was perhaps something of a risk, but it paid off. He laughed briefly, and was still smiling as he followed me into the kitchen.

I made him laugh again, later. After the macaroni cheese, I produced the cake – a jam and cream sponge, sprinkled with icing sugar, handing him a fork along with the plate.

"Use that if you think it'll save the dignity of your beard when the cream squidges out of the sides," I suggested. He accepted it with a nod, used it to sever the point of the slice, and put the portion carefully into his mouth.

"This is good!" he approved heartily, after a couple of chews.

"Thank you," I acknowledged, and followed his example. "Not quite up there with the best cake I ever tasted, but not bad," I admitted. "I don't have a particularly wide range as a cook, but the things I do, I do quite well."

"It'll do me," he said, continuing to eat with evident relish.

"Good-oh," I said equably.

After a short pause, he quirked an eyebrow at me and said, "So what was?"

"What was what?"

"What was the best cake you ever tasted?"

"Oh! Oh, a custard slice," I said immediately. "Mum and Dad'd been up to London for the day, and Mum knows I've got this weakness for custard slices, so she brought me one back from a Patisserie Valerie. Have you ever had one of their cakes?" The treasured memory of eating that slice accounted for the sudden enthusiasm in my voice.

"No," he admitted.

"Oh-h-h, Peter! You've missed out, big time! You must, one day. Mind you, it was just as well I was on my own when I ate it!"

He awarded me a slightly puzzled look. "Why?" he enquired.

I realized I'd dug myself into a hole with that careless comment, but I'd left myself with no choice but to go ahead with the explanation.

"The noises I made while I was eating it," I said. "I couldn't help myself! It was just too delicious not to! But if someone'd overheard me who couldn't see what I was really doing, they – um – might've been misled into thinking I was enjoying another type of experience entirely..." I grinned at him mischievously.

He threw his head back and laughed, and I took tremendous pleasure in the sight. He hadn't been so ready to laugh when I first knew him. "*You're good for him,*" Alan had said. "*He's a lot more relaxed. Laughs more. More like he used to be.*" I was so glad of it – especially knowing what I now knew.

"But it really was the most delicious thing I've ever tasted," I went on. "I keep promising myself I'll have another one, one day. But I don't get up that way much. Something to look forward to, though."

"If that's the effect they have, I'll definitely be having the one you had," he assured me.

Now it was my turn to laugh, and it started him off again, too.

"Indeed," I agreed, wiping my eyes at last. I looked at what was left of the sponge on his plate. "Sorry this isn't in quite the same league…"

"It'll do me," he said simply.

And for some reason, that one plain statement filled me with more pleasure than I could possibly have expressed.

Even more than the infamous custard slice! Which was saying something.

Chapter 12

About a month later I discovered the truth of Peter's warning that his talking about what had happened to his wife could be an uncomfortable experience for me. It was early November, but we'd arranged to go for a walk in some woods not far from Biggin Hill, and he came to pick me up and drive me there, as arranged.

The problem was that it was clear, from the moment he turned up, that he was in a pretty black sort of mood. I hadn't seen him for about a week, but his responses to my attempts at conversation were almost unrelentingly monosyllabic, so I knew the afternoon was likely to be hard going. But he hadn't called it off, which I would have expected him to do if he really hadn't wanted to come. I presumed the most likely explanation was that something wasn't going well at work. So I kept my conversational gambits to a minimum, by and large, and waited to learn if he would see fit to account for his ill humour at some point.

At least it was a lovely day, crisply cool under the almost cloudless blue sky. The hues of autumn were now past their best, but there were still enough golds, browns and reds for the sun to illuminate into a last gasp of beauty, and the ground underfoot was mostly firm, with only occasional reaches of muddier soil to be negotiated.

We walked mostly in silence, although I remained doggedly upbeat about pointing out things that took my interest, such as the occasional sightings of hedgerow birds, the colours of the fallen leaves, and so on. But in the end, casting a sideways glance at his hunched shoulders, the hands jammed deep into his jeans pockets, I decided I was going to have to grasp the nettle. Make an attempt to draw him out on whatever it was that was on his mind.

"I take it not everything in your world is the way you'd like it to be, then," I ventured after a particularly long silence, consciously not looking at him as I said it, though I caught the brief, sharp turn of his head toward me in my peripheral vision before he looked away again.

"No," he said flatly. For a moment I thought that was all I was going to get by way of response. But then he went on, his voice bleak. "We lost an informant a couple of days ago. An important one."

"Lost how?" I wondered which of the range of grim possibilities he was employing to mean 'lost' in this context.

"Not dead," he said grimly. "Not quite. But I don't think there're many parts of his skeleton that aren't out of true. Massive soft tissue damage. He'll be in hospital for months. They're taking out one of his kidneys, and part of his spleen. His girlfriend found him, beaten to a pulp, and after she'd got him to the hospital she was straight on to us. She knew he'd been talking to us, and she didn't like it – she was afraid something like this was going to happen. If he recovers, he won't be talking to us again – she was pretty clear on that. Lesser's issued one of his warnings, you see. Not just to him. To others like him. We thought we were on the verge of making some real progress this time. Not now, we aren't." He kicked savagely at an inoffensive chunk of ancient tree branch on the pathway, sending it skittering into the dying undergrowth.

I hesitated over how to reply, but it wasn't necessary. The floodgates were open now.

"It's always the same! One step forward, two steps back! Any time we're getting close to something we can use, this is what he does. Makes an example of someone. So everyone else knows what to expect. Like he did with me. Oh, yeah – I got that lesson by heart, all right! And now someone else's got it, too. Control by fear. '*Step over my line*,' he says, '*and this is what'll happen to you.*' It's very effective, I'll give him that." His voice was growing more savage with each passing second. Abruptly he stopped and looked me straight in the eye, his face set in hard lines, his eyes burning, his body rigid with emotion.

"Do you know what I wannae do, sometimes?" he demanded. "I wannae have him in front of me and just *smash his face in*! I wannae *hurt* him! I wannae *kill* him! *Kill* him!" I could see the tendons in his neck standing out, taut. "I imagine doing it, you know! See it all happening in my head. Think about how I wannae do it. All the ways I *could* do it."

I couldn't think of anything to say. I just stared at him, troubled for him, and – I have to admit it – taken aback by the sheer passion of the outburst. Even though it wasn't directed at me, it wasn't comfortable, being confronted with so much fury, so much hatred, and the realization of how close – and how constantly – it must lie under the surface to be so readily vented.

He spat out a travesty of a laugh, but it was disgust at himself, not humour, that he was expressing.

"I know it's stupid, and it's pointless, and it won't bring them back, either of them. I know it takes me down from a reasoning human being to the level of an animal. But still I just wannae *kill* him! Do to him what he did to them. Blot him out of existence. Because I *hate* him!" His voice rose in bitter, savage frustration. "I *hate* him for what he did to them! For what he did to *me*! Took from me! By what right? What right did he have?"

His eyes were swimming with furious tears, his mouth an ugly rectangular shape, revealing the clenched teeth through which he was forcing his words.

"No right," I said quietly. "None."

His eyes were dark with rage at the injustice of it. Who could blame him for that? I said nothing. What could I usefully say, that wouldn't sound trite and banal and even patronizing?

He turned abruptly away from me, and there was a long, long silence. I waited, with thudding heart.

When at last he turned back, it was evident that, having got it off his chest, he'd managed to calm down, quite a lot; now, as he looked at me, a different expression had replaced the anger.

"What, no platitudes?" He wasn't being sarcastic. I could see in his eyes that he was still feeling fairly roused – you don't recover from that pitch of emotion at the drop of a hat – but he was also looking at me with genuine curiosity. "You know, other times I've got like this, people've said, '*oh, you mustn't feel like that*', '*you've got to let it go*', and other damned rubbish. But not you." He said that last slowly, with the air of a man making a discovery.

"Maybe – if I'd ever experienced anything remotely like it – I might have some faint right to pronounce," I said, aware that I needed to tread carefully. "But I haven't. It's completely outside my experience. The best I can say is that I can only try to imagine what it must be like, and if I'm going to be honest, I don't suppose for a minute I can come even close. To pretend otherwise – well, seems to me like the height of presumption. So I don't want to be such a fool as to try to talk about something I know nothing about."

"Oh, you're not a fool," he said softly. "Definitely not a fool."

I didn't know what to reply to that, so I said nothing.

Abruptly he strode over and seized both my hands in his.

"Thank you," he said, unexpectedly. "Thank you." Those were the only words he used, but the strength of his grip on my fingers went on speaking for him.

I couldn't think what he could possibly be thanking me for. Personally, I felt as if my response had been woefully inadequate, though he didn't seem to think so. But what I'd told him was true. I could only try to imagine it. I *had* tried to imagine it. I'd closed my eyes and tried to picture Laura – *being* Laura – tied to those banisters.

Desperately struggling to free herself, abrading her wrists raw as her nostrils filled with the scent of smoke.

Able to hear the crackle of the flames, gradually growing louder, with all her instincts screaming at her to get away from the danger, but not able to act on them.

Starting to cough, choking into her gag, as more smoke filled the air.

The increasing desperation she must have felt.

The panic, the fear, the horror that anyone would have of burning alive.

But not just for herself.

The feelings of the mother of an unborn child, facing the prospect of that death, thinking of her baby dying that way.

The screams she must have tried to utter, muffled by the strip of tape around her mouth, the tears that must have streamed down her face because of the billowing smoke and the pitch of her terror.

Calling uselessly for Peter, over and over again.

The blood running down her forearms from the rings of raw flesh that her wrists had become as she continued to wrestle against the bindings.

The horror of knowing that, while her mind still shrieked out the need to escape, her body was succumbing to the smoke.

Fighting to extract enough oxygen from the grey clouds to go on breathing.

Knowing all the time she was going to lose that fight.

The despair of knowing that nobody was coming.

Not Peter, not anyone.

Gradually, despite her efforts not to do so, sinking into fatal unconsciousness.

Her final, jumbled thoughts; of Peter. Of herself. Of their child, dying with her.

Until, at last, mercifully, no more thinking.

No more breathing.

An end to the torment.

Nothing.

Oh, yes – I'd tried to imagine it. But, somehow, I'd failed. Not in the intellectual exercise of being able to imagine that those things happened; not in failing to be able to summon up the words that described them. But a rather worrying failure of emotional connection, somehow; being unable to replicate those emotions in myself to go along with the pictures in my head. Was that some kind of fault in my emotional makeup? Did I lack empathy? I hadn't thought so, until now, and yet – imagining Laura's death in such detail, still I found myself unable to experience, to induce in myself, the emotions that must have gone with it. Why couldn't I do that, when I willed to do it?

Perhaps it was some kind of self-protective mechanism kicking in. My psyche fending off an extreme experience of negative emotions. I'd already had more than enough of those in my time, albeit from a different source and because of a different set of problems, and sometimes they'd cost me dear. Perhaps I should be grateful for this failure to connect. Yet I remained unhappy about it.

Which was why I couldn't help feeling that my response had, indeed, been inadequate. But I decided I'd keep my reasons to myself. I didn't see any good purpose would be served by discussing them with Peter. What I'd said had seemed to suffice for him; let it stay that way.

"I don't know what you're thanking me for," I said lamely.

He continued to regard me, maintaining his grip on my hands.

"Don't you?" he said softly. "I do."

He let me go, and walked on, and I turned to go with him.

"Peter," I said after a while.

"Yeh?"

"Days like this. When it goes wrong, and it really gets you down. The job, I mean. What do you do? To help yourself cope? How do you wind down from something like that?"

"Besides unloading onto you, you mean?" Unexpectedly, there was a gleam of humour in his eyes as he said it. Joking. He was making a joke of it. More progress?

"Yeh, besides that," I agreed, shrugging as if it was a given. Then, more seriously, "I suppose different people do it different ways. Cope with what your job throws up at you from time to time. Things like – what you've just said. I can't imagine having to deal with things at that sort of pitch. How do you manage it?"

He considered.

"Ben goes fishing," he said reflectively. "Shoeshop – Cathie – she goes and buys another pair of new shoes every time. No idea where she puts them all. Brad's got a classic car he goes home and tinkers with. Abhik's still at the age where he thinks going out and getting smashed is the best solution. Kevlar does that, too, though you'd think he was old enough to know better—"

"Kevlar?" I interrupted.

"Nickname," Peter explained. "Kevin, Kevlar, see? Chris rows with whatever girlfriend he's currently with, then makes up with her again. He gets through them at quite a rate. And I don't know what Andy does." He frowned momentarily at the oversight. "Haven't asked," he ended, with a shrug.

"And Alan sketches, I suppose?" I added lightly. Peter shrugged, and grinned.

"Mebbe," he said. "Or watches a Bolton match, if he can catch one. Not that he exactly finds that a relaxing pastime, most of the time!"

If he thought that stream of colleague names had successfully distracted me from the fact that he hadn't answered my actual question – what did *he* do – he was wrong. But then, I'd picked up on that very first evening that he didn't seem to have much in the way of active interests. Not these days, anyway. I remembered his passing reference on that occasion to having learned to sail as a child, though, and by association of ideas instinctively looked up at the blueness of the sky.

"Pity you don't still sail," I commented. "Your friend Ben's got the right idea with fishing, I reckon. Being on or near water's one of the most relaxing things you can do. Always works for me. There's something about water…" I shook my head, reflectively. "Streams, rivers, lakes, the sea – it's just…" I shrugged, my powers of description inadequate to the task.

"Or listening to the rain fall?" he suggested.

I looked at him, and we shared a smile.

"But sailing would be even better, wouldn't it? I wish I could've learned to sail," I concluded wistfully. "I've always wanted to. Not sea sailing, necessarily, but on a lake, at least. Or the Norfolk Broads; somewhere like that. I'd've liked to be able to do that."

Peter didn't respond immediately. He gave me a glance, then stared into the middle distance, his eyes apparently fixed on something I couldn't see. Then he spoke.

"Teach you, if you like," he offered unexpectedly, his tone studiedly nonchalant.

I looked at him quickly.

"Do you mean that?" I asked, astonished.

"If you like," he repeated, with a shrug that was meant to look casual. But when he looked at me again, I saw he really was serious.

I was both astounded, and delighted. If I could get him sailing again, he'd have an outlet, something to calm him down when things got on top of him. Taking him up on his offer might do him so much good. Give him an interest, an ongoing commitment – because I didn't think it was an offer he would make lightly, and then renege on. Not to me. Oh, this could only do him good! So, yes, I was going to accept. Besides, I'd been telling him the honest truth – I had always wanted to learn to sail.

"Yes, I would like!" I said fervently. "Are you quite sure? You mustn't feel obliged…"

"Yeh," he agreed, smiling faintly. "Got that one the first time we met up for dinner, remember?" He looked at me more intently. "How much do you know about sailing?"

"Complete laywoman," I admitted. "Unless re-reading the *Swallows and Amazons* books a million and one times since childhood counts? I've got a layman's grasp on the principle of tacking, and if you give me a pair of oars I daresay I could catch you a fairly sizeable crab or two. I know a sheet is a rope, not a sail. I know odd bits of stuff, like" – I cast around for an example – "red for port, green for starboard. That kind of thing. But that's the level we're talking, I'm afraid. Not much good, by your standards, I don't suppose," I ended, slightly forlornly.

"No, that's okay," he contradicted. "It's a start. A good start." Encouragingly, he sounded as if he meant it.

"How would it work, though? I mean, where would we go? How do we get hold of something to sail?"

"Give me a few days. I'll sort something out," he said decisively. "Mind you, it's not the best time of year to start. You'll be pretty cold, sometimes, if we start now."

"I don't care," I said quickly, worried that he might be having second thoughts. I didn't want this thing losing momentum. "If you really mean it, I don't care how cold I get. I don't want to wait. Not if you mean it," I repeated.

"I mean it," he said flatly.

And from that, I knew he'd committed to it. I hugged my thrill of pleasure to myself. I was going to learn to sail! More importantly, Peter was going to get that emotional outlet, that external interest, that he so badly needed. Even if I ended up falling overboard and half-drowning myself making sure of it. And if that's what it would take, then I'd be doing it. Without a moment's regret.

He was better after that. Started to relax. Talked to me some more about sailing, what it would entail, what equipment I'd need. When I queried what it would cost, he told me not to worry about it, he'd got it covered. Despite his admonition, I did worry about that for a bit. After all, I had next to no spare disposable income myself, and I didn't expect sailing to be a particularly cheap leisure activity – not by my standards, anyway. I certainly didn't want to impose on his generous impulse simply because of a thoughtless comment on my part. But as he talked, I saw the pleasure he was getting from the whole idea, and let the worry go. I had the feeling that whatever it cost, he'd think it was worth it.

We were in the car and on the way back when I asked, without thinking, "Are there any clubs near where you live?"

It was only then that I realized that in all the months we'd been keeping company, I'd never enquired – and he'd never volunteered the information – where he lived. How strange that I'd never felt the need to ask! Somehow it hadn't seemed important. He wanted to see me, he rang up or texted, he came. That was the way it worked. Why had it never occurred to me to enquire about something as basic as that? Though – maybe it worked both ways. I hadn't asked, but, conversely, he'd never said, either. So perhaps he didn't want to tell me. He'd never revealed much about his personal circumstances, anymore than he did about his work. The nature of our friendship had never depended on knowing those things. I certainly hadn't intended to pry, but now, perhaps – inadvertently – I had.

I could feel myself colouring slightly, and he saw it.

"What?" he asked.

"I'm sorry," I stammered. "I didn't mean to pry. I mean – I only meant..."

By now he'd worked out what the problem was.

"Ah," he said. "You mean, are there many sailing clubs around Brixton?"

I nodded, wordlessly.

"Not exactly, but don't worry. I'll sort it, like I said." He looked at me with tolerant amusement. "Relax, Jenny! It's not a secret. Not from you! I just never got round to saying, that's all."

"So," I said hesitantly, but, now that I had clear permission, wanting to know, "where do you live?"

"Small flat in an old house. Not as nice as yours." He shrugged. "Not the most salubrious area, either, though some parts of Brixton are better than others. But it's somewhere to live."

"How many flats altogether?"

"Half a dozen. Mine's top floor, at the back."

"Have you got much of a view?"

I only meant it as a conversational gambit, but there was a pause so long I thought he wasn't going to answer. In fact, I began to wonder if perhaps I shouldn't even have asked. Then he completely surprised me.

"I'll show you," he said, and swung the wheel decisively to turn the car in a new direction.

Which is how, later, I found myself doing something I really hadn't expected to be doing when I'd got up that morning. Being ushered into Peter's flat.

The building itself had a distinctly shabby air about it. A dull green-painted front door apparently served the other flats, but some quirk of the architecture meant that Peter had his own front door, a narrow affair on the right-hand side of the house, painted the same dull green. The servants' entrance, once, perhaps, or tradesmen's? Inside was a poorly-lit passage which led to a couple of flights of stairs, and thence to the door of his flat, at the top of the house.

'Small' was how he'd described it, and I had to admit he'd been strictly truthful on that front. A tiny shower and toilet, a minuscule kitchen in which two people would be one too many, and a bedroom that seemed fairly full even with only a single bed in it; the most redeeming feature was the tolerably-sized living room area, with a narrow French window which opened out onto a tiny balcony that was clearly a more modern addition. Lots of the original features, like the picture rails and the ornate coving, were still present, but vanished abruptly into the later, less substantial walls that had been put in to convert what looked originally to have been two large rooms into the current four small ones. It had last been decorated some years ago, by the look of it, and in plain, pallid shades – peach, cream, and the like – presumably to try to make the living spaces look larger than they really were. The strategy hadn't entirely succeeded.

"I have to admit, you had just the right adjective for it," I said, trying to be polite. "Small you said, and small it is."

"Yeh, well – like I said, somewhere to live," he shrugged. "D'you want a coffee?"

"Thanks."

"Two minutes." He vanished into the kitchen.

"Can I use the loo?" I called after him.

"Try not to get lost while you're looking for it," he advised.

The sound of the kettle coming to the boil greeted me as I emerged again and walked along the tiny hallway back toward the living room. On an impulse, I paused again by the open bedroom door, and took another look. Something struck me that hadn't the first time, only minutes before.

And that was how spartan it was. Just a built-in wardrobe, a bed, and a bedside table, the only items on it a lamp and a radio alarm clock. So little in the way of personal belongings, even in this most intimate and personal of rooms. In fact, when it came down to it, nothing that conveyed any hint of being a *personal* possession at all.

I felt my brows contract into a slight frown, which didn't relax as I went back to the living room, and realized the same was true there. A television and DVD player; a music centre; a small bookcase, only partially filled. A tiny desk, crammed against one wall, with a laptop set up on it. A not very luxurious looking three-seater sofa was the only seating available, other than the two chairs belonging to the tiny dining table. No pictures on the walls. An overall feeling of – what, exactly? Emptiness? Sterility?

The only really personal touch was the one small framed photograph on the top of the bookcase. I didn't go to look at it close up, but I could see long dark hair, a laughing mouth and eyes. No question who it was a photograph of, but going to pick it up, look at it more closely, would have felt like an invasion of his privacy. If he showed me himself, fair enough. Otherwise...

I looked around again, still wearing a faint frown as I assessed the –

what was the right description? – the emotional *vacancy* of that tiny flat. So impersonal that it could have been a holiday let, rather than a man's home. Perhaps he didn't think of it as home. I remembered a friend telling me once that she'd lived in several locations, and while some of the houses felt like home, some of them had only ever felt like somewhere to live. The very words Peter had used. *"It's somewhere to live..."* Said with a shrug, as if it didn't matter.

Maybe this was Lesser's doing, too. Maybe he'd made Peter too afraid to have a 'home', to have a personal space, personal possessions which required or engendered emotional investment. That might make him too vulnerable to more loss. If he had nothing that couldn't be replaced, he could face losing what he had. In that way, Lesser had stripped him even of what he should have been able to have as a basic human right – a home, a place of refuge. Somewhere away from his professional life, where he could feel safe, at ease, relax. If he had such a place at all, it certainly couldn't be here, where he lived. No, not even 'lived'. This was a place to eat, sleep, keep his clothes – but not a place to 'live'.

Angry. That made me so angry! At this man I'd never met, but who had done this to Peter, put him in this intolerable situation. I could feel myself physically tensing with hostility. Then Peter's footstep sounded behind me, and I did my best to get my face into order before he caught sight of it.

"Here y'are," he said, handing me a mug.

"Thanks," I said. "Can I have a look outside? I still haven't inspected the view."

I think some of what I was still feeling must have come through in my tone, because he awarded me a keen look for a couple of moments. But he didn't follow it up.

"This way," he said, striding forward and turning the key of the French windows. He pushed both doors as wide as they would go, and made a gesture inviting me to step out onto the tiny balcony.

The garden, a plain area of grass with a couple of spindly trees and a few bushes of some sort or another to break up the monotony, lay immediately below; similar sized gardens queued to right and left, most more lovingly cultivated than this one, and ahead lay the back gardens and the rear elevations of the houses that faced onto the next street. Tall fences attempted to secure a degree of privacy for the residents, but the height of this top floor thwarted that in quite a few places. There were quite a lot of well-established trees, though. As with all groups of gardens, some were well-kept, others less so, but on the whole, the outlook wasn't bad.

I looked at the plant-holders hooked onto the rail of the balcony, the sere skeletons of dead plants populating them.

"What were those, when they were alive?" I enquired.

Peter looked at the lifeless detritus.

"Geraniums," he said succinctly.

"How traditional of you," I teased gently.

He uttered a snort of amusement.

"Jane, not me," he disclaimed. "She grows them, then insists I have them. Installs a new batch for me every year. I find it easier just to humour her on that one." He looked at the brown desolation. "About time I cleared this lot out, by the look of it."

"I hope she does you lemon-scented ones," I said. "I love the scent of lemon. It's one of my favourites."

He didn't reply to that, just nodded and drank some more of his coffee.

"Well, now you know what the view's like," he observed casually.

"Mmm," I agreed. Then, after a pause, I added, "Thank you for showing me."

"About time I did," he said, his eyes fixed on the house opposite. I couldn't quite work out what he meant by that, and decided I wouldn't ask.

When we went back inside, he shut and locked the French windows, then went past me and straight to the bookcase. He lifted the photograph frame from it and held it out to me.

"That's Laura," he said gruffly. I took it from him and looked at it.

She'd been beautiful, Peter's wife. Now I could see her closely, I could see how attractive she'd been, how pretty a smile she'd had, how intense a sparkle in the blue eyes. She looked altogether a lovely person. Sometimes you can tell just by looking, and know beyond all doubt that you're right, that someone is beautiful inside, whatever their outside appearance. Because what they are just shines on their face. Laura McLeish had clearly been beautiful both inside and out.

I looked up and found his eyes on my face, expectant.

"She looks lovely, Peter. I wish I could have known her," I said, simply and sincerely.

He didn't speak, but nodded, slowly. He knew I'd given him my honest reaction; he knew I didn't deal in anything but truth.

And everything else that either of us might have gone on to say was already understood, as I handed him back the photograph of his dead wife.

Chapter 13

I encountered a postscript to that visit to Peter's flat only a few days later. Jane sprang a lunch invitation on me for the Sunday, when Alan was going to be able to be there.

"Sorry, the kids won't be here," she apologized. "They've both got other things going on. You don't mind, do you?"

"Well, I'll be sorry to miss them, but apart from that, of course not," I assured her. As far as I was concerned, it was whether Alan was going to be there or not that mattered to me. There was something I wanted to talk to him about.

Inevitably, over the meal, the conversation turned to Peter. Which was Jane's doing, not Alan's, I noted. I supposed that now she was aware Peter was seeing me she couldn't help probing a little, though I could tell she was doing her best to keep it within acceptable bounds. For myself, I didn't mind telling her; my problem was deciding how much Peter would want me to say. But since they already knew he came to me, I conjectured that my visit to him would be a harmless enough conversational gambit.

"He showed me his flat the other day," I remarked. "Tiny little place, isn't it? Good job he doesn't want to swing any cats!"

The suddenness with which silence fell was almost palpable. I looked up, quickly. Alan had frozen in mid-chew and was staring at me with startled eyes. Then he looked at Jane; her expression was a mirror of his.

"What? What's the matter?" I demanded, perplexed.

Alan slowly resumed his chewing, and swallowed.

"Sorry... We're just – surprised," he said carefully.

I looked from one to the other.

"Because—?" I prompted.

"Because, as far as we know – apart from us – he's never taken anyone there," said Jane. "Ever."

I didn't know what to say. Alan saw my dilemma, and smiled.

"Don't worry about it, Jenny," he said. "As far as I'm concerned, it can only be a good thing."

"Well, maybe you'll think this is a good thing, too," I ventured. "He says he's going to teach me to sail."

Again they looked at each other, and back at me – once more surprised, but clearly delighted, too.

"That's – that's…" Alan was searching for the right superlative, but stalling over the task. Jane rescued him.

"That's wonderful!" she said with enthusiasm. "That'll be so good for him!"

"That's what I thought," I agreed. "It was worrying me that he didn't seem to have anything he did for relaxation."

"Other than seeing you, you mean?" she teased gently.

"You know what I mean," I said, reproachfully. "He told me he used to sail as a boy?"

"When he was a teenager," Alan amended, taking up my implicit invitation to expand on the subject. "He was about seventeen or eighteen by the time he stopped. Actually" – he corrected himself – " he must have been at least seventeen, because he went for his Coastal Skipper certificate as soon as he was old enough, and you have to be seventeen to try for that. But when he joined the service, he didn't seem to have enough time to keep it up regularly. And once he came down to London, that was that," he concluded ruefully.

"Well, I told him I wished I could've learned to sail. Because it really is something that interests me. And he said he'd teach me. Is, apparently, making arrangements with some sailing club or other even as we speak," I added, with a slight element of hyperbole. "Unless work ends up interfering, of course." I grinned at Alan.

"Not if I can help it!" he said quickly.

"Not that you always can," I pointed out. "But even so, it doesn't matter. We can always rearrange. The main thing is, he wants to do it. That's a result, as far as I'm concerned."

Alan smiled, and dipped his head in agreement.

"Well – coffee, anyone?" Jane said, rising from the table. "Yes? Okay. Won't be long…" She left the room.

As soon as she'd gone, I decided to take my chance. "Alan – can we talk?"

He caught my tone, and looked at me carefully. Then he nodded. Raising his voice, he called out, "Jane? Jenny and I are just going out into the garden for a few moments. I'm going to give her the guided tour."

"It's not looking like much at this time of year," she protested.

"She wants to see the fountain."

"All right, then. But don't get too cold. I know it's a nice day, but it's still pretty chilly out there! Coffee when you come back in?"

"Thanks. We won't be long."

The fountain stood in the middle of the lawn, two tiers of bowls in pale grey stone that emptied into a small pond. Alan switched it on, giving us our ostensible talking point. We strolled toward it in silence and came to a halt a few feet away, our backs to the house, looking at it.

"That was quick thinking," I commended him. "No wonder you've risen so high in the service."

He chuckled briefly, then became serious. "What was it you wanted to talk about?"

"I want you to tell me about Matthew Lesser," I said levelly, discarding my smile.

He cast me a quick and somewhat startled look.

"How do you know about Lesser?" he demanded.

"Because Peter told me. When he told me about Laura."

His eyes widened slightly, and he was silent for a few moments. Then he said cautiously, "How much has he told you?"

"I know the baby was going to be a girl," I said deliberately. "He said you and Jane are the only other people who know that."

He nodded, looking at me with a curiously intent gaze. "Then he's told you everything," he said slowly, evidently grappling with the revelation of how much Peter had confided to me. That he had confided in me at all on that subject.

"Not everything he could have," I disagreed. "Like what's been going on since then. Because that wasn't the end of it, was it?"

"What do you mean?" he asked, shifting uneasily.

"I mean, whenever he makes an arrangement to meet me other than at my flat, the way he never meets me in the same place twice. I mean the way he goes back to the entranceway of our drive and looks around before he comes up. At first I couldn't work out why he was doing that, but then I got it. He's checking to see if he's been followed, isn't he? I mean that wretched, soulless little place that's got nothing personal in it at all except one photograph of Laura. Nothing there that matters, that he couldn't stand to lose. That's not a home, Alan, it's a *cage*. And I mean the attack in Scotland. The point where I came in." I could hear the terseness of my own voice. "Lesser didn't murder Laura and leave it at that, did he?" I challenged.

His shoulders dropped slightly, and he stared at the ground for a few moments. Then he straightened, and thrust his hands into his pockets. The mannerism, unsurprisingly, was very like Peter's.

"More than ten years, and he's still on Peter's case," he said heavily. "An ongoing campaign of persecution. Just small things, most of them, but absolutely relentless. Peter never knows when he's going to find some note shoved under his door, or his headlights smashed, or an anonymous message on his voicemail. Sometimes weeks go by, sometimes months, but sooner or later… Just to keep reminding him. Petty stuff, but cumulative."

"And the shooting? Bit more than 'petty', I would've said." I could hear the slight edge in my voice.

Alan sighed.

"Yes," he agreed. "There've been one or two times when he's had more serious goes. Nothing on that level before, though. Peter and Mike'd been working on" – he hesitated over how much to tell me – "on a lead that looked fairly promising. They must've been getting too close. Lesser always provides an object lesson when that happens. And once word gets round, the leads evaporate. It's always for nothing," he said bitterly.

I was silent.

"Intelligence work," Alan went on, still with that bitter tinge in his voice. "The trouble is, intelligence is what Lesser's got – in spades. He never gives us anything we can make stick. Knowing it's one thing. Proving it's another. And the intelligence we do get… That's how Peter and Mike came to be in Scotland. We came into possession of something that seemed to make it worthwhile sending them up there. And all the time it was Lesser, setting them up. If I'd known it was him – him in person, I mean – I'd never have sent Peter, not in a million years. But I didn't know. So I was the one who told them to go. That's the fun bit of my job. Making operational decisions that mean Peter might—" He broke off.

The quality of the silence that followed overrode the glissando of the falling water, somehow deadening its beauty into futility.

"But Peter's still on the team," I said slowly. "Not because it isn't dangerous for him. And not even because your Commander Laird thinks that Peter's somehow got an edge that means you'll get Lesser in the end." Alan looked at me sharply, and I met his eyes squarely. My tone was flat and uncompromising. "You go on with him because you know Lesser won't leave him be, even if he's not in the job anymore. So he might as well be where he is. And because you know he'll never be at peace until Lesser is dealt with. Or else one of them is dead."

The implications of that last sentence quivered between us.

"You lay things on the line, don't you?" Alan said at last. His tone was heavy, but tinged with respect.

"I believe in telling the truth," I said. "Especially to friends. Everybody knows where they stand, that way. I've told Peter so, already. And now I'm telling you."

"Well, you're right," he said, his eyes turning to the fountain again, though not seeing it. "If he wasn't still on the job, he'd be more vulnerable to Lesser than ever. This way, at least I can keep an eye on him. Team him with one of the others when there's something needs doing. Cutting him adrift wouldn't achieve a thing. Even though there are some pretty senior people who'd like to see it happen."

"Why?" I asked, perplexed. "Can't they see what it would lead to?"

"They're just taking the pragmatic view. They think he's a weak point in the team. And, in a way, they're right. But as long as Laird's backing him, he'll be able to stay." He looked at me again, and his face was drawn in lines of stress. "I'd give anything for him to be safe, Jenny! Anything! But there's nothing more I can—" He broke off, shutting his lips into a hard line.

"I'm not criticizing you," I said quietly. "I don't see what else you can do. In the circumstances."

He looked at me swiftly, as if my validation really mattered, then away again, letting out a long breath.

"What about you?" he said, after a pause.

"What about me?" I frowned.

"Now you know all this." He was looking at me curiously. "Where does it leave you?"

"Peter's friend," I said flatly. "And that's not going to change. Whatever happens." It was more than a promise; it was a vow. And he knew it.

"When I heard what happened up in Scotland, I thought… Well, you can probably guess what I thought," he said. "That I should never have sent him up there. Now" – there was the hint of a smile in his eyes as he looked at me – "I'm glad I did."

Before I could react to the compliment, he turned decisively on his heel, and put a hand on my shoulder to turn me, too, back toward the house.

"Come on," he said firmly. "Coffee. Jane'll be waiting."

And as we started back, he kept his hand on my shoulder just long enough for his fingers to close briefly with the extra pressure that conveyed both gratitude and approbation.

"Here it is," Jane said a couple of minutes later, as she brought a tray with three cups on it into the living room. "You take sugar, don't you, Jenny?"

"Please."

"Well, help yourself." She sat down beside Alan. "So, what did you think of the garden? Not as big as yours, I'm afraid."

"Very nice. I'm not much of a gardener myself, but I appreciate the craftsmanship of those who are. I love the fountain!"

"That was Alan's contribution," Jane said. "Almost his only one! He doesn't get much time for it, generally."

"No, it's Jane who's the gardener," Alan agreed, sipping at his coffee.

"Lemon-scented geraniums, among other things, I'm told?" I suggested, archly.

Jane looked puzzled for a moment, then realized what I was referring to.

"Peter's been showing you his window boxes, then?" she smiled.

"It's a variation on etchings, I suppose," I said innocently. "Talking of which" – I turned to Alan – "what about this artwork of yours Sophie was boasting about? Am I allowed to see any of it?"

"Oh, that! Well, I suppose so. If you really want to," Alan agreed, with a tolerant shrug. He put his cup down on the coffee table and stood up. "I'll go and get my portfolio. Brace yourself…"

"Don't take any nonsense from him," Jane advised me as he left the room. "He's good. Better than he makes out."

"Ah, but he's British, and a man," I reminded her. "Not always a good combination for honestly admitting you've got a talent. And even worse when it comes to handling compliments, no doubt?"

Jane's chuckle was confirmation that I was right.

When Alan came back and laid a literal portfolio in my lap for me to look through, I couldn't be other than impressed. Pencil sketches only, as he'd said, but beautifully done – expert use of detail, yet enough left inexplicit for one's imagination to be able to fill in the blanks. All sorts of subject matter were portrayed: scenic panoramas, buildings, still life subjects, people. I didn't know most of the latter, but he'd done some very good likenesses of his children. And there was one – just one – of Peter; a head-and-shoulders portrait. I tried not to linger on it too obviously, while thinking how well Alan had captured him.

"This is a very good one of Craig," I said, turning to the next leaf. "How old was he then?"

Alan glanced at it.

"I did that a couple of years or so ago," he said. "He'd've been about thirteen, I suppose."

"Well, I'm sorry, Alan, but I'm going to be completely honest about these," I said somewhat sternly. He caught my expression and looked back at me with rather surprised apprehension. Jane, on the other hand, had already spotted that my tongue was firmly in my cheek.

"I've got to tell you these are" – I hesitated dramatically – "absolutely brilliant!" Alan relaxed and shook his head at me reprovingly as he realized I'd been pulling his leg. "They really are!" I went on. "You've got a real talent for this! When you get the chance to use it, I suppose," I qualified.

"Not as often as I'd like," he agreed. "But – thank you." His expression contained a hint of mischief. "Perhaps you'd let me sketch you, sometime?"

He was trying to get his own back for my tease, but I wasn't going to let him.

"Okay," I said equably. "Now, if you like."

I hadn't been sure if he was being serious, but he was. I chatted to Jane while he sketched, and while it was impossible to be totally natural and ignore the fact that he was doing it, I must have succeeded to some extent, because when he showed me the result I was both flattered and impressed.

"Well, that's me immortalized for posterity, then!" I joked.

"I'll let you know what our particular posterity thinks of it," Alan said, sliding the sheet of paper into the portfolio. "Sophie's very insistent that I have to show her everything I do. You can have a copy, if you like?"

"Actually, I might take you up on that. Not for myself," I added hurriedly. "But Mum and Dad would probably like it, so – thank you."

"My pleasure," he assured me.

"Besides, it's not every day I get my likeness taken by a police artist of your rank," I added drolly. Which got a laugh out of both of them, as I'd intended.

About a week later, Jane returned home from a shopping trip to find both Alan and Peter there, drinking coffee.

"Peter's eating with us tonight," Alan announced.

"Oh, good! I'll start it in a minute, but I want a coffee first." She got herself one from the percolator in the kitchen. As she came back in and plumped herself down in an armchair, she said, "By the way, I saw Jenny today. Gave her the portrait you did of her. She said to thank you for having it framed." She had one eye on Peter as she spoke, curious to see if he'd react. Which he did to the extent of raising an interrogative eyebrow in Alan's direction.

"I did a sketch of her the other day," Alan explained. "She thought her parents would like a copy. D'you want to see the original?"

"Yeh, okay," Peter agreed blandly.

Alan went to get it, and handed it over for inspection.

"What do you think?" he prompted.

"Yeh," said Peter, handing it back. "It's good."

"The kids liked it. Craig especially. He thinks Jenny's quite pretty, you know," said Jane, smiling. "He dropped it into a conversation we were having the other day. Quite casually, but I could tell he meant it. I told Jenny what he said, today."

A slight frown creased Alan's forehead. He wondered how his son would feel if he knew that particular confidence had been passed on to the person it concerned. At Craig's age, he was pretty sure he wouldn't have appreciated it, had his own mother done anything of the sort.

"What did she say?" he asked, a touch of reserve in his voice. Jane was enjoying herself so much, however, that she failed to pick up on it. She laughed.

"As near as I can remember, she said – now, hang on, let me get this exactly right – yes – *'It's very nice of him to say so – I've never frightened any cats, to my knowledge, but, on the other hand, no one's ever stopped dead in the street, struck speechless by my personal beauty…'*" She laughed again, catching the look on Peter's face out of the corner of her eye as she did so.

"You agree with him, don't you, Peter?" she said, turning to him. "Don't you think Jenny's pretty?"

Peter fixed her with his dark eyes for a few seconds, but now they were expressionless. Then he said, "Yeh," and looked away again. "Any coffee left?" he asked, a moment later.

"Of course! Help yourself," Jane assured him, and watched him leave the room with a mischievous smile. Which faded almost immediately, at her husband's next words.

"Jane. Stop it."

She looked at him quickly, surprised by the flat finality of his tone. He was frowning at her.

"What?" she demanded.

"Stop baiting Peter about Jenny. He doesn't need that. And if Craig told you that in confidence, I'm not happy that you passed it on without his permission. Did you?"

She was looking serious now, as the implications started to sink in. It was a long time since she'd heard him being so censorious with her.

"I suppose so." She met his eyes, and hers were contrite. "I'm sorry. I didn't think… I'm sure she won't say anything to him about it, though."

"I'm sure you're right," Alan agreed. "But that's not exactly the point, is it? And I meant it about Peter. Just leave it. Let him work things out in his own time, if that's what he wants to do. After everything that's happened, if he's made a friend of her, even that's more than we might've hoped for, isn't it? After all this time, it's the first time he's showed any signs of getting close to anyone. Don't put any extra pressure on him."

His concern for his cousin was clear and emphatic. She knew he was right, and felt a little ashamed of herself. She didn't usually make mistakes of that sort. She knew how protective Alan was of Peter's emotional wellbeing.

"I'm sorry, darling," she said, extending her hand out to him in apology. "I won't do it again. I promise."

He regarded her with a still face for a few moments. Then he relaxed, and took the offered hand, entwining his fingers into hers.

"I'm sorry, too," he said.

"No," Jane told him. "You were quite right. I'll be a good girl from now on, honest."

"Don't start making promises you won't keep," he said, but he was smiling at her, and his tone was light and teasing.

And she knew it was all right between them again.

That night, lying in bed, Alan's arm cradling her shoulders, she said thoughtfully, "You know, I think Jenny must have had quite a hard time with her marriage, in some ways."

"Why? She always talks about her husband very positively, I'd've said."

"Oh, yes," Jane agreed. "She does. We talked about him today. I don't think it was about loving him. It's pretty obvious how much she did."

"What, then?" Alan moved his fingertips gently up and down the smooth skin of his wife's arm.

"Well, he clearly suffered from a quite fundamental level of depression. But from what she told me, he'd never admit he had a problem."

"Like some alcoholics I know," Alan commented.

"I suppose so." Jane snuggled closer to him, her cheek warm on his shoulder. "But it meant he couldn't be helped. He wouldn't admit he was ill, so there was nothing she could do. That must be so frustrating! I think the thing she found hardest was that he had absolutely no self-esteem. She said he had to concede that she did love him, but she doesn't think he ever understood why. Virtually everything he said about himself had some sort of negative slant, by the sound of it, and she spent all her time reminding him that it was because of his good qualities that she loved him."

"Oh, he did have some, then?" Alan said dryly.

Jane snorted humorously.

"You should hear her! Intelligent – clever – brilliant sense of humour – attractive – by her account, he had the lot! But not according to him... So that was that! And he never really got it. So trying to convince him otherwise was a twenty-four-seven career, sounds like."

They lay in silence for a while. Then Jane spoke again.

"You know, in her place, I think a lot of people would have got out. I mean, imagine what that must be like, hour after hour, day after day. Year after year! No matter how much you love someone."

"So why didn't she?"

"I asked her that..."

Alan turned his head slightly; Jane moved her own head on his shoulder to look up at him in response, and saw his expression.

"You've got a nerve, Jane McLeish!" He was openly laughing at her. "So what did she say?"

143

"Oh, she didn't mind. She's a very open sort of person. Her reasoning was that when she got married she'd made him promises – for better or worse, in sickness and health, all that sort of thing. *'And I'm a woman of my word,'* she said. Not something up for negotiation, obviously. No matter how hard it got."

For while they lay in silence. Alan was thinking about what Jenny had said to him. *"I'm Peter's friend. And that's not going to change. Whatever happens."* A promise. Made despite knowing about Lesser. And she kept her promises, no matter how difficult it was. *"I'm a woman of my word…"*

Jane stirred.

"D'you know what else she said?" As if there'd been no break in the conversation.

"No-o-o…" Alan drew the monosyllable out with a clear implication of 'How could I?' in his tone, which Jane chose to ignore.

"She said she only had to live with him – she didn't have to *be* him."

Another silence ensued as they both contemplated the implications of that remark, but as the moments passed he sensed she still had something else to say.

"What?" he prompted, eventually.

"Well," she said hesitantly, "I couldn't help thinking that there was another aspect of the marriage that wasn't quite all it could have been. She didn't come out and say it directly, but – it's true, isn't it, that people with depression have a low sex drive?"

"So I believe," Alan agreed.

"Poor Jenny," said Jane softly, after a pause.

Alan looked down at his wife, and stroked her arm again. Then he shifted position more purposefully.

"Tell you something," he said. "That's not a problem I've got."

Jane looked up at him quickly, then matched the gleam in his eyes with one of her own.

"Lucky for me," she said, and turned her lips up to his as he rolled over and gathered her in his arms.

Chapter 14

Peter was as good as his word. Which I'd never doubted he would be. He found a small sailing club in Kent which would allow us to attend during the winter months. There was a lot of preparation involved before I got anywhere near an actual dinghy, though. There was theory to be studied, in which Peter gave me a good grounding, though he advised me to take one of the club's theory courses as well. Even for just sailing on a lake or a reservoir I'd need to know the principles behind rigging, steering, wind awareness, tacking, jibing, and the like. So there was a lot of reading to be done, plus verbal coaching from Peter. It was hard work, sometimes, but it was exciting, too.

"This is all a bit dismaying," I commented to him once. "I'd no idea sailing could be quite so lethal."

He frowned at me. "What d'you mean?"

"This." I gestured with the book I was reading. "All these ways you can end up dead or injured. Apparently" – I consulted the relevant page – "I can drown, capsize, get trapped under a capsized craft, get lifting injuries, head injuries – mostly from being hit by the boom – slip, trip, fall, get hypothermia, collide with fixed objects, trap my fingers in the winch, get rope burns, and if I fall in, I'm at risk from waterborne pollution and diseases." I cocked an eyebrow at him. "This is a sport you do for fun, yes?"

He laughed.

I'd been right in thinking that reawakening his interest in sailing would be good for him. He seemed so much more relaxed whenever he came round, and very keen; not an evening he came to me passed by without his initiating a theory session of some sort. I was delighted to see him so enthusiastic, so animated.

I spent a lot of December doing that, although I got seriously distracted toward the end of the month, as Dad's retirement date loomed. He'd been thirty-seven years in the profession, over twenty of them in the same school, and he'd made a lot of friends and admirers among his colleagues in that time, so there was quite a fuss over the occasion, with a couple of informal celebrations in addition to the official one at the school. David Hayward, the head, specially arranged for Mum and me to attend that one, as a surprise for Dad. David, a Welshman to his core, delivered, with a characteristically mischievous twinkle in his lively blue eyes, a valedictory that combined the bardic fluency of his forebears with statements that frequently verged on the libellous, and had every one of us in that staff room almost weeping with laughter throughout. Dad, of course, took it all with his customary aplomb, and riposted with a farewell speech so full of dry humour that it, too, had us all paralytic with mirth in places. David told Mum afterwards that Dad had had a rousing farewell from the kids at the last assembly before the end of term, too; he was a popular teacher, as well as colleague. At our own private celebration for family and friends, for which my brother David, along with Bronwyn and the boys, came over from Wales, Mum included Alan and Jane and Peter in the guest list. This time, Alan was able to come, and I saw, with immense satisfaction, that he and Dad were clearly getting on like a house on fire. It was a successful evening.

"And now your mother and I can start planning all those things we've been looking forward to doing while we both have still the money and the health to do them," Dad told me with satisfaction, when it was all over.

"You'll miss it, though," I predicted.

"The teaching, you mean? Yes, I shall miss the teaching…" he said, a little pensively. Then, emphatically, "Though not the accompanying bureaucracy, I can assure you! But I intend to be much too busy to miss it, and as quickly as possible!" He looked very happy; I was so glad for him, and for Mum. All those places they'd always planned to visit, all those things they'd wanted to do; all were open to them now. Indeed, within a very few days they'd taken advantage of the January sales to book a cruise for the coming September.

"Twenty-eight nights," said my mother happily, showing me the brochure. "Italy, Greece and Spain, and everywhere in between. Sunshine and sightseeing and lots and lots of lazing! Oh, it's going to be glorious!"

"And not a pupil nor a draft manuscript in sight," my father added with a smile. "A change that will definitely be not as good as a rest, but an actual rest."

"I hope you have the most wonderful time, I really do," I said emphatically, actively enjoying the pleasure they were taking in it. "You'll deserve it."

My father looked me with a tinge of regret.

"I wish you could come with us, darling," he said, not quite as happily.

"I daresay, but who's going to water the plants, if I don't stay home to do it?" I teased him. Then I dropped the levity. "It's all right, Dad, really it is. Maybe I can come another time. I think you and Mum owe this one to yourselves first, don't you? Just the two of you. It'll be great. Something you can look forward to, and back on."

"Oh, Jenny," said my mother with love, and gave me a hug.

Eventually the day came when Peter first took me out on the water. To sail proper, that is; he'd made sure to give me some pointers on rowing efficiently, before he let me loose in a sailing dinghy. That wasn't until the second week of January. It wasn't as cold as it sounds; we were having an exceptionally mild winter, so it wasn't too bad. Even so, it was quite cold enough, but I was determined to go through with it, for his sake. It also meant there were very few other boats out, which I told Peter I was definitely in favour of; fewer people to witness my mistakes, plus fewer chances of my steering us into a collision. He laughed at me for that, but I didn't care. I was nervous, but he was patient with me, and it went well, that first time; we both enjoyed it, though when we were warming up back in the clubhouse bar, I had the definite impression that the club staff thought we were completely mad for starting out at that time of year. The next day, I couldn't help wondering if I was mad for doing it at all, having discovered precisely how many muscle groups I had unsuspectingly possessed that I had never, ever used as a library assistant.

The second time things were going well enough, too – until I tried standing up at just the wrong moment, just as Peter was about to tack. I can't even remember why I did it, though I must have felt it was necessary at the time. But even though I can't remember the reason, I do remember Peter's exclamation of warning as he realized, too late, what I was doing.

Out of the corner of my eye I saw the boom swinging swiftly toward me. I instinctively tried to step back, but of course there was no room. My raised foot met the inner slope of the hull, sliding awkwardly downward and tipping me in the direction of the water. Already off-balance, I briefly registered the pressure of the gunwale against my calves. Then my own momentum carried me over. The boom never touched me; nevertheless, I tipped heels over head into the lake.

As I went under, I thought I heard Peter shout my name. He reacted quickly, putting the tiller hard over; by the time I bobbed up, spitting water and clawing my hair out of my eyes, he was already on his way back to me. As he brought the dinghy level with me and saw I was all right, he couldn't suppress the tolerant smile of an experienced sailor who's just seen a rank beginner go overboard for the first time.

"Shut up and get me on board again," I demanded, trying to grin back as I trod water, but unable to prevent myself gasping with the cold. "It's freezing in here!"

"Come on, then," he said, leaning over the side and putting his hand out. I spat again before taking a couple of strokes to the side of the dinghy. With his help I heaved myself back on board, tumbling inelegantly into an untidy heap across the thwart.

"You can wipe that grin off your face," I scolded cheerfully, righting myself, although already I was shivering noticeably. "You know perfectly well it was only a matter of time before this happened! Nobody in history ever learned to sail without falling in at some point, did they?"

"No," he agreed, still fighting down his smile. "Were you planning a career as a water sprite, at all?"

"Haven't got the right qualifications. Not graceful enough," I told him.

"Idiot woman," he said cheerfully. And of course I couldn't argue.

Then we were laughing again, laughing so hard we were almost crying. I was soaked and freezing, but it was one of the most joyous moments I'd had in a long time. And I was glad for Peter, because I had a feeling he hadn't laughed like this for a much, much longer time. Years, maybe…

There was a period in February where I didn't see him for a couple of weeks. He'd warned me it was going to happen; there was something going on at work which would keep him tied up for a while, he said. We'd have to postpone the next sailing lesson – sorry. He'd text, or ring – but only when he was able. I didn't ask what was going on, of course, but I couldn't suppress a twinge of anxiety. It had to be something serious, for him to be talking in those terms. I wondered if it was something to do with Lesser. But I didn't ask, just told him I'd wait to hear from him.

"Will it be all right if I text you, if I need to?" I enquired.

"I might not be able to answer straight away," he said.

"I won't mind that… But do you want me to? Or should I not?"

"No, do it if you want," he said. "Give me something to look forward to."

And yet he might not be able to answer straight away. But I just nodded, and smiled.

After which I had nothing from him for several days. I was dreadfully tempted to ask Jane whether she or Alan had heard anything more than I had, though I managed to fight down the urge. But after a week I couldn't stand it anymore, and sent Peter a one-word text.

OK?

Almost a day later, he replied.

OK.

And that was all.

I went to the window seat and sat on it, my elbow propped on the sill, my head resting against my hand, and stared unseeingly out at the garden. This was what it was going to be like, from now on. Being on the periphery of his life. His professional life, that was. I was pretty sure I was no longer on the periphery of his personal life, not in terms of our friendship; that was now too firmly established for me to doubt its value to him. He'd been wary of committing to it to start with, but then, with his history, who could blame him? But it couldn't be separated from the rest of his life. Not while he was still locked, both professionally and personally, in this feud with Lesser. Working in the type of job about which I neither could, nor should, know more than he saw fit to tell me. But knowing enough to be disturbingly aware of so many, many implications. Knowing that every day, any day, might bring – anything...

It was going to be hard. Hard in a different way from Alex, but still hard. Yet I didn't regret it. I had come to feel so strongly that I was doing him good, helping him to regain some sort of life for himself, that I couldn't possibly wish it had never happened.

But difficult? Demanding? Distressing? All of those things, I was sure, from time to time. Though it wasn't as if I was unfamiliar with such things, having lived with Alex's problems for all those years. And now, all over again with Peter, it seemed. Well, that was the way it was going to have to be. Because Peter was my friend. And I was his, no matter what.

"Where does it leave you?" Alan had asked me.

"Peter's friend," I'd replied.

I'd made that claim to Alan, but what did I mean by it? What *was* a friend? Just a word you used, casually, about a whole range of relationships. But what, really, was a friend?

Someone you knew well, perhaps even very well – yes. Someone you liked – yes. But what, exactly? What did you like about them? Their personal qualities and attributes? The fact that they enjoyed and appreciated the same things you did? That you could trust them, confide in them? That you had the power sometimes to bring contentment, joy, even happiness close enough for them to feel the touch of those things?

On all those counts, yes, Peter was my friend. And I, it seemed, must be his. Or why would he have persisted in coming to see me in those early days, allowed the relationship to develop despite what he evidently regarded as the potential risk to both himself and me? He must, surely, have found those things in me, too, to want them, and want them very badly, in spite of what had happened to him before – something that must have been always in the back of his mind, right from the outset. I remembered his initial hesitancy over taking my mobile number, as if it had been some incredibly big decision to do so. I hadn't known then, for him, just how big. Yet he'd still done it.

Then, out of nowhere, something came into my mind. Something I'd read once? No. No, it was something Mother had come across when she was proofing a book. What had it been called? I could feel my forehead furrowing as I strove to remember. Yes, that was it – *The Discourse of Loving*

– that had been the title. And in one of the chapters the author had stated that a friend was, literally, a lover, because the English word for 'friend' had come, via other languages, from an Indo-European word meaning 'to love'. Mother had mentioned the concept as a point of interest, and we'd ended up having quite a discussion about it. A friend being a lover. Which, because the author had described it in that context as a love explicitly exclusive of sex, had led to a fascinating debate about the different types and degrees of love that there are.

Which brought me back to Peter.

Yes, Peter was my friend, using the root meaning of the word. And I, his. But, if a friend is literally a lover...?

My anxieties were needless; a couple of days after that I got a phone call.

"I'm back," he announced, without preamble. "Can I see you tonight?"

"I think I can cope with the concept," I said dryly, while a wave of relief swept through me. "Want me to cook?"

"Up to you," he offered.

"Okay, then. There's something I've been thinking of trying out on you for quite a while, you being a Scot. I hope you like rumbledethumps?"

"Rumbledethumps! Are you serious?" He laughed, a laugh tinged with pleased surprise. "Haven't had them since I was a kid!"

"Well, I've no idea whether anything I produce will in any way resemble what a *bona fide* Scotswoman would do, but I'll give it a go," I told him. "See you about half-seven?"

"Yeh, right. Rumbledethumps!" he repeated half-incredulously, still chuckling, and ended the call.

I blew my cheeks out with relief. He was all right. He was coming back. This time.

March came, and the day I wasn't looking forward to was coming closer.

The day before, we'd been sailing, and I think I managed to mask my feelings from him; he didn't seem to notice anything, anyway. Too busy trying to hammer the difference between being close-hauled and reaching into my thick skull, probably.

But it was bad, the next day. Which I'd expected up to a point, but somehow it felt worse than I'd anticipated. I felt depressed, though I managed to hide it at work. At least, I think I did; no one commented, at any rate. Perhaps not depressed in the clinical sense, but low in spirits, definitely. I had no appetite for lunch when I got home. I knew I ought to find something to occupy me, distract me, but instead ended up sitting by the living room window, staring out ostensibly at the garden but in fact at nothing particular.

What I was steadfastly not looking at was the small framed photograph on the cabinet in the corner of the room.

When the impulse came, it felt so natural I didn't stop to analyze it for even a moment before acting upon it. I got out my phone, and texted Peter. Just a brief question; his hoped-for affirmative arrived only a couple of minutes later. Which lifted my spirits a little.

But though I didn't know it then, that text had caused him something of a problem.

He was in his office, at his desk, when it arrived. He saw who it was from, and opened it.

Can you come round tonight, please?

Just a brief question, and a commonplace enough request. But something about it – he didn't know what – gave him the feeling something was wrong. Not urgently wrong, perhaps, but wrong nonetheless. He started to reply.

And that was the moment Chris picked to notice what he was doing.

"Oi! You're doing a lot of texting lately," he said, too loudly. "Don't tell me you've got yourself a girl at last!"

Peter didn't look up. Ben did, though, sharply. One or two of the others stirred, uncomfortably.

I hadn't met any of the team at that point, though I did later. Chris Packer was in his mid-twenties, pretty full of himself; the one Peter had described to me as getting through girlfriends at quite a rate. Ben Sullivan was older, in his early fifties, experienced and reliable; he'd been in the team when Peter joined it; although as a sergeant he was equal in rank to Peter, his longer service meant that, to all intents and purposes, he was Alan's deputy in the ongoing absence of a Detective Inspector in the team, some administrator somewhere having decided to save on a salary by putting a replacement on hold. The rest, like Chris, were DCs. Colin Bradburn – Brad – was in his early forties, quietly good at his job; Kevin Jones, universally known as Kevlar, was similar in age, and displayed the same unostentatious efficiency. Abhik Malakar, a third-generation Brit whose forebears were Bengali, had just turned thirty. Cathie Angwin, whose nickname of Shoeshop was well earned, was just a couple of years older, while Pauline Roberts, whose grandparents had immigrated from Antigua to Britain in the Fifties, went by the nickname of Andy, which Ben had bestowed on her for reasons no cricket fan would need explained; she was the youngest of the team. And, of course, there had used to be Mike. Detective Inspector Mike Clifford. But not anymore…

For once, all of them were in the office at the same time – a rare occurrence.

"Am I right?" Chris demanded, cockily. Then, triumphantly, when

Peter didn't reply: "I am, aren't I? You've got someone, haven't you?"

Ben was watching Peter, who still didn't look up. He was apparently intent only on his phone, his face hidden by the sweep of his hair. But Ben could see the set of his shoulders.

"Leave it, Chris," he said quietly.

Chris turned round and grinned at him, failing to read the signals. Or to see the looks that the other members of the team were giving him.

"Hey, don't get me wrong," he said, still too loudly. "I'm happy for him! Aren't you? Peter McLeish, got himself a girlfriend, at last! About time, too!"

"Shut up," said Ben, still in that quiet voice. He glanced at Peter, who had completed his text; Ben saw his thumb punch the send key.

"Oh, come on, Ben! Don't be so miserable! Aren't you happy for him?" Chris was enjoying his tease too much to sense the atmosphere. Peter put his phone back into his breast pocket; his face still wasn't visible. He stood up abruptly, without looking at anyone, and strode out.

"What did I say?" Chris spread his arms in an exaggerated gesture of mystification, innocence itself. He swung round to assess the reactions of the others, and for the first time saw how they were looking at him. Abhik and Andy, the newest members of the team, had no idea what was going on, and were simply looking baffled, but the rest of them – the ones who did know, or who had worked out something close to the truth over the course of time – were managing to emanate disapproval despite carefully impassive faces.

Ben got up, in a very deliberate manner, and walked toward him. The grin on the younger man's face began to melt into uncertainty, then into downright apprehension as Ben thrust his short, stocky body right into Chris's personal space, backing him up against his own desk. His eyes were bright blue spheres of anger as his thick forefinger jabbed at Chris's chest.

"If you ever say anything like that to him again, I swear I will do you over *myself*," he said through shut teeth. "Got that? You stupid, crass—"

"What?" Chris wailed. "What've I done?"

"Do you wanna know why he hasn't had a girlfriend all these years?" Chris shook his head, dumbly. "Well, I'll tell you," hissed Ben, his eyes boring into Chris's face. "Because Lesser's had it in for him ever since he got out of prison. Because he got back at him by tying up his wife and leaving her in their house and setting fire to it. She was eight months pregnant, and she died. But it wasn't just to get back at him the once, see? It was a warning. *'Get close to anyone, and the same'll happen to them.'* Peter used to have friends, until things started to happen to them, too. Things that only stopped if he cut himself off from seeing them. See? *'Don't get close to anyone, or they'll suffer for it.'* Peter learned that lesson, all right. He's had to. So don't you ever – *ever* – have a go at him like this again. You got that?"

Chris licked his lips and nodded, ashen-faced.

"Ben?" A familiar voice broke in. "Everything all right?"

Chris's eyes flicked nervously to the speaker, who had just come into the room, and then back to Ben's uncompromising, hard gaze, still fixed on his face. Ben didn't move a muscle; his eyes continued to bore into Chris's.

"Everything's fine, Boss," he said levelly. "Just explaining something to Chris. In words of one syllable, so he'll be sure to understand. You do understand, don't you, Chris?" he asked, solicitously.

Chris swallowed, and nodded again, jerkily. Ben suddenly smiled at him, and patted his chest lightly.

"That's all right, then, isn't it?" he said cheerfully, and walked out of the office.

Alan eyed his departing back thoughtfully, and said nothing. But he saw, out of the corner of his eye, how shaken Chris looked as he sat back down. He glanced round at the rest of the team. Andy looked as if she'd bitten into something sour; Abhik was staring at Chris. The others met Alan's eye, one by one, then – ostensibly, at least – turned their attention back to whatever they had been doing before. Nobody said anything.

But then, nobody needed to.

Ben found Peter where he expected, up on the roof; it was a common refuge when any of them wanted a quiet moment. The building they were housed in harked back to the 1930s, when municipal architects favoured flat roofs; on fine days it was useful to the smokers to be able to come up here, rather than cluster out at the back under a tiny lean-to, as they had to when it rained.

Peter wasn't a smoker, but he was up here now. Alone, hands thrust deep in pockets, standing near the two-foot high parapet, complete with precautionary metal railings, that enclosed the roof area. Ben walked over and stood beside him, and for a couple of minutes they both surveyed the landscape of roofs offered by their vantage point, in silence.

"He won't be doing that again," said Ben at last, his eyes fixed on the horizon.

Peter didn't look at him. Ben caught the tiniest movement of his shoulders, which with sufficient imagination could be interpreted as a shrug.

"He didn't know," he said, sounding indifferent.

"Well, he does now," said Ben flatly.

And they went on standing there, in silence, looking out across the sprawl of roofs.

Chapter 15

My father was washing his car, making the most of the fading early evening light, when Peter pulled into the drive and got out, carrying a weighted carrier bag bearing a wine merchant's logo.

"Peter," he greeted him serenely. "I didn't know we were going to see you this evening."

"Nor did I," said Peter, a touch wryly. "Jenny asked me to come."

"Ah," said my father. Something about the way he said it got Peter's attention.

"What?" he prompted. Then, suddenly anxious, "She's all right, isn't she?"

Dad looked at him for a moment before replying.

"It's the anniversary of Alex's death, today," he said quietly. "Three years."

Peter's head slowly rose and then dipped in a gesture of comprehension, and he turned to stare up at the door at the top of the steps. Dad could tell he was no longer really aware of his presence; physically he was still there, but internally he had withdrawn from my father. Now he was focused on me, behind that door.

Without another word, Peter left him, and ran up the steps.

I heard the peremptory knocking, and felt a contraction in my chest. He was here. He'd come. I went to let him in.

"Hi," I said, with a small smile, trying – unsuccessfully, I suspected – to sound normal as I held the door open for him to enter.

He looked at me searchingly, but didn't say anything as he gestured to me to precede him along the passage and into the living room. There I turned to face him, but before I could speak, he did.

"Is it bad?" he asked gently.

I looked at him quickly. "How did you know?"

"I met your father on the way in."

"Oh."

I hadn't meant it to happen, but I couldn't control it. I turned away from him a little too quickly, and strode over to the window, but it was too late. He saw my hurriedly bowed head, my shaking shoulders, and knew. Instantly he was at my side, putting an arm round me.

"I'm sorry…" I choked, raising my hands to cover my eyes. "I'm sorry…"

He pulled me round and put both arms around me, so my face, my hands, were pressed against his chest as I wept. He didn't say anything, just let me cry, until gradually the need subsided. When at last I stood silenced and still, leaning against him and cherishing the sense of comfort I was drawing from his physical warmth and presence, he gently let me go, put his hands on my shoulders, and steered me down into a seat on the sofa.

"Wait," he said, and went out, to return a few seconds later with my facecloth, newly dampened under the washbasin tap. He knelt in front of me, took my chin in one hand, and wiped my face and eyes, as if I had been thirty years younger than I was. I couldn't help smiling. A watery smile, to be sure, but one meant to express the appreciation I felt for the motive behind the action.

"Thanks," I said, somewhat tremulously. I took the facecloth from him and applied it again.

"D'you need a towel?" he offered.

"No, it's all right, thanks." I let the facecloth hang limply from my hand, and looked at him sadly. "I wish you'd had someone to do this for you, when you needed it."

"Never mind about me," he said with the hint of a scold in his tone. "It's you I'm worried about. I got through it. You will, too."

"I know," I agreed quietly. "I know I will. It's getting better all the time. It's just that it was – today… You know what I mean, don't you?" Not that I needed to ask that. Of course he understood. Of course he did.

"Yeh, I know," he acknowledged heavily. "Tenth of June, for me. I don't… Well, not anymore. But I don't forget." He looked at me carefully, concern in the large, dark eyes. "Sure you're all right?"

"Hardly," I said, with an attempt at a laugh that sounded more like a gasp. "But I will be."

He knew I was telling him the truth, and nodded. He got to his feet.

"Won't be a moment," he said, and picked up something – a tall, thin bag? I wasn't paying much attention – that he'd evidently let drop on the sofa when he came to comfort me. He took it through into the kitchen. I watched him go, then became aware of the damp facecloth still in my hand. Feeling strangely lethargic, the way you do after a crying jag, I made myself get up, and went to the bathroom. I rinsed the facecloth, hung it back in its accustomed place on the bath rack, and went back to the living room.

A few seconds after I'd resumed my place on the sofa Peter came back, carrying two large glasses of wine.

"Here – you need this," he said, giving one of them to me.

"Where did this come from?" I asked, though it was an entirely superfluous question.

"I must've had a premonition you were going to need a drink," he said. "Come on, get that down you."

"Alcohol on an empty stomach. I haven't had anything to eat," I warned him.

"We'll fix that," he promised. He sat down next to me and held his glass up to mine; they touched briefly with a kiss of crystal. Then he took a mouthful, his eyes visibly willing me to do the same. I obeyed, and the flare of warmth in my throat and stomach was, as he obviously intended, both comforting and soothing.

"Right," he said decisively, after a few moments. "Now you eat."

"I'm not hungry," I told him, shifting restlessly at the suggestion.

"I don't care," he said flatly. "You need to eat something. You're going to eat something, even if I have to force it down you. Understand me?"

I began to cry again. Not because of what he'd said, nor even the way he'd said it. Crying because of why he was saying it. What he meant by it.

He put his arm round my shoulders and held me until I'd calmed down once more. Afterwards he wouldn't let me come into the kitchen, though I was allowed to stand in the doorway and watch him rustle up some tinned spaghetti on toast for both of us. I still wasn't hungry, but he was so determined I was going to eat it that I couldn't refuse him, and though I had to make a real effort to do so, I have to concede that I did feel better afterwards. Though that could have been the wine, of course.

"Very classy," I said, with a breath of laughter. "Tinned spaghetti and a good quality red, you Philistine. That a combination you use very often?"

One corner of his mouth curved upward. "Works for me," he said.

He sent me back into the living room while he cleared up, then came back to join me. He found me standing by the window, staring out into the darkness of the March night, my own reflection gazing crookedly back at me from the black pane.

"Better now?" he enquired.

I nodded.

"Here, have another one." He refilled my wine glass and topped up his own. We both drank; I put my glass down on the window sill.

"I'm sorry I'm like this," I apologized, not looking at him. "I – I wanted you to come, but I didn't mean to go all weepy on you."

"I'm glad I came," he said. And he meant it. "If it helps."

"Of course it does. *Because you know. You know what I'm feeling. You understand.* "But I *am* sorry. It's just – I thought after the first time it'd start getting better. You know – the first time you do something you used to do

156

together, and now it's the same day or the same place, but this time you're on your own." He nodded; he knew. "The first anniversary was difficult, but then, I expected it to be. But I thought the second one would be easier. And it wasn't. And this is the third one. But I keep doing the same stupid, stupid thing."

"What thing?" he asked gently.

"I start thinking about things. The wrong sort of things. I don't want to think about them, but I think about them anyway. I know it doesn't help, and it's only going to upset me, but I can't stop myself. So it's my own fault, really."

He looked at me intently. "What is it you think about?"

I swallowed. "I – I remember the wrong sort of things. I tell myself to try to think about the good things, and – I don't. I didn't. I started thinking about the – the other things. And I couldn't make myself stop."

"What other things?" he asked carefully.

"The times I let him down." I stared down at the glass I'd placed on the sill, the pool of dark liquid inside it. "The times I wasn't as patient as I should have been. The time I…" I faltered into silence.

He put his wineglass down beside mine. Then he reached out, gently took my hand in his, and just held it, motionless. He waited.

"You don't know what you're capable of until you're pushed to extremes," I said at last. "You know that."

He nodded, silently.

"Well, I found out something about myself once," I went on, sombrely. "He'd got really bad. Really low. For several weeks. And in the end, it just got too much for me. We were sleeping in separate rooms by then; he was such a light sleeper even my breathing used to keep him awake. Then he'd get irritable, and restless, so I'd get woken up too, and it could get quite – difficult, at times. It wasn't that we never shared a bed for other reasons, mind" – despite the use of the euphemism, I wanted him to be clear about that – "it was just that, for purely practical purposes, we had to do our actual sleeping in different rooms. But that night, I'd reached the end of my tether. Just completely lost it, and we had a blazing row before we went to bed. Separately, of course," I reiterated. I stared at my own reflection in the window, a tenuous outline against the blackness outside, without seeing it. Remembering.

"The stupid thing is, I can't even remember what the row was about! But I was too stirred up to sleep, and he was, too. I could hear him in the next room, tossing and turning. And then I heard him get up. There was something about the way he did it… I'll never forget the thump of his feet hitting the floor, really hard. He stamped out of his room and went down the stairs with such a – such an *angry* tread. Do you know what I mean by that?"

He nodded again.

"I felt as if I'd had enough. All those weeks. Everything mounting up till it got unbearable. I felt as if I just couldn't cope anymore. I lay in that bed," I said deliberately, "and I thought to myself, *He's gone to get the tablets to take with the whisky.* And I found myself thinking, *I don't want to know. If that's what he's doing, I don't want to know.* And I just lay there, and did nothing."

Now I could feel the first hint of a tremble in my body, hear it in my voice. Peter gripped my hand more tightly. I wondered what he was thinking about me, about this stripping of my emotions naked and showing this worst of myself to him. I didn't know if it was wise, but I did know I had to do it. No fakery, no deceit between Peter and me. I had to take the risk. This was something he had to know about me.

"As it turned out, that wasn't what he was doing. But he could have been! And if he had, I wouldn't have been there to stop him..." Now the tears were beginning to come again, and I clutched Peter's hand convulsively. I could feel my mouth trembling as I looked at him. "I keep wondering – what if he had? And I'd deliberately turned my back and just let him...? It's the thing I most hate myself for! But at the time I just – I couldn't..."

I'd done it. I'd told him the worst. Yet it might not be the worst. My throat muscles were tight with apprehension as I forced myself to ask him the question on which I was afraid our continuing relationship might now depend. "Do you think I'm a very terrible person, for feeling like that?"

He exclaimed something under his breath, sharply, and wrenched his hand free of mine – but only because he wanted to throw his arms around me, and pull me against him with breath-expelling force.

"Never!" he said vehemently. "Never, never, never!"

I began to cry again. Partly because I was already overwrought and therefore easily tipped over the edge of self-control, but partly with sheer relief. I'd told him what I felt was the very worst thing about myself, and he hadn't rejected me. I hadn't lost him, I hadn't lost his regard. I could tell that by the fierceness with which he was holding me. What I'd done didn't matter to him. Well, no, that wasn't strictly true; of course it mattered. But he comprehended, he accepted.

"You got driven too far," he was saying, urgently. "You put up with so much for so long, and you just ran out of rope, that was all! Anyone would, in those circumstances! No one could've blamed you!"

"Oh, yes, they could!" I contradicted hoarsely. He understood me instantly.

"No one else *except* you. Everyone's got their breaking point, Jenny! Don't savage yourself for discovering where yours was!"

"He didn't mean to make me feel like that," I sobbed. "He never meant any of it! It was the depression! And I tried so hard. I just wanted to make him happy! As happy as anyone could... But even I couldn't do it! It was an illness, and it had too strong a hold, and there wasn't anything I could do about it! Because he wouldn't let me!"

I began to cry in earnest again, and he kept hold of me, the way I had of him when he'd told me about Laura. Trying, as I had, to convey comfort through physical contact, one human being to another.

When I'd calmed down, he made me sit down and finish my wine. He sat beside me, not saying much, just being there. Which meant so much to me right at that moment.

"I'd better go and wash my face again," I said after a little while. "I must look an absolute fright."

He cocked his head to one side and considered me.

"Not the best I've ever seen you," he agreed, honestly. I caught the slight gleam in his eye as he said it, and couldn't help smiling.

"I'll see what I can do, then," I said. He stood up when I did, but stayed where he was, watching me leave the room.

I looked in the bathroom mirror, and winced. Definitely not the best he'd ever seen me. My face was a map of varicoloured blotches, white in some places, bright pink in others, and my eyes were rimmed with scarlet. Even my hair looked untidy. I was a complete mess. Not at my best? He'd probably never see me looking worse.

I shrugged, and set about trying to repair the damage. After a few minutes I went back to the living room. He'd gone back to standing by the window, and turned as I came in.

"Better?" he enquired.

"Half-way back to being human, maybe. Peter" – my tone caught his attention – "I'm sorry about this evening. I'm sorry you've had so much to put up with. I only meant to – well, to have your company."

"But it's helped?" The question was superfluous; he already knew the answer.

"Of course it has."

"Then I'm glad you wanted me here. I'm glad I came."

He meant it, yet there was something in the back of his eyes as he said it that made me wonder what else he was thinking. A troubled look, almost. I wondered why. But I didn't feel strong enough to ask. It was enough that he was here, and that he wanted to help.

"So – what do you want to do now? A DVD, or something?" I suggested as brightly as I could, seizing on something, anything, that might lighten the mood, shift focus.

When it came time for him to go, he paused on the point of stepping out through the front door, and turned back to me.

"Are you sure you're all right now?" he asked, studying my face intently. I smiled.

"As all right as I can be," I assured him. "And I'll be better still tomorrow. Thank you. I can't tell you – well, anyway, thank you. I'm so grateful."

"Shall I come round tomorrow evening?" Bless him, he wanted to be sure I was all right.

"Of course you can. You don't need to ask that, you dope. In fact—"

I broke off, thinking. Peter looked at me, evidently wondering what I'd been about to say.

"Wait there," I said decisively, and left him standing there. Thirty seconds later I was back, holding something out to him.

"Have that," I said, dropping it into the hand he automatically held out to receive it. "Then you can get in any time you like. Even if I'm not here."

He stared down at the key lying on his palm.

"Are you sure?" he said. That strange troubled look was back in his eyes, and I realized why. He was afraid that in some way he was making me vulnerable. To him? Surely not! Suddenly I intuited the real reason. Not to him, no – to *Lesser*. As if merely possessing my house key, which would be a totally anonymous artefact to anyone else, made that a risk. I didn't believe it, but that was irrelevant. He did.

"I'm very sure." I looked him in the eye, so he could see that I knew why he was asking – and had to believe me. "I've got another spare, besides that one. I want you to have it. I'd hate you to turn up some time and not able to get in just because I'd – oh, I don't know – run down to the shops, or something."

"I'll take good care of it," he said. "I promise."

"D'you really think I needed to be told that?" I enquired quizzically.

He hesitated, then said, "'Night, Jenny."

"G'night." I came out into the vestibule to watch him go down the steps and unlock his car. He paused before getting in, gazing up at me for a few moments. Then he gave me a brief wave, which I returned, and left.

I waited until the sound of his car had faded beyond hearing. Then I closed the door, shutting myself back inside, to get through the night.

Downstairs, in their living room, my parents heard the car leaving. My father lowered the book he was reading, and glanced over at Mum, who had looked up from her magazine.

160

"I wonder what kind of an evening they had," he speculated. "It had the potential to be quite – difficult, I suspect. For Peter, I mean."

"For Jenny, too!" said my mother indignantly.

"Of course for Jenny," said Dad patiently. "I mean that it might have been difficult for Peter if she was – emotional. And I expect she was. The potential was certainly there when I saw her this afternoon."

"Yes, I know what you mean," Mum agreed. "Still, she wanted him there."

"Mmm. I find it interesting," observed my father, "that it was Peter that she turned to for the occasion."

Mother looked at him.

"Do you mind?" she asked carefully.

My father caught her drift, and smiled reassuringly.

"Not at all," he said. "In fact, in a lot of ways I'm very pleased. I just hope it wasn't too uncomfortable an experience for him."

"Maybe she wanted to spare us, this time," Mum suggested lightly.

"Maybe she did," agreed Dad equably, and picked up his book again.

Unseen by him, my mother's mouth quirked briefly at the corners; and she continued to smile inwardly as she returned her attention to her magazine.

It was only when it was coming on to late afternoon the next day that I realized neither Peter nor I had specified his time of arrival. I wondered if I should text him, but then thought better of it. After all, he'd probably only say seven-thirty, as he usually did.

But seven-thirty came and went without a sign of him, nor any message. Eight… Nine… Ten… Nothing. Nothing, despite my trying to call him at about nine o'clock. Unsuccessfully. I'd given up on the idea that he was coming over at that point, but I couldn't help being anxious as to why. But there was no answer, nor to the text I sent him – *Are you OK?*

It wasn't much of an evening. Unconsciously I'd been pinning rather stupidly high hopes on seeing him again after yesterday. Instead, no Peter, and – what was worse – no explanation. I couldn't settle to anything; my mind kept going back to worry at possible reasons for his non-appearance. In a way, it was worse than the previous evening.

At eleven I couldn't bear it anymore, and rang Jane.

"I'm sorry to be ringing at this time of night," I apologized, "but Peter said he'd come round this evening and he never showed. Should I be worried?"

"I don't know…" she said slowly. Then, more briskly, "Probably not. Alan's not home, either, so they're probably caught up at work."

"But wouldn't he have let me know?"

"Depends on where he is," Jane said. "And who he's with. He might not be able to, you see. If it was something that blew up unexpectedly, and he's had to – well, he might be somewhere where it wouldn't be—"

Safe. Where it wouldn't be safe for him break off what he's doing to ring you. My mind completed the sentence that she hadn't.

"Of course," I said. "I hadn't thought of that. That's probably what it is, then."

"Sorry, Jenny," said Jane sympathetically. "This is the sort of thing you have to get used to. I *know*. Try not to worry. It doesn't do any good." Years of hard-won experience were in her voice.

"I'll try," I promised. "Thanks, Jane. Sorry my L-plates were showing." She laughed, and rang off.

Despite her attempts to reassure me, I found it hard to get to sleep that night, and hard to stay asleep when I did. Quarter to six found me awake for the umpteenth time, and this time, unlikely to drift off again. I gave up the attempt and just lay open-eyed in the dark, staring at the ceiling.

My phone, beside me on the bedside table, started to sound. In the early morning quiet it packed all the emotional punch of a firecracker suddenly going off. I instantly rolled over and seized it.

"Peter?"

"Sorry. On my way." And that was all.

I didn't know whether to cry or laugh. Cry with relief that he was, apparently, all right, or laugh with incredulity that he was on his way here at this time of the morning.

I flew out of bed and dressed hastily. Then I went downstairs and prepared two coffees, ready to be made as soon as the kettle boiled. After which I tried to school myself to patience by waiting in the living room, but I couldn't. I found myself continually going to stand in the vestibule and peer out into the early morning gloom.

It was sometime before seven when I heard the crunch of wheels on the gravel of the drive. He killed the engine, and got out. I couldn't see him clearly in the half-darkness, but what I could see was that he was moving more slowly than usual, and instead of running up the steps, as he usually did, his feet met each riser heavily. He didn't even look up until I opened the front door. When I saw his face clearly, I was shocked at how weary he looked.

"What on earth are you doing here in that state, you stupid man?" I demanded.

"I promised you I'd come," he mumbled.

"You shouldn't have," I scolded him. "Look at the state of you! You should be home in bed, not here!"

"I said I'd come," he reiterated, stubbornly. Then, more quietly, "I'm sorry, Jenny." He sounded very tired.

"Doesn't matter," I said quickly. "Come on. Coffee?"

"Yeh, thanks," he muttered.

He followed me to the kitchen. I switched the kettle on, then turned to look at him.

"You look terrible," I said frankly. And he did. He was paler even than usual, which only emphasized the dark circles under his eyes, the red rims of his eyelids. He looked, quite simply, exhausted.

"I've been" – he searched for the right euphemism – "busy."

"It shows," I told him. "To good effect, I hope?"

He rubbed his forehead tiredly with one hand.

"Yeh," he agreed. "Sort of."

"That's something, then." The kettle switched itself off; I made the drinks and handed his to him. "Go on in, then."

He nodded and turned back through the doorway. I was on his heels as he sat heavily down at one end of the sofa. I sat at the other end and studied him over the rim of my cup as I sipped my coffee.

"Are you all right?" I asked. "Other than being completely shattered, that is?"

He gave me a half-smile.

"Yeh, I'm all right," he said. "You're right about being shattered, though. Yesterday was a long, hard day, and it ran into a long, hard night."

"Does this—?" I broke off and changed what I'd been going to say. "Do you get nights like that very often?"

"Not too often," he shrugged. "Fortunately. But they happen." He raised those red-rimmed eyes to look at me. "I'm sorry I couldn't let you know. What I was doing – it wouldn't have been…"

"I know," I told him. "It's all right. I do know. Jane's explained it to me. I was only worried about whether you were all right, that was all."

"I would've let you know, if I could," he said, looking troubled.

"Well, I know it now, so don't worry about it anymore. I mean it, Peter. It's all right."

He searched my face, and believed me, visibly relaxing. Tiredly he sank back, cradling his mug in his hands, and rested his head on the back of the sofa. His eyes closed. I watched him without speaking for a minute or so, identifying each mark of exhaustion on his features. Then I realized his head was sagging to one side, and the mug was tilting dangerously sideways in his lax fingers. I let my breath out in a quick hiss, and he started awake again just as I snatched it from his hands, milliseconds before it reached the point of no return. He blinked at me as I leaned forward and put it down on the coffee table with a sharp movement. We stared at each other for a few moments.

"Oh, for goodness' sake!" I exclaimed in sheer exasperation. I reached over and grabbed his shoulders, pulling him sideways toward me. He didn't even make a token protest, just yielded to my insistence with a sigh, folding his long legs up onto the sofa, his eyes already closing. Within just a few seconds, the rhythm of his breathing had changed, and he was asleep again, his head heavy on my lap.

I looked down at him, almost absently brushing some of the strands of his hair back from his temple and into better order. When a cat falls asleep on someone, it's supposed to indicate a profound degree of trust. Was this a similar thing? I supposed so. But I prepared myself for a long wait. Someone as exhausted as he was wasn't going to wake up again anytime soon.

And so, for the second time since I'd known him, I watched over Peter McLeish's sleep.

It was close to eleven before he began to stir. I could only see one side of his face, but I saw when his eyes opened, heavily, and his initial confusion over where he was. Then I saw recollection hit. He hurriedly levered himself erect, staring at me with dismayed apology. I was aware of the warmth where his head had lain on my lap already starting to dissipate.

"How long—?" He broke off, and started again. "What time is it?"

"Nearly eleven."

"Eleven? That's" – he laboriously worked it out – "that's four hours…!" Something else struck him. "I've made you late for work…!"

Clearly he was still too blurred with sleep to have worked it out. Or else, despite it, still too tired for his brain to be functioning properly.

"No, you haven't. Friday," I said laconically. "Non-working day. You're the one who's late for work," I added, making sure I hit the right note of prim smugness.

He stared at me for a moment, then let out a breath of laughter, and relaxed.

"I won't get fired for it," he said, rubbing his right eye with the heel of his hand. "Odd hours can be par for the course in our line of work."

"I'll bet," I remarked. "You'll have time for breakfast, then. Might as well, if you're this late. In for a penny, sheep for a lamb, and all that."

"A coffee'll do fine," he demurred.

"Not if you had the kind of day you evidently did. I'll bet you didn't stop to eat anything, did you? Let alone a proper meal."

"No, but—"

"You're quite right," I said promptly. "No 'but'! I don't care if you are a Scot – you're getting a full English, see? Even if I have to force it down you. Understand me?"

He recognized his own words being quoted back at him. "Okay, I surrender. Can I use the bathroom?"

"Don't ask silly questions," I said cheerfully. I got up, rather stiffly; I had been locked into the same physical position for close to four hours, not daring to move in case it woke him, and now my body was feeling the consequences.

Peter saw it, and winced slightly. He opened his mouth to speak, but I cut in ahead of him.

"Don't," I said firmly. "You're only allowed to speak if it's not an apology."

Which, of course, silenced him.

"Good. Now, let me go to the loo first, and then you can have the run of the bathroom." I studied him critically. "Do you want a bath, while you're here? You look as if you could do with one."

"Thanks," he said wryly, but his eyes had lit up at the suggestion. Showers are all very well, but they're just not the same as a good soak in a hot bath.

"Take as long as you like," I told him. "Just give me a yell when you're getting out, so I know when to start frying the eggs. There's a clean towel on the rack you can use."

He took me at my word; he was in that bath a long while. By the time we were ready to eat the meal had effectively changed from breakfast to lunch, but it didn't matter.

When he was on his second cup of coffee, he suddenly said, "Jenny—"

"Yes?"

"I'm sorry you were worried." There, again, was the troubled look in his eyes.

"I'm sorry it's worrying *you*," I said. "Especially if it makes you drive half-across London in the early hours of the morning in a positively dangerous state of exhaustion, just on my account."

"I didn't want to let you down," he muttered. "Not after how you'd been the day before."

I sighed. I didn't know whether to be exasperated with him, or pleased that he'd gone to so much trouble to keep his word to me.

"Look, I know worrying goes with the territory. I know that sometimes what you do is dangerous. How could I not?" The way we had met was in both our minds as we looked at each other. "And I know your time isn't always your own. Not for personal concerns. You've got enough on your plate, without me adding to it. So I'm sorry. But it can't be helped. There are – oh, I don't know how many! – people all over the world who do jobs that are potentially dangerous. Like soldiers, or bomb disposal experts, or lifeboat crews. They all have families – and friends – who must worry about them sometimes, too. It's just – it's what happens, all right?"

"But I don't want you—"

"Tough. Get used to it," I said flatly. "Outside of my parents, you're my best friend. Don't expect me not to worry about you from time to time. Not with your history."

He hadn't been ready for such frankness, and for a few moments didn't know what to say. Then his shoulders sagged slightly.

"Okay," he conceded, and let it lie.

Good enough. Except that neither of us realized it wasn't just him I should have been worrying about.

Chapter 16

It was a month or so later that Peter fell ill. First he cancelled a sailing lesson because he wasn't feeling up to it. Then he pulled out of coming round to my place the next day. Seemed to have a bit of a cold, he told me. And then didn't get in touch for the next three days. So, in the end, I rang him.

As soon as I heard his voice, I knew he was in a bad way.

"You sound awful!" I exclaimed. "What's wrong?"

"I'm fine." As blatant a lie as I was ever likely to hear from him. "Don't worry." His voice sounded anything but fine; weak and breathless was more like it, as if his nasal passages were blocked solid.

"You're not at work, are you?" I challenged. "Tell me you're not at work, sounding like that! Are you at home?"

He hesitated, clearly reluctant to admit it, but forced to. "Yeh. But I'm all right," he repeated. "You don't need to worry."

I was worried, though. He really did sound very rough indeed; worse by the time the call ended than when it began. I sat thinking for a few minutes. About how fragile he'd sounded. About the fact that he was a man, and hence unlikely to admit how ill he was. About the likelihood of him looking after himself properly in that horrible little flat.

And when I'd thought about all those things, I collected a coat and my car keys.

I didn't tell him I was coming. He'd only have tried to talk me out of it, and I wasn't having any of that. My most pressing worry was that I was going to have to cruise the streets of Brixton for hours to find somewhere reasonably adjacent to his flat to park; my memory of the one time I'd been there was of a road lined absolutely solid on both sides with cars. But my luck was in. I spotted a parking space only a few yards from his front door and hurriedly reversed into it, earning myself a dirty look from the driver of the car behind me, who'd obviously had the same ambition.

What I didn't see was the man – the tall, powerfully built man with short-cropped fair hair – sitting in a 4x4 parked a few yards up the street, who leaned forward with sudden recognition in his hooded blue eyes as I marched purposefully to the side door and rang Peter's doorbell.

Nor, when he finally answered the door, did Peter. He wouldn't have noticed a troupe of can-can dancers wearing fluorescent yellow, by the look of him. His black-circled eyes looked muzzily at me from an uncharacteristically flushed face; he was clearly feverish, and looked as if he was barely able to stay upright. His forehead was damp, and his untidy hair clung to it in lank strands. He opened his mouth to speak, but had to cough first.

"Jenny," he panted. "What are you doing here?"

"Proving you're a liar. You told me you were all right, and you're not," I said flatly.

"You'd better not come in." He coughed again. "You might get it, too."

"Tough," I said, and pushed past him.

He shut the door, and I led the way relentlessly upstairs, into the flat and into the living room, where I saw the rumpled pillow on the sofa, the thin duvet that had been thrown back when he rose. He hadn't even gone properly to bed. I turned to face him.

"What is it?" I demanded.

"Flu, I think," he said huskily, giving up any attempt to deflect my enquiries.

"Are you aching?" I asked quickly. He nodded, reluctantly.

"The real thing, then," I said sombrely. "You've been coming down with this for the last four days, haven't you? When did it get bad?"

"Yesterday. Alan sent me home half way through the day. Told me I wasn't well enough to be at work."

I looked at him for a long moment, biting my lip. He wavered slightly, and folded down onto the sofa as if his legs wouldn't hold him anymore.

"Right," I said decisively. "That does it. You're coming home with me."

"What...?" He sounded confused.

"If you've got the real thing, you're going to be pretty ill for several days. I'm not having you here, not looking after yourself properly. You're going to stay in my spare room, so you'll only be alone for the mornings. Then I can be there the rest of the time to make sure you're getting enough fluids and anything else you might need."

"You don't need to do that," he protested, as I'd known he would. "I'll be all right."

"Please don't argue, Peter," I told him impatiently. "That's not just a bad cold. That's real influenza. Real influenza can kill people. And while I don't expect it to kill you, I do expect you to be ill enough to make it worthwhile having someone there to look after you, at least to start with. Do you seriously think I could leave you like this and then live with myself? Now I've seen the state you're in, I'd be worried sick about you all the time! If you're where I can keep an eye on you, I won't be so worried.

D'you see?" My tone had changed from decision almost to a plea.

"I shouldn't impose on you," he muttered; clearly his defences were breaching.

"You're not. I offered. And I don't regard helping a friend who needs it as being imposed on," I said firmly. "Shut up, and come on. What do you need to bring with you? And what do you want me to pack it in?"

Once in a while, Matthew Lesser would do this. Idly, for his own pleasure, when he had some free time and the inclination. Drive to McLeish's flat, and, if he could find a parking space from where he could see it, sit for a while, watching it for any signs of activity. He'd very rarely seen any over the years – a very few times he'd seen McLeish going in, a few times coming out. But almost always alone.

This, though, was new. This was different. Other than the occasional postman, and Alan McLeish on a few occasions, he'd never before seen anyone else even approach the flat, let alone go inside it, as this woman had done. When she'd first emerged from her vehicle, he'd merely registered her existence, as he would have any presence on the street, not analyzed her as an individual. But when she'd made for the flat, that had brought her into the sharp focus of his full attention. And once that had happened, it had only taken him a second or two to recognize her. He'd only seen her once before, of course, but he had an excellent memory.

"Well, hello, Jenny Gregory," he murmured aloud. "What brings you here, I wonder? Keeping in touch with Peter, are we?"

He watched her vanish inside, then leaned back again and waited, his eyes on the narrow door. His patience was rewarded after about ten minutes when he saw her ushering an obviously ill McLeish out of the flat, down the steps, and into her car, where he sank limply into the passenger seat, his head thrown back against the headrest, his eyes closed.

"Ah, I see," breathed Lesser. "Still being his ministering angel, Jenny. How very kind of you."

Oblivious to his presence, she hurriedly threw the carryall and carrier bag in her hands into the back of the car, then got into the driver's seat and started the engine.

Lesser waited until she was about fifty yards down the road before he started to follow her, anonymously unobtrusive. If McLeish had been alert, he might have spotted the 4x4 that stayed on their tail all the way to Croydon, but he had looked ill enough for that not to be probable; his companion was unlikely to have any suspicion that they were being followed.

At last, on a road lined with solid-looking detached villas, her car turned into one of the driveways. He calmly drove on, assessing the neighbourhood

– big houses, lots of mature trees, large gardens. He made use of a small cul-de-sac about a quarter of a mile further on to turn round, then drove at a leisurely pace in the other direction, slowly enough to have a good sight of the house, and the tall figure stumbling up the steps toward the door of a half-glassed vestibule at the top, escorted by the anxious woman with that memorable corn-straw hair.

So – still seeing her, then, Peter? Know her well enough to agree to stay with her? That's interesting. That's very interesting indeed...

A smile of satisfaction curving his lips, Lesser drove on.

I can see I'm going to have to find out a bit more about you, Jenny Gregory...

I was pretty ruthless with poor Peter. I drove him with verbal whips up to the spare bedroom, and told him in no uncertain terms to get himself undressed and into the bed by the time I came back up.

"If you don't, I'll come up and undress you myself," I threatened. That got a weak smile out of him.

"Well, it wouldn't be the first time," he pointed out.

"No, it wouldn't, would it?" I agreed, quirking an eyebrow at him. "Your dignity, your decision!"

I left him to his own devices and went back downstairs. By the time I returned, carrying a tray, he was lying under the duvet, his eyes closed. They opened again as I came in and put the tray down on the bedside cabinet beside him. A jug of water and a glass; another glass, with guava juice in it; a small bottle of paracetamol; a box of tissues and an old plastic carrier bag.

"If you blow your nose, put the used tissues in that," I told him. "I'll get rid of them later. Now, take a couple of these" – I handed over two of the paracetamol, then poured out half a glass of water and gave that to him, too – "then, drink this." I picked up the guava juice and waited while he propped himself back up into a sitting position and obediently took the tablets, then handed it to him. It would be cool and soothing to his sore throat, I hoped.

He drank it down, and handed the glass back to me.

"Are you going to be all right for temperature?" I asked. He wasn't wearing anything on his upper body; he might very well not be wearing anything at all. Which didn't worry me, unless it meant he wasn't going to keep warm enough.

"Yeh," he said, sliding back down under the duvet.

"You'd better be telling me the truth," I warned him.

"Wouldn't dare do anything else." He gave me a weak half-smile. "You can be quite a harridan, you know that?"

"If driven to it," I agreed. "So behave yourself!"

He'd thrown his clothes carelessly on top of the ottoman under the single window that had been built into the slope of the roof. It made the room the same odd shape as my own – you had to remember not to knock your head against the sloping ceiling on that side of the bed – but it had been the only practical way to have a window at all.

"D'you want me to pull the blind down?" I asked him, gesturing at the window above his head, but he said no.

I tidied his discarded clothes and unpacked the contents of his carryall, telling him where I was putting everything, and draping his dressing gown on a nearby chair; no pistol to deal with, this time. I came back to the bedside, looking down at him.

"Right; that should do, for now. Are you hungry?"

"No," he said, almost flinching from the idea of food.

"Well, the way to get over this as quickly as possible is to get plenty of rest, and drink plenty of liquids. I'll go out and get you a glucose energy drink or something, later."

"Haven't had that kind of thing since I was a kid…" he said, with a weak chuckle.

"Well, until you feel more like eating, hopefully it'll keep you alive long enough to get as far as your second childhood. If there's anything else you need, just yell. Or thump on the floor. And if not, try to sleep as much as you can. That'll do you more good than just about anything else. I'll come up and check on you before I go out. I won't be long."

He gazed at me for long moments with heavy-lidded eyes. Then he mumbled something I didn't quite catch, but I did detect the word 'kind'.

"It's not being kind, it's being practical," I said matter-of-factly. "Now go to sleep, for heaven's sake."

His eyes were already closed by the time I pulled the door to behind me.

My next move was to go down to explain to my parents what had happened.

"He was never going to look after himself properly," I declared. "Not with real influenza. So I've kidnapped him."

"At gunpoint, by the sound of it," commented my mother. I glanced at her. *He's the one with the gun, Mum, not me.* But I didn't say it aloud.

"Very nearly," I admitted. "So I'd better keep away from you after this. I'll be keeping away from him as much as possible, come to that! But I had to do it. I'd've been so worried about him, otherwise."

"Of course you would," my mother agreed. "And it's not as if you don't have some experience of a man who won't look after his health properly."

"Well, I might not have been able to persuade Alex to medicate for depression, but at least I can physically pour drink down Peter's throat."

"Just make sure you don't choke him," Dad advised.

"Be a bit self-defeating, wouldn't it? So I'll try not to. And now I'm going down to the supermarket to get some supplies in. He's going to need more paracetamol."

"Is he a whisky man?" Dad enquired.

"Not with paracetamol, I hope!" I quipped. Echoes of the episode with Alex that I'd confessed to Peter quivered in the back of my mind momentarily.

"I think it's aspirin you'd need to worry about," Dad pointed out. "And I was thinking more in terms of medicinal purposes."

"D'you know, I don't know the answer to that?" I admitted, having thought about it. "I've never seen him drink it, but usually he's doing the driving, or else he's up with me, and I don't keep it in. But he's a Scotsman born and bred, so I'd be pretty shocked if he didn't drink it."

"Find out from Alan," Dad suggested. "If he is, take this" – he extracted a couple of notes from his wallet, and held them out to me – "and get him a decent single malt. A gift from me. Give him something to look forward to, when he gets better."

"Thanks, Dad. I'll let you have the change later. If there is any!" I lifted my phone to my ear. "Alan? Got a question for you…"

Two days later, Alan was at his desk when he was interrupted.

"Boss?"

Alan looked up. Ben was in the doorway, looking grim.

"What is it?"

"Mark Walsh in e-Crime just tipped me the wink. Jenny Gregory's original email account – someone's hacked it, as of yesterday."

Alan frowned.

"Lesser?"

Ben shrugged.

"But why wait until now?" Alan asked, mystified. "He took that laptop months ago. What's brought that on?"

"Dunno," said Ben. "But it's a bad sign, if he's suddenly started taking an interest in her."

Alan met his eye, and nodded slowly.

"See if there's anything else you can find out," he said. "And, Ben – I know he won't be around for a few days, but – don't say anything about this to Peter. Not yet, anyway."

Ben tilted his head slightly as the implications of the request sank in.

"Is it her he's been seeing, then?" he enquired casually. Alan was startled.

"How did you know—?"

"Oh, I dunno. Just one or two things I've picked up about the way he's been lately. Not so uptight. Just got the idea he might be seeing someone at last. Didn't ask," said Ben succinctly.

"Does anyone else know?" Alan felt unreasonably anxious about the possibility. The last thing Peter needed was pressure from his colleagues, even if it was well-meant.

"Not until that little episode with Chris the other day," Ben said grimly. "Think I was the only one who'd worked it out before that. He doesn't give much away. But don't worry. They won't be asking, either."

One corner of Alan's mouth quirked momentarily.

"Well, keep a lid on it as long as you can, will you?"

Ben cocked a reproving eyebrow at him. *As if you needed to tell me that,* his look said.

"Yeah," he grunted. Then, in a different tone of voice, "What's she like? She all right for him?" He'd been in the team a long time, had seen what Peter had gone through at Lesser's hands. Since Laura's death he'd been quite protective of Peter's wellbeing in a paternal sort of way, but he rarely showed it as obviously as now.

Alan considered his reply before delivering it.

"I think she's the best thing that could possibly have happened to him," he said levelly.

Ben raised his eyebrows momentarily, assessing Alan's judgement, accepting it. He nodded.

"Worth looking out for, then. Okay, I'm on it."

Alan watched him leave, thinking hard. Lesser following up on Jenny. He didn't like that. He didn't like that at all.

Peter was pretty ill for the best part of a week before he began to pick up. Mostly he slept, to start with. On the whole I left him alone, just checking on him from time to time; before I went to work, when I came back, that sort of thing. I'd top up his supply of drinks before I'd leave, as well as threaten him with bodily violence if he hadn't drunk his assigned quota by the time I returned, and on the whole he was fairly good about it. Gradually the muscle aches receded, though he got through quite a few packets of paracetamol before they did, and he began to improve, though he was still fairly weak. I had the feeling he'd been pushing himself hard for quite a while, and his body was taking the chance to vent its reaction. I'd expected him to be fighting me to get up as soon as possible, but surprisingly he didn't; he seemed to want to just lie there, safe, warm, relaxed, as if he valued the opportunity to really wind down for once. Being waited on hand and foot probably didn't come amiss, either. I didn't mind. There wasn't much extra work involved, and I was glad to be able to do something useful for him.

But I learned something else about him that I hadn't known before, though I suppose I might have expected it.

It first happened six days in, in the early hours of the morning. I was jerked awake by the eerie sound coming from the next room. The hoarse, rising howl of someone having a nightmare. The pitch went up and up until he was screaming incoherently.

In seconds I was out of my room and in with him, switching on the bedside lamp.

"Peter! Peter!" I kept repeating, not loud enough to startle him, but enough to wake him as quickly as might be, I hoped. The screaming broke off, and he lay on his back, panting, while he came to full consciousness. He turned his head slowly, saw me kneeling beside the bed.

"Jenny…" he mumbled. A pause, as he worked out what had happened. "Sorry – I…"

I reached out and gripped his bare shoulder reassuringly.

"Okay – it's okay. Don't worry about it."

"But—"

"Doesn't matter!" I insisted. "As long as you're all right."

He moved his head slightly. "Yeh, I'm fine. Go back to bed."

"Sure?"

"Yeh. Go on. Go back to sleep."

I smiled at him. "I will if you will." I withdrew my hand from his shoulder, and stood up. "Do you want me to leave the lamp on?"

The smile he attempted was something of a travesty, but it was a valiant effort. "No, thanks, Mum."

I gave him an old-fashioned look, and left him to it, pulling the door to but not closed behind me.

I took him up some buttered toast and a coffee the next morning before I left for work – he was beginning to feel like eating again by then, though he wasn't back to full appetite. He looked at me remorsefully when I came in.

"Sorry about last night," he said, with an air of getting it in first.

"No need," I said cheerfully, putting the tray down on the bedside cabinet for him. "No lives were lost in the making of this episode."

His face lightened momentarily at my disclaimer, but then grew serious again.

"I should've warned you, though," he said.

I sat on the edge of the bed. "Does it happen very often, then?"

He shrugged. "Sometimes." Which I interpreted as an admission that it did.

"Well, don't let it worry you. If you do it again, I shall simply come in and wake you up, like I did last night, and then go back to sleep. Also like I did last night! What is it? Stuff from work?"

"Sometimes. But sometimes it's Laura."

I nodded. Hardly a surprise. But I felt unreasonably pleased that he could confide it to me so readily.

"Well, any time you need to let rip, go right ahead," I assured him. "I shall simply come in and tell you to shut up and let decent folks get their sleep. Now eat that toast before it gets glacial. I'm off now. I'll see you later. For the waking nightmare that will be lunch."

As I left, I heard a quiet burble of laughter behind me. I was glad of that.

He only did it once more while he was staying with me, as it happened. But the ground rules were in place by then, so it wasn't so bad for either of us, the second time. Early in the second week I drove him to the doctor, who promptly signed him off work for a further seven days, and I insisted that he stay that time out with me.

"I want to make sure you're properly fuelled up by the time you're released back into the wild," I told him. "Then you can go back to your single-man-alone eating habits as much as you like."

He didn't take too much persuading, which was a pleasant surprise; again, I thought he'd insist on going as soon as he could, but he didn't. He still slept on for quite a while in the mornings, but he was usually up and about by the time I got back from work, though never doing much more than watching television or listening to music. I even caught him listening to more Chris de Burgh, which I valiantly forbore to comment on.

"Do you ever go on holiday?" I enquired over lunch one day. "A real holiday, I mean?"

"Do you?" he parried. Which was revealing enough to constitute an answer.

"Not abroad. Not since Alex died," I said. "Sometimes I go and stay with David and Bronwyn. You can do some great rockpooling in St Bride's Bay! Or sometimes I go up to the lodge."

Thank heavens I do. Or I wouldn't have been there when you needed me...

If he was thinking the same thing, he didn't say it aloud.

"So you don't go away, then," I commented. "Thought as much." He shifted uncomfortably. "Do you bother taking leave at all?" I knew what the answer was going to be before he gave it.

"Not much," he shrugged. He didn't look at me, so he couldn't read my expression, though I suspect he could sense my disapproval. But the next thing he said surprised me.

"Might do soon, though."

"Oh?" I wondered why he sounded quite so definite about it.

"When you've finished your lessons. We could go sailing somewhere. Lake District. The Broads. Somewhere like that." He glanced at me diffidently. "Would you – d'you think you might like that?"

I could not possibly have expressed adequately how delighted I was at that moment. So I took refuge, English-wise, in self-deprecation.

"Well, I suppose I could be useful as ballast," I mused.

"Shut up!" he grinned. "Is that a 'yes'?"

I gave in.

"Yes," I said. "I'd love to." It was worth saying it, if only to see the look on his face. "Separate berths, of course," I threw in lightly, as a reminder, then went on, "But only when you're really sure I'm ready! I'd hate to be a liability."

"You wouldn't know how," he said, so matter-of-factly that it would have been quite easy not to notice what a compliment he'd just paid me; but I did notice.

"Talking about water-based activities – can I have another bath this evening?" he said. "I won't have that many more chances. You've spoiled me. You know that, don't you? Baths instead of showers."

"Not many more chances?" I queried, unable to suppress a twinge of disappointment. Though it had been inevitable, of course.

"Well, I thought maybe I should go back to my place soon." How significant that he didn't say "*home*"; just "*my place*." It was hardly even that. "I'll be back to work Monday."

"You might as well stay until Sunday then, mightn't you? And of course you can have a bath. As many as you like! And you can come back and have one any time you want, in any case," I said cheerfully.

"You know how to tempt a man, don't you?" he remarked. "Thanks. Might take you up on that."

"Good," I said, because I could tell he meant it. Somehow I always knew when he really meant what he'd said. "Better not forget your whisky when you go," I added flippantly.

He gave me a considering look.

"No," he said. "You keep it here. Don't want to start drinking alone, do I?" He offered it as a joke, but I wondered if, underneath, there was something more serious. "*I tried diving into a bottle,*" he'd said about the time after Laura's death. Perhaps he still felt capable of that behaviour if alone, and with the means to hand.

"Okay," I agreed equably. "It'll be safe enough with me – whisky's not my tipple. I know that's a terrible admission to make to a Scotsman, but there it is. But don't forget you can come and claim it whenever you want, even if I'm not here."

For a moment my meaning escaped him, and he frowned an enquiry.

"I gave you that key for a reason, you know," I said smugly. And he had to laugh.

That evening, when he'd had his bath, I put a CD into the music centre, and we sat in front of the fire, chatting idly as we listened. That is, I sat, and he stretched out on the sofa, his head resting on one of the arms; he was improving, but he still took every opportunity to lie down that offered. I'd opted to sit on the floor, leaning back against the end of the sofa nearest the fire, which put me comfortably close to the heat but meant I was blocking it from reaching his bare feet, which were also at that end of the sofa, behind my shoulders.

I don't know what prompted me to say it, but – I don't know why – this felt like the right moment.

"Peter – what was Laura like?"

He didn't answer straight away, which made me turn my head and scan his face, abruptly anxious that I'd misjudged my timing, after all. But it wasn't that; I could see he was simply considering his answer.

"She was – not fragile – delicate. Not physically. Just – her personality. Like bone china. Beautiful, but – delicate. Gentle. And she was kind. Like you are. Always kind. And she was a *joyful* person," he went on. "She – *sparkled*. Do you know what I mean?"

I thought of the photograph he'd showed me, that beautiful smile, and nodded. "Where did you meet her?"

"Party at a friend's," he said simply. "I saw her, and" – he shrugged, as if the outcome had been inevitable – "I liked her. Straight away."

"So" – I was getting it straight in my mind, gradually – "you were with the police. What did she do?"

"She worked for a baker and confectioner. She did cakes – you know, wedding cakes, that kind of stuff."

"What, decorating them, you mean?"

"Yeh. Oh, you should've seen them, Jenny!" His eyes kindled with remembered enthusiasm. "She was so talented at it! She made the most beautiful flowers, all out of icing, but you'd never know they weren't the real thing. And not just flowers. All sorts of things! Just about anything you could conceivably want on a cake, she could make it out of icing. I've still got some photos of some of her stuff. Next time you're over at Alan's, get him to show them to you. You'll like them." He was in no doubt about that. But I was slightly confused.

"Alan's…?"

"Yeh." His face changed slightly. "There wasn't much left after the fire – not burned, but smoke damage, you see – but what there is, he's got. Safer with him than with me."

There wasn't much I could say to that. Except get angry at Lesser all over again. The man had prevented Peter from keeping even his most private and personal possessions and mementoes close at hand.

"She wasn't especially academically inclined," he went on, the slight hint of tension vanishing from his face and voice, and I did my best to banish thoughts of Lesser and go on listening to him. "She was just – well, a natural homemaker, I suppose. I mean, she did go out to work, but homemaking was her nature."

"It's underrated, these days," I said thoughtfully. "Everybody acts as if making money is the most important thing there is. But all the money in the world won't help you if you haven't got a good home. A happy home, I mean. So if you had someone who was good at making a home, you were lucky. Anyway," I said, looking across my shoulder at him, "if two people are together, it takes both of them to make a good home. So you must have had something to do with it, don't you think?"

He studied me for a few moments, the orange glow from the fire making warm pinpoints in his irises.

"You always look for the best in people, don't you? Try to make them feel good about themselves." He spoke slowly, as if realizing he'd made some sort of discovery, and with such profound sincerity that I had to look away quickly, feeling self-conscious and hoping the glow from the fire would account for the additional colour in my cheeks.

"Beats the alternative," I shrugged, to hide my discomfiture.

"I wish you could have met her," he said softly, after a pause. "She'd've liked you."

I didn't say anything to that. I wished it, too, but it was impossible, and always would have been. Because I could never have met Laura. She would have had to be alive for that to happen. And if she had been alive, why would my path ever have crossed Peter's? Laura's life was the price that had had to be paid for Peter and me to meet in the first place. So better to say nothing, and ignore my awareness of the sudden and unaccountably insistent thudding of my heart against my ribs.

Chapter 17

On the Thursday I warned Peter I was liable to be late back from work; I had some shopping I wanted to do.

"You'll have to crack open your own tin of soup, this time," I told him, as I left.

But instead he ended up having lunch with my parents. Mum, out in the garden, caught sight of him at the window and gesticulated that he should open it. When he did, she called up, "Peter, I know Jenny's going to be late home – would you like to come and eat with us? It's just a salad, so there's plenty to spare."

Peter later commented to me on how widely his own definition of "just a salad" differed from Mum's. But even more than the food, he enjoyed their company; the range of topics covered by their conversation was both catholic and interesting, and even when asking him about his own views and opinions, they were never even close to intrusive.

"And are you sure you're well enough to go back to work?" Mother asked eventually.

"Yeh," Peter said. "Jenny's a good nurse."

"Well, you certainly seem to give her enough chances to hone her skills," Mum observed comfortably. She was clearly referring not just to his flu, but back to the events at Guithas Lodge, and she did it with such transparent good nature that Peter found himself smiling at her almost in spite of himself.

"I'll try not to keep her so busy in future," he promised.

"Now, would you two like a coffee, in the living room?" Mum suggested. "It's about time I went back to work. I've got quite a big segment to proof this afternoon."

Once she was gone, the two men went on talking, on various subjects. Eventually, of course, they got round to me.

"How did Jenny come to be a library assistant?" Peter asked. "I'd've thought she could've been doing something more – I don't know – more high-powered than that."

"She could indeed," Dad agreed indulgently. "She certainly has the intellect and the capacity. But I'm afraid she has two fatal flaws in terms of pursuing the sort of career you're thinking of."

Peter frowned at him. "What d'you mean?"

"She entirely lacks a sense of materialism," said Dad, shaking his head mock-sadly. "So she seems to be completely unmotivated by any desire to accumulate money. She was also born without the least trace of ambition. In the sense that she's not driven to climb any of the ladders that anyone who wants to progress to the top of their chosen field needs to scale. Both profound handicaps to what is classed as success and the pursuit of happiness in the modern world, you'll appreciate… All her teachers, including myself – in my professional capacity, you understand – fully expected her to go to university and to go on from there." Dad shrugged, and Peter sensed there was an element of disappointment as well as resignation in it. "She wasn't the least bit interested. Not that she didn't think about it. Carefully, too. She just decided that wasn't the kind of life that she thought would make her happy."

"Did you mind?" Peter asked, interested in the implications of that shrug.

"A little," Dad admitted. "At first. Both Beth and I had followed that route, and so had David, and I suppose we were afraid she'd be missing out on so many opportunities. But I've come to realize that she did do the right thing – the right thing for her. She's always loved books, and reading. So she went for a City and Guilds, and got taken on by the library service. She was able to transfer up here when she left Hampshire. She's only-part time, and it's not a particularly well-paid job, but…" He shrugged. "She's perfectly content doing what she's doing, and I think she thought that supporting Alex was far more important than anything else she might have done with her life. If she was ever driven in any way, it was to try to help him." He caught Peter's eye. "I want to tell you, Peter, how grateful I am that you were there for her to turn to when the anniversary of his death came round. For providing an outlet. You did her immense good, and I want to express my appreciation to you."

Peter dropped his eyes, and said nothing for a few moments. Then he said, in a low voice, "Did she tell you she's given me a key to her flat?"

"No," said Dad, slowly. "No – but, in one way, at least, I can't say I'm surprised."

Peter looked at him quickly, then away again, but not before Dad had caught the expression in his eyes. He regarded him thoughtfully for a few seconds, then leaned forward purposefully.

"Peter, I want to ask you something," he said. There was no particular change in his tone, but Peter looked at him warily.

"I want to understand what's going on in your head," my father said. "You wouldn't have kept coming to see Jenny if you didn't have some very strong motive for it. If you simply weren't interested, you'd have eased out of her life by now. But you haven't. Yet you seem to me to be" – he paused, to identify the most accurate phrase – "holding back in some way. I think I may understand why, but I was hoping you'd tell me yourself, if I asked you. What *is* Jenny to you?"

Peter was silent for a while. Dad waited, patiently.

"Jenny is…" Peter hesitated, as if having difficulty bringing the words out. "Jenny is – important to me. But…" He trailed to a halt.

Dad decided to help him out.

"You're afraid, aren't you? Peter, what is it you're afraid of? What is it I don't know? Can't you tell me?"

Peter looked at him, and didn't speak at first. But then he began. Hesitantly at first, and fighting down his emotions throughout. But at last he told Dad what he'd already told me. The whole, terrible story.

When he fell silent, my father drew in a deep breath, and thought for some seconds.

"I – see," he said slowly.

"I – I care about Jenny," Peter said, looking at him anxiously. "A lot. I don't want to lose her" – he hesitated for a fraction of a second over the description – "her friendship…"

My father knows a euphemism when he hears one, though he forbore to remark.

"But I don't want her caring too much about me," Peter went on. "In case—"

My father shook his head.

"Much too late to worry about that," he said matter-of-factly. "I doubt she'll say anything if you don't, but I know my daughter very well. Let me tell you something about her. Somehow, between us, my wife and I managed to create a very remarkable person. I would say that, wouldn't I? But it's true. Though I didn't realize it fully until after she married Alex. It soon became evident that he had problems, quite fundamental ones. She was very young to be dealing with that kind of thing – too young, some people might have thought. Young people can be quite remarkably self-centred, even when they love. But what I learned about Jenny, as I watched how things went, was that when she commits her love, it's outgoing. With Alex, she didn't complain about all the things he couldn't give her, didn't have it within him to give. Or not often, anyway, though sometimes she did confide in us. But where others might have given up on the relationship because they weren't getting what they wanted out of it, she chose to concentrate on what she could give, not what she could get. Acknowledged his difficulties, but focused on his good qualities. Of which he did have many, I can assure you. And because of that the marriage survived, and was even happy, right up to the end."

"Do you think his death was an accident, or deliberate?" Peter asked, carefully.

My father shook his head heavily.

"I don't know. I shall never know. What I am sure of is that it wasn't because of any failing in their relationship. But" – he looked at Peter directly – "the reason I'm telling you all this is because I can see – I *know* – that things are already past the point where you could hope she doesn't care 'too much' about you."

Peter's face, as Dad later described it to me, was a curious mix of joy and distress. He held his head between his hands, clasping at his skull as if it was trying to burst outwards.

"What am I gonnae do?" he pleaded. "What if he—" He bit down on what he was saying. And my father realized what that was.

"You're afraid Lesser might use her as a way to get to you, aren't you?" he said softly, unable to mask his own reaction to the possibility.

Peter raised miserable eyes to his, and they gazed at each other for long moments. At last my father spoke.

"I don't see there's anything you can do about your feelings or hers," he said quietly. "Things have gone beyond that. But there's something you can do. The only thing you can do, now."

Peter gestured with his head as if to say, *What?*

"Stay away from her, you mean?" he asked, anguished.

My father shook his head.

"Catch him, Peter. Stop him. It's more vital than ever. Not just because of your wife and child. For Jenny's sake. And even more, I think, for your own. That's the only way you can protect Jenny now. From all of it."

And instead of crying out, *What do you think I've been* trying *to do?*"– as he would have been quite justified in doing – Peter looked at my father and nodded, slowly, as if making a vow.

At that point the phone rang out in the hall.

"Excuse me," said my father, and went to answer it.

"Hello?" he said.

"Dad, it's me." My voice sounded in his ear. "I'm home. You haven't got Peter with you, by any chance? I seem to have mislaid him."

"Yes, he's here," Dad assured me. "Do you want him back?"

"Only if you've finished with him." He could hear I was smiling. "How did he end up down there?"

"Your mother lured him down with promises of lunch," Dad explained.

"She there, too?"

"Gone back to her proofing. A deadline is beginning to loom, so she left us to our own devices."

"Oh, right. Well, no hurry, but tell Peter, when he's ready to come back up, I'm here."

"I'll tell him," Dad promised, and hung up.

He went back into the lounge.

"I'm sure you heard that," he observed mildly, resuming his seat. "Jenny asked me to let you know she's back."

Peter was searching his face, still intent on the last thing he had said before my interruption.

"Are you sure you don't want me away, Richard?" he pressed anxiously. "Away from Jenny?"

Dad looked him soberly.

"No father worth his salt wants his daughter in difficulty, or in danger," he said. "But nor does he want her to sacrifice her friends – her real friends – for anything other than the most extreme of reasons. I do not" – he weighed his words carefully – "consider that that situation has yet been reached. I should be most sorry to lose you as a friend, Peter. Not just as Jenny's friend, but as a friend of our family. As a friend of mine." His tone didn't change as he voiced the accolade, but he marked the effect of its delivery on Peter's expression.

There was a short silence. Then Peter stood up.

"Well, I'll – I'll go back up, then," he said, a little at a loss as to what to say.

"I'm glad you came down," Dad said. "I've appreciated the opportunity for this conversation. And the chance to get better acquainted."

"Yeh. Me, too," said Peter, and started to leave. When he'd got halfway through the door, he paused and turned back, his great, dark eyes locked on Dad's face.

"I *will* take care of her," he vowed, urgently.

"You don't need to tell me that," said my father gently. "I already know."

A week or so after Peter had gone back – to his own flat, and to work – Craig got in touch with me. The new school term had started, and his Media Studies teacher had set them a fresh project to work on, which would involve the whole scripting, shooting and editing process from beginning to end. The film had to be no more than three minutes long, and it had to be a documentary of some kind.

He was a little awkward over coming out with it, but essentially what he wanted to ask me was, could he make his documentary about me? Working in the library? Could I find out if he'd be allowed to film me at work? Or, if he couldn't get permission to come out and film during the school day, which covered my usual working hours, was there some other time we could do it?

I was charmed by the diffidence with which he presented the request; I was aware, from what Jane had told me, that he had a bit of a crush on me, and I'm not too proud to admit I was rather touched by that. I was happy to help him, provided my line manager at the library was willing, so I promised him I'd find out what she thought of the idea.

"He'd probably just want to come in and film me doing a bit of stuff like putting books back on the shelves, processing new stock, giving advice on using the computers," I said to Elizabeth. "Taking books back in and issuing them out. All the standard stuff. I could come back and do that sort of thing later in the day, after work? He might not be able to come until after school in any case. If we made sure we weren't in anybody's way...?"

She considered, then nodded.

"Yes, I don't see why not," she said. "As long as you weren't using any of the computers when we or the customers needed them." She regarded me with a twinkle in her eye. "It'd be good advertising for the library. Might get some of his classmates away from their screens and back to reading real books, you never know!"

"Optimist," I grinned.

But it meant I was able to go back to Craig and tell him that as far as the library and I were concerned, the project was on a green light, so it was up to him what he sorted out with his teacher. As he'd suspected, he wasn't allowed out to film in school hours – that part of the project came under the heading of homework – but we could do it after school. Plus he'd rope Sophie in to play the role of someone using the enquiry desk – whether she wanted to do it or not, was the feeling I got, suppressing my amusement.

"What about someone needing help with the computer?" I asked. "Sophie wouldn't be convincing casting for that. Nobody's going to believe in an IT-illiterate thirteen year old! Would you like me to see if Mum or Dad would do it for you?"

Even over the phone, I could sense his grin.

"He's a teacher. He might not like to be seen being helped to use a computer," he chuckled.

"He's not a teacher anymore," I reminded him. "And I still reckon he'd be up for it, if you needed him to be. Let me know if you want me to ask him."

"Could I – could I meet you at the library on Saturday some time? It's" – he stumbled over the admission, slightly embarrassed by it – "it's been a while since I was last there. I'd kind of need to do some location research..."

184

I smiled to myself.

"Of course. How about twelve? We might be able to hunt up a decent lunch after that, if you'd like?"

I could almost hear the way he was striving not to sound too pleased.

"Yeh, that'd be fine," he said, with studied casualness. "Twelve, Saturday. See you then."

Twelve, Saturday, turned out to be the moment Ben took a call from DI Lorna Templeman.

"Hello, Temp!" he greeted her. "It's been a while. How's life in Homicide and Serious Crime?"

"Got something I need to ask you about," she said tersely, ignoring the pleasantry. "Can you come? Now?"

"Where?"

"Battersea." Ben wrote down the address she gave him.

"On my way," he said.

"Oh, Ben—"

"Yeah?"

"Bring Peter, if he's there. He might want to know about this." She rang off.

Ben looked across at Peter. Peter caught the movement in his peripheral vision and looked back at him, antennae suddenly a-quiver.

"Temp's got something she wants me to see," Ben said, standing up and retrieving his jacket from the back of his chair. "And she seems to think you ought to be there. Not going to disappoint the lady, are you?" He walked out without so much as looking back to see if Peter was following.

It had been a productive visit to the library. I'd shown Craig round, and told him what was encompassed in the job; we'd discussed possible shot setups for some of the things I did. Quite a lot of the admin tasks were done on computer, so we concluded that a voiceover might be the answer to describing some of them: sending out overdue notifications, researching availability for inter-library loans, that kind of thing. He'd taken a lot of photos for reference, and I'd briefly introduced him to Elizabeth, who had been very encouraging in her endorsement of his project. He was bubbling with enthusiasm as we left.

"D'you still fancy lunch, before you go home?" I offered, as we walked out of the library. "Or will it destroy all your street cred with your mates, if we get spotted together?" I halted on the pavement, awaiting his decision.

He grinned, and shrugged. "I'll risk it."

"Good man! There's a pretty good place I know, not far from here.

185

That do you? Okay, then. So – I take it the photos'll help with the storyboarding?" I enquired, as we began walking.

He pulled a face. "Yeah. That's the bit of the project I like least. It's quite hard getting what you can see in your head sketched out, sometimes."

"I presume you just do a rough version first, though, don't you? I mean, it doesn't have to be perfect, does it? Just the general idea? Or does he expect you to get the artwork very detailed?"

"As detailed as I can get it," he confirmed, without enthusiasm. "I just wish I was a better artist."

"Don't worry too much. I expect it's the ideas he's after. If you get into a real job doing this, they'd have a specialist storyboarder working from the script anyway, wouldn't they? And if you do end up as a cameraman, you'll be working from someone else's storyboarding, not your own."

"Yeah, but I've still got to do it for now," he pointed out, slightly plaintively.

"Well, I think—"

And at that point our conversation was abruptly terminated as, completely without warning, everything around us erupted in a blur of violence.

When Peter and Ben arrived, Detective Inspector Templeman – inevitably and universally known to her colleagues as Temp – was there to greet them. Booted and suited in disposable coveralls, they ducked under the cordon tape wreathing the perimeter of the crime scene and walked toward where she was standing in the open doorway of an empty shop premises. She was keeping the muscles of her face fairly successfully expressionless, but the look in her eyes told a different story. Temp by name, but not by nature; she was an experienced officer, and had been in Murder Investigation for almost ten years, so whatever was making her look like that wasn't going to be good.

"In here," she said briefly. "And I hope you haven't had your lunch yet."

Peter exchanged a grim glance with Ben before he scanned the shabby facade of the tiny, ancient shop. The *To Let* sign pasted onto the boarded-up window was weathered almost to the point of unreadability. No one had been taking any notice of this place for years.

But someone had found a use for it now.

They followed Templeman inside, through the shop itself, past the stairs which implied a flat on the floor above, and through into what had once presumably been the stockroom, pausing to make way with a nod of acknowledgement to the pathologist who was just coming in the opposite direction, having completed such of his job as he could do at the scene.

Dust-laden, splintered shelving lined the walls on both sides the entire length of the room, which led from the door they had come in by to the one at the back that allowed exit from the building.

Or would have done, had it not been for what was lying on the floor in front of it, partially propped against it. Now they knew why Temp had that sick look in her eyes. Peter flinched, and even Ben, who'd seen most things in the course of his career, involuntarily snapped out a profanity.

"Hardly looks human anymore, does it?" Temp commented, striving for professional detachment.

"Do you know which human it was, before that happened to it?" Ben growled.

"We think so. But I thought you might be able to confirm it for me quicker than the pathologist can. I think you know him."

"His own mother wouldn't know *that*," Ben snorted.

"What if I were to tell you it was Jimmy Ademola?"

Peter had heard of him — he was a minor member of a Nigerian gang that dealt mostly in drug trafficking — but had never encountered him personally. Ben, however, had, and took another look at the thing on the floor.

"That's Jimmy Ademola?" he demanded.

"We think so," Temp repeated.

Ben continued to stare, then nodded again, slowly.

"Could be," he said. "Hard to tell, but — yeah, could be…"

"What made you call us in?" Peter asked.

"Thought you ought to know," said Temp. "He was a courier. Only he decided to go into business for himself. Thought he could take a few bags and no one'd know the difference. Only someone did. And this was the result."

"So why do we want to know?" Ben growled.

"Thing is, that 'someone' didn't wait for us to find him," Temp went on, as if he hadn't interrupted. "We got a tip-off. Supposedly anonymous, but we're pretty sure who it is, even though we can't prove it. And our intel is the news is already doing the rounds among the gangs."

"So who's the someone?" Peter asked harshly, already suspecting the answer.

Temp looked at him.

"Guess," she said. "Just guess."

Chapter 18

Toward the end of the afternoon, I rang Peter.

"What's up?" he asked quickly; I sometimes texted him, but didn't usually ring him during working hours. Which I'll grant were a bit difficult to predict in his case. I had to be careful about my answer; I didn't want to set his professional antenna quivering.

"It's just... I don't know if you were thinking of coming over tonight, but just in case you were, I thought I'd better tell you I – well, I've not had a particularly good day. So I thought I'd get an early night tonight. Do you mind?"

"Why?" he demanded. "Has something happened?"

So much for not alerting the professional antenna.

"Well, like I said," I temporized. "Not a good day. I'm not feeling a hundred per cent at the moment. But don't worry. I'll feel better tomorrow."

"Jenny, are you all right?" He sounded quite sharp.

"D'you want to come over tomorrow evening and prove it to yourself?" I suggested, simulating a teasing tone.

"Yeh," he said flatly.

"Okay. When you want. You've got the key, after all. See you tomorrow. When I've had a good night's sleep. Bye." I ended the call. I felt a bit uneasy about misleading him like that, but I didn't want to tell him anything over the phone. What had happened had only been bad luck, after all, and he had enough to worry about without adding me to his list. I didn't want him reading more into it than was really there.

What I hadn't taken into account was that he was going to find out because of the phone call Craig had made to his father earlier.

Alan was alone in his office, head down in administration, when his mobile rang. His attention still focused on the paperwork in front of him, pen poised to continue the margin notes he was making, he glanced at the call display and frowned momentarily before he answered.

"Craig, this had better be important," he said sternly. "I've told you before about ringing me at work—"

"Dad, it's Jenny!" The stress and anxiety in his son's voice instantly got his full attention.

"What's happened?" he asked sharply.

"She's – they've taken her to hospital…" Craig was audibly fighting to keep his voice calm. "I think she's all right, but – they wanted to make sure…"

"What's happened?" Alan asked again, tautly.

"Well, we'd done the stuff at the library – we were going for lunch – and we were just" – his voice wobbled slightly, then he fought it back – "walking along the street, and – and all of a sudden we were in the middle of a fight!"

"What do you mean, in the middle of a fight?" Alan's pen dropped to his desk unheeded as he sat bolt upright, quite unaware of the fact that he'd done so.

"These four blokes came charging out of an alley, or something, and they were fighting each other – and – I don't know how it happened, Dad, but there they were, all round us, and they started hitting *us*."

"Are you all right?" Alan demanded sharply.

"Me? Yeh, yeh, I'm fine – I just got pushed to the ground. But Jenny – she got hit in the face, and one of them pushed her against the wall, really hard, and she fell down. Then they ran off. I phoned for an ambulance, and they've just taken her away. They don't think she's seriously hurt, but they said they'd make sure."

"Where are you now?" Alan snapped.

"I'm still here – where it happened," said Craig. "There's a couple of your blokes here with me. I told the 999 woman I wanted police as well. There're some other people here who saw it, and they want us all to make statements. But I thought…" His voice wavered again, then came back to full strength. "I thought I ought to tell you. And Jenny said—"

"What did Jenny say?"

"She said – not to tell Peter. She didn't want to worry him. But she didn't say not to tell you. So – I thought I ought to."

"You did right," Alan told him, his mind racing while he strove to keep calm, and to convey to his son, without openly saying so, how proud he was of him. "Does your mother know?" he added quickly.

"No, I haven't… I rang you first," Craig said uncertainly.

"Good. Don't worry, I'll warn her. You're sure you're all right?"

"Honest, Dad." He wasn't, entirely; he might not have been hurt, but he was clearly shocked – though no more than that. He would be all right, Alan felt sure, once he'd got over that. He and Jane between them would see to it, once he got home.

"I'll try to get away early today," he said. "Check you out for myself."

"I keep telling you I'm all right, Dad," Craig said, with a very teenage touch of exasperation in his voice. "What about Jenny, though? And Peter?"

"I'll get in touch with her, and then we'll see about Peter," said Alan. "Don't you go worrying about it. Will you be all right for getting home? If not, I'll get someone to give you a lift. In fact, hand me over to whoever you're with, will you?"

"Okay, Dad. See you later." He heard Craig passing on the request, then spoke to the officer who took the phone, finding it was Sam Lambert, whom he knew slightly. Sam reassured him about Craig's wellbeing, and promised to drive him home when they were finished with him, with all the respect due to a Detective Chief Inspector making a request of that nature.

Alan phoned Jane next, then me. I assured him I was as well as could be expected, and I'd already been in touch with Peter, but without telling him what had happened – yet.

"I've got to go and give a statement tomorrow," I said.

"Are you going to be all right to do that?"

"Yes, of course. I'll freely admit I'm glad I don't have to go into work tomorrow, though. I think I need a bit of recovery time. I have this tendency to weepiness when I've been under stress, you'll remember?"

"I remember," he agreed; I could tell he was smiling. "Well, you look after yourself."

"I will," I promised. "What about Craig? Is he all right?"

"Bit shaken, of course. I've only spoken to him on the phone, but he sounds as if he will be. All right, I mean. He was more worried about you than he was about himself."

"Oh, bless him! Well, tell him I'm going to be all right. Bit bruised, but still fairly functional, on the whole."

"Okay, I'll tell him. He'll want to know that." Then something else struck him. "Are you still at the hospital?"

"Yes," I confirmed ruefully. "The 'accident' bit of A and E can be achieved very quickly. The wheels grind somewhat slower in the area of 'emergency'! Still, I daresay they'll get round to letting me go before I reach pensionable age."

"So how are you getting home? You're not driving yourself?"

"No, Dad's coming for me. He should be here any minute."

"All right, then. And I'll ring you again tomorrow. See how you are."

"You needn't," I demurred, "but – thanks."

"You look after yourself, Jenny," he repeated, and ended the call.

It was Sophie who blew the gaff. Without meaning to, of course. But she didn't know I'd been hoping to break it to Peter myself, and gently. Instead, when he turned up unannounced in the early evening, and she opened the door to him, he could see at a glance that something was up. Her colour was high, her eyes shining with excitement.

"What's going on?" he demanded, as he came in past her.

"Craig's been in a fight!" she announced, almost proudly.

Peter's frown contained more than an element of surprise; Craig wasn't that sort of boy.

"Who with?" he enquired.

"Some blokes in Croydon," said Sophie, bursting with self-importance at knowing something her adored second cousin didn't know. "And Jenny had to go to hospital!"

Her excitement died abruptly as Peter rounded on her with a look in his eyes she'd never seen before.

"Jenny? What's Jenny got to do with it? What happened?" he demanded harshly.

He was suddenly a stranger. Sophie blanched, but before she could answer, Alan appeared from the living room.

"It's all right, Sophie," he said. "I'll tell Peter all about it."

"Alan, what's going on? What's happened to Jenny?" Peter stalked towards him.

Behind him, Sophie stared at her father with huge, anxious eyes.

"I'm sorry," she quavered. "I didn't mean…"

Her father pushed past Peter and came to her. He put his arms round her and dropped a kiss on the top of her head.

"It's all right," he repeated. "Don't worry. I'll tell him. You go back in with your mother and Craig. We'll be there in a minute."

She nodded tremulously and retreated into the living room.

Peter locked eyes with Alan.

"Tell me what?"

The sound of the front door opening and closing – with a jerk and a slam respectively – made me start, though I immediately realized who it must be. My heart sank slightly; I'd hoped to avoid this, or at least postpone it until tomorrow. But no hope of that, now. This was the down side of his having his own key. I went very still for a few moments, my hands submerged in the washing-up bowl, my dinner plate in one of them, the dishcloth in the other. Then I looked back down into the bowl and went on with what I was doing, only glancing up briefly as Peter stalked through the living room door into the kitchen.

"Why didn't you tell me?" he demanded angrily.

"Because I had the feeling you'd be like this about it," I said, not looking at him as I rinsed the washed plate under the tap and put it into the drying rack. "How did you find out?"

"Did you seriously think I wouldn't?" he said in a tone very close to a sneer.

"I told Craig not to tell you," I said a little crossly, disappointed.

"He didn't," said Peter flatly. "But he did tell his parents. And his sister," he added meaningfully.

"Oh," I said slowly. "Well – I suppose he would've… Look, what I didn't want" – I changed what I'd been going to say – "what I didn't want was you worrying about me when there wasn't any real need for it. It was just an accident, and it's only bruises…"

"Show me," he ordered, and reached out toward me, hooking a finger under my chin. The gentleness of the pressure he used to turn my face fully round to him was at odds with the harshness of his tone. He swore as he took in the extent of the damage: the bruising and abrasions on right temple and cheek, the swollen and already blackening eye, the small cut on the cheekbone, held together with butterfly stitches.

"Remember how you told me in Inverness you were going for all the colours of the rainbow?" I said, trying to be casual. "I think, if you give me a few days, I might be able to give you a run for your money on that one, don't you?"

He ignored that.

"Alan said something about your back, as well," he said, still in that harsh tone.

I sighed, dried my hands, and turned my back to him, lifting my blouse – a loose-fitting one – for a few moments so he could see me from the waist to just under my bra strap. A fairly extensive area of bruising where my assailant had thrown me against the wall, but at least no broken skin.

"So there you have it," I said, letting the blouse drop, and turning back to face him. "I'll be stiff and sore for a few days, but no real harm done."

"Tell me exactly what happened," he demanded.

I gave him more or less the same version of events Craig had given Alan. "It was just an accident," I assured him. "One of those 'wrong time, wrong place' things. I'll be all right, Peter – really, I will be."

"You're gonnae have to be more careful—" he started, heatedly – and all of a sudden it was more than I could bear. My eyes filled, my face crumpled, and I was crying. I covered my eyes with my hands, but that didn't stem the tears abruptly flooding down my cheeks.

He exclaimed, realizing how much he was upsetting me. One step forward, and his arms were round me.

"It's just reaction," I sobbed. "Shock, or something. Sorry! I'm sorry, Peter!"

"*I'm* sorry," he muttered contritely. "I didn't think... I..."

"It's all right," I wept. "It's all *right*..."

I seemed to reassure him, but after I'd calmed down I went on trying to do so until he left, because, even though he appeared to relax a little, underneath he was still tense; he did his best, but it didn't make him especially good company. I assumed it was because he was worried about me, so I was ready to excuse him. I had no idea that in his mind, visions of me having been attacked kept merging with the image of the battered corpse of Jimmy Ademola. If I had, I'd have understood a lot more than I did.

It was close to midnight by the time Peter got back to Brixton. Just about every parking space was already occupied; he had to leave his car quite a distance from the flat, and after the day he'd had, the walk seemed particularly onerous. He approached his front door with a heavy, tired tread. Listlessly he fished out his door key and turned it in the lock.

As he went in, something on the floor rustled. He looked down, and in the dim light of the hallway saw a folded sheet of paper caught under the bottom of the door. He bent down and freed it, then shut the door behind him before unfolding it.

He stood very still; he could almost feel the blood leaving his face as he read the single line of print. The paper crumpled in the suddenly convulsive grip of his fingers.

Dear, dear! How unfortunate! Was she very much hurt, Peter? it said.

"So it wasn't an accident, after all," said Alan grimly. He looked again at the paper, angling it to the early morning light coming in through his office window, and muttered something blasphemous under his breath as he re-read the message. He could almost hear Lesser's voice, posing the question with urbane but counterfeit concern. He looked up at Peter. "Have you told her?"

Peter shook his head.

"Then don't," Alan advised him. "You were the target here, not her. Don't give her something else to worry about."

"I wasn't going to," said Peter brusquely.

Alan got up and opened the door.

"Ben," he said, and jerked his head. He left the door open and went to sit behind his desk.

Ben came in.

"Close the door, will you?" Alan said.

Ben did so. "What's up?" he enquired.

"Lesser's on to Jenny."

Ben looked sharply at Peter, but Peter was staring at the floor. Ben's lips tightened.

Briefly, concisely, Alan told him the whole story. At the end of it, he handed the paper to him.

Ben scanned it, and swore, briefly and bitterly. He looked up quickly. "What about Craig? He all right?"

"Yeah," said Alan, expelling a heavy breath like a sigh. "Or will be, once he's calmed down. He got pretty pumped up about it."

"And Jenny?" Ben looked at Peter again, but he was still staring down at the floor, and didn't respond.

"She'll be all right, too," Alan answered for him. "Nothing worse than bruising."

There was a short silence, in which the words 'This time...' hovered like harbingers.

"What do you want me to do?" Ben asked gruffly.

"CCTV," said Alan tersely. "I want to see exactly what happened."

"On it," Ben agreed. He put the paper down on the desk, gave Peter another searching look, then left.

It was early afternoon when he caught Alan's eye through the glass of his office, and crooked a finger at him. Alan responded with alacrity. Peter, slumped in his seat, looked up quickly as he saw Alan heading for Ben's desk.

"You, as well," Ben said to him, tersely. "You'll need to see this."

They stood, one either side of him, looking over his shoulder at the screen. The view they were looking at showed a wide angle shot of both sides of the street outside the library, which was about thirty yards beyond the camera point, on the right. Two figures came out of it and paused on the pavement, making other pedestrians divert around them.

"That's Jenny and Craig," said Ben. "But look there." His thick forefinger pointed at the opposite pavement. Four young men, anonymous in hoodies, were grouped there, one facing the library, the others facing him in a loose semi-circle. When Jenny and Craig turned and began to walk toward the camera, the first youth made a gesture with his head in the same direction. Immediately all four of them turned and began to walk along their side of the road, tracking the oblivious pair, and carefully keeping slightly behind them.

Both groups vanished out of the view of the camera, but Ben switched to another shot, from a different camera, showing the four youths still trailing Jenny and Craig. In the next shot Jenny and Craig were heading away from the camera, still at a leisurely pace, and at first it seemed as if the pursuers had vanished. But then the group of four came into view, still on the opposite side of the road; they had picked up their pace, drawing well ahead. Suddenly they ran across the road, dancing somewhat dangerously through the busy traffic, back onto the same side as the two conversing figures. Just four dark blurs in the distance, which vanished as they abruptly turned to the left and out of view of the camera.

"That's where the alley is, where they came out of," said Ben. He looked up at Alan, then at Peter. "You won't enjoy the next bit, either of you."

Peter said nothing. His face was set in hard lines. Ben glanced at Alan for confirmation that he should go on, and got it with a curt nod.

Ben pursed his lips and switched to the next shot. This camera was on the opposite side of the road to where all the protagonists now were, about eighty feet from the dark maw of the alley. Jenny and Craig, oblivious, were approaching it, obviously engaged in animated conversation. Nothing could be seen in the gloom of the alley entrance. Then, as the two of them drew level with it, four figures came bursting out in a tangle of arms and legs. Three of them surrounded Jenny, who automatically threw her arms up in front of her in a defensive gesture. The fourth cannoned into Craig, making him stumble heavily backwards. He recovered himself and came forward again in a rush, but the same man deliberately shoved him backwards, so hard that this time he crashed heavily to the pavement.

Peter only noticed this with a fraction of his attention. The rest was on Jenny, in the middle of the fracas. It was only too clear that the youths weren't fighting each other at all; they were simply out to get her. His guts clenched as he saw the punch land on her face that sent her reeling into the arms of the man behind her, who caught her and swung her round backwards, like a travesty of a folk dance, and slammed her, full force, against the wall and its iron downpipe. She doubled up in pain, sliding down against the brickwork to end up hunched in a sitting position against the wall.

By this time Craig was on his feet again, yelling something and launching himself at the attackers with no evident thought for his own safety. All the nearby pedestrians were staring, but only two came to help; two young men, following in Craig's wake. The four youths hesitated, glancing at each other. One of them gave a brief nod and a sideways flick of his head; all four instantly turned on their heels and fled. Pursued and pursuers vanished out of shot.

A few of the onlookers came over to cluster around Jenny, still slumped against the wall, but, as always, the majority of passers-by chose to ignore the fact that anything had happened, and kept walking. Even among the few that gathered, nobody appeared to do anything until Craig ran back into view, pushing through them to drop to his knees next to Jenny. He spoke to her, and she shook her head, wincing. Craig got out his phone, thumbing it urgently, and put it to his ear. While he was speaking, the two men who had given chase came back to join the group. He looked up at them, but they both shrugged, and one of them shook his head. He threw up a hand in acknowledgement, and went on speaking into the phone.

Ben stopped the playback. There was a short, unpleasant silence.

"Planned," said Alan grimly. "Waiting for them. For her, anyway. Waited to see which way they went, got ahead of them, ambushed them. Every bit of it, planned."

Peter remained silent.

Ben glanced at him, face impassive but raging inwardly. As ever, nothing they could use. Four anonymous youths, no identifying features, faces hidden, all vanished. And even if they'd caught any of them, there wouldn't have been anything tying them to Lesser. There never was. Everything known, but nothing provable. Again.

Chapter 19

I'd been to give my statement that morning. Jane had rung up to find out how I was, and when I'd assured her I was as well as could be expected in the circumstances, she'd volunteered, since Craig had to do the same, to pick me up so that we could go and do it together.

"That way you can let him see you're all right," she told me. "You'd be doing me a favour. He's been on a real downer today over not being able to do more to stop it."

"But he couldn't have!" I exclaimed, indignant that he should think anything of the sort. "He ought to be proud of what he did do, not having a go at himself over what he didn't!"

"Of course he should," Jane agreed. "But he won't have it from me. He might from you, though."

So that was what we did. For all that his father was a DCI, it was Craig's first experience of being in a police station officially, so to speak, so although he tried to hide it, underneath, in a rather endearingly teenage male way, he was quite excited about the whole thing. A new life experience for him, and one with a bit of street cred, I supposed. For myself, having been through the process before, and remembering how painstaking I'd had to be, I didn't especially feel up to it; I was still slightly in shock, probably. Still, it had to be done. So I did it, and did my best. For the sake of the young constable tasked with dealing with me, as much as anything; I got the impression she, like Craig, was fairly new at this, and did my best to be helpful for her.

Back home, I didn't feel much like lunch, and went to bed for a while in the middle of the afternoon; I was shocked to find I'd slept for three hours when I awoke. Though that wouldn't hurt; it had probably done me a lot of good, and I might be on better form for when Peter came over, which I expected would be before too long. We'd been due a sailing lesson today, but of course we hadn't gone. I hoped he'd remembered to cancel it, and not forfeited his money. Nevertheless, I hadn't expected him to be as late as he turned out to be. When the evening began to draw in, I concluded that he must have been called into work, Sunday or no Sunday.

In point of fact it was about half-past eight – just past sunset – when he finally arrived.

I'd been down to put a rubbish bag into the wheelie bin, and had just reached the top of the steps again when I heard a car turning into our drive. I turned. The car was Peter's.

From the moment he emerged, my antenna was on alert and quivering. The violence with which he slammed the car door. The tense set of his shoulders. The way he replied to my greeting with nothing but a surly grunt. All clear danger signals that, once again, something was not as it should be. He took the steps two at a time, barely glancing at me, and pushed past me into the flat. I felt my brows contract as I followed him in at a more modest pace, but I made sure the frown was gone from my face by the time I'd located him in the living room, flinging his jacket over the back of the sofa with an abrupt gesture and throwing himself roughly into a seat.

"How're things?" I enquired carefully.

"Fine." Which was so clearly untrue it was hardly worth commenting on.

"Have you eaten?"

"No."

"Do you want anything now?"

"No."

My attempts at normal conversation were wilting in the face of such an unrelenting barrier of clipped monosyllables. I'd never seen him quite like this; I wondered what the cause was. Something, I suspected, was not going well at work. Which meant I couldn't ask.

"So what do you want to do?"

"Nothing." He said it curtly, without looking at me.

I thought of Alan, saying, *"Bear with him, Jenny. Be patient…"*

"Well, that's easy enough," I responded lightly, lying through my teeth. Nothing about this conversation was easy. "Do you want a coffee while we're doing it?"

At that his glance flicked toward me, and I thought I detected a touch of shamefacedness in it.

"Yeh, okay," he muttered.

"Hold your breath, then," I said, summoning up a slightly forced smile. "Won't be long."

I left him there, and went into the kitchen, speculating furiously, and anxiously, on what could have happened to put him in this sort of mood. When I went back in he was still slumped in the armchair, staring at the floor with brooding eyes. He took the mug I offered and immediately took a large swallow, so fast that he must have been in no small danger of burning his mouth with that much hot liquid. But if he had, he didn't show it; indeed, I'd hardly had my first sip before he'd emptied the mug with another couple of gulps.

"How're you feeling?" An expression of concern delivered with all the delicacy of a machine gun.

"Sore. But all right apart from that…"

"D'you wannae go for a walk?" It was not so much a question as a demand, and he didn't look at me as he said it, his Scots accent noticeably broader than usual.

I felt anxious. The aura he was radiating had so much anger, so much frustration, in it, I felt as if virtually anything I said or did might be the wrong thing. Clearly something was seriously disturbing him, and if he thought that going for a walk would help, I wasn't going to do anything other than agree. But I'd never felt so uncomfortable in his presence.

I put my virtually untouched coffee down and rose.

"If that's what you want to do, yes. I'll get my coat," I said.

When we got out to the road, I asked carefully, "Where do you want to go?"

"Don't know," was the terse reply. "Anywhere."

"There's a footpath up that way that goes alongside a stream," I suggested, gesturing.

"Yeh, fine." Before the last monosyllable was out he was turning on his heel and stalking along the road. I had to walk faster than was comfortable for me, in order to catch up and keep up with him. After a few moments he seemed to realize that, and slowed his pace a little. But he didn't speak to me, hardly even looked at me.

Dusk was falling as we walked; the street lights were on, and so were those along the footpath, which turned off the main road between two of the houses; if you didn't know it was there, you'd hardly notice it. We didn't encounter anyone else, not even when we reached the stream; the footway along it was also well lit, and usually it was a popular route with dog walkers and joggers. At this particular time, on this particular evening, it was uncharacteristically deserted.

Peter turned to the left, without consulting me, and continued to walk, but now much more slowly. Almost as if he'd lost his way, or his sense of urgency, or whatever it was that had been driving him. His body language had changed, too; his head was bowed, his shoulders slumped. Then he stopped entirely, and just stood, staring at the tarmac of the path.

I took the extra pace or two that allowed me to turn and stand in front of him.

"Peter," I implored. "Talk to me! What's the matter?"

He stood mute and unmoving.

"Peter, please! You're worrying me!"

His head flew up and he looked at me, really looked at me, for the first time.

"Yeh? Well, maybe I'm worried about *you*. Had you thought of that?"

"But why? I've told you I'm all right. What's the *matter*?"

There was a long pause before he answered.

"Not being fair to you," he muttered.

Sudden irritation flared inside me. Perhaps because he was frightening me, and fear and anger link so easily. I wanted to help, but he wasn't letting me, and it was beginning to make me resentful. I'd had too much of that with Alex, and I didn't like it.

"Well, since I'm clearly not in possession of facts you apparently are, that's hard for me to comment on," I said, rather tartly.

"Maybe there're things you shouldn't know," he said belligerently.

"Maybe there are!" I snapped. "But then, maybe there're things I should know, too! So why're you being like this? Why aren't you telling me what they are?"

With a violence that both startled and frightened me, he seized me, his hands gripping my shoulder joints, the fingers digging into my flesh, and leaned down to press his forehead against mine with painful force. I instinctively stiffened my neck muscles, to stop my head being forced too far backwards; he might have been preparing to wrestle with me. He was certainly wrestling with something. His eyes were tight shut and his lips parted over clenched teeth, as if he was in pain. His breath hissed out in savage eruptions of sound.

He stayed like that for several seconds. He didn't move, I didn't move. Then, abruptly, he straightened up and released me. The cessation of the pressure against the bone of my forehead was sheer physical relief.

There was a long silence. I stared up at him, but I couldn't see him clearly; he had his back to the nearest street light and his face above mine was in shadow. I realized I was trembling.

It must have shown, because he suddenly uttered a sound of distress deep in his throat, and for a moment covered his face with his hands.

"I'm sorry," he said, his voice muffled. "I'm so sorry."

His anguish was evident and real, and almost instantly my fear and my lingering anger evaporated in a rush of concern. Instinctively I reached out my hand and laid it on his sleeve. He dropped his hands from his face, and I could see the gleam of his eyes in the shadows as he stared at me. Then he seized me in a fierce embrace. I couldn't quite suppress a gasp of pain as he gripped me around my bruised shoulders, but he was so wrapped up in his own distress that I don't think he heard it.

"I'm sorry," he said again, whispering into my hair.

I hugged him back, that way trying to convey my forgiveness, my anxiety, my care.

After about half a minute his arms briefly tightened, then released me. I looked up at him anxiously.

"We'd better go back," he muttered, turning for home.

Neither of us said a word on the way back, though it was a different kind of silence from the one on the outward journey. When we got to the driveway he stopped by his car, and I wondered if he was simply going to leave. But he didn't. Instead, he walked slowly forward to the steps up to the flat, hesitated, then turned and sat down on them, deliberately leaving room for me to join him.

I accepted the implicit invitation, and sat down beside him in the semi-darkness; the street lights, the light emanating from next door's upstairs bedroom window, the general light pollution of a built-up area, all provided a degree of subdued illumination. Both our faces were blurred by shadows; I watched his, and waited for him to speak.

When he did, it was in such a low voice that even if anyone else had been near, they wouldn't have been able to hear him.

"Somebody got murdered yesterday," he said. He bowed his head for a moment, apparently studying his clasped hands, hanging between his knees. He wasn't looking at me, but at least he was talking to me. Communicating. Apologizing, even, perhaps? "An ugly, brutal, savage murder."

"By Lesser?" I whispered, after a pause. I was having a flashback. The November day we'd been walking in the woods. The day he'd told me about a man who'd been beaten nearly to death. "*We lost an informant a couple of days ago...*"

He nodded.

"Won't be able to prove it, of course," he said. "Never can, with him. But he did it. We know he did it. Ordered it, anyway. But there's nothing other than circumstantial."

"Was it someone" – I wasn't sure how to frame the question – "someone known to you?"

"Professionally, you mean? Yeh. A poor devil out on the fringes of one of the other gangs, got in out of his depth. Got in Lesser's way. Like Mike and I did. He doesn't like people in his way. So he takes steps. Like he did with this one." He let out a shuddering breath. "I hope you never have to see a sight like the one I saw yesterday, Jenny. That informant I told you about, got beaten up?" So he'd remembered that, too. "Love taps, compared to that. I—" He tried to keep going, but his voice choked off.

I put my hand on his shoulder, and let it rest there. I began to see why he'd behaved the way he had, why he was so angry. *Fear and anger link so easily.* He'd been so angry because he was so afraid.

201

For me.

Because he'd been reminded, in raw, red terms, just what Lesser could do – had done – and might do again. Though why he should be so worried, I had no idea.

"Then there was what happened to you," he went on. "It just kind of topped off an already bad day. And I suppose" – he hesitated – "I suppose I still haven't got over it."

"Peter!" I reached down, and he had to unclasp his hands as I seized the one nearest to me, his right hand, in a fierce grip. "Don't worry about me! I'll be all right. That was just an accident! It could've happened to anybody!"

Just for a second or two he turned a strange, intense look on me, a wild, hard glitter in his eyes.

"What're you looking like that for?" I demanded, startled.

His lips thinned into a line, and he quickly looked away. He clearly had no intention of answering me, so there was no point in pursuing it, but I didn't like it. What did he—? *No use. Leave it. Say what you were going to say.*

"Look," I said sharply, "don't forget what I told you before! One day, you'll get him. You will get him."

He flung me a glance in which scepticism and irritation were combined – the sort of look any professional has the right to give an amateur who's pronouncing on his specialism – but it still wasn't an expression of wishful thinking on my part; it was something I was sure of, deep down in my soul. Very sure.

"Yes, you will," I said, contradicting the words he hadn't said. "Nobody's luck holds forever! Okay, he's clever, and he's careful, and that's why he's got away with it for so long. But for it to be this long, with all of you working so hard to get him, he has to have had luck, too. And sooner or later it'll run out. Because it must. It does. Good or bad, luck runs out! So one day, he'll make a mistake, at last. Or else something'll happen that's out of his control. And then you'll get him. You'll get him, Peter! I know it! One day, it *will* be over!"

I gripped his hand more tightly, communicating my conviction. And just for a brief moment, his hand responded with a tighter clasp of its own. He covered his forehead and his eyes with the palm of his other hand, and for a while sat motionless, in silence.

When he did speak again, he surprised me.

"Once it is over, I'm gonnae resign," he said in a low voice.

There was a pause. For some reason, I hadn't been expecting that. I waited, my heart hammering.

"It's what I've always been gonnae do. I promised myself. Because

202

that phase of my life'll be over. I will start again. I will rebuild my life. Eventually. But when I do, I don't want the people I care about being hostages to fortune again. I'm not gonnae run that risk. Not ever again. So I'll be needing a change of direction. Different job. Different way of life." He looked at me. "But I can't do it, until it's over. Until we've got him, once and for all. And it's not over."

I nodded. I think he could see that – as far as anyone could, who hadn't been through what he had – I did understand. Or at least accepted his reasoning. He relaxed slightly, and dipped his head in response, as though I'd spoken.

"But it will be," I told him again, firmly.

He let out a muffled snort of laughter, and shook his head.

"You're mad," he said, helplessly.

"Have you only just discovered that?" I demanded with mock censoriousness. "You can't've been paying attention, Mr McLeish!"

"Yeh, I have, actually," he contradicted.

"Well, then, had you noticed how far it is into the evening and you've not yet been fed?" I realized I was still holding his hand, and let it go. "What about an omelette, or something?"

He shook his head again, but not at the offer of the omelette.

"I still think you're mad," he said.

"Oh, definitely. Deep into box-of-frogs territory," I agreed. "But I promise not to put any of them in the omelette. Come on. Eat, then go home and sleep. Tomorrow's another day, Scarlett."

I hope he got more sleep that night than I did. I couldn't stop thinking about what he'd said – or, rather, what he hadn't said. Playing back the look he'd given me when I'd told him that what had happened had been an accident. No agreement, no reassurance. Just that look.

The pointers were percolating through. He knew something I didn't know; he'd as good as admitted that. And he was clearly worried. About me. Or – should that be *for* me...? Link those hints with his personal history, with the way he always checked the street when he arrived – the way we'd met...

I was beginning to get the first inkling of what might be going on. Lying there in the dark, going over and over the scraps of evidence in my mind, I wondered if I was being over-imaginative, over-dramatizing. But then I remembered the last time I'd wondered about that. In the lodge, staring at the wrecked telephone junction box. I hadn't been imagining things then. Maybe I wasn't now.

And if I wasn't? Then I'd no longer be on the periphery of his professional life, where I'd thought of myself as being, until now. I'd be right at the heart of it, with a vengeance.

I drew my duvet tight up under my chin, clutching at it with both hands to keep it there. As if the less of me that was visible, the less likely my suspicions were to be true.

Yeah, right, Jenny. That'll really help.

Except that it didn't, of course.

I was somewhat abstracted for the next couple of days; they even noticed it at work, and Dad definitely did. He asked me if I was all right, and I told him not quite, I did have something on my mind, but I'd talk it over with him if I thought it would help. Not a lie – I've never lied to him, about anything – but an evasion, certainly. Until I knew for sure if my suspicions were true, I had no intention of worrying him or Mum unnecessarily. But not yet could I ask Peter if they were. I was relying on him telling me if there was anything I needed to know. Or maybe even more on Alan, who'd made a promise to that effect up in Scotland; I hoped he'd remembered it, and would keep it. Well, no, that wasn't quite true. I didn't want him to have to keep that promise. Because what I was really – desperately – hoping was that I was mistaken, that my reasoning was all wrong. That the fact neither of them had said anything was simply because there wasn't anything to say. But, somehow, deep down, that wasn't how it felt.

And if it wasn't – if what I suspected was true – what was I going to do?

I had to shelve that line of thought when I went over to see Craig on the Wednesday evening. I'd got in touch to ask him if we needed to do some more planning for his project, but I didn't want him picking up on my preoccupations.

"D'you still want to do it?" he'd blurted, sounding astonished.

"Why not?" I'd said lightly. "Shall I come over, so we can talk about it?"

So I did. I even turned Peter down, when he wanted to come over to me; he wasn't happy at first, until I told him where I was going. Somehow, I didn't feel ready to face him just yet. And Alan wasn't there, which in a strange way was a relief; I ran no risk of having my suspicions confirmed. Not yet, anyway. But Jane was delighted to see me, and made something of a fuss of me. The bruising was turning multicoloured, making it look much worse than it really was.

I had to reassure Craig on that point, too, when we went up to his room to conduct our discussion.

"I'd like to wait another few days till the swelling's gone right down," I said. "And the butterfly stitches are gone. But after that – well, you can keep pretending my left side is my best side. And I'll try to cover the worst of the bruises with makeup."

"Are you sure?" He didn't know whether to be pleased that I still wanted to go ahead with it, or incredulous that I was prepared to be filmed when looking less than at my best.

"Of course! I don't want to derail your project at this stage in the proceedings. Anyway, it'll be a talking point, won't it? Make your film stand out from all the others. You can always tell your teacher some of the library users get violent if they can't find the exact book they want."

He saw the twinkle in my eye, and laughed, in spite of himself. Then he grew serious again.

"One of the girls in my class is pretty good with makeup," he suggested diffidently. "She might even end up doing it professionally. Or wardrobe, maybe. She likes that side of things. If I asked her, she'd probably help…"

"He means Emily," Sophie announced, appearing in the doorway. "He *likes* her," she added, in a very little-sister sort of way.

"Shut up, you," he said, flushing slightly. "She's good with makeup, that's all."

"Hmmm," said Sophie, prolonging the syllable archly. She came in, ignoring her brother's scowl, and plumped herself on the floor at my feet; I was sitting on the edge of Craig's bed, while he occupied the chair in front of his computer.

"Nothing wrong with liking someone, Sophie," I pointed out placidly. "That's how friendships usually start."

"Bet it's not friendship he's thinking about!" she said provocatively.

"Shut *up*!" Craig snarled. "Who asked you in here, anyway?"

"Not a bad thing if he is, you know," I said, still trying to keep the peace. "Friendship isn't as susceptible to hormones, so it's likely to last longer. My husband was my best friend, you know. I just happened to love him, as well. It was a good combination."

"Do you think you'll ever find anybody else?" Sophie asked, rushing in where angels might have feared to tread. At thirteen, many of the realities of life haven't yet sunk in.

I shrugged. "Don't know. It's not as easy as you might think, you know – finding a right person."

"*A* right person?" she queried, picking up on the phrasing. "I thought it was supposed to be *the* right person."

"There's bound to be more than one person in the world who's right in some way or another," I pointed out pragmatically. "The trick is finding even one of them! And, what's more," I added with a grin, "finding them before someone else does."

"But why wouldn't it be easy? There are millions of men about!" She threw her arms dramatically wide to demonstrate just how many there were. Craig glowered at her, definitely unimpressed.

"When you get to my age – which is thirty-five going on thirty-six, you'll remember," I inserted parenthetically, before going on, "what you generally find is that the men who are available are mostly either the ones who don't want to commit to a long-term relationship, or else they haven't made a success of the ones they've had. Neither of which I regard as a sound basis for operations."

"Can't be all of them!" she protested.

"No, not all of them, of course," I agreed. "By far the majority, though, I suspect. But among the rest, I'll grant you, are the ones who are the type who commit, but they've just had bad luck."

"Like Peter," she said.

"Like Peter," I agreed.

She put her head to one side, and regarded me for a moment or two. Then she said, with unexpected gravity, "And like you."

I hadn't seen that coming, but it was true, I realized. I hadn't expected that maturity of insight from her.

"Yes," I agreed. "And like me."

"Well" – Craig cleared his throat, then went on, wanting to inspire optimism, "maybe you'll both get lucky! One day..." he finished awkwardly.

"Maybe," I conceded non-committally. "But not until my film career is over, of course," I went on, lightly. "The acting profession can be very hard on personal relationships – you must know that! So, one thing at a time, I think..."

A couple of days later, I texted Peter.

He was with Alan when he got it. Alan saw him smile as he read it, and enquired lightly, "Something funny?"

"Jenny," said Peter, and handed his phone over so Alan could read the message.

Anniversary of our meeting today. You had a black eye then, I've got one now. Imitation is the sincerest form of flattery.

"She's got a seriously quirky sense of humour, that girl," Alan commented dryly, handing the phone back. "No text-speak, either," he added casually, apropos of nothing. "Everything properly spelled and punctuated to a fare-thee-well."

"I teased her about that once," Peter admitted. "Got read the riot act on how English was the most marvellous language and she was never going to write it anything other than properly, no matter what. And then she pointed out she was the daughter of an English teacher and a proof-reader, and what did I expect?" His tone accurately mimicked the indignation of the original comment. Alan chuckled, then eyed him speculatively.

"'*Anniversary of our meeting today...*' Marking the occasion in any way?"

There was the faintest of gleams in Peter's eye. "Mind your own business," he retorted.

Alan suppressed a smile; that was a 'Yes', then. He wondered exactly how far things had gone between them. Not that he was going to ask. But, with all his heart, he wished them well. And hoped that Lesser wasn't coming up with a way to spoil things. Not today... Though that was something he definitely wasn't going to say aloud. Not least because – from the look on his face as he put his phone away – Peter was probably already thinking the same thing.

That, by the way, was the day I got home from work and found Peter had been making use of his key. When I went into the kitchen, I found a pot plant sitting on the kitchen table that hadn't been there before, with a note.

Thought you might like this. See you later.

It was a geranium. A lemon-scented one.

I didn't usually ring him during the working day, but this felt like a special occasion. I rubbed one of the leaves between my thumb and forefinger, inhaling the scent while I waited for him to pick up.

"Hi," came his voice after a few seconds.

"Hi," I echoed. "Doing anything special?"

"Just tweaking a report."

"Tweak when you're twoken to," I advised him.

He laughed.

"I just wanted to say thank you," I went on. "It smells beautiful."

"S'okay. You said you liked lemon, and I was out your way anyway – for something else – so..."

I couldn't let that pass. "Peter," I said firmly.

"What?"

"Do you remember how I told you that I'd always behave as if I believed you?"

"Yeh," he said, more warily.

"Well, this is one of those times."

He laughed again.

"I'll see you later," I said, and rang off.

Chapter 20

Another couple of weeks went by. Craig shot his footage; Dad gamely stepped up to the plate and did his cameo as a computer user in need of advice. Sophie performed her role, too, though, as I remarked to Jane afterwards, she showed a distressing tendency to argue with the director. I met Emily, and she was not only a nice girl – as I informed Craig, to his great gratification – she was also very good at what she did, and made a brilliant job of masking my bruises; they hardly showed on the edited film.

Peter was around more than ever. When I thought back to how, to start with, we'd only meet every few weeks, and contrasted it with now, when, sailing lessons aside, he was making arrangements to see me, either out or at home, virtually every night, I couldn't help feeling it was confirming what I feared. And still I couldn't bring myself to ask him; still he didn't volunteer any information. It wasn't a comfortable time. He, I suspected, was still hoping I was in ignorance that anything was wrong. I, on the other hand, was watching for confirmation of the suspicions I didn't think he yet realized I was harbouring. It made for an element of constraint between us that hadn't been there before.

But then it all changed.

It was a Thursday, and Peter had arranged to meet me at home, though I'd told him I'd be a bit later getting back from work than usual, because I had a bit of shopping to do first, so he'd better arrange his own lunch. His car was there when I got back, but he wasn't in the flat; he must be down with Mum and Dad. I went down to find out. I had something to tell him, and it couldn't wait.

I used my 'back door' and went down through the house. Voices came from the living room. Dad, Mum, Peter. I opened the door.

"Hello, darling—" Dad began cheerfully, but stopped as he caught sight of my face.

"Jenny?" Peter was onto it almost as quickly as Dad. "What's wrong?"

"Something rather funny happened while I was out." I tried to keep my tone light, but from the way they were all looking at me, I wasn't fooling anyone.

"What sort of funny?" Mother enquired.

"Odd funny. I got approached by some bloke I'd never seen before.

No, Dad, not like that!" In spite of the seriousness of what I had to say, a flicker of humour touched my tone for a moment. Then I banished it. "What I mean is, I don't think I've ever seen him before, but he seemed to know me. He walked up to me and said, '*Hello, Jenny – hope you're having a lovely day.*' Which took me a bit by surprise. I didn't get a chance to ask him who he was; he'd gone." I left it at that.

I saw the look on Peter's face, and also on my father's. I could have cut the atmosphere with a knife. They looked at each other, and I could see the silent communication of alarm passing between them. Peter leaned forward, his eyes huge and dark.

"What did he look like?" he demanded hoarsely.

I'd known the question was inevitable, so I'd rehearsed the answer.

"He was big. Not just tall, but big; well, sturdy, anyway. Mid-fifties, quite fit-looking. Fair hair and blue eyes. Or grey, maybe. And well-spoken."

Having delivered the information, I waited for his reaction, feeling the building knot of tension in my stomach. Make or break time. He knew it, too; his face was suddenly drawn and pale.

"Come with me," he said, and it wasn't a request. "There's a photo you need to look at." He stood up, and so did my father. We all looked at each other, but none of us spoke; words aren't necessary when you already know what the other person is thinking.

"Where are you going?" Mum asked. The pitch of her voice had risen slightly, as she sensed the change in atmosphere. She got up, too, looking around at the three of us with some anxiety.

"To the office," said Peter tersely. He looked at Dad.

"I'm gonnae do what you told me, Richard," he said. "It's the only way, like you said."

My father nodded.

"Richard, what's going on?" Mum pressed. He gestured at her, as much as to say, *I'll tell you later*, and came to me.

"Go with Peter," he told me, giving me a quick but intense hug. "And be careful."

"He won't let me be anything else," I said.

It was an uncomfortable drive, that journey to Peter's office. The atmosphere in the car was tense, and the silence virtually unbroken. I did try, once.

"Perhaps it isn't him," I suggested, tentatively.

All that got me was a look of disgusted disdain, and, really, I couldn't fault him.

I didn't believe it, either.

The door of the building where Peter's team were housed opened initially into a small section of corridor with a cubicle on the right containing what I assumed to be – given what little I knew about the nature of the work his team did – a security officer, rather than a receptionist. He looked up as Peter swept through the door, relaxed as he recognized him, then came to the alert as he saw me. He half-rose as it became clear that Peter had no intention of stopping and identifying me to him.

"Hang on – who's—?" he began, but Peter gave him short shrift.

"She's with me," he said curtly, and took me by the arm, sweeping me past the confused guard and through the electronically locked door into the next section of corridor with a brief wave of his ID card at the sensor. I could feel the man staring after us as the door swung back and locked behind us.

Only four of the team were in the office when Peter burst through the door. Andy saw him first, and raised her eyebrows.

"Peter? I thought…" Her voice trailed off as she caught sight of me behind him. Brad caught her tone, and looked up, too.

Peter ignored them both, and headed straight for his desk. I threw them both a tentative smile as I followed him. Then, as I looked round the room, I saw Alan staring at us through the glass wall of his office, another, older man standing beside him, doing the same. Within seconds they were both out in the main office. Alan strode toward us.

"Jenny?" he queried, concerned and alerted. "Peter, what's going on?"

Peter didn't answer; his flying fingers were busy with keyboard and mouse. Alan's lips tightened momentarily, then he said to the room at large, "Everyone – this is Jenny Gregory. That's Brad, and Andy, and this is Ben."

"Hi," I said, with a nervous little smile and wave of one hand. Andy and Brad nodded at me and continued to study me with overt interest, while Ben came to my rescue. He put out a hand to shake mine.

"Hello, Jenny," he said. "Good to meet you. What's this strong, silent type doing, bringing you here?"

"There's a photo he wants me to see," I said. "Somehow I don't think it's one of his holiday snaps."

Alan and Ben looked at each other quickly, then at Peter, then back at me. None of us needed to telegraph our suspicions.

"Here," said Peter abruptly. He gestured me peremptorily round to his side of the desk, and pointed at the record displayed on the screen – specifically, at the head and shoulders photograph at the top right. I looked at it, my stomach churning with dread that what I feared was going to be confirmed. It only took a couple of seconds for me to be sure of the short-cropped fair hair, the hooded blue eyes. I let out a short, shaky breath, and nodded.

"Yes," I said heavily. "That's him."

Peter looked up at Alan with burning eyes.

"Lesser's tagged her," he said. "Spoke to her. Today."

"Today?" Alan exclaimed. He looked at me sharply. "Where? When?"

I repeated my story. "I didn't have a clue who he was – then," I concluded, glancing back at the screen. I wondered what my face looked like to everyone else; to me it felt stiff, as if the muscles were too tense to move. "I do now."

There was a short silence. Ben was watching me; Peter and Alan were staring at each other.

"Well, now what do we do?" Peter's voice was close to a snarl.

I'd been wondering that myself, on the drive to the office. What we would do, if our suspicions were confirmed. As they now were. I'd been thinking about it, hard; especially what Peter would do, how he would react. His tone of voice told me I'd been right in my private predictions on that front. Above all, I wanted to keep his response within reasonable bounds. For his sake.

"Well," I said as composedly as I could, intervening before Alan could reply, "it's not really all that unexpected, is it? Given the history. So I think" – I caught Peter's eye, and held it as I spoke – "in the time-honoured phrase, we keep calm and carry on. Don't give him the satisfaction of an overreaction."

"Overreaction?" he snapped indignantly, his voice nearly cracking like an adolescent boy's.

"She's right," Alan said quickly. "I know you're worried, but – it won't help."

I glanced at Ben and found he was regarding me with a gleam of approval in his eyes.

"Maybe we should go into your office and talk this over, Boss," he said to Alan. Alan nodded curtly, and gestured to me to precede him. The sensation of Andy's and Brad's eyes boring into my back was almost tangible as I obeyed.

"Take a seat, Jenny," Alan invited, gesturing at the chair positioned in front of his desk. Ben shut the door behind us and watched with suppressed, if somewhat grim, amusement the way Peter immediately came and stood protectively alongside me, one hand on the back of my chair.

"Now, tell me again what happened, in as much detail as you can," he said, and I did my best to comply.

"And you've never seen him before today?" he pressed, when I'd finished.

I shook my head. "Not to my knowledge. But then, I wouldn't have known if I had seen him, would I?" I spoke reasonably, but I felt Peter shift as if I'd accused him of keeping me in ignorance.

"I wonder how he—" Alan began to speculate, then cut off his own sentence, abruptly. I caught his eye, and read the rest there. Lesser would have known who I was from having seen me in Scotland; it was as near to definitive confirmation as anyone was ever likely to get of whose footprints the forensics team had found outside the living room window. If he'd somehow seen me in Peter's company here down south – as he could have on any one of numerous occasions, despite Peter's precautions – he was sure to have drawn the obvious conclusion. No matter how dismayed Peter was about it.

"Never mind how," Peter snapped, with the anger of a man who is irrationally blaming himself for something he couldn't reasonably have prevented. I recognized the tone; Alex had used to use it too. So often! Blaming himself and his own perceived flaws for imagined failures that were nothing of the sort; just accidents or circumstances over which he could have had no possible control. Which he nevertheless felt responsible for having failed to prevent, or bring to a different outcome. I would just have to bear with Peter over this, as I had had to bear with Alex before him. I knew full well, from bitter experience, I wouldn't persuade him it wasn't his fault. And I supposed that if you looked at it harshly enough – as he was sure to be doing – it *was* his fault, in that he hadn't stopped seeing me after that first time.

Knowing what I now knew, his hesitation to arrange even that first evening at the restaurant had become explicable. He'd taken what had appeared then to be an unconscionably long time over issuing the invitation, but it no longer seemed surprising. It must in reality have been a horrendously difficult decision to come to, if he'd sensed that something could be started by it that he might not want to stop. I remembered the way he'd always hesitated when committing to those early meetings between us. Not, I now knew, because he was reluctant to be with me, but because he was afraid of the potential consequences for me. And yet – and yet! – some connection had been made between us, by the nature of that first, violent encounter in Scotland, that had persuaded him – compelled him, even – to proceed with the relationship despite his fears. Fears that had turned out to be all too real. But even now, I couldn't be sorry about any of it, even if this was where it had led.

"What're we gonnae do?" Peter was still demanding, above my head.

"Well, keep calm, for one thing," said Ben definitely. "Jenny's right about that. He might not know he's been recognized yet. He couldn't be sure she was even going to mention it to you. So he might not be in a hurry."

"You know better than that," Peter snapped. "He's going to assume I've told her about him. He probably counted on her telling me. So I'd know he knows."

Ben was silenced.

"Now I do know who he is I can be on the lookout for him," I suggested. "Let you know if he tries it again."

"It may not be him," said Peter sharply. "He's got other people he can use for that."

There was a brief silence.

"I don't think there's a lot we can do, at this stage," said Alan heavily. He looked at me, and there was both concern and apology on his face. "I'm sorry, Jenny. What I'd like to do is put you under twenty-four hour surveillance, but I don't have the manpower. And nothing's actually happened yet. I'd need more than this to get budget committed for that sort of cover."

My heart was pounding, but I was proud of the way I managed to keep my voice calm when I spoke.

"Of course not," I agreed. "Wouldn't need it twenty-four hours, anyway. Presumably the best thing is not to go anywhere alone. I won't be alone when I'm at work. And my parents are just downstairs at home. And if I may be allowed to speculate" – I glanced up at Peter, then back to Alan, with a touch of black humour – "I suspect that Peter will provide as much personal surveillance as he can. Probably to an unreasonable degree, in fact."

Alan and Ben both tried to hide their smiles, and when I glanced back up at Peter, even he couldn't suppress the twitch at the corner of his mouth as he admitted the truth of my conjecture.

"So I'll just have to be very careful about where I go, and make sure I go with someone else whenever possible. And other than that, carry on as near normal as I can," I concluded, still looking up at Peter, as if making him a personal promise. "What else can I do?"

He had no answer, but briefly squeezed my shoulder; whether the reassurance was intended for himself or me, I couldn't have said. Maybe both. With a prayer added…

"And now I'm sure you'll want to subject this development to professional analysis," I said. "Which is a convoluted way of saying you'll want to talk about it without my being here!" I threw a meaningful glance at Alan, whose eyes flickered briefly in acknowledgement. "So, in view of my promise, could I borrow Peter to take me home so you can do it in peace?"

"Actually, I'd rather Ben did it," Alan said quickly. He saw Peter's instinctive movement of protest, and went on, firmly, "It's you I want to talk to. And Ben can look over where Jenny lives, for future reference."

Ben nodded. "Come on, Jenny. Might have to be quick. Probably need to come back wearing my referee's hat, if these two really start fighting."

"Never let it be said I impeded an emergency service," I said lightly, rising to my feet. I looked at Peter, who was looking back at me with a troubled face. "Don't worry; Ben'll look after me. He looks like the sort of man who can, don't you think?"

"He'd better," Peter growled. Ben made a dismissively scornful noise and ushered me out of the office, closing the door behind us. As we went, I threw a quick glance back into the office; Peter was already leaning on the desk toward Alan, speaking vehemently.

"They've started already," I said to Ben, with a jerk of my thumb back over my shoulder. He looked, and grinned.

"Nice to have met you, even if briefly," I said to Andy and Brad, pausing as we passed them on our way to the door. "Still – better go… Don't want to keep Ben waiting!"

"Right," agreed Brad. Andy smiled tentatively at me, and gave me a little wave of farewell. As I followed Ben, I wondered what kind of an impression I'd given them.

"What's going on, Richard?" my mother repeated, more urgently.

Dad didn't answer until Peter's car had vanished out onto the road. Then he turned back from the window.

"Sit down, and I'll tell you," he said. He sounded his normal, unruffled self, but Mother knows him very well. Still, she sat down on the sofa and schooled herself to patience, while he resumed his seat beside her.

"Peter and Jenny have a bit of a problem," he began.

"What sort of problem? Not between themselves?"

"Not exactly…"

"But I thought—"

Dad cut across her, which he doesn't do very often.

"I suppose it's more accurate to say that it's Peter's problem, and now Jenny might be affected by it." Mother was bursting with questions, but forced herself to wait for him to explain it his own way. "It's – complicated. I can only tell you so much. But it may be as a result of their relationship."

He paused, and in spite of her resolve, Mother had to ask.

"But she *is* in love with him, isn't she?"

Dad considered that carefully.

"Not sure about *in* love," he said with reservation. Then, more definitely,

"But if your question is '*does she* love *him?*', then, in my opinion – yes, without question."

"Has she said so?"

"Not as such. She keeps talking about being his friend. But I think her behaviour generally, her whole attitude to him, makes it very clear – to me, at least – that she loves him. Loves him in the ultimate sense – that his welfare and happiness are more important to her than her own."

Mother was silent for a few moments. Then she said, "Do you think they *are* lovers? I know what Jenny's always said, but—"

"Not yet," said my father. "Not knowing the strength of her convictions on that particular matter. Though I think – I hope – there's every chance that they will be. Eventually. And if that's what happens, I've no doubt it'll only be on Jenny's stated terms. But I also think it's up to Peter. He wants her, I'm sure of that. But he's also afraid to want her."

"Afraid?" Mother was surprised. "But why?"

Dad leaned forward to prop his elbows on his knees, interlocking his fingers and bringing them up to rest against the lower half of his face for a few moments, while he thought deeply. Then he lowered them again, to speak.

"I can't give you details, because what Peter's told me he's told me in confidence. All I can tell you is that there's someone who is" – he selected the right word carefully – "persecuting him, the reason for which lies in his professional history. And he's afraid, for very sound reasons, that Jenny will suffer by association. Which is why he's in such a dilemma. He wants her, and he's afraid for her."

My mother's face was anxious, troubled.

"Does Jenny know about this? This – history?"

"Oh, yes," said Dad, gently. "She's known for quite some time. She's fully aware of the implications, I've no doubt. And it's made no difference to the way she feels, that I can detect. If there's any holding back, it's not on her side. It's Peter."

"But if he's holding back, don't you think—?" began Mother, doubtfully.

"I think," said my father, cutting across her again, but weighing his words carefully, "that his very hesitation is the giveaway. Because if he didn't care about her, he would simply cut loose, to ensure her safety. And the reason he can't bring himself to do that is because in fact he cares too deeply to let her go. Which is why he is in such a dilemma. He's afraid he'll be damned if he keeps her, and, in a different way, damned if he loses her."

There was a pause.

"And this man she was talking about?"

"May be a part of the problem. But I can't tell you any more. Not yet."

There was another silence. After a while, Mother put her hand out, and Dad accepted it.

"Is there anything we can do, Richard?" she asked, simply.

"Nothing," said Dad heavily. "Nothing except support them both, whatever happens, whatever decisions they make. And hope that there'll be a happy ending, after all." He sighed. "Poor Jenny. She chooses well, yet it always seems to turn out to be so complicated for her. But I hope they manage it. Peter's a good man, Beth. If they did end up together, I'd be happy she was with him." He tightened his grasp on my mother's hand. "I want her to be happy the way we've been happy. We've had our moments, of course, but, by and large, we've been so lucky, you and I. Right for each other. I so want Jenny to have what we've had."

"Still do have," Mother pointed out, her throat slightly tight with restrained emotion.

Dad raised her hand to his lips and kissed it.

"My love," he said, so low as to be hardly audible. But Mother heard him, and brought her head down to rest on his shoulder, while he put his arm round her and held her tightly against him, bracing both of them against the burden of anxiety weighing so heavy upon them.

Chapter 21

In the car, I gave Ben the necessary directions. Once we were on our way, to get the necessary conversation going between newly-met strangers I used the ploy of asking about his fishing. Not something I knew too much about, so I was able to keep things going with a lot of questions; he played along, letting me get used to him. But when the subject had come to a natural end, after a slight hesitation I said tentatively, "Ben…"

"Yeah?"

I hesitated, not sure how to put what I wanted to say.

"I suppose – I mean, we're all assuming Lesser's going to do the same as he did before. When he stalked Laura. There's no possibility he's not going to—?"

"No," he said flatly. "Not if it's a way to get to Peter." He slid a sidelong look at me, in which there was a tinge of sympathy, but no hint of doubt.

I drew in a long breath. "Well, thanks for being honest."

I could sense him assessing me, my reaction. I wondered if he'd expected me to be panicking by now. Maybe I should have been. If I'd had any sense, I probably would have been. But I found that all I could think about was Peter.

"How long have you known Peter?" I asked, after a few moments.

"About fifteen years," he said briefly.

"So you were around when…?" I let the question trail off.

He glanced at me, then returned his attention to the road. "Yeah," he said.

"Then – you know what happened," I ventured, slightly uncertainly. "You've seen what it's done to him."

"Oh, yeah. I've seen that, all right," he said. There was an edge of anger in his voice. "I saw a man who used to laugh a lot stop even smiling. I saw a man who'd been able to take everything the job had thrown at him disabled by grief. I saw a man who'd had more friends than you could count forced to isolate himself from everybody. I saw a man who had to go on living when his life had been destroyed. Yeah, I've seen what it's done to him, all right," he said.

There was an uncomfortable pause.

Then he added, "And I've seen what you've done to him, too."

"What d'you mean?" I felt my stomach clench with sudden alarm. "*What you've* done to him." Did he think I'd inflicted Peter with an unnecessary Achilles' heel? I discovered that even on such a short acquaintance I had an unreasonably intense desire to have Ben's good opinion, but was instantly afraid that maybe I'd already lost it.

"I mean, that's how he's been since it happened." He paused. "Till you came along."

It took me a second or two to take in what he'd said. The implication he was making. When I did, I had to look out of the window for a few moments, until my suddenly blurred eyes could clear again.

"It ain't gonna be any fun for you, this," he went on, after a pause, still in that level tone. "You know how it went with Laura, do you?"

"Yes," I said, trying to loosen my throat muscles. He glanced at me for a moment.

"Then you know what to expect. You going to be able to handle that?"

"How do I know?" I protested, with a sort of plaintive indignation. "I've never been in a situation like this. But I'll tell you one thing." I could hear my tone harden with determination. "I'm going to do my damndest. Because he doesn't deserve what's happened to him. And if I've been able to help with that in any way at all, then I'm glad. Glad! And I'll do whatever I can to go on helping. In spite of – in spite of this. Everything I can."

He threw me another brief glance, then nodded, with an air of satisfaction. As if he was thinking, *You'll do...*

There was quite a long silence, after that.

When he dropped me off, he parked up and took a look at the house. I didn't take him inside, but I explained the layout, and took him as far as the back garden so he could see the flat from the outside.

"Have you only got the one way out?" he queried, with a tinge of professional disapproval.

"No." I explained about my 'back door'. "And not if you count the roll-up chain ladder up on the very top landing. The sort you can hang out the window in case of fire."

"Right," he acknowledged. "And your parents're mostly at home, are they?"

"Not always, but mostly," I agreed. "One, if not both. We'll just have to hope it's enough, won't we?"

He looked at me with a quizzical half-smile.

"You're taking this all pretty calmly," he said, but not with disapproval.

"You think? That just proves you can fool all of the people some of the time, and some of the people all of the time," I told him, and he emitted a brief snort of laughter.

218

"Are they in, now?" he asked, gesturing at the house.

"Yes. But no doubt Peter'll be here as well. As soon as he and Alan have finished arguing," I added dryly, and he laughed again. Then he sobered.

"The Boss was right," he said seriously, warning me. "About not being able to do anything. Not yet."

"I know. Economic constraints forcing you to operate a 'close the stable door' policy," I commented, with gentle irony.

He smiled grimly, and there was a brief silence, before I broke it.

"This is so – I don't know how to say it," I said, drawing a deep breath. Now I was the one who was serious. "I hate to deal in clichés, but – I never thought anything like this would happen to *me*. *Could* happen to me. It's – I don't know – I'm suddenly in a different world, but I've got the feeling it hasn't really struck home yet. Here, maybe" – I touched my temple briefly with my index finger – "but not – here." I balled my fist and rested it against my chest, over my heart, for a few moments. I looked at him anxiously. "I just want to say – I hope I don't let you down, Ben. When the realization really kicks in."

"You won't," he said with assurance. "Because of Peter." I was torn between pleasure at such an expression of confidence, from such a source, and envy that he could apparently feel quite so sure about it.

He turned and began to walk back towards his car. "Time I got back. Make sure the office is still standing."

"Tell Peter I'll try not to let anything exciting happen to me before he gets here," I told him.

"You'd better not," he growled.

"Anyway, if Lesser's watching me at the moment, he'll have seen you, too. He'll know you're on the case," I said lightly, as he got into the car. "That ought to frighten him off, don't you think?"

He looked at me, but he wasn't smiling.

"I wish it worked like that," he said. "But it doesn't."

As I watched him drive away, I became conscious that I was standing alone – unprotected – on the pavement. Not that there was anyone nearby; no pedestrians, and, just then, no cars either. But this, I realized, was exactly the sort of thing I'd promised I wouldn't do from now on. Not if I could avoid it.

It wasn't a cold day, but still I shivered, and retreated, hurriedly.

When Ben got back, Brad was still there, but Andy had gone, replaced by Kevlar. Through the glass walls of the office Alan and Peter could be seen, still head to head, their body language more than expressive.

Ben glanced at his wristwatch, then cocked an eye in their direction.

"Still at it, then," he remarked, entirely without surprise. "How's it going?"

"It's going," said Kevlar, with a characteristic economy of words.

"I think you could describe it as a robust discussion," Brad said, straight-faced.

Ben allowed the ghost of a smile to flit across his features.

"Better check there's been no actual bloodletting, I suppose," he said with resignation.

As he slid into the office, both men ignored him. Peter was in full cry, castigating himself.

"I should never have got her into this! She's – she's – know what's so good about her?" he abruptly challenged Alan, his voice taut with emotion. "She doesn't pretend to *understand*. That's what everyone else does. They think it'll make me feel better." His voice became a caricature. "'*I know what you mean. I know how you feel. I understand what you're going through.*' Well, they don't! But they pretend they do. They think they're being kind, and they're not! But she never does that."

"Then you should be grateful," said Alan, shortly.

"But I shouldn't even be seeing her! I should never have started it! It's too dangerous for her! But now" – Peter looked up, wretched – "I can't *not* see her. She's like" – he fumbled for the words – "she's like a respite. A haven. From the filthy world we work in – a filthy world with filthy people who do filthy things…" He kept giving bitter emphasis to every repetition of the adjective. "She's separate from that. She's never been touched by it. She said so herself, once. Thanked me for being someone who protected her from it!" He gave a short, humourless bark of sour laughter at the irony. "She knows it's all there, it all happens, but she's never been touched by it. She's" – again he was searching for the right words – "she's *clean*. She's *peace*. She's *contentment*. All the things I lost…" His voice took on a tinge of desperation. "And now I can't give that up. Not anymore. I didn't mean it to get this far. But it's too late. I can't give it up. I can't give *her* up. I can't!" It was a wail of protest.

"Then don't," interjected Ben, bluntly.

Peter looked at him with something close to a snarl on his face.

"But I've got to!" he contradicted himself. "What if something happens to her because of me?"

"You can't live the rest of your life like that," Alan told him, brusquely. "You do, and Lesser's won."

"Better he wins than she loses!" Peter retorted. "He's never touched you or Jane or the kids because he knows that'd be too big a risk. He's not that stupid! But anyone else – if they're someone I care about – they're at risk. I'm not doing that to – to anyone else. I *mustn't*." The ghost of Laura looked out of his eyes.

Ben intervened again.

"I think you're forgetting something," he said evenly.

"What?" Peter snapped at him.

"How Jenny feels. She's got a stake in this, you know."

"What d'you mean?"

Alan exchanged glances with Ben, and leaned forward.

"Ben's right. Look, she knows about Lesser, doesn't she? She was in that place up in Scotland with you, knowing he was out there. Barricaded in and scared half to death, by all accounts. And she knows about Laura. So she knows what he might do. Does do! And has she shown any sign of backing off?"

Peter stared at his cousin with dark brows drawn together, and remained silent.

"No," Alan confirmed, just as if he'd spoken. "She hasn't. Think about that! She's not stupid, Peter. Do you really think she hasn't worked out what's going on in your head? Look, I respect that woman utterly. And, knowing what she knows, her judgement is that she still wants to – well, be your friend, if that's what you want to call it. Despite the risk. Think about it! People like her don't come along every day! I know why you're afraid, but if you go through the rest of your life turning down the chance of friends like Jenny Gregory, then Lesser will have won. Is that what you want? D'you think that's what she wants?"

Peter looked rebellious, but still said nothing.

Time to drop the matter.

"Look, get lost, will you?" Alan said, sounding weary. "Go back to Jenny, and I don't want to see you again until Monday, all right?"

"And what about when Monday comes?" Peter demanded, stiffly.

"We'll try to work something out. We will, Peter." He made Peter meet his eyes. "D'you really think I'm going to let something happen to her, if there's anything I can do about it?"

"Or me," Ben interjected. Peter looked quickly at the sturdy figure leaning against the door, the folded arms, the steady blue eyes. But still the desperation he was trying to suppress was clear, even though he knew the worth of a promise from that source.

"Go on," Alan urged. "Get out of here. We'll come up with something, I promise."

Wordlessly, Peter stood up and went out; he looked tired, defeated, dispirited. Alan and Ben watched him go, each nursing their own misgivings. When he'd gone, Alan turned to Ben, and silently invited comment.

"Think Jenny might be in for a tough time this evening," Ben observed.

Alan nodded heavily. "He'll be having the same argument with her he's just had with me," he agreed. He thought about that, then amended it. "With us."

"Don't worry," said Ben comfortably. "He won't win."

Alan looked at him quickly, then more thoughtfully.

"Didn't take you long to make up your mind," he commented. Ben shrugged.

"With some people, you don't need long," he said. "So – what *are* we going to do?"

Alan sighed.

"I think I'd better brief Robert," he said. He was always careful, for the sake of team discipline, not to refer to his superior as 'the Laird' – except to Peter, and then only in private. "It's a development he'll need to know about."

"Yeah? Well, don't forget to ask him if he's going to let it happen all over again!"

Alan was surprised by the unexpected, barely suppressed savagery of Ben's tone. He'd never been aware that Ben had ever held Robert Laird responsible for Laura's death, and what it had done to Peter. More than once, he'd told Alan that Laird couldn't have foreseen Lesser's reaction. But it sounded as if he'd feel very differently if Lesser employed the same strategy with Jenny Gregory, and Laird chose to do nothing to prevent it.

"You think Lesser'll go the same route with Jenny?"

"Why wouldn't he? It worked last time," said Ben harshly.

"Well, let's hope forewarned is forearmed, this time," said Alan. But he didn't feel much in the way of hope on that score.

Ben was right; I did have a tough time, that evening.

When I came back toward the house from having seen him depart, I saw my father watching me through the living room window. As soon as he saw that I'd seen him, he vanished; moments later, the front door opened, and he stood there, looking at me. I met his eyes, and nodded, heavily. He drew in a long breath. For what seemed a long time we stood, him in the doorway, me on the drive, just looking at each other.

"He has told me," he said at last, a slight emphasis on the 'has'. "All of it."

"Oh…" I stared at him. "How long have you known?" I managed.

"He told me when he was staying with you."

So Dad had known all that time, and said nothing. I nodded, wordlessly. There didn't seem to be much to say.

"Who was it brought you home?" he asked, after a few moments.

"One of his colleagues. Ben Sullivan. Alan wanted to talk to Peter." I allowed a wry half-smile to cross my face. "Probably needed to, the state Peter was in." I looked down unseeingly at the gravel beneath my feet. "I suppose I'd better brace myself. He'll be back later. And he won't be a happy bunny." What a childish phrase to use for such a situation. A thought struck me, and I looked up, quickly.

"Does Mum know?"

Dad nodded, heavily. "Not the detail. I told her it was a confidence. But that Peter has been harassed by someone and that that might now be extended to you, yes."

"Don't tell her any more," I said. "Not unless" – which I knew was not the right word – "you have to. I don't want her more worried than she has to be."

He nodded, half reluctant to keep her in ignorance, but half wanting, like me, to protect her from it for as long as possible. "What are you going to do?" he asked, carefully.

"The best I can, Dad," I said simply. "The best for him, the best for me. I've just got to work out what that is."

"Good luck, darling," he said quietly. I felt a lump rise in my throat. I smiled at him – doubtless a rather lopsided smile, but a smile nonetheless – and headed for the stairs to my flat. I could feel his eyes remain on me, like a physical touch of support, until I passed out of his sight.

I don't know how long it was, between then and the time that Peter came back. I do know I spent the whole time sitting on the window seat, staring at nothing, trying not even to think. Once or twice my eyes filled with tears, and I let them flow; as I continued to sit, motionless, they dried by themselves while I went on trying not even to think...

At last I heard the key in the door. The key I'd given him just over a month before. So he could come and go as he pleased. That he'd taken with a reluctance born of the fear that in some unnameable way his having it would make me more vulnerable. It was the same sort of irrational reasoning Alex might have used; the automatic assumption that if anything happened, anything went wrong, it would be his fault. Well, that wasn't how I felt about it. I felt safer, knowing he had it, knowing he could get in to me at any time he needed to. Or that I needed him to.

He appeared in the doorway, but didn't come in. He just looked at me, his eyes huge and dark. There was a silence.

"What are we gonnae do?" he said at last. It was always such a giveaway, that particular idiom. Most of the time his phrasing was completely English, even though his accent was definitely, beautifully Scots. It was only when he was under some kind of stress, whether good or bad, that 'going to' became 'gonnae', or 'want to', 'wannae'.

"Have a coffee," I said as calmly as I could, getting up. "I expect you've shouted your throat dry at Alan, haven't you?"

He couldn't help but smile ruefully.

"You're amazing, you know that?" he said, shaking his head in wonder.

"Thank you, kind sir," I said lightly, going into the kitchen. "Want anything to eat?" I called back, as I began to spoon coffee into the mugs.

"No, thanks." From the sound of his voice, he'd come in from the hall, into the living room. Neither of us said any more while, in different rooms, we waited the couple of minutes it took for the kettle to boil. When I went back I found him sitting on the window seat, staring out into the garden. He took the mug I offered him with muttered thanks, and put it on the window sill. I sat down at the other end of the seat, cradling my mug between my hands, and waited. At last he brought his eyes round to mine, and I felt my heart go out to him; he was so profoundly distressed.

"I never meant this to happen," he said.

"Of course you didn't," I agreed. "Stuff happens without people meaning it rather a lot of the time. Had you not noticed?"

"Yeh, goes with the job," he said, with a feeble attempt at jocularity. A quite valiant one, given how miserable he was feeling. Then his face darkened. "Except, this time, I forgot to notice. I *chose* not to notice. And this is the result. Oh, Jenny" – he looked so wretched – "the last thing I wanted was to do this to you."

I put my mug down – I was never going to drink that particular coffee – and leaned forward earnestly.

"Peter, it's all right. Really. It's all right."

"All right?" His voice cracked with incredulity. "Lesser's got you on his radar, and you're trying to tell me it's all right?"

"No, of course it isn't! What I'm trying to tell you is, it's all right between *us*! I don't blame you for this. None of this is your doing. What you did twelve years ago – the consequences – everything since – it's all Lesser's doing, not yours! It's what he's done, what he's doing, that's making this happen. He's the instigator, not you!"

"What difference does that make? The point is, he's on to you! I've put you in danger. You!" His face contorted momentarily, then he got himself back under control. His face became expressionless, as he brought himself to the point of saying what he'd come to say. "There's only one thing I can do, now."

I looked at him warily, suspecting what was coming. "What?"

"I'm gonnae have to keep away. It's the only thing I can do."

My heart sank.

"Peter, that's not the answer." I fought to keep my voice calm. "All that would do is score him a point he hasn't had to earn. By making us more unhappy than we already are. I don't want to give him any ground I don't have to. Do you? Besides, it won't stop him – well, trying anything…" I declined spelling out what 'anything' might cover. "All it would mean is that you wouldn't be here when he did, wouldn't it?"

He looked at me with tortured eyes, then buried his face in his hands with a groan.

"If only I'd left you alone!" His voice was muffled by the heels of his palms. "I should have left you alone! How could I have been so stupid? I'm sorry, Jenny!"

I moved quickly, dropping to my knees in front of him and seizing his wrists, pulling his hands away from his face, forcing him to meet my eyes.

"You listen to me, Peter McLeish," I said firmly, looking up into his face with an unblinking stare. "Maybe you *are* sorry. But for myself, I am never going to be sorry that I met you and got to know you. Never. *Whatever* happens next. Do you know what I'll say to him, if I see him again? I'll say, '*Thank you, Matthew Lesser!*' Because if it weren't for him, we'd never have known each other. And I will never be sorry about that, no matter what. Got me?"

He stared at me, longing and dread fighting each other in his eyes. Then he slid off the window seat to kneel with me, his arms going round me, and I held him there while he cried, the way he'd cried the night he told me about Laura. And I cried, too. How could I not, when I was so afraid, and the man I loved was having his heart broken, so steadily and systematically, day after day?

If Peter was quiet in the office the next day, nobody commented on it. Not even Chris, who wasn't exactly noted for his discernment. Sometimes sympathy doesn't get expressed in words, but there are other ways to get the message across. Everyone kept their head down and got on with business as usual.

By the late afternoon, Peter and Ben were the only two at their desks. The computer screen was on, there was the occasional rustle of papers, but Ben could tell, by the occasional glance over at the other side of the room, that not much useful work was being done over there.

"Peter," he said eventually, breaking into the silence. "About Jenny…"

Peter looked up, quickly. Ben regarded him levelly.

"You've got a good one there," was all he said.

From that source, a seal of ultimate approval, delivered with all the finality of a fact beyond dispute.

Everything else that might have been said on the subject didn't need to be said aloud. They could just look at each other, and say it that way. So Peter didn't reply – not in words. After a couple of seconds Ben nodded, then dropped his eyes back to the notes he was making. But Peter spent a long time staring at his own desk after that, without really seeing what he was looking at.

Chapter 22

Life was a strange experience for a while, after that. Intellectually, I understood the situation I was in; emotionally, it felt so – so theoretical. But I began to find myself looking at other people – on the bus, in the tram, on the street, anywhere – and taking more notice of them than I would normally do. Looking at faces, and wondering to myself, *Are you the one who's watching me? Is it you? Is it you? Is it you…?*

I was beginning to realize what sort of pressure Laura must have felt herself under; the sort of pressure Peter must still be under. Had been under for years. Alan had told me that Lesser continually reminded him he was still watching him. I wondered if so many years of it had made him any more accustomed to it now than he had when it began. Then I remembered how he'd always check the street when he arrived at my place, and thought again. The trouble was convincing myself it was real, that I really did have to watch what I said to people I didn't know. To keep on the alert for people who might be following me, watching me. As Peter had said, Lesser wasn't likely to be doing it himself; he had minions for that, and I didn't know any of them. Yes, I had to behave as if I was being stalked, because I probably was. But it didn't come naturally.

At work was the most difficult. So many people use a library, and some of them regularly come in and hang about literally for hours, sometimes, reading the supply of magazines and newspapers, or sitting at the computers. How was I to know if any of those people were on Lesser's payroll, and were only using the library facilities as a cover for watching me? It was a bad dream, one that could so easily become a nightmare. And nothing had even happened yet. But if I found myself forgetting, dropping my guard, I had only to think of the anguish on Peter's face, replay the agony in his voice from that night when he told me what Lesser had done to Laura, and the reality of it would resurface again…

With my heightened awareness of the behaviour of complete strangers, I began to notice one man, maybe thirty years old or so, who seemed to me to frequenting the library a great deal, all of a sudden. Was that true, or was it just me being hyper-sensitive? No; he was there just about every day, so it wasn't my imagination. But I soon realized it wasn't me who was the focus of his attention. He kept using every opportunity he could to monopolize

Moira. She was only just turned nineteen, an open, bubbly personality. Like me, she hadn't got a degree, and had become a library assistant through the route of an NVQ in Information and Library Services; she was now working towards her City & Guilds 7371. I assumed he must be a new boyfriend, who couldn't resist hanging round his girl when the nature of her workplace made her so very accessible during the working day.

"Got an admirer, then, Moira?" I teased her.

"Yeah," she giggled, her face lighting up. "His name's Joe. We've been going out for a couple of weeks. He's nice," she added gratuitously, as if I could be in any doubt of her opinion.

"A gentleman of leisure, I take it, if he's got this much time to spend loitering in your vicinity?"

She giggled again, then shrugged cheerfully. "He's got a part-time job, I think."

"You think?"

She giggled again. "I've been concentrating on other things."

"I'll bet," I said dryly.

The next time he came in, leaning over the counter to chat to her, I caught him looking at me a number of times. I let him see that I'd noticed it, then ignored it thereafter, but later, in a quiet spell at the counter, Moira said, "I told Joe you were asking about him."

"Ah," I said. That would have been why he was checking me over, then.

"I asked him what his job was. He said he was in removals."

"Really? He doesn't look the type."

"What type do you have to be?" she demanded, slightly indignantly. Then she let out one of her habitual giggles. "He moves me, I know that!"

"Thanks, Moira – little bit too much information there," I told her.

She grinned, and changed the subject.

"So what are you doing over the weekend?" she asked.

"I'm—" I began, hesitated, then went on, with a dismissive shake of my head, "not doing much, really."

That wasn't true, but I was trying to get into the habit of not gratuitously disclosing my activities to other people. Especially people like Moira, who could gossip for England without batting her heavily mascara'd eyelashes. I didn't mind her knowing, but if she knew, everybody would know. And now I had to keep it in mind that I didn't know who that 'everybody' might be. It takes a lot of concentration, I was finding, to retrain a lifetime's habits of thought and behaviour.

When I got home from work, Dad also raised the subject of the weekend with me.

"In the light of the new situation," he said, picking his words delicately, "should I come with you?"

Poor darling. He wasn't sure where the line between protective and over-protective was, now.

"If no one else volunteers," I said cheerfully.

"Ah," he said. "You haven't yet told Peter, I take it?"

"I know this is a somewhat novel concept, but I do believe he might come over this evening... So I thought I'd tell him then."

"Well, let me know if you do need me," he said, and let it go at that.

Over dinner that evening I enquired casually, "Are we sailing this weekend?"

"Yeh," Peter said. "Sunday afternoon." *Why wouldn't we be?* asked his expression. *You know that perfectly well already...*

"Right," I agreed. "In that case I'll go tomorrow, then, not Saturday. Then I'll be back in good time."

"Back from where?" He looked at me quickly, his fork arrested in mid-air. The slightest hint of my going anywhere he didn't know about, and this was the result – instant concern, bordering on alarm. Poor Peter. Lesser was a devastatingly effective puppet master.

"I'm going down to Hampshire," I explained. "Wearing my landlady's hat. The cottage is between tenants at the moment, so the agent's been doing a bit of maintenance work in the interregnum. He's got a new let lined up, but he wants me to go down and approve what's been done before he goes ahead with it. So I'm doing that tomorrow."

"I'm coming with you." His response was instant; not even a suggestion, but a flat statement of fact, with no admittance of contradiction. As far as he was concerned, it was automatically a given. He didn't even ask if I'd already asked anyone else to go. My going anywhere without his being there if he was able to be was simply not up for debate.

"I hoped you would," I said cheerfully, attending to my plate. "I'd rather like to show it to you. It's very close to the coast, just a couple of miles or so from Lymington, on the east side of the river. You ought to like it, so near a navigable river. And the Solent. Anyway, I hope you do." I went on eating with a composure that I hoped would influence him to be calm, too. It seemed to work; the arrested fork went back to doing its job. "I could leave it all to Mr Snell to approve, but – I don't know – it was my home, once," I said, wanting him to understand. "It's probably silly, but I like to look it over myself, whenever any work's been done on it. Just to make sure..." Sure of what, I couldn't have defined, but, because of the way he nodded, I knew he did understand.

"What time d'you want me to pick you up?" he asked, still intent on practical matters.

"Oh, I'll drive," I demurred. "The car could do with a decent run. Could you get here about nine? The worst of the work traffic should be gone by then."

"Okay," he said. "I'll tell Alan where we'll be."

I didn't comment on that, but it did occur to me in passing – though, given his mood, I thought it wiser not to voice the thought out loud – that it was really rather more usual practice for a senior officer to tell a junior what he was going to do, than the other way round... Well, that was Alan's problem. I just hoped that what amounted to police protection would turn out to be more of a day's holiday, instead – for the man who never took one.

I don't know if Peter knew how glaringly obvious it was to me that he was checking out the traffic around us as we drove, at least to start with. Or, if so, whether he would have cared. I could tell by the slight movements of his head how frequently he was glancing in the door mirror; being so tall, he couldn't do it without leaning down and forward slightly. But after about half an hour or so he seemed to relax, and only kept it up thereafter on a kind of autopilot basis. Evidently he was fairly satisfied we weren't being followed. Not this time, at any rate. For which I was duly thankful, though I didn't say so aloud.

"It's quite isolated, really," I said, trying to describe the cottage to Peter. "It's not actually that far from the next houses in either direction, but because of the trees you just can't see they're there. It's fairly flat round there, of course, because of being a floodplain. We get a bit of protection from the Isle of Wight, but you can still get some fair old south-westerlies and easterlies coming up the Solent and Spithead from time to time." I flicked a glance at him. "Probably why it's called *Fair Winds*. Though when they kept up for long enough, Alex used to say it should have been called *Unfair Winds...*"

We weren't that far from our destination when I made my mistake. We were only making desultory conversation from time to time; I decided to idly remark on the remarkably traffic-free journey we'd had.

"I'm glad we've had such a good run. And alone! Just imagine – if Lesser was watching us now, he'd be rubbing his hands with glee," I commented without thinking, imagining I was being humorous. "Both his eggs in one basket."

Instantly Peter turned on me with sudden rage.

"Don't be so damned stupid!" he yelled at me savagely. "Don't you know how much danger you're in? I told you what happened to Laura! Start taking it *seriously*, damn you!"

For a moment I was simply shocked at the instantaneousness and violence of his reaction to what had been intended as nothing more than a moment of levity. Then my lips compressed, and sudden anger rose in my throat. For long moments I couldn't even speak. Fortuitously, a small layby offered a place to pull off the road at that exact instant. I swung the car into it violently and braked, then turned to face him with a look that – well, I don't know exactly what my face was showing, but it dissolved his rage into astonishment in only a couple of seconds.

"Don't you ever tell me again that I'm not taking it seriously," I said, my voice dangerously quiet. He'd never heard that tone from me before; he stared at me. "*Ever*," I repeated. "You listen to me, Peter McLeish. I'm assuming that Matthew Lesser means me harm. Serious harm. Because he'll see that as a way of getting to you. And I'm assuming he knows everything there is to know about me. Maybe he doesn't, but I'm going on the assumption that he does. Where I go, who I see, when I do it. Everything. Because I'm assuming he's got the kind of resources that means he can find out all those things if he wants to. Well, I can't do anything about that. What he does, or when he might choose to do it, or even where. I've got no control over his choices. Only over my own."

He opened his mouth, about to interrupt me, but I pointed at him sharply.

"Shut up," I said, with that same quiet intensity. "I haven't finished… So it seems to me that the only choice I've got here is how I react. How I cope with it. So what are my options? Do I go to pieces? Do I ignore it? Do I run away? Which means running away from you? Which means he wins? Or do I try to live as normal a life as possible? Trying not to be alone, trying to be with somebody as often as I can work it that way. Using my sense of humour to try to keep me sane in an impossible situation. Which option do you think I should take?"

He was silenced.

"So don't you ever tell me again that I'm not taking it seriously," I repeated harshly. After a tense pause, I restarted the engine, and swung back out onto the road. Perhaps fortunately, no car happened to be coming down our side of the carriageway just then, or they might have been badly startled by the speed of my manoeuvre.

The silence after that persisted throughout the remaining time it took us to reach the cottage. I veered into the small drive, pulled up before the front door, and switched off the engine. Without looking at Peter, I got out; he did the same. Then we faced each other across the roof of the car.

"I'm sorry, Peter," I said quietly. I'd had time to think, and I'd realized a few things that had been obscured by my anger.

"No, you were right," he demurred. He must have been going through the same process. "It was my fault."

231

"Not in the way you mean it," I contradicted him. "It's not your fault that this has happened – not when it comes right down to it – and I'll argue that one with you every time." I smiled at him, acknowledging that he would deplore my resolve. "But I should've remembered how you'd be feeling about it. And that you get so angry because you're worried about *me*. I do *know* that. When I'm being rational! But it's hard to be rational all the time. It's just – humour is a way I deal with it. But I realize it was a bit misplaced this time. So I'm sorry. I don't want to make you feel worse than you already do."

"I wish there was something I could do," he said in helpless frustration.

We looked at each other, but there was nothing to be said.

"Let's go inside," I said. "If we're in luck, we can have a coffee. The makings should be there; I asked Mr Snell if he'd arrange for some milk to be in the fridge."

"You're good at thinking ahead, aren't you?" Peter approved, embracing the change of subject gratefully.

I need to be, now, I thought. I hoped he hadn't read my mind.

"Come on," I said, fishing in my handbag for the front door key.

I showed him round first, of course. Two up, two down, plus bathroom and a utility room built onto the kitchen diner as an extension. The exterior was unadorned brick. I'd never found out how old the cottage was, but because of the small dimensions of the windows and the fact that they had leaded panes, probably a couple of hundred years, at least. The back faced south, and when we were up in the main bedroom, I drew Peter's attention to the view. Looking as if it was not so very far away, the dark hump of the western shoulder of the Isle of Wight rose from the horizon above the fields.

"If the trees weren't in the way, you'd be able to see a flock of masts over there," I said, pointing westward. "That's the mouth of the Lymington. It's a pretty busy marina. Ever been there? No? Well, we can drive over and take a look before we go back, if you like… Ready for that coffee now?"

"You check what you came to look at, first."

"Sure?"

"Go on." He was still taking in the view. "I'll be down in a minute."

"Well, roam around as much as you want to." I left him to it, and set about checking over the list of items Mr Snell had sent me – new washer-dryer and chest freezer in the utility room, replacement soft furnishings, fresh tiling in the kitchen, that sort of thing. It didn't take too long, and, as I'd told Peter, I could have left it to Mr Snell, really. But this had been my husband's home before it was mine, and I felt I owed it to Alex to make personally sure it was being kept in good condition. When I had just about finished checking the kitchen I heard Peter coming downstairs, so I put the kettle on. When I went to find him, he had come to rest in front of the window in the living room, studying the garden. He glanced round at me as I came in, accepted his coffee, then went on staring out of the window.

"Jenny..." he said hesitantly.

"Mmm?"

"Sorry I lost it." His voice was very low.

"Water under the bridge. You don't need to apologize again."

"Yeh, I do. You didn't deserve that." I wished he knew how much pleasure I got from hearing that 'deserve' come out as 'desairve'. "I just" – he groped for a way to express himself – "I just feel so damn helpless. I wish there was something I could *do*. Really do."

I looked at him sombrely.

"There is," I said. "If you can manage it."

His eyes fastened on mine, demanding an explanation.

"I'm going to be honest with you," I said. "Because this – thing – is hard enough as it is. But you don't help, Peter. I'm sorry, but you don't. You're like a coiled spring all the time. I know why, but" – I didn't know how to put it so it would come out the right way – "if you could just ease up a bit? Somehow? It's..." I cast about for a meaningful analogy. "Look, I don't like heights, right? And it's like standing at the top of a cliff. I'd be all right as long as I didn't look down, but not if there's someone standing right behind me, telling me how far down it is all the time. I don't need you to keep telling me that, Peter. I need you to help me cope. We need to help each other cope. But that way won't do it. Not for either of us." I was just about pleading with him by the time I'd finished.

He dropped his eyes, accepting the truth of what I was telling him.

"I'm sorry," he said in a low voice. "I've just been so – afraid..."

"I know. I *know*..."

"I've been trying to think of a reason why I should ever forgive myself," he said, still not meeting my eyes. "For getting you into this."

"Maybe you did," I said. "Get me into this. From one point of view. Which isn't mine. But let's say you did. Well, what's got to happen now, then, is that you – and the team – have got to get me out of it. And the only way I can see of doing that is, somehow, to get him. Get him, so he can't get me."

He looked at me ruefully.

"That's exactly what your father said," he commented.

"He's a very wise man," I said, attempting a brief smile. "Not that I'm biased, or anything, but – don't you think? It's got to be the answer! Because it wouldn't just get me out of it. It would get you out of it, too. And that's what matters to me most."

233

"Yeh, I know," he said, in such a low voice I hardly heard him. He dropped his eyes for a moment, then went back to looking out of the window again.

"Let's take a proper look outside," I said. "Might as well, while you're here."

The garden isn't large, but it's usually fairly tidy. Because of the succession of lets, I'd made sure, when I left it, that it was planted with low-maintenance shrubs and flowers that grew quite happily unsupervised; weeding is just about all the upkeep that's needed, except for the occasional hedge trim. I couldn't expect tenants to invest themselves in a garden that wasn't theirs. Mr Snell arranged for someone to come to do the hedge on the infrequent occasions when it became necessary, but that was about it.

It was a gorgeously warm day, and the sun – when not masked by one of the lazily-moving flotilla of white clouds overhead – showed it all to best advantage. From one corner a mass of pale mauve thyme extended three or four feet along each border, beautifully scented and alive with various species of bee, while in the other corner the enormous buddleia – that had been so small, when Alex and I had planted it – flickered all over with butterflies of every hue and description.

We stood together in silence for a while, each, for our own reasons, assessing the house and the garden over the soporific background drone of the bees. After a while Peter nodded slowly, several times.

"You're right," he said, delivering his verdict. "This is a good place." He paused, then went on, "It's got a good feel to it. You can tell, straight away. It's one of those places where you know right away you could be happy."

I think by 'you' he meant 'anyone', but I said, "I was. Not every moment, of course, and with some very hard moments indeed included in that, but, under it all, yes – basically happy." I caught his eye. "If you ever needed to, you could come and be happy here, if you like," I went on. "One day, when it's all over, you could come and live here." It came out sounding like an offer made on impulse, but somehow it didn't feel like that; it simply felt like a perfectly obvious solution. "Get yourself a little yacht and keep it on the Lymington or the Beaulieu. New start."

He stared at me for a moment, then began to smile quizzically. "Are you offering to be my landlady?"

"Better than being your landlubber," I retorted. "Which is still what it feels like, despite all the lessons."

He laughed.

"You're better than that, and you know it," he said, with a hint of reprimand in his tone. Then the smile faded slightly into an intent regard. "Are you serious?"

"Of course I am. I've told you before – say what I mean, mean what I say. Less complicated, remember? When you're ready to leave that rather bijou residence of yours" – *that ghastly, wretched little hole you spend your nights in, and eat your breakfast in* – "this'll be here for you. When it's over."

"When it's over," he echoed softly. He came closer, halting only a couple of feet away from me. "Do you know what a kind person you are?" he asked, with a strange, almost detached curiosity.

I shook my head at him. "You make me sound like it's some kind of altruism. And it isn't. Some people get a kick out of getting things; I get a kick out of giving them, that's all. Makes me feel good. In fact, sometimes I think it feels selfish to feel that good! So it's not for you at all, really." I grinned at him. "It's for me. It's just self, self, self, all the way."

"Oh, yeh," he said, still in that quiet, soft voice. "That's you, all right. Selfish to the core."

"Well, I'd rather you weren't under any illusions." I was still making light of it, but I could feel my heart starting to thump against my ribs. Time to change the subject again. "Right – I'm done here. So what about going to the marina? It'd be an awful waste to be this close and not have a look, don't you think?"

We must have spent a couple of hours or more in that marina, and I don't think I'd ever seen him so relaxed before. Pointing out to me the yachts he liked the look of. Explaining to me the reasons for his choices, their good points and their bad points. His face was more animated than I'd ever seen it. Just for a short while, he'd forgotten himself, forgotten Lesser, forgotten everything in the pleasure of sharing his reawakened passion for sailing and sailing craft with me. I could have wept with pleasure for every moment that look was on his face, that note in his voice. This was a glimpse of the real Peter McLeish, the one Ben had hinted at, the man he'd been before. I knew, of course, the Peter that Lesser had created would be back soon enough. But not now, not here. And he'd have this to remember, when he became that Peter again. Maybe it would help, a little.

Chapter 23

I'm not the first to use the simile, but the situation now was like living on the slopes of a volcano. Even though it seemed dormant, knowing that at some point, inevitably, it would blow. Never knowing if today would be the day. But people are endlessly adaptable. Even living on a volcano can become normal, and you carry on, day after day, without even looking at it after a while, no matter how large it looms. It became the norm that Peter would come over every evening, even if his work made him late. On the occasions when it prevented him from doing so altogether, he'd always ring me. Make sure I was all right. That nothing had happened.

So that became what passed for normal. I went to work – observing Joe's persistent attentions to Moira with tolerant amusement – I sometimes went to Alan and Jane's, often ending up closeted with Craig and his editing software, or I stayed at home, by myself or with Peter, when he came. After Alex's death I'd more or less let going out with friends or the people from work go, so there was no particular change in behaviour for anyone to remark upon there. But I did go out with them from time to time, and one of those times was Elizabeth's fortieth birthday. Which, of course, meant there was going to be a lunchtime get-together at her favourite pub. Her actual birthday had been the week before, but she'd taken some leave, so this was the first most convenient day for all of us; the fact that it was now seven calendar days later was not, in her book, a reason for not celebrating anyway. Not all of us could get there, of course, but cover had been fixed so that as many of us as possible could. Moira and Steve and Patti were all going, besides me.

Trying to keep my promise, I was training myself into the habit of telling my parents where I was going, on the infrequent occasions I went anywhere at all. When I mentioned it to them, it turned out they were going out that same afternoon – some friends' pearl wedding anniversary, deep down in south-east Kent – and they wouldn't be back until late. Still, Peter would be over later, so I wouldn't be alone for that long. And no matter what I'd promised, there were sometimes going to be times like this, when it couldn't be avoided for a few hours. At least I wouldn't be on my own at the pub.

It was a Friday, my non-working day, so I was going to have to make a special trip, but something I could avoid was paying a car parking fee. The pub in question was in the middle of town, but an erstwhile schoolfriend of mine ran a little car repair business in an out-of-the-way back street not far away – just himself and his younger brother – and he always let me use his spare parking bay if it was free. When I rang him to check, he said, "Yeah, no problem. We'll be shut on Friday, Jenny – we got a funeral to go to – but yer can park in the usual place."

"Oh, Nick! I'm sorry to hear that! Who is it?"

"Me aunt. Cancer," he said succinctly. "Good thing, in the end, I reckon. It wore her away till she weren't 'ardly there, come the finish… Anyway, point is, like I said, yer can park like usual. Won't exactly be in our way, will yer? Me'n'Robin won't be there."

"Well, all right – thanks. But I am sorry. I do hope it goes all right."

"Yeah, thanks. Enjoy your get-together, anyhow. More fun than mine's likely to be! See yer." He rang off leaving me with the impression that he was more cut up than he was letting on. Poor Nick.

Still, the parking bay would be free. Which would leave me something less than a five minute walk from there to the pub. It was all falling into place very nicely.

And so it was – but not just for me.

The big, fair-haired man waiting in the 4x4 a few yards down the road was checking his watch. According to what he'd been told, she should have been on her way by now. Where was she?

Ah – there! There was her car, pausing in the mouth of the driveway while she glanced up and down the road, too intent on locating moving traffic to notice him, sitting there anonymously. She pulled out to the left, heading away from him. He let her get a safe distance ahead before he set off in her wake.

He was confident, as he had been the first time, that she wouldn't detect his presence. Not even when she'd threaded her way through back streets to pull into the yard of a nondescript garage premises. She clearly wasn't aware of him as he drove sedately past while she got out of her car and locked it; his was just another vehicle, not to be consciously noticed.

He smiled. All exactly as he'd been told. Yes, it was all falling into place very nicely.

As I neared the pub, I spotted Moira. And, of course, Joe. Why would I be surprised? These days, anywhere she went, he went.

"Hi, Jenny!" Moira called, waving as expansively as if I was on the other side of a valley instead of just a few yards away. "I brought Joe," she added, superfluously, as I closed in on them.

"So I see," I observed cheerfully, and held out my hand for him to shake. "Hello, Joe. Nice to meet you officially, at last. And you've met Elizabeth, have you?"

"Not yet," he disclaimed. "Moira's pointed her out, but that's about it."

"You're in for an experience, then," I commented cheerfully. "After you…"

This particular pub was especially well patronized at lunchtimes, but we spotted the others through the crowd, already in place in an alcove over to the left, and made our way across. I greeted them above the babble of conversation arising on all sides, and dropped into one of the empty chairs. Moira paused before sitting down, hovering possessively at Joe's side.

"Elizabeth, this is Joe. Joe, Elizabeth." They exchanged affable nods. "That's Steve, and you've met Patti…" Moira went round the table making the introductions, although there were a couple of people there she, and I, didn't know, but who introduced themselves in turn as friends of Elizabeth. Shyama, who had used to work at the library and had left a few years ago but who still kept in touch with Elizabeth, I knew vaguely, but not Ian or Wendy or Jason. "And whatever you do, don't call her Liz," Moira supplemented in a stage whisper as she sat down. "Full name only! She's got a thing about it."

"Oh. Right," he agreed, a little nonplussed. Elizabeth grinned at him.

"It's how I keep order in my life," she explained. "Rule by terror, at home and at work. Helps professional discipline no end."

"You should ask Geoffrey," Patti chipped in mischievously. "That's her husband."

"Doesn't work with Steve, though, does it?" Moira teased. Steve, who was twenty-seven but misleadingly still looked about nineteen and whom nature had gifted with a naturally impish expression, instantly raised innocent eyebrows, as if to say, '*Who – me?*'

"Don't worry, he's still paying for that," Elizabeth assured her, the mock severity in her voice contradicted by the ready sparkle in her eyes. "And will be, for some time!"

"For what?" Joe asked.

"Show him the photo," I chuckled. Elizabeth promptly got out her smartphone and pulled up a photograph, which she brandished at Joe. I'd already seen it; it was of her desk at work, all done up with balloons and banners.

"That was my fortieth birthday," Elizabeth said. "Last Friday."

Joe frowned at the photo. Most of the balloons had '40' on them, but he'd spotted the odd one out.

"Why's there a balloon saying '*Happy 50th*', then?" he asked, perplexed.

"That was Steve's rather novel way of handing in his resignation," said Elizabeth, with heavy significance and a quirked eyebrow. Everyone laughed, and Steve grinned mischievously.

"Of course, the real celebration was when she went up to Liverpool on Saturday," I said.

Joe looked perplexed again.

"Liverpool? What for?"

"She supports Everton," I explained. "She's a real supporter, not an armchair one." Joe looked at Elizabeth with renewed interest.

"You a Scouser, then?" he enquired. "Don't sound much like one."

"No," she agreed. "I'm from Kent, originally."

Joe's forehead creased. "How come Everton, then? Why not one of the London clubs?"

"Because my dad's a Liverpool fan," she said, as if that should have been obvious.

"From which single statement you can deduce the nature of their entire relationship," I chipped in.

"Oh, right," said Joe, suitably amused. "So, how was the game? Did they give you a proper birthday present?"

She pulled a face. "A draw," she said, disgusted. "A bad one. I tell you, if they'd been playing in the garden, I'd've pulled the curtains!" Which got her a huge laugh from around the table.

Steve started teasing her about Everton, whereupon she, as she always did, started to roundly abuse him, with her tongue firmly in her cheek, for being such a Philistine as not to be interested in football at all. People started taking sides, and the conversation got definitely rowdy, after that. A few very lively photos got taken by various phones as things proceeded.

"Did the problems yesterday get sorted?" I asked Moira after a while. Joe looked at me.

"What problems?" he asked.

"Techie ones," she explained. "The computer system."

"It was very sad," I said mournfully. "The network was mucking about, but when I told them I was three icons short of a desktop, nobody seemed in the least surprised."

Joe laughed. "I'd better not comment," he said. "So – in a complete change of subject – where's the loo in this place?"

"Over there." I pointed helpfully.

He followed the direction of my finger. "Right, thanks."

"There y'go," I drawled.

"Literally," Elizabeth quipped. "It's what a toilet's for, after all."

That started another ripple of laughter around the group. Joe winked at Moira, got up and headed for the door marked 'Gents'; in my peripheral vision, I was vaguely aware of him being followed in by another man who'd risen from a nearby table at the same time. A tall man, fair-haired…

When Joe came back he found Steve in the middle of taking orders for another round.

"We've got to get them in, Joe," Moira explained. "Got to get back to work soon, remember? We've only got an hour, all told."

"Let me, then," Joe offered.

"No, my shout," Steve told him. "But thanks."

"Well, tell you what, I'll help you carry 'em back," Joe said, and followed him to the bar. The rest of us went on talking. It was only subliminally that I was conscious of the same man who'd followed him into the toilet now standing next to Joe as the girl serving him lined up the drinks. When Joe and Steve handed them round, I did catch a gleam of what I took for amusement in Joe's eyes as I accepted my glass from him and downed a long swallow, and I wondered briefly what he found so funny. But I forgot about it; Elizabeth was making us all shout with laughter again.

All in all, it was a short but intense occasion, and great fun. But at last it had to break up, and people began getting their coats on. I downed the last of my drink and put the glass back onto the table.

"Right, have a lovely afternoon, everyone," I instructed merrily. "See you on Monday! See you whenever, Joe."

He nodded a cheerful acknowledgement. A chorus of, "See you, Jenny," expressed in various forms, accompanied me to the door as I left and began to head back to Nick's garage.

But as I walked, I began to feel as if something wasn't quite right. A bit lightheaded, as if I'd been drinking alcohol and the effects were just beginning to kick in. But I hadn't been, so it couldn't be that. Maybe I was coming down with something. Didn't feel like a cold, though.

I walked on, but the nearer I got to where the car was, the more difficult I found it to concentrate. Lightheaded, indeed. I couldn't seem to get my thoughts in order. And I was beginning to feel an odd sensation of floating, as if there was a strange, empty gap between my feet and the rest of me. In these blank-walled streets of office units there were few pedestrians; one or two of the ones I did pass gave me sidelong looks, as if they could see something wasn't quite right. But none of them spoke to me.

There was the garage, at last. The car, where I'd left it, only a few yards away now. But I couldn't see it clearly; it was as if I was trying to look at it through a soft focus filter, so soft that not just the car but everything was blurring.

I stumbled and nearly fell; my head seemed full of cotton wool. I finally realized something was wrong. Really wrong. I fumbled in my bag for my phone, but couldn't seem to direct my hands properly. With a growing sense of anxiety I tried again, and this time I got it. Instinctively, I found myself calling Peter.

My hand felt incredibly heavy as I lifted the phone to my ear. My legs seemed not to want to obey me, as I still tried to walk toward the car. I was only feet away from it when Peter answered. I found I had to stop. Talking and walking at the same time was suddenly much too problematical to attempt.

"Hi, Jenny. What's up?"

I opened my mouth to reply, but I found it difficult to speak.

"Peter..." I managed, but my voice sounded slow and slurred.

"Jenny?" He sounded puzzled.

"Peter..." Why was it going dark? It shouldn't be going dark in the middle of the day...! "Pe-e-e-ter..." The dimming world was wheeling around me. Now the angles were all wrong. The car shouldn't be stood vertical like that... The sky shouldn't be on its side... What was happening...?

Someone, somewhere, their voice faint and frantic, was shouting, "Jenny! Jenny!" I couldn't work out why.

I gave up the fight to understand. My eyes felt as if they were rolling in my head, turning over and over and over, out of my control. It made me feel sick and dizzy and I wanted it to *stop make it stop make it stop make it stop...*

When everything went black, it did.

Stop.

Nobody in the street had paid any attention to the woman who had walked out of the pub, brushing a stray lock of her golden brown hair out of her eyes. Nor to the man who followed her out just a few seconds later, stood for a moment watching her, then turned to walk along the street in her wake. But he had been paying her attention, all right.

Lesser watched the progress of his victim as she retraced the route to her car. From his point of view, it was immensely helpful of her to have left it in such an out-of-the-way spot; the likelihood of someone seeing her and coming to assist was low. Given the dose she'd had, and the timing involved, he found it interesting to speculate whether she would even make it that far.

As she turned down into the side streets he could see the effects beginning to kick in. She shook her head once or twice, as if trying to clear it, and her walk was gradually becoming stilted and awkward, as if her control of her body was lessening. He smiled. All according to plan.

At the last, of course, she tried to phone. As he'd hoped. And when she spoke, her voice thick and indistinct, he knew she'd phoned exactly who he expected.

Then she went down, dropping heavily onto the rough tarmac, her inert hand still cradling the phone.

Lesser stopped and looked around, but there was no one in sight. He walked into the yard and stood looking down at her for a few moments. He could hear McLeish's frantic voice coming from the phone, calling her name. He bent down and took it from her limp fingers, and lifted it to his ear.

"You should come and find her, Peter," he said, cutting across McLeish. He could clearly hear the indrawn breath as his voice was recognized. "She's really having a lovely day, you know." He ended the call with an abrupt motion of his thumb, and looked down.

"Aren't you, Jenny?" he added, addressing the unconscious woman.

He bent down again and picked up her handbag, putting the phone into it and taking her car keys out. He unlocked the car and opened the passenger door, and put the handbag down on the floor of the footwell. Then he came back, crouched down, and picked her up, her arms helplessly spread wide, her hands dangling limply from her wrists, her head lolling loosely from her cruelly angled neck. He carried her to the car and then, carefully, as if anxious not to damage her, he put her into the passenger seat, meticulously fastening the seat belt across her body.

He got into the driver's seat and put the keys in the ignition. The car moved off to its next destination, unremarked by anyone.

But as he drove, there was a quiet smile of pleasurable satisfaction on Lesser's face.

He was imagining McLeish, going frantic somewhere.

Which he was.

Still clutching his phone, he burst into Alan's office as if all the hordes of Hell were on his tail.

"He's got Jenny!" he ejaculated.

Alan froze for a moment. There was no need to ask who 'he' was. For Peter, there was only one 'he' in a context like this.

"What do you mean?" he demanded.

"Phone call. I heard him! He's got Jenny!"

"Where?"

"*I don't know!*"

"What happened?"

"She rang me. She sounded strange. Like she couldn't speak properly. I think she collapsed. Then he was there. On her phone. '*Come and find her,*' he said. '*She's having a lovely day.*'" Peter stared at him with something close to terror in his eyes, as he leapt to conclusions. "He's drugged her. He must have drugged her! And now he's got her somewhere! And..." He couldn't finish the sentence.

Even if Peter was still in denial about the exact nature of his feelings for Jenny Gregory, they were now completely transparent to his cousin. But this wasn't the time to remark upon it. Alan clenched his jaw, then reached for the phone. A full search. The works. Especially mobile tracking. He issued his orders swiftly and concisely while Peter watched him with wild eyes, his hands clutching the door jambs, panting as if he'd been sprinting. At the end of the conversation Alan slammed the phone back into its cradle, and thought swiftly.

"'*Come and find her*,'" he repeated. "Sounds as if he expects you to know where to look. Is he taking her somewhere you've been together? Some special place you go often? Where might that be?"

"I don't know – I..." Peter's face distorted with concentration as he tried to think.

"Is there a pub you go to? A park? A landmark of some kind? Come on, Peter – where do you take her? Where did you take her last?"

"I don't know!" Peter said again, clutching at his head. He sounded close to tears, and he clearly wasn't thinking straight. All the qualities he needed at this moment – that he had under normal circumstances, that made him the excellent officer he was – were now in abeyance, scattered into incoherence just when he needed them most. Completely, utterly understandable, of course. He'd already lost one woman he loved in the most terrible way, and now the whole appalling nightmare might be playing itself out again, at the hands of the same man. He'd need to be more than human not to react as he was now doing. But it wouldn't do. Not for him, not for Jenny. Alan decided his best course of action was some tough love.

"Peter!" he snapped. "Pack it in and get your act together! Do your job! This is *Jenny*!"

"I know it's Jenny!" Peter yelled, savagely. "D'you think I don't know that? Why d'you think—?"

"Then start being professional, right now," Alan cut across him coldly. "You're about as much use as a damp rag in a flood, like this! Or, given the way you're behaving, should I start wondering exactly how much you really care about her?" The goading was deliberate, and it was working.

"*Mind your own business!*" Peter yelled.

"You're a subordinate colleague, you're my best friend, you're *family*!" Alan shouted back. "And Jenny is *my* friend! *Our* friend! On how many of those counts, exactly, is this *not* my business?"

243

There was a silence.

"Sorry," Peter muttered at last.

"I should damn well think so!" Alan snapped, but with frustration rather than anger. "Look, she needs your help. Now. She needs you to calm down, think straight, and be as good at what you do as we both know you are."

After a short silence, Peter said hoarsely, "I've always gone to different places. Different times. Tried not to set a pattern. So I don't know, Alan. I don't! Could be anywhere. Any of the places we've gone. Sometimes we've gone back somewhere we've been before, but never regularly. I don't think she knows why."

"Don't be stupid," Alan retorted. "Of course she knows! She's known for months! She's got her head screwed on, that girl. All right, then we'll have to see if tracking her mobile gives us any clues. Where do you think you're going?" he added abruptly.

"To look for her," said Peter, already half-way back through the door.

"Where, exactly?" Alan enquired acidly.

"I don't know! But I can't just sit here while he's out there doing who knows what with her!"

Alan stared at him with a steely eye for a moment, then relented.

"No, I suppose that would be asking too much," he conceded. "But stay in touch! If something comes through, I'll need to talk to you." He followed Peter to the door. Shoeshop, Kevlar and Ben were all staring at them. Clearly they'd heard every word.

"Ben, you go with him," Alan ordered.

"I don't need a nursemaid," Peter snapped savagely.

"You're not getting one," Alan snapped back. "But if the Laird hears I let you go off after Lesser on your own, it'll be my job on the line, not just yours."

Peter was compelled to recognize the truth of that. After a couple of seconds he nodded in reluctant acquiescence, then stalked out. Alan gave an expressive sideways jerk of his head at Ben, who was already rising, grabbing his jacket. He gave Alan a reassuring nod and went after Peter.

Ignoring the others, Alan turned back into his office and shut the door behind him. His right hand balled into a fist, and he pressed the back of it to his mouth for a moment, feeling the pressure of his teeth against the taut knuckles. He thought about Peter, and about Jenny. About what Jane and the kids would be feeling if they knew. About Richard and Beth Taylor.

Then he thought about Lesser, and his face darkened.

"We are going to *get* you, you son of a bitch," he muttered.

Ben didn't ask where they were going; he sat silent and let Peter go where he would. It didn't take long for Peter to realize he had no real idea what to do.

He didn't even know where he was going. Other than towards Croydon. But when he got there, where would he look? Lesser might have taken her anywhere by now.

Even so…

Please don't let him hurt her. Don't let it happen again. Not because of me. She doesn't deserve it. Please. Had his thoughts been coherent, that might have been how they would have sounded to the recipient, though he didn't have any clear idea who, or what, he was addressing. He was only conscious of an intense need to make the plea.

Please.

Alan's desk phone had only emitted one ring before he'd got it to his ear. His eyes lit up.

"New Addington? You're sure? Right. I'll see if I can get you any specific locations. Get back to you."

He broke the connection and redialled Peter's car phone.

"Come on, Peter, pick up," he muttered impatiently, even though only a couple of seconds had passed. Then the line buzzed into life.

"What?" Alan could hear the tension in Peter's voice.

"Mobile tracking have got a tentative location. New Addington. Have you been there with her lately?"

There was an edgy pause. Then Peter said, "Addington Park. We walked round it a couple of days ago. Went for a meal in a pub there – the Cricketers, it's called, or something? I – I can't remember."

"Anywhere else?"

"No."

"Right, I'll pass that on."

"Look – if they've picked up a signal, she's used her phone, hasn't she?" Peter's voice contained desperate hope.

"Somebody has," said Alan, dampingly. "I hope you're right. But maybe he's up to his usual games. Playing with us. Teasing us to come and find her. Look, I'll be in touch as soon as I know anything."

Suppressing his awareness of how superfluous that last sentence had been, he cut the connection and redialled.

"McLeish," he said tersely. "Addington Park. And maybe the Cricketers pub. Get someone to both places right away. Got the registration? Right. I want to know the second you know anything – got that?"

A nail-biting ten minutes later, another call came through. Alan seized the handset and listened, tautly.

"Where? Alive?" He let out a long breath at the reply. Then another difficult question. "Has she been assaulted in any way?" A pause. "You're sure?" Another pause. "Well, get the paramedics to see what they think and let me know as soon as you can. There's someone who needs to know."

He put the phone down, and buried his face in his hands for a few moments.

Then he squared his shoulders, and got on with his job.

When Peter's car phone rang he immediately answered it, with no diminution of his driving speed.

"Peter." Alan's voice came over the loudspeaker. "Where are you now?"

"On the way to New Addington." *Where did you think I was going?*

"Pull over."

"What?"

"Pull over. Now. I need to tell you something and I don't want you on the move while I do it."

Peter's heart lurched. Without regard for any other road users who might have happened to be in his proximity, he swerved into the side of the road and hit the brakes. Ben grabbed at the side of his seat with one hand, the dashboard with the other, as the car bumped to a ragged halt, half-mounting the pavement. Which was, fortunately, free of pedestrians just there. A car swept past them, the driver leaning on the horn, but Peter wasn't even aware of it.

"What is it?"

"She's been found."

Peter gasped violently, a sensation of piercing intensity in his guts, as if his relief was pain. He heard Ben expel a sharp breath. *Please.* He swallowed, and forced himself to ask the question.

"Alive?"

"Yes. And apparently unhurt."

"Then, she's not been—? He hasn't—?"

"No. They'll need to check to make really sure, but as far as they can tell – no. Just drugged. She hasn't come round yet."

Peter had to gather himself, breathing hard, before his next question.

"Where was she?"

"Addington Park."

Peter swore under his breath. "So he did know."

There was a short silence while both of them took in the implications.

"Where is she now?"

"They're taking her to Croydon Hospital. See you later." Alan rang off.

Peter sat rigid for a few seconds, staring at nothing. Then his face crumpled. He leaned forward, his fingers clutching at the top of the steering wheel, his head pressing down on his forearms, and gave way to one racking sob after another, his shoulders violently shaking, heaving gasps forcing their way up through his throat. He felt Ben's hand on his shoulder, relief and reassurance in the touch.

Thank you. Thank you.

But it wasn't Ben he was thanking.

Chapter 24

Peter was there to take me home when the hospital finally let me go, some hours later.

I covertly studied his profile as he drove. I'd already registered that his eyes were red-rimmed, and the lids slightly swollen. But now he stared ahead at the road with a fixed, burning intensity that couldn't be mistaken for anything but anger. The scream of the engine when he accelerated, the cavalier way in which he was handling the car, communicated his mood clearly enough.

By the time it became obvious that he wasn't going to speak, I was feeling very uncomfortable. Besides still feeling fairly dopey; whatever I'd had, the effects were dissipating, but it was still making its presence felt. I felt tired, and still shaken. I didn't think it was me he was angry with – I didn't *think* so – but I decided the assay needed to be made.

"You're very quiet," I said. "Am I in disgrace, or something?"

"Danger," he said, biting the word off. "You're in danger. And it's my fault. I shouldn't see you again."

I tried to suppress the immediate reaction of alarm, of instinctive protest, that quivered inside me.

"Bit late for that," I observed, trying to sound matter-of-fact. I had the strongest feeling I needed to keep as calm as possible, or one of us might end up saying something we'd regret.

"Is it," he said harshly; it was phrased as a question, but it was nothing of the sort. It was a plain, flat contradiction.

"Yes," I said, still trying to keep calm. "Nothing we can do about it now."

"Isn't there?" he challenged, in the same harsh tone. "Like I said, I could stop seeing you. That's something I could do. That'd do it."

I couldn't help myself.

"No, it wouldn't, and you know it," I snapped. My nerves, like his, were over-taut. "We've had this conversation once already, and nothing's changed! Do you really think it'd make any kind of difference now? He's already made the connection! Think not seeing each other'd suddenly convince him otherwise? And, anyway" – my voice was becoming as clipped as his; I was angry, like him, and afraid, like him, though not for the same reasons – "if you think I'm going to agree to stop seeing you, as if

I didn't" – I broke off, then changed what I had been going to say – "well, you can damn well think again!"

He swore under his breath, savagely. Then, with a violent movement, he swung the wheel. Accompanied by an angry blare from the horn of the vehicle behind us, its driver taken unawares by the unsignalled manoeuvre, the car shot into a small cul-de-sac, which had once been the entrance to a business premises of some kind; it was now closed and derelict, but while the building itself was ringed by chain link fencing, some of the parking area in front of it was still accessible. Still handling the controls with that same savagery, he swung us into it, braked fiercely to a halt, and leapt out, slamming the door behind him.

Almost as angrily, I did the same.

He'd stalked off a few paces and was standing with his back to me, his hands clutching at his hair. Then they balled into fists at his sides as he abruptly rounded on me.

"You stupid, stupid woman!" he shouted, desperately. "Can't you see? I'm trying to protect you!"

"Well, maybe I don't want to be protected!" I retorted. "Not if it means not seeing you again!"

"D'you think I could bear it, if anything happened to you?" he snarled.

"D'you think *I* could bear it, abandoning *you*?" I snapped back. "Thinking about you all alone? Under siege for the rest of your life, scared to be with anyone? Think I can just walk off and leave you to that kind of life?"

His brows contracted momentarily into a clench of pain.

"It's what you'd do if you had any sense," he said flatly.

"Well, maybe I haven't got any sense! And, look – I'm not making any decisions about anything while I'm not yet thinking straight. And neither are you." I paused, and we stared at each other, panting with the expenditure of emotional energy. His eyes were desperate and pleading; mine were implacable in their resolve. Poor Peter! The weakness of his position was that however volubly he argued his case, it wasn't what he *wanted*. He didn't want to stop seeing me. He was just so afraid of the possible consequences if he didn't. It wasn't that I wasn't afraid of those myself. Because I was. But he was more important to me than they were.

"Look, I'm not going to live my life on 'maybes'," I said, still angry, but trying to tone it down. "Neither of us knows what's going to happen in the future. Maybe I'll get food poisoning from my dinner tonight. Maybe we'll go for a walk in the park and a tree will fall on us. Maybe some idiot'll drive head on into us round the next corner. Maybe anything! But I can't live my life afraid to go out the door in case any of them do happen! Maybe

Lesser *will* have another go at me! But I am not going to abandon you just because he might!"

Peter stared at me, silenced, still breathing hard.

I took a deep breath. "Look, we've both had a fright. Why the hell d'you think we're going at each other like this? Is this what we'd normally do?"

Momentarily, his expression relaxed; he even got fairly close to a smile, though not quite all the way. Then he looked away, thrusting his hands deep into his trouser pockets.

"No," he conceded gruffly, after a few moments.

"No!" I agreed, instantly, still angry. "Because this isn't a normal situation. So what both of us should do is shut up, calm down, and *then* decide what we're going to do. Except that not seeing you is not an option on the table as far as I'm concerned, and it's never going to be! Quite apart from anything else, I'm not going to give him the satisfaction! Got that?" My voice had risen close to a shout again.

"Got it," he said, in a strange voice. I looked at him sharply, ready to fight on – only to realize that, quite unexpectedly, he was laughing. Even though I was still boiling inside, I felt a slash of relief cutting through the maelstrom. From what could have been a really serious quarrel, it had magically become one of those wonderful moments where we were on the same wavelength. The corner of my mouth twitched in response.

"Glad to hear it." I tried to sound stern, but my anger had subsided into relief, and I found myself smiling back, ruefully.

"Oh, Peter," I said contritely. "I'm sorry."

"I'm not! I should be," he added. "But I'm not."

Which was, in its way, a recognition of how everything stood between us. Not how it could have been – or, if sense or reason were applied, even how, perhaps, it should have been.

But, in spite of everything, how it was.

"Come on," he said. "Let's get you home."

Of course, a few minutes later, without warning, I started to cry. Peter glanced at me anxiously several times, his attention divided between my distress and the need to watch the road.

"What is it?"

I tried to swallow a sob, and waggled one hand in a negative gesture until I could speak.

"Don't worry," I said tremulously, once I could get my words out. "It's just reaction…" I looked at him, trying to smile even while the tears coursed down my cheeks. "I don't know what you were expecting! I've been kidnapped today, and we've just had a blazing row! It's just reaction, honestly. Please don't worry! I don't want you worrying. You've got enough on your plate." I hadn't known my eyes could produce so much water. Where was it all coming from?

He shook his head, helplessly, a wry amusement fighting with concern for the dominant expression on his face.

"You never give up, do you? Always worrying about me, when you should be worrying about yourself."

"I don't have to worry about myself," I retorted, with a loud and most unladylike sniff. "I've got you to do it for me, these days." I wrestled my handbag from the footwell onto my lap, and rummaged around inside it for a clean handkerchief. I wiped my eyes – to little effect, as fresh tears immediately brimmed and began to overflow – then blew my nose. I dared not think about what a mess I must look. Very few women have the knack of being able to weep without their faces becoming ugly and blotchy and distorted by it. And I'm not one of them.

"Do Richard and Beth know what's happened?" he asked abruptly.

"No. They're at a wedding anniversary party. They won't be back until late." I glanced at him. "I don't want to spoil things for them. There'll be plenty of time for that tomorrow," I added heavily.

Peter didn't answer that.

The empty driveway, when he pulled into it, made me realize that my car was absent from its usual place. *Of course it is, you idiot. What did you expect?* It must still be at Addington Park, where they'd found me.

"I suppose I'll need to go and get my car back, at some point," I remarked.

"Not till we say you can," said Peter briefly. "We've got a forensics team going over it at the moment."

I felt subdued. I'd forgotten that possibility.

He followed me so closely up the stairs it was a wonder he didn't tread on my heels. He was urgent to get me inside, but I was beginning to feel more tired than ever, and it almost seemed to require more energy than I possessed to raise each foot and put it on the next step. He pushed past me in the hall and vanished into the bathroom; as I took my coat off and hung it in the cloak cupboard, I heard the sound of water gushing into the bath. He reappeared in the doorway and looked at me almost sternly.

"Right," he said. "You're going to have a bath."

"So I gather," I acknowledged weakly.

"Bath, food, bed," he said implacably, laying down the timetable. The last thing I felt like doing was eating, but I didn't try to argue. I so wanted to sleep, now, but the thought of a bath was too attractive to refuse. Though there were things that had happened to me today that water couldn't wash away... I turned toward the bathroom, then paused, my hand on the door jamb, and met his eyes.

"Thank you, Peter," I said.

We looked at each other, and no more words were necessary. I went on into the bathroom, shutting the door behind me. The water level in the bath was creeping upwards, mounds of bubbles heaped on the rising surface; he'd gone a bit mad with the bath foam. By the time I'd stripped off my clothes, it was as full as it could safely be. I sank into the enclosing warmth as if I was entering a refuge.

I must have been lulled toward somnolence in the hot, scented water, because the knock on the bathroom door made me come to with a jerk.

"What—?" I began, momentarily disoriented.

"I'm trying to find your nightclothes." Peter's voice was muffled through the heavy wood of the door. "Where do you keep them?"

"I don't usually wear any," I said, before I thought. *Listen to yourself. Lying naked in a bath behind an unlocked door and telling him that...*

There was a slight pause. Then he persisted, "So what should I get you?"

I struggled to make my weary brain function.

"In the left-hand wardrobe in my room," I said. "There'll be some caftans. One of them'll do."

"Right," he said.

A couple of minutes later: "I'm just going to throw this inside, okay?"

"It's all right," I told him. "You can come in and hang it on the back of the door, if you like."

"Are you sure? Are you—?"

"Don't worry, it's all right," I said again. My modesty was safe enough, given the amount of bath foam he'd put in, but I sat up and leaned forward, bringing my knees up to my chin and embracing them, so that all he would see would be my back and shoulders, deep in scented bubbles. Tired as I was, I couldn't help smiling; he was being so protective of me, so solicitous. How could I feel anything other than touched by that?

There was another pause. Then the door opened, slowly, as if he still wasn't sure I meant it. I didn't turn round, but I heard the slight sounds as he stepped in, and hung the caftan onto the hook on the back of the door. There was a momentary silence; I could almost feel his eyes on my naked back, like a touch. Then he moved, and the door was pulled to behind him.

"What can I get you to eat?"

"Oh, Peter, don't," I pleaded. "I couldn't face anything. I just want to go to sleep."

There was a pause, as if he wanted to argue. "I'll get you something to drink," he compromised.

By the time I emerged from the bathroom, he had it ready for me; a large, heavily sugared hot chocolate. He hovered over me while I drank it. I felt so tired I hardly had the energy to finish it, but for his sake I ploughed on to the end. He took the empty mug from me and followed on my heels as I plodded up the stairs. But when I drew level with the spare room, heading for my own, he stopped me.

"Not your room," he ordered, taking me by the arm. "This one." He was pushing me through the door.

"But—" I began to protest.

"You bullied me into this bed last time," he said, propelling me toward it. "My turn."

Why it was important to him that I slept in the double bed and not my own, I could no longer be troubled to ask. All I wanted was to sink my head into the pillow and let go. I climbed in and immediately rolled over onto my left side, the side I always go to sleep on. I felt him pulling the duvet up to cover my shoulders, but that was the last thing I was aware of. I never even heard him leave the room.

If, indeed, he did.

When I came to, I didn't move at first. The light coming through the sloping window, falling onto the bed, had the look of early morning about it. I was still lying on my left side; perhaps I'd slept so deeply that I'd never moved at all during the night. My eyelids felt heavy as I gazed vacantly at the pillow on the other side of the bed, and I didn't register what I was seeing at first. But gradually it seeped into my comprehension. The dent in the pillow that had been pristine the night before. The indentation of a body into the surface of the duvet on that side of the bed. The faint warmth still detectable when I put a hand out to touch the rumpled cotton.

I let the hand lie there while I worked it all out. He must have been there all night. That was why my own bed wouldn't have done. He couldn't have watched over my sleep, been right there beside me, in my room. He'd been able to here; not in the bed with me, but on it. Making sure I wasn't left alone for a moment. I wondered who he'd intended to reassure. Me, or himself?

I felt my eyes start to brim. Then I got control of myself, rolled over and got out of bed. I went to the head of the stairs, and listened; I could hear no movement.

"Peter?" I called. No answer.

I went downstairs; he wasn't there. I went to the window and looked out, but he wasn't in the garden, either. Thinking he might have had to go for some reason without telling me, I went to the front door and looked down at the driveway. His car was still there.

So there was only one place left that he could be. And probably only one reason for being there.

I went slowly back up the stairs, to get dressed.

In my parents' part of the house, my father had already had his breakfast, and was now making his way into the living room. As he glanced out of the window, something caught his eye, and he looked with more attention.

Alongside his own car, he'd expected to see only mine, in place of Peter's which had been there last night, even though it had been very late when they'd returned from the party. But my car wasn't there. And Peter's still was. Which was puzzling. My father regarded the scene thoughtfully. Knowing me as he did, some of the apparent implications surprised, or at any rate unsettled, him.

Then, while he was still staring abstractedly out at the cars, a familiar, tall figure suddenly appeared from the right, the side of the house where the stairs led down from my flat, and strode purposefully across the face of the window. A few seconds later, there was a knock on the front door.

My father went out into the hall and opened it.

"Peter," he said, striving to keep his voice uninflected. My choices were, after all, my own. "I wasn't expecting to see you here at this time of day."

Peter looked at him with dark, serious eyes.

"I've been in Jenny's flat all night," he said.

"Oh?" One of my father's eyebrows quirked slightly in response to such a blunt declaration; this time it was harder to keep his tone level. It wasn't very difficult to deduce what he was thinking.

"I wasn't sleeping with her," said Peter bleakly. "I was guarding her."

My father's expression changed. He stared at Peter for a couple of seconds, implications beginning to coalesce in his brain. Then he opened the door wider.

"You'd better come in," he said.

It was already warm in the garden. A slight breeze stirred the leaves of the trees; sparrows and chaffinches chirped, mostly unseen, in the foliage. A blackbird perched on a low bough of one of the flowering cherries, alternately releasing bursts of beautiful song and then relapsing into silence, occasionally meeting my gaze with the impersonal black orb of his eye.

I continued to watch him without moving as my father came and joined me on the garden bench. I was at one end; he sat at the other, crossing his legs casually and stretching one arm out along the back of the bench. Almost touching me, but not quite.

We sat without speaking for a couple of minutes before he broke the silence.

"I find myself in something of a dilemma," he observed with a veneer of clinical detachment. As if we were mid-conversation; as if we'd been saying aloud what we'd been thinking. "Intellectually, I know there's nothing more to be done, in practical terms, than Peter and his colleagues are already doing. And that you're a sensible person, and I can trust you to behave accordingly, and take all the precautions you can. Yet" – he paused, then went on in that calm, collected voice, that he must have been exerting such self-control to maintain – "emotionally, I find I want to snatch you into my arms, the way I did when you were a little girl, and hold you very close. Protect you. Keep you safe from every bad thing in the world."

I smiled wryly, still watching the blackbird.

"You'd have your work cut out," I said. "There're rather a lot of bad things in the world these days."

"I know," he acknowledged heavily. "But it doesn't stop me wanting to do it."

"Oh, Dad," I said sadly, and lifted my right hand back and up to find his where it lay on the back of the bench. His fingers curled around mine, and held them hard.

"Are you all right now?" he asked.

"Physically? Yes, I think so. Emotionally…" I let that one lie. "Where's Peter?"

"Still talking things through with your mother."

"Is she all right?"

"Not exactly. I think you'll find she's in much the same case as I am over this."

"I'm sorry, Dad."

"Hardly your fault, darling."

"I know, but – I'm sorry I can't stop you being distressed by it. I wish it could just be me. After all, I'm the one really involved."

"Ah-ah-ah," he reproved. "No man is an island. Neither you, nor Peter. You're our daughter, he's your friend, therefore he's our friend. That's the way it works."

"I know," I repeated, with a sigh.

"Just take care, Jenny, please." He stared down at his right hand, lying in his lap, as if it was something useless to him. "Take every possible care. And so will we." He tilted his head back to look up at the sky, and drew in a deep breath. Then he looked at me, and smiled – anxiously, even sadly, but still a smile. "And now I think I'd better go back and make sure your mother's all right. Or as all right as she can be, in the circumstances." He gave my fingers another squeeze, and released them. As he rose, I looked up at him.

"There's one thing you haven't suggested," I said, cocking an eyebrow at him.

"What's that?"

"That I stop seeing Peter."

"No," said my father instantly. "Nor will I. Nor," he added, "are you such a shallow person as to take any notice of me if I did."

He held my gaze for a moment, then walked behind the bench, evidently about to go back into the house. Just for a moment he paused behind me, and I felt the kiss he dropped onto the top of my head, the hand he laid momentarily on my shoulder, the brief pressure of his fingers before they were withdrawn. Then he walked on, leaving me as he'd found me, listening to the blackbird, still singing with heartbreaking beauty in the flowering cherry.

Chapter 25

I knew there'd have to be an interview, of course. Alan would need to glean from me anything that might be of use to him and the team. I wondered if he'd do it himself, as he had up in Inverness, but of course he didn't. That had been a procedural aberration, arising in very specific circumstances from a crossover of his professional and personal relationships with Peter. This time he got Ben to conduct it, but he sat in, observing and listening; he certainly had no intention of having Peter there, getting himself uselessly worked up.

"Just tell us everything you can remember," he told me quietly, deliberately wearing his professional face – as he had to, in the circumstances – before he nodded to Ben to proceed. So I did, whilst painfully aware that memory, even recent memory, can be such an unreliable function. Something I'd picked up from more than one science documentary over the years was the way the brain edits memories to make them bearable, or links together unconnected details and presents them as one coherent memory, when in reality they belong to totally separate occasions, essentially creating false memories and presenting them, quite sincerely, as truth. That's why you can have ten eyewitnesses of an event who give ten different versions of what happened and each one be completely sincere in the belief that they are telling the absolute truth.

So I could only give him my truth. But I did my best, describing the occasion as accurately as I could, listing who had been there, what we had done, any slight detail I could remember. They were recording the whole thing, of course, but Ben still made notes as he listened and questioned; Alan watched, and listened, and correlated.

"The photos that got taken," Ben said, looking at what he'd written. "We'll need to contact everyone who was there, get copies of them. There might be someone caught in the background we can identify."

"I'll give you Elizabeth's number," I said. "She can put you in touch with all of them."

"Tell her to keep it as quiet as possible," Alan interjected, catching Ben's eye. "She doesn't even need to know anything happened to Jenny. I don't want a lot of unhelpful attention being drawn to her. Just say we've had information that something happened in the vicinity of the pub and we heard their group were taking a lot of photos, so we'd like to see them in case, etcetera, etcetera."

Ben nodded, and regarded me thoughtfully.

"Who knew you were going to be there?" he asked. "Did you tell anyone?"

I frowned. "Outside of work, you mean? Not knowingly. Apart from Mum and Dad. I'm not sure I even mentioned it to Peter. But as many of us as could, were going. And everyone knew about it for at least a couple of weeks beforehand. So anyone could have said anything to anyone. It wasn't exactly a secret." I paused, then added, "And no one would have known there was any reason why it should've been."

"No," Ben agreed, non-committally.

"Something else you should know," I said. "There was a call on Dad's answer phone. Yesterday, fourteen thirty-seven. No voice, just silence." I looked over at Alan. "For about half a minute."

"Making sure we had every chance to track your phone," Alan observed with leaden calm. He looked at Ben. "Like I said. Teasing us." Ben met his eyes impassively before adding to his growing list of notes. Then he glanced back at Alan, silently asking if there was anything else. Alan gave the tiniest shake of his head. Ben turned back to me.

"He's had access to your phone," he said. "You'd better get a new one. And make sure you use a security code. Were you using one already?"

I shook my head, ruefully. Like a lot of people, I'd never bothered; I'd never thought of any of the numbers on it as needing protection. After all, who was going to be interested in what was on *my* phone? My mistake.

"Will he already know your number, and Peter's?" I asked Alan. "They're on there."

"I'm sure he does," Alan agreed. "But don't worry about that." He glanced at Ben; they consulted each other silently again, after which Ben closed his notebook decisively.

"That's it for now, then," he said. "When we've got the photos, you'll come back and go through them?"

It wasn't really a question, but I nodded as if it was.

"Thank you, Jenny," said Alan, and that was all. But it wasn't just the thanks of a high-ranking officer presiding over a specialist police team seeking to procure the conviction of a clever and serious criminal. It was the thanks of a personal friend, concerned about my welfare and that of the man who had, since our unconventional encounter at the foot of that hill in Scotland, linked us. A delicate balancing act for him to get right. It was probably tough enough doing it with just Peter, in the normal course of events; I must complicate the equation noticeably. But he'd showed every sign of being equal to the task so far.

"Try not to worry," he went on, though his expression betrayed the knowledge that it was probably a useless piece of advice. "Go home. Relax."

"I can guarantee the going home bit," I agreed. "The relaxing bit might not be up to just me."

He smiled understandingly. "Well, try to get *him* to relax. Then your chances might be better."

"I'll try," I promised.

It didn't entirely work, though.

"Ben…"

Ben looked up in response to Andy's summons. Shoeshop, the only other person there, was on the phone to someone and ignored them both. Andy gestured at her computer; Ben went over.

On the screen was one of the photos he'd rounded up from the group at the pub. It showed Elizabeth on the left, her back to the bar, with Jenny alongside her on the right of the shot, sideways on to the camera, laughing. Behind Jenny, one of the booths that lined the right-hand wall.

Silently Andy pointed at the man sitting on the outer edge of the half-circle seat that ran around the inside of the booth, a partially empty lager glass on the table in front of him. A big man, fair-haired. His back was to the camera, and only the left side of his body was clearly visible – shoulder, arm, leg – but his head was turned slightly to his left, so that his face was almost in profile.

Andy zoomed in until the increased pixelation threatened to make the resulting view meaningless.

"It is, isn't it?" she said tentatively.

Ben nodded. It wasn't identification absolute, not in terms a court would accept. But there was no doubt in his mind.

"It's him," he said flatly.

Shoeshop had finished her call, and was blatantly eavesdropping.

"Who?" she asked. Ben gestured at the screen, and she came over and looked.

"Lesser," she said immediately.

"Any more shots like this?" Ben asked.

Andy shook her head. "None that show his face. Just the back of his head."

Ben muttered a blasphemy under his breath. That was Lesser all over – you knew, but you couldn't prove. It would be coincidence – of course it would. After all, he had a right to go into any pub he chose and have a drink, any time he wanted. This just happened to be the one, and the time, when Jenny Gregory was there, too. Of *course* it was coincidence!

Even the greenest defence lawyer would be on to that one, like a shot. Oh, yes, you knew. But you could never prove. And the Crown Prosecution Service wouldn't accept straws in the wind, no matter how many of them there were. Only the whole haystack, right there in their laps. And then only when its really being a haystack had been attested to by reliable expert witnesses, of course.

Ben swore again. Then he put a hand on Andy's shoulder for a moment.

"Okay, thanks," he said. "Send that one to the Boss, will you?"

She nodded.

There was a short silence.

"Are we ever going to get him, Ben?" Shoeshop asked, though not as if she really expected an answer.

"We'd better," Ben said promptly – and so grimly that both women looked at him, startled by the bleakness of his tone.

"Because, particularly—?" Shoeshop prompted.

"Because her life depends on it," Ben said, gesturing at the screen, his tone robbing the statement of any hint of cliché.

Andy and Shoeshop stared at him, then at each other, before looking back at the photograph, and the laughing face of Jenny Gregory.

Some persecutors don't hesitate, once they've started; they pile attack upon attack, overwhelming their prey by the very relentlessness of their victimization. Matthew Lesser, it seemed, was not such a one. His favoured approach, apparently, was to give you time after each encounter to think about what had happened, think of all the implications, and let them work on you before his next strike, while leaving you achingly aware that that might happen at any moment. A couple of weeks went by with no further move from him; if that was his strategy, it was an effective one. I tried not to show it outwardly, but I couldn't help thinking. Not about what had happened to me. About what had not happened to me – but could have. And still might. I couldn't prevent myself from being unsettled by the images my mind persisted in creating.

Peter, for one, must have recognized the signs; he'd seen it happen to Laura. But he tried hard to keep his promise not to continually articulate the obvious, but to help me cope. I could see the effort it cost him sometimes, but he kept trying, bless him. And I loved him for it.

I know the exact moment when I acknowledged it openly to myself. That I loved him. It wasn't a particularly remarkable occasion; he'd come to me after work, as he did every day now, and let himself in. It was a warm July evening; he hadn't bothered to put his jacket on after parking his car in the drive. When he came into the living room, I looked up to greet him, and that was when I felt, quite unexpectedly, a physical jolt, as if something had hit me in the pit of my stomach. Why that evening, and no other, I shall never be able to explain. But as he stood there, tall and slim in black jeans and a plain white cotton shirt, the sleeves half-rolled up over his forearms, dropping his jacket casually over the back of the sofa, something changed for me.

He must have detected a shift in my expression, because he looked at me enquiringly.

"What?" he prompted.

"I was just thinking you look good in that shirt," I said honestly. He wore a look of slight surprise as he glanced down at it.

"It's just a shirt," he shrugged, slightly bemused.

I smiled, and didn't comment further, just told him I'd start on dinner and he could do what he liked meanwhile.

"Have I got time for a quick bath?" he enquired.

"Of course," I told him. "Help yourself."

A little while afterward I heard the sound of the bathwater emptying down the pipe, followed a few minutes later by his return to the living room and the almost undetectable noise of his weight settling into the armchair. He didn't speak to me, and just at that moment I couldn't leave the cooker. A couple more minutes, and I could; I went to the open doorway between the kitchen and the living room.

"Peter—" I began, but broke off. It was instantly evident that, sprawled in the receiving softness of the armchair, warmed and relaxed by his bath, he had fallen asleep.

I stood in the kitchen doorway for a long time, leaning against the jamb, looking at him. Just looking at him. For the pure pleasure of doing so.

He was half-turned in the chair, his right leg flung over the arm. His left foot was flat on the floor, but the knee was leaning over to the right, tending to turn the whole leg in the same direction. His left forearm lay along the other arm of the chair, his hand dangling loosely from his wrist over the end of it, his long, beautiful fingers limp and relaxed. His right hand lay palm up in his lap. His face was three-quarters turned towards me, the features relaxed and at ease in a way they never were when he was conscious. Stray, damp strands of his long, dark hair trailed lightly across his forehead and his bearded cheek. The collar of his shirt was turned back, and my eyes followed the compelling curve of his neck and shoulder until it, and the pale skin stretching smoothly over the collarbone and upper chest, was concealed by the clean white cotton.

I looked at him, and I wanted him. I knew I wanted him. I wanted him emotionally, and I wanted him physically. That was the plain truth.

But it wasn't the only truth. There was another truth, one that had to take priority. And that was that I could not – and must not – put the pressure on him that would inevitably result from my telling him, or in any way consciously showing him, what I felt. Whether I might give myself away unconsciously was another matter. He must be good at reading people; he couldn't be a good detective without having that skill. So maybe I would betray myself without meaning to. Maybe I already had. But I feared that to say it, to declare it or demonstrate it overtly in any way, would, in some way I couldn't define, bring something out into the open that he wasn't yet ready to deal with.

I loved him. That was blindingly clear to me now. But as long as there was Lesser, I couldn't tell him.

Could not, and must not.

They must have picked up on my mood at work, too; Moira certainly did, and I didn't have her down as one of the most perceptive people in the world.

"Are you all right, Jenny?" she asked. "You don't seem your usual self, somehow."

"Yeh, well – I've got something I've got to sort out," I admitted. "It's preying on my mind a bit."

She looked sympathetic.

"You need a break," she advised me. "I'm on the Saturday morning shift this week, but why don't we go out somewhere on Sunday?"

"What sort of somewhere?" I enquired, trying not to sound cautious. What Moira, at nineteen, might class as somewhere to go out might not necessarily be the sort of place I'd choose to go...

"What about Kew Gardens?" she suggested brightly, to my relief. "I went there last year, but you can't see the whole thing in one day, no chance. So I did the Palm House and all the stuff down that end, but I've never seen any of the rest of it – you know, the bits up near the Thames. D'you fancy that?"

I thought about it, and I did.

"Yes, I do," I said, more animatedly. "Thanks. What time, Sunday? And who drives?"

"Oh, me," she said immediately. "After all, it's my idea, isn't it? You tell me when to pick you up."

"Okay," I agreed.

She looked smug. "I tried asking Joe, but he said he was busy. So now I can tell him I'm going anyway. With you. So there!"

"Hello – some of the gloss wearing off?" I enquired mischievously.

She grinned. "Not where it counts!"

So early Sunday morning found us together in Moira's car, heading for Richmond. The forecasters were predicting a change to very warm weather on Monday, but for today it was a sunshine-and-showers forecast, though with the showers more likely later on, so we'd decided to take the risk. I'd told Peter where I was going, and with whom, so he knew I, in turn, was keeping my promise. But I had to get Moira to help me keep it, too, and without arousing her suspicions.

"Kew's a big place," I said casually, as we drove. "You won't go wandering off anywhere without me, will you? I want us to stick together."

"Yeah, of course," she agreed readily. "Mind you, if it gets much warmer than this, I'll be sticking to my own clothes! I didn't know it was going to be this humid today, did you? Dunno why you're worrying, though. We can always phone each other if we get separated."

"I know, but I'd rather we didn't," I said, trying to sound as if it was just a preference. "It'd be tricky getting home if I did lose you! So let's stay together. Promise?" I added lightly.

She gave me an odd look, but shrugged amiably.

"Yeah, promise," she said, humouring the eccentric old lady. I was sixteen years her senior, after all.

The threat of showers seemed to have put people off; there were fewer visitors in the gardens than I'd expected, certainly far fewer than would normally be there on a Sunday. I didn't care; I liked it that way. Less people to wander into my photographs and camcorder shots. Moira smiled as I dug both devices out of my shoulder bag.

"Might have known!" she sighed, pretending resignation.

"Well, this is me we're talking about," I pointed out amiably.

It was beautiful and peaceful, as it always is at Kew, if you ignore the constant traffic on the flight path to Heathrow overhead every couple of minutes. You soon tune it out, though. We opted to go in at the Lion Gate, near the Pagoda, so we could go straight up the Cedar Vista. Well, I say 'straight up', but my photographer's eye wouldn't let me pass much without wanting to get it on record, so it took us quite a while. Moira good-naturedly constrained her pace to a leisurely amble, allowing me the time to repeatedly stop, shoot, and then catch up with her again.

From the Waterlily Pond we diverted to the right to walk down along the side of the long, islanded lake and over Sackler Crossing. The lake displayed its usual healthy population of waterfowl; there was an abundance of coots, moorhens and various species of duck, some of them very exotic-looking. One coot swam right past us, so we could see the movement of its feet clearly in the water; Moira had never seen the size of a coot's feet in relation to its body before, and thought it was very funny.

"Where shall we go next?" she asked, still smiling as she leaned over the side of the bridge, watching the little bird paddling away for all it was worth, intent on some priority of its own. I consulted the colourful map issued to us with our entry tickets.

"What about the Rhododendron Dell?" I suggested.

Moira looked doubtful.

"Won't be any blossoms at this time of year," she demurred. "You'd need to be here in the spring for that."

"It'll still be worth a look, though, I'll bet. Look" – I brandished the map at her – "if we cut across this way, we can come up on this end of the Dell and work our way back to the turn-off into the Bamboo Gardens."

She brightened as she studied the map. "That's true. I love bamboo, don't know why. And what's this Minka House? Chinese or Japanese, or something, by the sound of it… Yeah, let's do that. Okay, then – onwards and upwards!"

"Something every pilot leaving Heathrow probably says to himself as soon as he gets into his slot on the runway," I muttered, as yet another enormous airliner sailed overhead. Moira laughed.

The Rhododendron Dell, despite its name, isn't populated purely by rhododendrons; there are some wonderful trees and shrubs there, too. Some of the rhododendron bushes themselves swell into huge mounds fifteen feet or even more in height, their broad leaves and tangled branches forming apparently impenetrable walls of vegetation – walls which, at the right time of year, would be covered with the most enormous and beautiful blossoms. Benches, distributed at intervals along the pathway, doubtless offer springtime visitors the opportunity to stop and take them in.

"Look!" said Moira, pointing to the left, where a brown roof rose above the greenery. "That must be the – what was that place called, again?"

"The Minka House," I reminded her obligingly.

"Yeah, well – I want to see that, but let's sit down for a minute first," she suggested. "Honestly , you'd think being on your feet all week would set you up for being on them all weekend as well, but it doesn't seem to work like that!"

I chuckled, and joined her on her chosen bench, one of two positioned close to the turn-off signposted to the Bamboo Garden and the House. The map showed the route through the Dell almost as a straight line, but in fact it snaked ever so slightly in places, so that the view along the path was cut off after a certain distance. Our particular bench was on a fairly long stretch between two such curves, but even so there was not another soul in sight; just now, we really did have the place to ourselves. Perhaps the piling clouds above had something to do with it; it looked as if it might be working up to a fairly heavy shower before long.

We sat chatting, keeping an eye on what could be seen of the sky from where we were, and reviewing some of my photos. After a few minutes, however, something caught my attention.

"Can you hear that?" I looked to our left, where one of the biggest walls of rhododendron we'd seen lined one side of the path. "Some sort of bird singing... I wonder what it is?"

Moira shrugged; flowers were her thing, birds were not. I stared along the pathway, trying to identify where the song was coming from; curiosity was getting the better of me.

"I'm just going to see if I can spot him, all right?"

"Yeah, you go ahead," Moira agreed. "Personally, I'm staying right here. Unless it rains," she qualified, glancing again at the darkening grey above. "In which case I'll be bolting for this Minka House of yours."

"Okay," I agreed almost absently, already rising, my attention focused on the sporadic, joyous little song. Stills camera for plants, camcorder for moving subjects. Almost before I had finished getting to my feet my camcorder was in my hand.

Moira watched me for a while, as I became engrossed in the hunt. Then a movement to her right from the direction of the Bamboo Garden registered in her peripheral vision, and she glanced that way.

Her jaw dropped. A few feet away, Joe was standing in the middle of the path, a finger to his lips and a mischievous look on his face.

Moira glanced for a split second in my direction, but from where I was standing, he would have been out of my line of sight, even had I been looking that way. Then she looked back at him, almost indignantly. He was still holding his finger against his lips in a 'hush' gesture, but with the other hand he beckoned her toward him. With another quick glance in my direction, she got up and went to him.

"What are you doing here?" she demanded. "You said you couldn't come!"

"Change of plans," he said, grinning. "Why? D'you want me to go away again?"

She thrust out her lower lip for a moment, then admitted, "No..."

He put his hands on her waist, and gave her a quick kiss.

"Come on," he said. "Ever been kissed in a bamboo grove?"

"Wouldn't you like to know?" she teased, archly.

"Well, even if you have, it wasn't by me," he said. "Time we put that right." He slipped his hands around her to pull her closer against him.

"I promised Jenny I wouldn't wander off," she protested, but without noticeable conviction. His physical proximity was having its usual effect on her.

"You're not," he said. "We'll only be just over there." He nodded behind him. "Not far, see? Come on. Let's see if you kiss better in the middle of all these bushes, eh?"

He released her from his embrace, took one of her hands, and started to pull her after him. She hesitated, with one more glance behind her, but already I was out of her sight. Then she acquiesced, and followed him. Within a couple of minutes, her promise to me was the last thing on her mind.

And I, meanwhile, had located the songster; a little bird I didn't recognize. A visitor from overseas, maybe? Whatever else he was, he was definitely hyperactive, leaping animatedly from twig to twig between bursts of song. At that moment, all I cared about was getting him on camera. So, intent on my filming, I never saw Moira go, or realized I was now completely alone on that section of the path. I didn't hear or sense anything, until someone spoke from immediately behind me, with shocking unexpectedness.

"Please don't move, Jenny," said the voice, quietly. "I really don't advise it."

Even as the words were spoken, something small, cold and hard touched the back of my neck and rested there, aborting my instinctive movement to turn round and see who was addressing me.

Though I didn't need to. I recognized the voice instantly – and realized what the thing touching my neck must be. So I tried to obey, not to move, but I couldn't prevent myself flinching, or the shudder that passed through me. The only movement I did make was to drop my hands to my sides, the camcorder still clutched in my right palm.

I couldn't remember ever feeling so scared as I did that that moment. That sensation of my mouth going dry, that I'd experienced only once before – it was back. More intense than before. And that time, too, this man had been the cause.

"Nor do I advise attempting to call out," he went on.

I wasn't sure I could produce a sound, in any case. Quite apart from the fear-induced dryness of my mouth and throat, my neck muscles were painfully taut, clenched in useless reaction to the menace of the metal muzzle lightly touching my skin.

"Let's get off the path, shall we?" The gun prodded me toward the huge stand of rhododendron. "We don't want anyone interrupting our little tête-à-tête…"

From a distance the tangle of leaves looked impenetrable, but close to, a small gap no more than three feet high and a foot wide disclosed itself. My legs felt stiff and clumsy as I bent down and pushed through. He followed me closely, the small, hard metal mouth never leaving my neck.

Beyond the outer curtain of leaves, instead of a tangle of branches, there was, unexpectedly, a large, virtually empty space where you could stand upright and still be clear of the surrounding shrubs; the crown of the bush rose well over our heads. Underfoot was a carpet of brown, discarded rhododendron leaves that rustled slightly as our feet disturbed them. The ground slanted gently uphill, and the space was bounded upslope by a wall of smaller shrubs and bushes.

"There, that'll do," he said when we reached them. I stopped. We were only about twenty feet from the pathway, yet completely hidden from view by the curtain of dark leaves.

"I don't need to remind you not to draw any attention to us, do I, Jenny?" he said smoothly, keeping his voice to a murmur. "You wouldn't want anyone to become unnecessary collateral damage, would you? It could so easily happen, you know. If you weren't sensible. But of course you are sensible, aren't you? I know that much about you."

He was right. I couldn't do that, no matter how much my instinct was screaming at me to summon help. I could call out, of course I could – if anyone passed by, at that distance they'd hear me even if I spoke at normal volume, let alone shouted. But because of the gun, I couldn't. I'd already seen his willingness to harm others in pursuit of his main target; Mike Clifford was a clear example of that. No, I couldn't risk the life of some innocent passerby, and he knew it.

Not that there was likely to be a passerby at the moment. They'd all be trying to find somewhere to shelter; it had begun to rain at last. There was a spatter of sound as rain began to hit the leaves all around us; lightly at first, then with more vigour. We were fairly protected here, under the edges of the stand of rhododendron, but even so, I could feel some of the drops getting through.

"I thought perhaps it was time I formally introduced myself. Matthew William Lesser, Jenny…" He deliberately moved the muzzle of the gun delicately up and down over the nape of my neck in a ghastly perversion of a caress, inducing another involuntary shudder from me.

"That camcorder," he continued. "Perhaps you'd like to put it down. And your bag." As if it was a suggestion.

Moving slowly, I looked at the camcorder as if I'd never seen such a thing before, couldn't understand what it was doing in my hand.

Then, for a few moments, a very strange thing happened. Or it seemed strange to me, though I understand a human being reacts in some remarkable ways to the prospect of imminent death. Maybe it was just adrenalin, or something. Whatever it was, my mind, briefly, became very focused, my thinking very clear and precise. And – just for those few seconds – I knew exactly what to do.

Carefully, deliberately, I closed the viewing screen into the body of the camcorder, allowing the click to be clearly audible. I then closed the lens cover, again with a definite click. Then, still moving slowly – the gun's muzzle never leaving my neck, moving with me as I moved – I sank down into a crouch, slid my handbag off my shoulder onto the carpet of dry leaves, and placed the camcorder with meticulous care on the ground beside it.

But not before, with a surreptitious movement of my thumb when the camcorder was momentarily out of his sight in front of my body, I'd pressed the 'Record' button.

Whatever he said – whatever he did – there'd be a soundtrack.

I slowly rose erect again, wondering briefly if I'd just set up a recording of my last moments of life. A macabre thought. If I had, I could only hope it would provide evidence against him. It was all I could do. For myself. For Peter.

"What—?" My voice came out as a high, undignified squeak. I stopped, swallowed, and tried again. Whatever I did, I had to remember to keep my voice down. "What do you want?" I managed, in a hoarse whisper.

"Oh, I just thought it was time we had a little talk." It felt surreal that a man of such violence, such emotional and physical brutality, should have such a cultured and pleasant voice; it was like listening to my father speaking. Though my father doesn't have that what I can only call 'gravelled' quality to his voice. "The last time we met, we weren't able to hold a conversation, were we? For reasons I'm sure you remember. But I felt the right moment had come. We both have an interest in the same man, after all. I've been trying to decide whether you're more use to me alive – or dead."

He delivered this chilling summary in a detached tone, as if it was merely an intellectual problem to be solved. I found my eyes instinctively screwing shut, my body locking into rigidity, anticipating the explosive passage of the bullet through my throat.

"I've almost come to my decision, but I thought it would be only courteous to discuss it with you," he went on quietly. "Since it concerns you so closely."

Discuss? Perhaps, then, I still had seconds – even minutes – to live.

"I was really quite annoyed with you, to start with." He sounded like a grieved parent, chiding me for some minor misdemeanour. "I'd gone to all that trouble, and then you went and saved his life. Very inconsiderate of you! Of course, it was partly my own fault. I really should have checked. But, there you are – these things happen, don't they?"

I was silent, my fists clenched at my sides. Around us the rain continued to patter a gentle but steady percussion on the leaves.

"You're not saying very much, Jenny," he reproved me, rubbing the barrel of the gun gently up and down the right side of my throat. No, not the gun itself; the length was wrong. It must be a silencer that was being stroked so tenderly against my skin.

"What – what do you expect me to say?" I said hoarsely.

"Ah! You feel the circumstances aren't conducive to conversation, I take it? Well, I suppose that's not an unreasonable point of view for you to take. But I'm afraid I must insist. I really would like to know what you're thinking…" The gun had travelled round to the back of my neck again, and prodded gently. *Answer me, Jenny.*

And, to my own astonishment, I found there was something I did want to say.

"Did you start the fire that killed Peter's wife and child?" I asked abruptly.

He uttered an unspellable snort of sound that gave nothing away.

"Why do you keep going after *him*? There was a whole team involved. Why just him, out of all of them?" I persisted. What did I have to lose? I couldn't stop him killing me if he chose to do so. This way, Peter might learn something.

That he did answer, in a suddenly savage tone that made me jerk with fright.

"Because I trusted him! I *trusted* him! He *made* me trust him!" Just for a moment, he'd forgotten his own injunction; then he remembered to lower his voice again. "And all the time, he was *lying* to me."

I swallowed. I was so frightened! But I had to keep him talking. As long as he was talking, he wasn't killing me…

"I didn't think people in your line of business were big on trust." My voice quavered in spite of my efforts to hold it steady.

"No," he agreed, more calmly. "We aren't. I'm not. Except this one time. This one man. And I let him through my guard. Never again. *Never again.*" He sounded as if he was speaking through shut teeth. "He *betrayed* me. He betrayed *me.*"

There was a short silence. I knew we were on desperately thin ice here. His professional pride, his estimation of his own judgement, had been fundamentally violated, and even though he'd done it to himself, he'd made it Peter's fault. Yet I couldn't stay silent. I was driven to defend Peter, in spite of the danger.

"Do you know what I think, Mr Lesser?" I emitted a momentary travesty of a laugh, wondering what my parents would think of my childhood indoctrination in forms of address holding true at a moment such as this. But why not tell him? In the circumstances, what did I have to lose? I paused, wishing my mouth didn't feel so dry, but the gun prodded at me again, urging me to continue.

"You're a professional – of your kind. So's he. You're good at your job. So's he. So perhaps you shouldn't think of it as betrayal. Perhaps you ought to pay him the professional respect of admitting he was simply doing his job and doing it well. When it comes right down to it, he wasn't breaking faith with you. All he was doing was keeping a different faith. One that came before the one with you."

He drew in a sharp breath, and the muzzle of the silencer was pushed with painful force against my vertebrae. I gasped, and tensed. *Done it now,* I thought. *Gone too far...*

But after a few moments, the pressure relaxed, and the quality of his silence changed.

"You're an unusual woman, Jenny Gregory," he said at last, his voice tinged with a new interest. "Here you are, caught up in a world that's quite alien to you and your way of life. And you're terrified that at any moment I may choose to put those few extra ounces of pressure on this trigger, and kill you – I can feel you, literally shaking with fear. Yet you retain enough self-possession to argue the ethics of my – profession – with me while a gun is held to your head."

He moved it gently over my skin again, and once more I shuddered. I think he knew the instinctive physical reaction that the touch was causing each time – and was enjoying it.

"If you really intend to – to kill me" – my voice faltered for a moment before I could continue – "why not? There's nothing I could say that would change your mind."

There was another short silence.

Then he remarked, almost conversationally, "As it's turned out, you're quite wrong about that... So – goodbye for the time being, Jenny. Enjoy the rest of your day, won't you? Oh, and please don't turn round or call out for the next two minutes. Or I may have to change my mind again." The implication of the slight emphasis he put on that final word was chilling.

The touch of metal against my neck vanished. So did the sense of his presence behind me. A slight rustle of leaves, then silence.

I have no idea whether it really was for two minutes that I stood there without moving, as he'd told me. It felt like forever. I do know that I spent the whole time trembling violently, tears pouring down my face, unsuccessfully trying to choke back a staccato series of sobs. The pattering of the rain began to subside; the shower was finally passing over.

It was quite a while before I could summon sufficient courage to turn round. By the time I finally forced myself to the risk, Lesser was long gone.

I found I'd been holding my body so tensely, the muscles clenched so tightly, that now the tension was relaxed a wave of physical weakness threatened to overwhelm me. My legs refused to hold me upright any longer, and I folded to the ground with a thump and had to sit there, trembling, for quite a while before I could move again.

Eventually, with shaking hands, I got out my phone. My fingers were so unsteady I could barely punch the right buttons. And although in reality it was only a few seconds before Peter answered, it felt like an eternity.

"Jenny?"

"P-Peter..." I quavered.

"Jenny! What's wrong?" He was onto it like a shot.

"Peter, he was here! He... Please – can you come...?" Moira never even entered my head.

"Where are you?" he snapped, and cut the call almost before I'd finished telling him.

Then I bowed my head and began to cry in earnest.

It was only several minutes later that I remembered the camcorder, assiduously recording every gasp, every sob. Fumblingly I picked it up, hardly able to see it properly through the film of salt water, and ran it back a little way to check that it had, in fact, recorded.

A bit muffled, but, yes – my weeping was faithfully on record. I was probably going to be quite irrationally embarrassed about that, later on. But, by implication, my conversation with Lesser was also on record. Which had been the point, after all.

Maybe, just maybe, the risk had paid off.

Chapter 26

He came; he found me. He put his arms round me, and spoke to me, but I don't remember what he said. I do remember the anger and the fear that leaked through into his voice even as he was trying to comfort me, but it was the sense of care communicated by his touch that meant more than anything he said.

He got me back to his car. Where Moira was, or why she'd vanished, or what she'd think when she couldn't find me again, I couldn't have cared less.

As we drove – more or less in silence – it began to rain again. I remember looking out of the window at the streets, the cars, the people; they were all blurred, muffled, but not by the rain. I felt as if I were disconnected from everything. On the outside, looking in. As if ordinary life, where ordinary things happened and were what mattered, was somewhere near – on the other side of a glass wall – and I could see it, but I couldn't reach it, or touch it. Could see it all though the glass – but couldn't pass through the barrier to get back to the other side, to where everyone else was.

When my phone sounded, that, too, didn't feel particularly real, but I picked it up automatically and looked at the screen.

Moira.

"Hi," I said. My voice sounded somehow blank, empty. Even to me.

"Jenny? Where are you? I can't find you anywhere!" She sounded half excited, half guilty.

"Oh. Sorry." I fumbled for words. "I – I met a friend. One of my other friends, I mean… I'm afraid I've—"

"Seriously?" she squealed, not giving me time to finish; there was excited pleasure in her voice. "What are the chances, eh? So did I! You'll never guess what – Joe turned up after all! And then of course it started to rain. That Minka House came in really useful while that was going on, I can tell you! So we – well, anyway, when we came to look for you, you were gone. Is everything all right?"

"Yes. Yes, it's fine."

"Are you sure?" She sounded concerned. "You sound a bit – odd, somehow."

"No, I'm – I'm fine…" Not convincing, no; even I could hear the tremble

272

in my voice. My brain felt woolly and disconnected; I strove to pull a strand of plausibility out of the tangle. "Well – that is… I did start not feeling very well. But my friend's going to take me home, all right? So don't worry about me. I'll see you tomorrow. You can tell me about it then." It felt like such hard work, summoning up the words, trying to make them sound coherent, normal. They must have sounded more convincing to her than they did to me.

"Oh – all right, then," she agree blithely. "See you tomorrow. Hope you feel better soon. Bye!" She rang off.

"Moira?" Peter asked, as I put my phone away.

"Yes. Joe turned up, apparently."

"Right."

Silence fell again.

When we got home, he made me sit down at the kitchen table while he made us both coffee.

"I suppose you'd better take me in to the office so I can get it all down on tape while it's fresh in my mind," I said as he sat down opposite me. He looked slightly shamefaced.

"Professionally, that's what I should be doing," he agreed. "But are you sure you're up to it?"

"Yeh, I'm all right now." Which was a barefaced lie, but we both let it pass. I gave him a faint smile, touched with wryness. "At least I'm used to the procedure by now. I'm getting enough practice, let's face it."

"Sure?" He didn't look convinced, but started to get his phone out. "I'd better tell Alan, then."

I put out a hand out across the table to touch his wrist, stopping him from making the call.

"Before you do," I said. "Something else, first."

He looked at me sharply. "What?"

I reached down into my bag, which I'd dropped to the floor beside my chair. When I straightened up again, I had the camcorder in my hand. I put it onto the table between us.

"You'll want the tape," I said. "Or a copy of it, at least. I don't know if it's going to be of any use, but I hope so. But I thought – I thought you should listen to it with me, first. Before anyone else hears it."

"What is it?" His brows were drawn together as he looked at the camcorder.

"Lesser. What he said. I recorded it. He didn't know. He thought I'd turned it off."

Peter stared at me. "You did that?"

"No film, just a soundtrack. It was all I could do."

"Oh, Jenny!" Impulsively he reached out and grabbed my hand, squeezing my fingers hard. I wasn't sure if I was being reproved for the risk I'd taken, or commended for that brief moment of quick thinking. Maybe both.

So we sat together, side by side on the sofa, and listened to the playback. I tried to ignore the content and my own strained voice, and listen to it objectively. To my intense relief, on the whole the sound quality was of a reasonable standard, certainly good enough for any use the team might want to make of it. At least I'd achieved what I'd set out to do. And was still alive to know it. It would be overstating things to say the result was worth the fear I'd felt, but at least it hadn't been an opportunity missed.

Peter found it harder to be objective. As soon as he heard me speak for the first time, heard the distress in my voice, he snatched at my hand again, and held it tightly – sometimes too tightly – while he listened. Once Lesser had said his last words, I stopped the playback.

"It's just me crying, after that," I said. It wouldn't do him any good to hear it for himself.

Neither of us spoke for a while after that. He'd heard it for the first time; I'd had to re-live it. Both of us needed time to climb down from the tension; both of us knew how close I'd come to being dead.

"I might think about raiding your whisky bottle, after all," I said at last, in a feeble attempt to break the ice. His fingers, interlocked with mine, tightened momentarily, and he let out a snort of what might, with a valiant stretch of the imagination, be a warped kind of amusement.

"You and me both," he said. "The bottle and two straws between us. That should do it." His eyes were large and luminous. "I'm sorry, Jenny. I'm so sorry."

"Shut up," I said. "We've had that conversation." I released my fingers from his grasp, and stood up. "So you'd better take me in now, hadn't you? Get it done?"

He let out a sigh. "Yeh," he agreed, without enthusiasm. "I'll tell Alan." He rose to his feet, too, and got out his phone. But he didn't use it straight away. Instead he hesitated, and drew a quick breath as if about to speak. I looked at him, waiting to hear what it was.

"You do know what it was you did today, don't you?" he said at last. "How much courage that took? You do know that, don't you?"

Courage? When I'd felt the way I had? He'd got that one wrong, big time. I shook my head wordlessly, denying it.

"Don't you shake your head at me," he told me, more sharply. "I know what I'm talking about. Facing up to Lesser? That takes courage, and don't you try to tell me otherwise!"

I was caught between pleasure that he thought so, and irritation that he thought so. I felt as if he was trying to make me out to be something I wasn't.

"Courage? When all I do is collapse into tears every time?" I retorted, with a savagery that was directed at myself, not at him. I was still upset, of course, and this was how it was coming out. "It's so stupid! It's so useless! I'm so useless!"

"No, you're not!" he contradicted me, almost angrily.

"A quivering wreck with nerves about as sturdy as a wood pigeon's, who needs a box of tissues every time something happens?" I almost wailed. "What good is that?"

"Jenny! Jenny, listen to me," he said sharply, grabbing me by both shoulders and forcing me to meet his eyes. "Doesn't matter! Doesn't matter about feeling afraid. That's normal! If you weren't afraid, there *would* be something wrong with you. But there isn't! Being afraid is all right! It's okay! Doesn't matter that you have a reaction afterwards. That's normal, too. You *should* feel like that, you *should* cry and let it all out. That happens for a reason, you know! It's a natural safety mechanism." He shook my shoulders gently. "It's what you do that counts. Not whether you're afraid during, or emotional afterwards. It's what you do. What you've *done*. Okay, maybe some people would've been able to do what you've done with a stiff upper lip and you've had to do it with a trembling lower lip – right, fine! But you've still done it! And what you've done's been" – he cast about for the right word – "brilliant! Just brilliant! Every time!"

I looked at him with eyes still sheened with tears, unconvinced.

"Look, you're not a professional," he said, gripping my shoulders more tightly and beginning to sound more than a little exasperated. "You've not been trained to deal with situations like this. You're a library assistant, damn it! What makes you think that'd prepare you for dealing with professional criminals and assassins and what they do? Just – just think *straight*, will you?"

I wiped my eyes with the back of my wrist, in a childlike gesture. "D'you mean it?"

"Of course I mean it, you stupid woman," he said curtly. "You've been more use than I could possibly tell you! So shut up about it, all right?" He really did sound genuinely exasperated.

Abruptly I let out a sob of laughter. To be sure, I was being hysterical, but something about his irritation struck me as genuinely funny, and I couldn't help myself. Another followed, then another. Then I buried my face in my hands and literally cried with laughter, my body shaking with paroxysms. He pulled me tight against him, and I could feel him begin to shake, too. Even hysterical laughter could be infectious, it seemed; he simply couldn't suppress his instinctive response to what I was doing. And when we separated, he, like me, was wiping tears from his eyes.

"Very professional," I remarked, with a watery grin.

"I told you to shut up," he reminded me cheerfully. "Come on. You need to wash your face."

"I hate to dent your male pride, but − so do you," I said, the corner of my mouth twitching again. "So come on. You can't go into the office looking like that. They'd never let you live it down."

Déjà vu. Ben and Alan and me, back in that little room with the recorder going. Except that this time Alan had had to interrupt his weekend − I hoped Jane would forgive me − and Peter, I knew, was behind the two-way mirror window set into the wall facing me. Alan still didn't want him in the room, which was fair enough, but this time he was at least being allowed to observe, to watch and listen from the room beyond.

"That's the tape," I said, handing it over to Ben. "Can I have it back when you've finished with it? I've got some good footage on that. Craig might like to see it." I offered Alan a weak smile. "Not all of it, obviously."

"Maybe. Eventually," he agreed, but not with conviction.

There was a pause. I wondered if I myself would ever be able to watch any of that film again, even the ordinary bits. Or ever go back to Kew. For both, the associations might be too strong.

"How did he know where you were going to be?" Ben demanded gruffly. "Who knew, besides you and Moira?"

Déjà vu, indeed.

"Dad, Mum, Peter," I said. "I don't know if Moira mentioned it to anyone else except Joe. You'd have to ask her that. But" − I thought back − "we were both out on the desk when we made the arrangement. I suppose anyone who was near enough could have heard us, if they'd been listening." I tried to visualize who else might have been around, but I couldn't summon up the necessary detail. "I can't remember if there was anybody nearby, or not. Sorry."

"So someone might have overheard you," Ben summarized, "or maybe he just had you followed."

Alan looked grim. "There's a third possibility," he observed, and caught my eye. "You do realize, don't you, that someone could have deliberately tipped him off as to where you were going to be, and when?" he said, with professional as well as personal sympathy.

I nodded glumly. I had realized that, and it wasn't a pleasant thought. Because, having thought about it, it seemed to me that if that was the case, there were two only alternatives. Option One: that Lesser, or someone in his employ, had made the acquaintance of someone in my circle of friends, and that that someone, quite oblivious of what was happening, was being pumped for information about me. But that was infinitely preferable to Option Two, where the someone in question knew exactly what they were doing, and were doing it deliberately. Whether because they chose to of their own free will, or whether because Lesser had a hold over them in some way, was in practical terms a distinction without a difference. The outcome was the same: it was possible that someone I knew, whenever I interacted with them, was presenting to me the face of a friend, whilst knowingly putting me in Lesser's hands.

"Maybe we should have a word with your friend Moira," said Ben.

"That'll mean letting her know something's going on," Alan reminded him.

"I think we're getting close to that point with a lot of people, don't you, Boss?" Ben's tone was respectful, but there was a hint of steel underneath.

"We'll see," Alan temporised. "Maybe you can do our job for us there, Jenny. You'll see her at work tomorrow, won't you? Maybe just drop it into the conversation. Find out if she told anyone else."

I smiled briefly. "It's worth a try," I agreed.

Both men rose, indicating the interview was terminated, but I put out a hand toward Alan to stop him leaving.

"Alan, could I have a private word with you and Peter?" I asked.

He looked down at me, then nodded, and looked at Ben. "Would you excuse us, Ben?" Ben acquiesced with a brief smile, and left. Alan looked over at the blank window and beckoned. "Well, come on," he said, raising his voice. "In you come!"

Moments later Peter joined us. He pulled a spare chair over and sat beside me, without speaking, though he was clearly wondering what this was about. Alan resumed his own seat.

"So what is it, Jenny?" he prompted.

I drew a deep breath; this might be a tricky subject. But I might as well come straight out with it.

"How much do Jane and the children know about what's happening?" I asked directly.

Alan paused before answering.

"Jane knows," he said. "The kids don't."

"And how much do they know about Laura?" I glanced at Peter as I asked that. He met my eyes sombrely, but let Alan answer.

"Everything," he said heavily.

"Even though they were so young at the time?" I wasn't criticizing; I simply wanted to know, to understand how things stood.

"Only what they could understand, then. But as they got older, we told them everything. As it's turned out, Lesser's never gone near them, or even Jane. But at the time, we couldn't know that. Every parent has to make sure their kids don't talk to strangers, but we had to make really sure. Really sure." Alan's eyes were filled with remembered anxiety. It must have been horrible for him and Jane, not knowing if their children might become a target for the man who had murdered Peter's wife, a means for him to cause further torment to Peter. And even though the threat had never materialized, it must still have been in the background all the time. Why Lesser had decided not to touch them, I didn't know. Perhaps he'd concluded that targeting the family of a DCI would have been a step too far, might have provoked consequences he viewed as disproportionate to what he wanted to accomplish. But even so, Alan and Jane must never have been entirely able to dismiss the possibility that at some point, especially as the children grew older, he might not change his mind.

If there was one silver lining to this particular cloud, at least it might be that because now he had me to focus on, he would go on ignoring them.

"But they don't know about – now? About me?" I probed.

Alan shook his head.

I took another deep breath.

"Well… I was wondering if it might not be time to say something. Because I wanted to say that, if you were thinking about doing that, it's all right with me. I appreciate it's your decision – yours and Jane's and Peter's" – I glanced from one to the other – "but – well, he's had two goes at me so far. I don't want them upset any more than you do, but… if something does happen to me, and you haven't told them… Well, I wouldn't want to be you, faced with Craig asking you, '*Why didn't you tell us?*'"

Alan nodded heavily in agreement.

"I know," he said. "I've been thinking about that, myself."

"Well, I just wanted you to know that, if that's what you decide to do, it's all right with me," I repeated. "You still might decide not to, but if you do, can you let me know? In case they say anything to me? I'd like to be forearmed." I attempted a faint smile, then remembered something else that needed to be said. "Although – in the circumstances, do you think I should stay away from them? To be on the safe side?" I felt a sharp pang of internal protest even as I made the suggestion; I didn't want to forego the pleasure I got from being with Alan's family, especially Craig. But who knew what Lesser might take it into his head to do? "I don't want anything happening to them because of me."

Alan and Peter looked at each other. Alan seemed to be asking a question, silently; Peter nodded, heavily. Alan turned back to me.

"I'm afraid we're already too late with that one," he said. "He hasn't just had two goes at you. He's had three."

I frowned at him, puzzled. What on earth was he talking about? Then I realized. The youths in Croydon. No wonder Peter had been in such an angry mood the next day. He'd known, as I hadn't, that what had happened to me had been no accident. And Craig had been there.

There was silence for a few moments, as they let me take it on board. There were a lot of implications to be absorbed. But I found the one that predominated was what had happened to Craig during the attack. And, if I was right, there was some hope to be had from it.

"They could have laid into Craig, too," I pointed out, tentatively. "But they didn't. They just pushed him out of the way. Maybe – maybe Lesser told them to lay off him? For" – I hesitated over which word to use – "for policy reasons?"

Alan's look lightened momentarily; clearly it was something that hadn't occurred to him.

"Maybe…" Then, with more feeling, "I hope you're right."

"Why didn't you tell me, at the time?" I asked, looking at Peter, and hating myself for asking something that sounded so critical. It wasn't meant to be. I knew he would have had a reason, just not what it was.

"No hard evidence it was him." Peter was evidently hating himself just as much, but for different reasons. "Not then. But there was a note under my door that night. And the attack – had his stamp all over it. But we didn't know until then that he'd tagged you. I just – didn't want you worried for no reason. Not – till you had to be." The sentences were staccato, hard for him to say.

But it hadn't been for no reason, as the look on his face told me only too clearly. Even without any hard evidence, he'd known in his gut that it was Lesser. After so many years, he knew the smell of something that Lesser was behind. But he'd been trying to shield me from the knowledge as long as possible. And it hadn't just been me he'd been thinking about. He'd had to come to terms with the idea himself. Adjust to the jolt. The knowledge that Lesser knew about me, and how I could be used.

"I don't know if that was the right thing, or the wrong thing. But it was a kind thing," I said gently, trying to reassure him. To reassure both of them. "As kind as the circumstances allowed, anyway. So – thank you." I turned at Alan. "You'd better talk it over with Jane and let me know what you want me to do. What you decide to tell the kids."

He nodded, looked at Peter, then back at me.

"Tell you what," he said. "Tell Ben to take you for a drink over the road. He'll know where. Can you find your own way back to the office?"

Clearly he wanted to talk to Peter about it now, and in private.

"Can do," I said. "See you later."

When I reappeared in the office, Ben saw my solitary state, and raised his eyebrows.

"They've got things to talk over," I explained. "Apparently you're to take me for a drink over the road while they're doing it, and you'll know where that is."

It turned out to be a little pub only a few yards down the road which rejoiced in the very traditional name of The White Lion and was, Ben explained, the team's weapon of choice when it came to drinking in the immediate vicinity.

"Have you had any lunch?" he enquired. I shook my head; I think he could see I hadn't, and still didn't, feel much like eating. When I asked for a soft drink, he pressed me to be sure I didn't want anything stronger, but I didn't. He accepted that, and went to the bar. In a couple of minutes he was back, with two orange juices. Of course; he was on duty.

He put my glass down in front of me; I picked it up as he seated himself beside me. As I did, my eyes lifted – and I felt my face go blank with shock.

Not thirty feet away, seated facing us in one of the booths, Matthew Lesser, his eyes on us – on me – sipped comfortably from his pint glass, quite at ease. He must have followed Peter and me, to be here, now. And only a few hours ago he had been holding a gun to my head, musing over whether to kill me.

The sheer, brass nerve of the man! Sitting there knowing there was nothing I, or anyone else, could do about it. Because he had a perfect right to be there, didn't he? A perfect right to look at whom he wished. And he was looking at me. He could see I had recognized him, that I knew who he was. And he was waiting to see how I would react.

How *would* I react? For long seconds, I didn't know the answer to that, just continued to stare at him, while Ben, still oblivious, started to talk to me about something – I didn't hear a word – and Lesser slowly began to smile in triumph.

But then something came back to my mind. When I was at school, about fourteen years old, there was a boy a year above me who was known throughout the school as a bully, except that he was always too clever to get provably caught at it by the staff. He cast his net quite wide, but one of the people he picked on was a friend of mine. He never touched her, but I know what a brutal time he gave her verbally, because sometimes I was with her when he crudely exercised what passed for his wit on her, to the sycophantic amusement of his little band of cronies. But I've always remembered what she did, because she never reacted in any of the usual ways; she never rose to his taunts, never cried, never shouted abuse back at him, never even tried to avoid him.

What she did do, every time she encountered him, was smile at him. Just smile at him. Really pleasantly, as if they were the best of friends. Never spoke to him, just smiled.

And it defeated him. He didn't get the hoped-for rise out of her, she gave him nothing to feed off, and she wasn't retaliating in a way he could take exception to. And gradually he gave up and, in the end, left her alone.

Now I was a similar target, and Lesser was sitting there, expecting me to be afraid. Waiting confidently for me to show fear.

And I was afraid, of course I was. Perhaps that was all I should have been feeling. Instead – and somewhat to my own astonishment – what I was feeling was not just, nor even primarily, fear. What I was feeling most was anger. A rising sense of anger. At what he was doing to me, and what he had been doing to Peter for all these years.

So what reaction was I going to show him?

Well, what did I have to lose?

My eyes locked on his, I smiled, and raised my glass to him.

For a moment – for one wonderful, superb moment – he was taken by surprise. I'd wrong-footed him, and it showed, just for one fleeting second. Then he, too, began to smile. A smile of genuine amusement; tinged with a shade of respect, even? And as I had to him, he raised his glass to me.

Ben had, of course, seen my gesture, and had followed the line of my eyes to see who I was acknowledging. Now I heard him hiss an obscenity through clenched teeth as he realized who I was looking at, who was looking at me.

"What the hell—?" he exploded. For a moment, words failed him. Lesser looked on, blatantly amused. Ben slammed his glass down on the table and swore some more. But then he realized all the same things I had; that there was nothing he could do. Except the obvious thing, of course.

"Let's get out of here," he muttered grimly. Then he tore his eyes away from Lesser and looked at me, took more notice of my expression. As he interpreted it, I could see his surprise. Like Lesser, he'd expected me to be afraid.

"No." I shook my head with a definite gesture. "You've bought me this drink, Ben. I'm not going to waste your money. I'm going to stay here until I've finished it. Why should I let him make me be the one to leave? Why should I let him think he's already won?"

Ben glanced at Lesser, who was still watching us with that slightly amused look on his face. "Sure you know what you're doing?" he probed.

"Probably not," I said bleakly. A resurgence of very sensible apprehension was tugging at my resolve. "I'm just the amateur caught in between all the professionals. And I don't see how I can win. If he really wants to get me, there might not be anything any of you can do about it, no matter how hard you try." I could see by the look on his face he wanted to contradict my bleak realism, but couldn't. He was too honest for that. "But I'm not going down without a fight, Ben." I was quaking inside, but then my voice hardened as the anger came back, pushing the fear down again, shoring up my determination. "For my own sake, yes. But even more, for Peter's."

As I spoke, I looked over at Lesser again, and it was as if he'd heard me. This time, our eyes met like the touch of rapier blades. Battle had been joined.

"Well, for Peter's sake, I think you should drink up and we should get back," Ben growled. "What if he comes in and finds *him* here? We probably wouldn't be able to stop him murdering him on the spot."

I hadn't thought of that.

"Good point," I conceded. I raised my glass to him. "Cheers," I said acerbically.

Chapter 27

It was late afternoon when Peter got me back home again. He turned off the engine, and we sat for a moment in silence. My father's car was in its usual place on the drive. Which meant he and Mum were at home.

Peter glanced over at me.

"Are we going straight up?" he asked.

I shook my head.

"Something else we need to do first."

He said nothing, but his sympathy was like a touch.

We got out of the car and went to the front door. Dad opened it. His smile of welcome congealed almost instantly; he could see something was wrong.

"Dad," I said. "There's been – a development. Got something we need to tell you."

Alan looked at his wife and drew a deep breath. "Ready?" he asked.

Jane nodded sombrely. "As I'll ever be," she qualified. "I'll get them." She got as far as the door, then turned back.

"They're just children!" she burst out, in helpless outrage. "They shouldn't have to be dealing with this sort of thing at their age! They should never have had to!"

"Think you need to tell me that?" he returned.

There was nothing else he could usefully say, and she knew it. She went out of the living room and to the foot of the stairs. "Craig! Sophie! Come down a moment, please, both of you!"

Alan heard Sophie's voice respond in complaint mode, though he couldn't make out the exact words. Jane's tone became sharper.

"No, *now*. It's important. We need to talk to you."

Alan heard the familiar thump of his son's feet on the stairs.

"What's up, Mum?" he asked. From his tone, it was evident he'd detected that there was something serious going on.

"Mu-u-um!" Sophie's voice followed, an outraged wail of objection. "I was right in the middle of—"

Jane cut her off. "I don't care what you were in the middle of. This matters. Come on – your father's in the lounge."

They came in. Sophie threw herself down in a protesting sprawl on the sofa, looking annoyed, but Craig sat forward, alert. Jane sat down, too, watching her children, but Alan remained standing in front of the mantelpiece.

"There's something you need to know," he began.

"Is it about Peter?" Craig asked. He was quick, that boy, no question. Alan felt a momentary upsurge of pride in his son.

"In a way, yes," he confirmed cautiously. "How did you know?"

"Dunno," Craig shrugged. "It's just – the way you said it. It's the voice you use when something's happening with Peter."

Alan hadn't been aware he used a special tone of voice for that, but however Craig had picked up on it, he was right.

"So what is it?" Craig persisted. Even Sophie had picked up on the tenor of the conversation now, and her expression was tinged with unease.

"Peter's all right, isn't he?" she asked quickly.

"Yes, Peter's fine," Alan assured them. "It's – Jenny."

Two pairs of eyes stared at him apprehensively. Alan shoved his hands in his pockets, and glanced at his wife before proceeding.

"What happened to Laura," he said heavily. "It's happening again. Lesser's found out about Jenny. He's attacked her three times already."

They both looked horrified, but, at the same time, Craig was still making connections.

"When those blokes beat her up?" he asked quickly.

Alan nodded. "And twice since then. One of them was earlier today. She's all right" – he quickly forestalled Craig's next question – "but she thought you ought to know, in case something else happens." *Something worse...*

From the expressions on their faces, they didn't need it spelled out.

"But – what are you going to do?" Sophie demanded urgently. "Can't you stop him?"

"Shut up," said Craig briefly. "What d'you think he's been trying to do all this time?"

Sophie looked ready to cry. With a slightly reproving look at Craig, Jane left her chair to kneel at the end of the sofa next to her, and put a hand on her arm.

"Your father's going to do everything he possibly can," she said firmly. "But we all need to be careful. And we need you to be careful. Even more careful than you usually are. You haven't accepted any new friends on Facebook lately, have you? Ones you don't know personally?" She included Craig in the question. They both shook their heads, decisively.

"We never do that, Mum," he said. "Honest." Sophie nodded in confirmation.

"Well, if anybody tries, I need you to let me know," said Alan. "Or if anyone starts asking you questions about Peter or Jenny. No matter how harmless they seem. And" – again he consulted Jane with his eyes – "we think it's best if you don't see Jenny outside of this house."

"You're not stopping us seeing her?" Craig protested quickly. He looked stricken at the idea.

"Not at all," Alan corrected him. "But only here. Or maybe if you go to her house, with us or with Peter. But not alone. And no more filming in Croydon." He tried to inject a tinge of drollery in his tone; as he spoke, he met Craig's eyes, inviting him to be complicit in his black humour. After a few moments, he could see that, with some reluctance, Craig was responding.

"Is she all right, Dad?" he asked, sounding so much more like a man than a boy.

"So far," Alan said. "She's quite a strong person, Jenny. I think she's coping very well. But there's no blinking the fact that she's in danger. And you two need to know that. Because she needs to know that she's not putting you in danger as well, because of being your friend. Our friend. It'll help her, if she knows that. So can I tell her you'll be careful, both of you? And you'll be on the lookout for anything unusual? No matter how small or unimportant it might seem? Anything might help."

Subdued and sombre, his son and his daughter both nodded.

"Thank you," he said, as he would to adults. "Peter and Jenny will both be happier, knowing that. And so will your mother and I."

For a few moments, nobody spoke. But then Craig looked up again, and this time his expression was implacable.

"Get him, Dad," he said grimly. "Just get him."

Alan didn't answer, not in words; but his eyes spoke for him, and Craig was satisfied.

That night, in his flat, Peter alternated between perching on the edge of his sofa, elbows on knees, hands clenched together and pressed against his mouth, or pacing restlessly like a caged animal. Sleep was out of the question. What was he going to do? *What was he going to do?*

At length he slumped down on the sofa again. He held his head in his hands, and groaned softly.

When he raised his eyes again, he caught sight of a CD on the top of his bookcase. One Jenny had lent him. Chris de Burgh – *The Power of Ten*. One of her favourites; she loved *Heart of Darkness* best of all de Burgh's songs. He shrugged, got up and slid the disc into the player. He associated it with her, with good things. Maybe listening to it again would distract him from bad things. Worth a try.

And he found it did work, a little. He could just imagine what Abhik or Chris, for instance, would say, if they caught him listening to it. He no longer cared. De Burgh's voice summoned up images of Jenny. Jenny laughing. Smiling. Making coffee in the kitchen. Curled up on her sofa, watching the television. Sat on the window seat, looking out at the garden. Listening to the rain...

He'd never had Chris de Burgh's music on his personal radar until Jenny had come into his life. But now, at this moment, he found himself thinking about the recurring themes in de Burgh's songs. The loyal, steadfast support of the woman in your life. Being not only your love but, even more crucially, a friend you could depend on lifelong. The meaning, the inspiration that gave to your life. Making her someone you would fight to keep, whatever obstacles were placed in your way.

With that skill that poets have of providing the right words for the right moment, de Burgh was describing with eerie accuracy the standing of the relationship between Jenny and himself. And he realized the man was right about something else. That the possibility of a future with such a woman was in his own hands. The chance of a love and a life with someone the like of whom he might never find again. But did he have the courage? The courage to risk loss? Again?

He'd have to. Because the idea of letting her go, the idea of losing her, wasn't to be borne. His brows drew together.

Watch out, Matthew Lesser. Because Jenny Gregory has become my war cry. And you brought it on yourself. Because you're the one who made her that way.

Next morning, the forecasters were vindicated; the temperature was beginning to climb. And not just out in the open. In the office, Shoeshop had laid herself open to the rest of the team by declaring to Andy her intention to buy another pair of shoes before the day was out, the twin of a pair she'd only bought the previous week – "No, but they're really fantastic, honest!" – and now Abhik and Chris were ragging her mercilessly.

"It's not that I don't know people need new shoes," said Abhik. "I get that. I do! What I don't get is that you need them every week."

"Every day, more like," Brad muttered, *sotto voce.*

"Then you're still not getting it," Shoeshop retorted. "Blokes never do. Do they, Andy?"

Andy looked up from her screen long enough to give her a brief smile, but declined to comment.

"But why do you need another pair exactly the same as you've already got?" Chris demanded. "You've only got one pair of feet, like the rest of us!"

"Yeah, but these are blue," Shoeshop explained with forced patience. "The others are black."

"What, with all those shoes you've got, you haven't got a blue pair already?" Abhik challenged.

"Of course I have." she acknowledged scornfully. "But not like these! And I've got a pair of blue slacks I want to wear them with. I can't wear black shoes with blue trousers!"

"Why not? I do!" Chris said, shrugging.

"Yeah, and look at you!" Shoeshop crowed derisively. "No wonder you get through so many girls! None of 'em can put up with your dress sense, I shouldn't think!"

"I think I can fairly safely say that's not what they see in me," Chris boasted smugly.

Shoeshop wrinkled her nose with distaste. "Oh, *please*! Let's not even go there! Come on, Andy, back me up," she demanded, looking to her sister officer for support. "You've gotta have the right shoes, haven't you?" But Andy shook her head.

"Sorry, Shoeshop," she apologized. "I know I'm a girl, but even I don't understand a ratio of two hundred shoes to one person."

Chris and Abhik grinned triumphantly, Kevlar snorted, and even Brad treated himself to a brief smile.

"Traitor!" Shoeshop accused, rounding on her indignantly. She opened her mouth to continue her rearguard action, but just then Peter walked in.

Used as they were to his occasional moodiness and tendency to turn monosyllabic, even they couldn't fail to notice the almost tangible aura of infuriation which seemed to sweep into the room with him as he stalked in and slammed down into his seat. He started riffling impatiently through the piles of paper on his desk, but couldn't seem to find what he was looking for. He said something short and virulent that was clearly audible to the whole room, then threw himself back in his chair, brooding blackly.

Everyone else glanced at each other, and there were some raised eyebrows, but no one commented. The sudden silence was noticeable through the open door of Alan's office and caught his attention despite the consultation he was holding with Ben. They both turned to scan the office, and swiftly identified the source of the disruption; Peter's scowl was fierce enough to attract anyone's attention.

The next moment, with startling speed, he was back on his feet.

"Chris, you're with me," he ordered savagely. "Now!" The word was snapped out like the crack of a whip, as Chris looked at him blankly.

"What for?"

"To follow up that Ackerman lead. I wannae know more about it. We're gonnae talk to your man. And we're gonnae do it *now*." And without another word, he stalked out.

Chris stood up and looked around the team with a shrug, but he didn't say anything, and neither did they. He caught up his jacket from the back of his chair and hastily shrugged it on as he hurried to catch up with Peter.

Alan and Ben watched the little scene from the office door.

"That's one very angry man you've got there... You know, I think Lesser's made a mistake, at long last," said Ben, thoughtfully.

Alan looked at him quickly.

"What d'you mean?"

"I mean, last time Peter didn't know what the score was. About Laura. That's why I think Lesser's made a mistake. Starting in on Jenny. Because this time Peter does know." Ben looked at Alan with years of experience in his eyes. "I don't think Lesser knows what kind of a fight he's in, now." He paused. "But he's gonna."

Moira was in the staff kitchen when I got into the library that morning. When I went in she had her back to me, putting the kettle on to boil for the coffee she always had before starting work.

"Make one for me, will you?" I requested cheerfully. That is to say, acting my head off so as to sound more cheerful than I actually felt.

She turned round.

"Jenny! Is everything all right? It all got a bit messed up yesterday, didn't it?" She sounded apologetic. "It was just that Joe turned up, you know, and—"

"Don't worry about it," I shrugged. "After all, I did a bunk, too, remember?"

"Yeah!" she realized. "So who did you meet?"

"Just a friend. One I hadn't seen for a while." In point of fact, not since the previous evening, and he'd left quite late, too. That still met the definition of '*a while*', didn't it? If you took it literally enough?

"Isn't it funny how things turn out?" Moira delivered the truism with her native cheerfulness.

"Good job you didn't tell all your friends where we were going, or we might have ended up swamped!" I cast my line casually, wondering if she'd bite, or whether I'd need to prompt her. "Who else did you tell about going to Kew?"

"Oh, just Joe," she said brightly.

Just Joe. A faint sense of uneasiness began to stir in the pit of my stomach. Surely not! And yet – *why* not...?

"Just Joe?" I repeated. "Doesn't sound like you! I'd've thought you'd spray it round more widely than that, knowing you!"

She grinned, unoffended. "No, just him," she confirmed. "He was the one I wanted to go with in the first place, remember? I only thought of you because he said he couldn't come. And then it turned out he could've come all along!" She was still a bit indignant about that. "You didn't mind being second choice, did you?" she added, looking slightly worried that she might have hurt my feelings.

"Not a bit of it," I assured her, still thinking furiously. "Gave me an opportunity I might not have had otherwise."

More to the point, it had given someone else an opportunity he might not have had otherwise, too.

"We were talking about you yesterday, you know," Moira went on conversationally, pouring hot water into the cups. "Joe was asking about you. Wanted to know if you've got a boyfriend."

Just a simple comment; not even a very remarkable one. But it set an alarm shrilling in my head. I was glad she had her back to me.

"Did he? Hope he's not eyeing me up, when he's going out with you!" I said lightly.

She giggled. "I hope not, too!" She didn't sound as if she felt threatened by the concept; I was a decade and a half older than her, after all.

"What did you tell him?" I tried to sound as if it didn't matter.

She shrugged.

"I said I didn't know. Do you?" she asked, eyeing me curiously.

"You tell him from me," I said firmly, pointing an emphatic finger at her, "my motto is, '*Better unhappily single than unhappily married.*'" Which was perfectly true. It just didn't answer the question.

She didn't seem to notice. "Never mind; you'll find someone eventually. You're bound to," she said consolingly, with the confidence of youth. "You're too nice not to."

Bless her. She had such a sweet, sunny nature. I hoped my fear for her would prove to be unfounded; that that good nature wasn't being taken advantage of. Abused. But I couldn't let it drop now.

"Aagh! Look at the clock!" she shrieked in alarmed realization. "Time we were out on the desk!"

"I know, but – can you cover for me a moment? I've just realized I've got a phone call I need to make first. Won't take me long."

"No problem," she said. "See you in a minute." She swallowed the last of her coffee and dumped the mug on the draining board. "I'll wash that up later," she promised, and was gone.

I stood for a few moments, thinking about what I'd heard, reviewing everything I knew about Joe. And a pattern did begin to emerge. Elizabeth's birthday, Kew… I got my phone out, and made the call.

"Alan? Sorry to trouble you, but I thought I ought to ring you instead of Peter on this one. I've been talking to Moira, like you asked…"

Alan acted fast. Ben and Shoeshop were there within half an hour. When they turned up, asking to speak to Moira and me, I told Elizabeth, who had to organize cover for us on the desk while we were being interviewed.

"What's it about?" she wanted to know, naturally enough.

"Something that happened yesterday," I said. "When Moira and I were at Kew. I suppose they're going to ask us if we saw anything. Something like that." I shrugged, as if it didn't matter much. "Anyway, hopefully they won't keep us long."

"Okay," Elizabeth agreed. "Bit exciting, isn't it?"

"More excitement than I was hoping for today," I told her, and went back to the kitchen, where Ben and Shoeshop were waiting for me. Moira was looking apprehensive, not knowing what it was about.

"Mrs Gregory," Ben greeted me. "Detective Sergeant Sullivan, Detective Constable Angwin." He made the introductions as if I didn't already know who they were. Therefore he was playing this so as not to tip Moira off. I merely nodded politely, and saw the gleam of approval in his eyes. Shoeshop gave me a slight smile, also recognizing that I was going along with the strategy, and I returned it; I hadn't met her before, but, after Peter's description, I couldn't think of her by any other name.

Ben turned to Moira.

"Miss Ward," he said. "We have reason to believe you might be able to help us locate someone who can assist us with some enquiries. Do you know a Joe Robertson?"

"Joe?" Moira repeated, bewildered. "Yes, he's my boyfriend. Why, what's he done?"

"Don't worry, Miss Ward, we only want to ask him a few questions," Shoeshop said, professionally reassuring. "Could you tell us where we might find him? His address? His place of work?"

"He does removals, but I don't know who for. I've never asked…" She coloured slightly as she realized how lame that sounded.

"Well, perhaps you can tell us where he lives?" Shoeshop pressed in a carefully casual tone.

Moira looked at her uncertainly, but gave her the information, looking to me for support.

"Now, we understand you both saw him yesterday, is that right?" Ben knew it wasn't, but he looked in my direction, prompting me to speak my next set of lines.

"I didn't actually see him myself," I said. "I've seen him here at the library a few times, but the only other time I've seen him anywhere was when we went to the pub once. Our line manager's birthday. He came along with Moira then. I only knew he was there yesterday because Moira told me so. We got separated, you see." I was proud of the way I managed to keep my voice uninflected as I said that.

"I see. And what time did you meet up with him, Miss Ward?" Ben turned back to Moira.

"I dunno. About half-ten, eleven, maybe? Sorry – I wasn't thinking about what time it was." She blushed again.

I'll bet you weren't, I thought. *I'll bet he was doing everything he could to distract you. If he was there for the reason I think he was.*

"And you were with him then until – when?"

"Oh, I dunno," she said again. "We had lunch there, then we walked round a bit more. I suppose we left at about half-three, something like that? Definitely before four, I do know that. I remember hearing the on-the-hour news on the radio when we were in the car."

"Was that your car, or his?" Ben enquired casually.

"Mine."

Ben assumed a look of puzzlement. "Kew's a fair way from this address," he said, gesturing with his notebook. "How did he get there, if he didn't come in his own car?"

Moira looked puzzled. "Actually, I don't know," she said. "He didn't say."

No? I'll tell you how he got there. He came with Lesser. And Lesser left him to come back with you. Giving him an alibi so we wouldn't suspect any connection between them. Oh, Moira…

"Never mind," Ben said comfortably. "It's not important. Well, thank you, Miss Ward, Mrs Gregory" – he included me in his glance – "you've both been a great help. But I would like to ask you a favour, Miss Ward. Could I ask you not to get in touch with Mr Robertson until we've spoken to him? That would be very helpful."

Moira looked at him with sudden wariness, but nodded.

"Thanks again," Ben said smoothly. "We appreciate your help."

"I'll show you out," I offered quickly. "I'll see you back on the desk in a minute, Moira, all right?"

She nodded uncertainly, and silently watched us leave.

"You can be a bit of a charmer, can't you, Ben?" I said lightly, as we halted in front of the main door; he grinned. I turned to Shoeshop.

"Hello," I said, and offered my hand. "Jenny. And you're – Shoeshop, yes?" I offered the epithet with a slight hesitation, but she smiled immediately.

"Peter's been telling tales, then," she said lightly.

"Well, yes," I admitted. "But it's nice to have met you in person! And now I'd better get straight back, if you don't mind." I jerked my thumb over my shoulder. "I've caused enough disruption in there for one morning."

"We'll be in touch, Jenny," Ben called after me, as I turned away.

When I got back, Moira still wasn't on the desk. Patti, who was covering for us, threw me a look as much as to say, *Aren't you back yet?*

"Be right there," I mouthed to her, and headed back to the kitchen. The door was ajar, and I could see Moira, standing with her back to me, phone to her ear, speaking in a hushed and anxious voice.

"Joe, it's me! Whatever have you been up to? I've just had the police here, asking about you! Is everything all right? Look, give me a call as soon as you can, will you? Let me know what's going on?"

She ended the call, then looked up and saw me. She blanched, guiltily.

"Moira," I said resignedly. "They asked you not to do that."

"Well, what did they expect?" she demanded, defensively.

"They did it for a *reason*," I said, not trying very hard to keep the exasperation out of my voice. I looked at her pityingly. "Do I really have to tell you what's going to happen next?" I added.

She stared at me.

"I'm sorry, Moira," I said. "I know you liked him."

She was still staring at me, her phone clutched in her hand, as I gave her a sad smile and turned away, leaving the door ajar behind me.

Of course, by the time Ben and Shoeshop got to Joe's address, he wasn't there. And never was again. Vanished. Comprehensively.

Poor Moira.

Stupid Moira.

Chapter 28

"Well, that was a waste of time!" Ben announced with disgust, dropping into his chair. He glanced at Alan's office; Alan was on the phone, but looked an enquiry at him. Ben shook his head. Alan's lips tightened, and he went on with his call. Ben looked over at Brad. "Jenny rang not five minutes after we left her. That girl tried to phone him. Gone!"

"Pity," Brad observed. "Seems we could've had a very interesting chat with him."

Shoeshop, hanging her jacket on the back of her chair, turned to look at him. "Why? What've you got?"

Brad jerked his head in an invitation to join him at his desk. They both went over, and scanned the record Brad had on screen; the criminal record of one Joseph Martin Collinson, age thirty-one.

"Not Robertson after all, then," Shoeshop observed calmly. "How'd you find him?"

"Looked up some of those photos from the party at the pub," said Brad. "Thought he looked a bit familiar, so I thought I'd see if I could find any matches. And eventually he popped up."

"Several convictions for assault and aggravated assault," Ben summarized. "Three prosecutions for manslaughter, two for murder. None successful." He looked again at the photo; dark eyes stared balefully back at him.

"He must've started young, to get that lot fitted in by the time he was thirty," Shoeshop observed.

Ben glared at the screen. "And somebody must've had damn good lawyers to keep him on the streets, with that little lot to his credit. '*In removals!*'" he snorted, half amused, half indignant.

"Well, accurate job description," Brad pointed out dryly. "It's just that he removes people. Problems. Not furniture."

"That girlfriend of his might've had a lucky escape," Shoeshop commented.

Ben looked at her grimly. "It's Jenny who needs the lucky escape," he said.

They looked up as Alan came out of his office.

"What happened?" he asked. Ben told him. Alan looked at Brad's screen.

"Didn't we know Collinson was one of Lesser's?"

"Not till now," Brad said. "He must have changed employers fairly recently. He was with the same lot as Jimmy Ademola until about two months ago."

"Maybe that was how Lesser got Ademola," Ben theorized. "If Ademola knew Collinson, but didn't know he'd switched, maybe that's how he got caught out. Thought he was meeting a colleague, only to find he was working for a new boss. With new orders."

"But wouldn't Temp's lot have found Collinson's DNA somewhere?" Shoeshop objected.

Ben snorted. "If there's one thing you can bet on, it's that anyone Lesser uses for anything like that'll be more forensically aware than you are of all the shoe retailers in London," he grumbled. Shoeshop pulled a face at him.

"Well, you can all take it from me he's definitely on our wish list," said Alan firmly. He looked at Ben. "I've just got off the phone. The Commander's called a meeting the day after tomorrow. Here. Him, me, Peter. You. And Jenny."

Ben regarded him with a degree of gratification.

"About time," he remarked. "He's heard the tape, then?"

"I played it to him this morning," Alan said.

"Well done, Jenny. Got some action out of him at last," Ben muttered softly, under his breath. Alan looked at him levelly.

"Three o'clock," he said, a hint of censure in his tone, as he turned back to his office.

"I'm gonna ring her." Ben raised his voice slightly at Alan's retreating back. "Promised I'd tell her how it turned out with Collinson. D'you want me to tell her about the meeting?"

"If you would," Alan agreed, without turning round, and still in the same tone.

Brad and Shoeshop looked at Ben, but he remained unrepentant.

"About time something got him moving on this," he muttered, to no one in particular, as he went back to his desk. But he didn't mean Alan.

"The proverbial clean pair of heels, then," I said. I wasn't surprised.

"Yeah," Ben's voice growled in my ear. "The Boss still wants him found, but don't hold your breath."

"What do you think will've happened to him?"

I could almost hear Ben's shrug. "Depends how useful he is to Lesser. It's not the first time he's used someone and then they vanish off the radar. He usually spirits them away somewhere else, once their cover's blown. Unless he thinks it's safer to remove the removal man, of course. It's been known." It sounded so callous – but then, he was talking about someone who habitually displayed callousness at a very fundamental level.

"Well, thanks for letting me know, anyway," I said.

"You all right?"

I let out a breath of laughter.

"Given the context in which you're asking, I expect so. It's a bit hard to know what all right's supposed to be, though."

"You're doing okay," he said, with gruff reassurance. "Look, I just wanted to say… If there's anything else you think I can do to help, you tell me, right? And I don't mean just in working hours."

I was touched. "That's – really kind of you, Ben. I will if I need to, I promise. Though" – I used a lighter tone – "I didn't think in your job there *was* anything except working hours."

He chuckled. "It can turn out that way," he agreed. "See you Wednesday."

"Can't wait," I said dryly. He laughed again, and rang off.

I put my phone down on the kitchen table, where I was sitting. I'd been in the middle of balancing my bank statement, and all the paraphernalia that accompanied the task was spread on the tabletop – my chequebook, my service till receipts, all the shopping receipts for where I'd used my debit card, my calculator, my pen. Balancing wasn't something I'd bothered to do as a teenager, but after I married, Alex had gradually trained me into doing it; he'd always been very particular about monitoring expenses. I wished I could tell him how grateful I was to him for it, now that I was on my own and had to keep careful track of such income as I had. Even though my part-time job was supplemented by the rents from the cottage, it still didn't leave much to spare; I couldn't afford to let any of it go unaccounted for.

But I didn't pick up my pen again. I stared unseeing out of the window, thinking about Alex. I had so much more than that to be grateful to him for. Dad had said as much, the previous evening. After Peter had finally gone, he'd come up to see me. Poor thing, he was so anxious for me; they both were, but Mum had let him come up alone to talk to me. Not that there was very much to be usefully said. But during the conversation he'd come out with something I hadn't expected – that having lived with Alex was helping me to deal with what was going on now.

I'd looked at him, surprised. "What do you mean?"

"Because, to cope with this situation with Peter, you're using all the same qualities you had to develop to cope with Alex. Patience. Understanding. Empathy. A determination not to give up on someone just because it's not easy. It always seemed to us that the more difficult things got with Alex, the more determined you were to do everything you could for him. And I know sometimes you got to the point where it felt like more than you could take – I could see it on your face. But you never gave up. You always tried again. That's a kind of courage, you know, and it wasn't something anybody else could give you; you had to develop it for yourself. You had a long, hard training in those things, but they paid off for you. For both of you. And now – I think – those qualities are coming in useful again. This thing with Peter is in a different league, I know, but you're coping now, because of then. That's Alex's doing. Or partly. Wouldn't you say?"

I'd had to wait for a moment or two before I could reply. When I did, I said, not without difficulty, "You know, towards the end, there were quite a few people who couldn't see why I stayed with him, why I put up with the problems. They thought I should just cut loose and leave him to it. They didn't get it." I looked at my father with a troubled expression. "How could I possibly have been happy, if it had been at his expense? He depended on me. He depended on the support I gave him. And I'd promised. What kind of person would I have been to abandon him just because it would've been more convenient for me? I couldn't have done it and kept my self-respect intact. But they didn't seem to get that once you've lost your self-respect, it's one of the most difficult things in the world to get back. And it can't ever be quite the same. Like gluing a broken chip back into a vase. I couldn't do that. Not just to him, but to me. They couldn't see it, but – I could never have done it. Maybe other people can, but not me. Not and been happy. Never, Dad."

"I know it, darling," he'd said, taking my hand. There'd been a pause.

"I used to get so angry sometimes," I'd said in a low voice. "When it got really hard. I'd smile at him, and try to say something that I hoped would encourage him. And then I'd go into another room, where he couldn't see me, and I'd be so angry! Sometimes I'd cry, you know? Because it wasn't fair! *Why* did I have to keep putting up with all this stuff? Why *should* I? Why not shout at him, or scream at him, or nag him to be different than he was?" I'd gripped my father's hand more tightly, and he mine, as he listened. Then I'd shaken my head helplessly, and wiped my filling eyes with the back of my other hand. "But when I stopped thinking about myself, and remembered what it must be like to be him, I'd simmer down. Keep going. Because he didn't choose to be ill. Even if he chose the wrong way of dealing with it. But you can't expect someone who's got a broken ankle to run a marathon. And you can't expect someone who's got a broken mind to behave like someone who hasn't. I knew that most of the time. It's just that sometimes it was harder to remember than others. But I did try, Dad. I did."

"I know you did," he'd said, squeezing my hand. "In the circumstances, I don't believe there was anything more you could've done, beyond what you did."

"But you're right... It's sort of like that now," I'd gone on, slowly. "It wasn't fair about Alex, and it's not fair about Peter. That he should've been persecuted the way he has been, all these years. It's not fair that I should end up being used against him the way I am being. But I've got to see it through, Dad. Not just for him. For me, too. You do know that, don't you?" I'd sought his eyes, urgently seeking his comprehension, his approval.

"Because you love him," my father had stated. I'd nodded silently. I remember the way his eyes searched my face. "Have you told him so?"

A silent shake of my head.

"Why not?"

I'd had to think out my answer.

"Because he hasn't said how he feels, and I think... I think he has to say it first. I can't tell you why, exactly, but – that's what I feel. Does that sound stupid? But that's how it is. I can't say I love him, not until he says he loves me."

"And does he?" Dad hadn't been being intrusive; he'd been trying to get me to analyze it objectively, I could tell. His fingers never once relaxed their hold on mine.

"I think so..." I'd looked up. "No, that's not true. I know so. I know he does. But he never says it. He never even gets close to saying it. But I'm sure he does..." My eyes had began to well up again. "So why doesn't he say it, Dad? Why?"

There'd been a short silence. He'd stared down at our linked hands, deep in thought. I'd waited. At last he'd spoken again, with slow consideration.

"Some cultures – ones that have a belief in magic, for want of a better word – have a superstition about words. That words have a power that can be invoked by using them. And particularly names. They believe that if you know someone's true name, and you speak that name out loud, it gives other people power over that person. A power that can be used for evil purposes."

I'd nodded.

"I wonder if something like that is going on in Peter's head," my father had continued, quietly. "Even if he doesn't realize it. If he admits to himself that he loves you, the logical corollary is that he has to say it. To you. But once he's named it to himself – named it to you – perhaps he's afraid that makes him – and you – even more vulnerable to Lesser, in some way he can't even explain. Not exactly a rational reaction, but if his reactions aren't entirely rational in the circumstances, who could blame him?"

I'd stared at him for a long time, thinking about what he'd said. And it had made sense. A weird kind of sense, to be sure, but – plausible, yes...

"I'm not saying that *is* what he thinks," my father had added. "But if it is, it might explain why he can't bring himself to say what he so evidently does feel about you. I've seen him, Jenny; I've seen the two of you together. I've watched him when he's with you. And it's blindingly obvious to me that he loves you. He wants to be with you. If he hasn't said so, it's because something is holding him back from saying it. What I've suggested is just one explanation; there could be many others. But whatever it is, there is a reason in his own mind for not saying it. It's not because he doesn't feel it."

I'd been silent again for a while, absorbing his words, wrestling with the implications. Eventually, I'd offered him a watery smile.

"In that case... As you were, then," I'd said, as lightly as I could.

My father had raised my hand to his lips, and kissed it. "You have such courage, Jenny. And such loyalty. When I saw what you went through with Alex, I didn't think I could ever have been more proud of you than I was then. But I am now."

Which had reduced me to tears again, of course. But I'd been thinking a lot about what he'd said, since then. I'd never thought of it before, but I'd realized he was right about how living with Alex then was helping me with Peter now. I wished Alex could know how grateful I was. In spite of his problems, he'd given me so much. I simply hadn't realized until now just how much. And that he still was, even though he was dead.

I was still staring out of the window, thinking about what Dad had said about Peter and wondering if it was true, when my mobile rang again, jerking me back to awareness. I picked it up.

"Jenny?" It was Craig.

"Hello, Craig. How are you?"

"That's what I was going to ask you." He was trying to sound casual, but there was a slight crack of anxiety in his voice that gave him away. "Dad's told us," he went on.

Ah.

"Yes." I tried to strike the right note of regret. "No more filming in Croydon, that's for sure!"

He couldn't bring himself to laugh about it.

"Are you all right?"

"Everyone keeps asking me that," I said wryly. "I keep saying yes, but... I suppose I don't know, really. It's hard to know."

"Yeh," he said. There was a pause, as if he desperately wanted to say something, but didn't know what it was. To offer comfort, without knowing how to say it.

"I'll still be over to see you," I said, divining what the cause of his concern might be. "And you can always come over to me, if you want. Provided it's with someone. I've just got to be careful, that's all. You're used to this. I'm not. Not yet. So you're going to have to help me. Remind me what I should be doing, if you need to." I wasn't patronizing him; I meant it. He'd lived with this – with the potential of it – almost all his life, because of Peter; what had become second nature to him had to become second nature to me, too. I needed to learn from him.

"Course I will." The boy was becoming a man; I could hear it in his voice, buoyed by my expression of trust in him at an adult level.

"I don't think you'd be in any real danger, yourself," I said, not prevaricating. As with Peter, I wouldn't deal in anything but truth with Craig. "But there would be a risk you could be collateral damage. You do understand how I'd feel if that happened, don't you?"

"Yeh," he said, with sober maturity. "I get it."

"Craig – I'm sorry." *Sorry you're worried; sorry that by coming into Peter's life I've complicated yours, too. Sorry that liking me, caring about me, has become this problem for you.*

"Not your fault," he said quickly. "And they'll get him! You'll see! They'll get him, and you'll be safe again!"

If only life was that tidy. That fair. Still, I couldn't blame him; that was what I'd been telling Peter, wasn't it? Sometimes we believe because of the facts, sometimes we believe in spite of the facts.

"Well, I hope they get on with it," I said, trying to sound cheerful. "I'm depending on you for my burgeoning film career, and it's going to put a real crimp in my meteoric rise to stardom if we can't do location shoots."

This time he couldn't help laughing.

Always leave them laughing. If you have to leave them.

It was only six o'clock when I heard Peter's key in the door. He must be leaving work a lot earlier these days. The way he was behaving, he must be thinking I was safer when he was with me than when he wasn't. So he was putting himself under the pressure of having to be with me every minute he could. Poor Peter. But I couldn't put my hand on my heart and say I didn't want him with me, either.

He appeared in the kitchen doorway, and we looked at each other for a moment.

"Ben told you?" he said dourly.

"Yes," I said. "He rang."

He stared at me. Then his face contorted and he smashed his fist against the door jamb with such violence it made me jump.

"*Dammit!*" It was a yell of pure rage and frustration. Yet another lead evaporated, another hope gone. The disappointment was too much.

Then he saw the look on my face, and his expression changed. With a swift movement he came to me, put his arms around me, and held me in an embrace so strong it was almost painful.

"I'm sorry," he murmured contritely. "I didn't mean to frighten you."

"It's all right." I clung to him, trying to reassure him. "Peter, it's all right."

"Oh, Jenny," he whispered into my hair. "So nearly lost you. You came so close…"

The intensity of his hold on me, the crack of tension in his voice – it was so evident what he was saying to me. And yet he still wasn't saying it in words.

It was a moment that – well, it wouldn't be accurate to say it changed everything, because, in all essentials, it didn't. But I now knew Dad had been right. What Peter didn't say, wouldn't say – couldn't say – must be for the reasons he had outlined. And it gave me a new understanding of our relationship. I knew how I felt about Peter; I no longer doubted how he felt about me. Even though he couldn't bring himself to articulate it. But because I now felt I understood why, I was willing to take it on trust. I could cope with it, on that basis.

So – thanks to my father's insight – it made a difference, what passed between us that evening. After that conversation, we did know exactly how things stood between us.

But it wasn't spoken aloud, not in the usual sense. Not by either of us. Because, as I now understood, it couldn't be.

But then, it didn't need to be.

Next morning, when Ben came in, Peter's computer was on, but he wasn't at his desk. Ben looked at the empty chair across the office for a while. Then he got out his mobile and rang Peter's number.

"Yeh?" came the response.

"Where are you?"

"Roof."

Ben ended the call, and left the office, unremarked by the others.

He found Peter up on the roof, sitting on the left-hand parapet just where it joined the one along the front, his back to the railing. This was a different man from the one who had come bursting in yesterday, full of anger and energy. He was leaning forward tiredly, his elbows resting on his thighs and his hands dangling loosely from his wrists, in a posture of despondency. He looked up as Ben appeared, but didn't speak. Ben came and sat beside him.

"What is it, then?" he asked, after a few moments.

"Jenny," said Peter simply, as if that was all there was to say.

"What about her?" Ben prompted.

"Something that happened last night. We did a lot of talking about — things…" He clearly wasn't going to specify what they were. "But it was something she said after we'd done all that. It got me thinking, that's all."

"So what was it?"

Peter hesitated before answering. "It'll sound stupid."

"Try me."

"She doesn't pay for her own mobile contract. Richard — her father — he pays for it. To help her out. You know why?" Peter looked away into the middle distance. "Because she's on such a tight budget. She doesn't even do voicemail because of the cost. She's got a laptop, yeh, so she doesn't really need it. But you know what else? She said, *'I've got you to feed.'*" He looked back at Ben, his disgust at his own obtuseness more than evident. "I've been going round her place every night, and I never thought of that. That she was paying out for two, not for one anymore. So I said I'd start giving her something toward the food."

"Sorted, then."

"Yeh, but that's not the problem. The thing is, she didn't *mind*. She wasn't just pretending; she really didn't mind. She's just been doing it all along, and — happy about it. She'd never have said a word, if I hadn't." He shook his head.

"And that's what it was? That's what was worrying you?"

"Yeh. Said it'd sound stupid, didn't I?"

Ben ignored that.

"Look, you're there every waking moment you're not at work. You're paying toward the housekeeping. Why don't you just move in?" he asked, only half joking. Peter looked at him.

"I can't," he said in a low voice. "You know I can't."

Ben wanted to argue. But he couldn't.

Silence.

"Besides, she told me," Peter said after a while. "She doesn't sleep with men she isn't married to."

"So marry her!" Ben erupted, instantly.

"*I can't*," Peter said again, the words fraught with desperation.

There was a further silence. Then Peter spoke again.

"You know what he's started doing?"

301

No need to ask who 'he' was. "What?"

Peter got out his phone, pressed a few keys, and held it up so Ben could see the screen.

A text message. *Are you sure she's all right?*

Another one. *Have you checked she's safe today?*

Another. *Is she having a lovely day?*

"You get the idea," said Peter, and put his phone back in his pocket. "Sometimes it's voicemails instead – unidentifiable voice. All anonymous, all from different numbers, so no point trying to trace them. Every day. All on the same theme. And every time I have to phone her and make sure. In case this time it's for real."

"Does she know?"

"She worked it out, after the first few times. Telling her I was just checking for no reason didn't wash."

"What did she say?"

"You know Jenny. Told me to ring as many times as I needed to. Reassure myself. But if it happens when she's at work, she can't always get back to me right away. She tries to be as quick as she can, but sometimes, it feels like forever... And then she gets upset if she thinks I'm getting upset." The strain was clearly telling on him.

Ben fumed inwardly. Lesser had done much the same the first time, and Laura hadn't coped well with it. This time, neither was Peter, it appeared. Foreknowledge was no help in this circumstance.

"It's all my fault," Peter went on. "If only I'd just let it be! I mean, I could hardly ignore her, could I? Not after what she did for me. But I should have just met her the once, said my thanks, and left it at that. Left her to live her nice, safe life..." His features contorted, and his head sank forward as he covered his face with his hands.

Ben hesitated. He'd never had a son of his own, but over the years this man beside him had come to fill that place, as far as he was concerned, though he'd never have expressed it to Peter in those terms. And the woman at the heart of his dilemma was one he, Ben, utterly approved. But in all the years since Laura had been killed, Peter had never laid himself open to a relationship of any kind, even in the slightest degree. Not until now. He'd been too afraid of the consequences. And yet, with Jenny Gregory... This was a question he'd wanted to ask, and there might never come a better moment.

"So why didn't you?" he asked. "What made the difference, with her?" He didn't know if Peter would answer him. If he even knew the answer himself. He probably wouldn't even have entertained the question from anyone else, except maybe Alan. But he didn't immediately reject it. After a few moments he raised his head again, staring at nothing, and Ben saw his brow creasing into a frown he was probably entirely unconscious of, as he strove to articulate a response.

"I don't know, exactly... I was in trouble, and she was there, and – she wanted to help me." He was struggling to define his reasons, to describe what he felt about what she'd done. Spelling it out not just for Ben, but for himself. "I mean – not that lots of people wouldn't've done the same, I suppose. But there was just – something about the way she went about it... Not just the practicalities – it was more than that, somehow... I can't – I can't—" He broke off.

Ben didn't attempt to break into the pause; this thread of communication was too fragile to risk.

"It was as if I really mattered to her," Peter went on, at last. "Right from the very first. She didn't know anything about me, but, even so... It just felt as if I did. Then, when I took her out that first time – to say thank you – she was so—" He glanced at Ben. "Up front. Alan said that was what Jane said about her, the first time she met her. Up front. Honest. Open. But even that first time, she was thinking about me, about how I felt... She asked me, straight out, if we should talk about what happened, or not. And if I'd said no, she wouldn't have, I know that. But I didn't say no..."

Another pause.

"She's always been so straight with me. Such a straight talker. I never have to guess whether she means what she says. And she's never once asked me about the job. No details. To this day she still doesn't know what the name of the team is. Because she's never asked. Not that, not anything. Well, maybe a couple of times – just generalities – but that's it. She's never tried to find out anything she shouldn't. And I've never had to warn her off that, you know? It's just like she – she knows what not to ask. And sometimes I've been downright foul with her. On bad days. She's still never asked why. Just – taken it. Let me unload it the way I wanted to. And I have. Pretty selfish, huh?" He looked up at Ben again, and this time his eyes were over bright, sheened with upwelling tears. His voice was thickening. "Really proud of myself, yeh? But I didn't have to bottle it up anymore. Not with her. I could let it out! And *still* she... That much kindness – that was just – too much to let go of. Too much to – to renounce. I wasnae strong enough, and I couldnae do it."

The Scots accent was suddenly at full strength and tears were trailing down his cheeks. It was all Ben could do not to wince at the sight of those tortured eyes. He put an arm round Peter's shoulders.

"Know what I think?" he asked. "I think any man with his head screwed on right would've done exactly the same as you. A woman like that?

You'd've been mad not to." He gave the tense shoulders a brief shake. "The kind of people who can happily live as hermits're few and far between. And you're not one of them! You need companionship, just like anyone else. Of course you went for it when you saw it! You're only human, damn it!"

"But I should've—"

"Should've what? Just stuck to us, in the team? Because we're professionals? Pretty small pool of people to be picking your friends from! And why would you want to, when you see us all every day anyway? Because if you're telling me you'd *choose* to spend time with Chris when you didn't have to, I'm sorry, I'm not having it!"

Peter couldn't stifle a brief gasp of laughter at that, even as he wiped his face inelegantly with his sleeve.

"It's not the same, and you know it," Ben concluded firmly.

"But what'm I gonnae *do*?" It was a cry from the heart. The anguish in Peter's eyes was heartbreaking. Ben's grip round his shoulders tightened momentarily.

"Make the most of what you've got," he said. "Anyone can lose anyone at any time, for all sorts of reasons. It's just most of the time they don't have any idea it might happen. Just because you do, doesn't mean you shouldn't value what you've got. I'm getting to know Jenny, you know. And I can tell you, she isn't going to go away. She's going to stick with you, because that's the kind of woman she is. Can you imagine how many people would give – I don't know what, for what you've got? Make the most of it, Peter! While you've got it! That's all you can do. And I'll bet you anything you like that's what she wants for you. You hear me?" He gave one last, emphatic shake, then let his arm drop from Peter's shoulders.

Peter covered his face with his hands, and sat like that for a while. Ben didn't speak. At last, Peter sat upright, and wiped his eyes with the heels of his hands. Then he looked at Ben, and gave him a watery smile.

"I hear you," he said.

"Good. Then come on. Let's get on with solving the real problem," said Ben gruffly.

"Right," said Peter.

Chapter 29

The heat really began to build during the day. Being south-east England, it didn't just get hot; it got humid. Enervatingly so. And continued on into the night. It was going to be even hotter tomorrow, the forecasters were promising. The heat in that meeting room was going to be crippling by three in the afternoon, but Peter wasn't thinking about that.

He lay awake under a single sheet, and that thrown down as far as his waist. It was much too hot to wear any clothing; even the sheet was almost too much covering. Hands behind his head on the pillow, he stared at the ceiling of his bedroom reflecting the first hint of light beginning to pale the pre-dawn sky as it came through the window above the head of the bed. The stars still twinkled through the glass, but he didn't see them. He was thinking about corn-straw coloured hair, about brown-lashed hazel eyes, about the curve of neck into shoulder, about a smiling mouth, about the delicate shaping of hand and wrist and forearm...

The day Lesser had abducted her; that moment when she'd told him to come into the bathroom, to hang the caftan on the inside of the door. Herself, bent forward and hugging herself protectively in the warm water. She had been at her most vulnerable at that moment, both physically and emotionally, yet she'd trusted him in there with her at a time like that. That brief glimpse of her... He'd remembered that moment more than once. He'd honoured her gesture of trust. Yet the sight of her back and shoulders, glistening with water, had created an almost physical sensation in the palm of his hand, an urge to reach out, to touch her, to experience the sensation of stroking his fingers across her skin. And he had fought it down, and left.

Now the image was there in his mind once more. Again, the desire to touch the smooth skin with the touch of a lover spread through him, with a heightened sense of awareness that made him feel as though his own skin was more sensitive than usual. Yet an unformulated protest instantly rose to deny the image. An inchoate fear that, if he ever acted on that desire, it would somehow make her vulnerable to Lesser. And he *must not* make her vulnerable to Lesser.

Therefore he *must not* touch her.

He must *never* touch her.

Not with the touch of a lover.

Despite which, his body was filled with a desperate longing for her that he dared not – *dared not* – acknowledge. Not to her.

And most especially not to himself.

4.30 am. Still unable to sleep. He got up, took a shower. Then, wearing only a pair of jeans, he opened the door to the tiny balcony and stepped out, the stone tiles cold under his naked feet.

He spread his hands onto the black metal railing, leaning slightly forward as he stood looking at the paling sky, the dawn air still cool as it touched his wet hair, his damp, bare skin.

He watched the light in the east growing, trying hard to make his mind a blank, to relax, to not think about anything at all.

Miles away, I, too, lay awake, staring through the skylight at the dimming stars, feeling a nagging sense of incompleteness, an unfulfilled yearning. For Peter. Wondering what it would be like if he were ever to approach me as more than a friend. Wondering if it was a yearning that would ever be satisfied.

I knew, for so many reasons, some of them still unformulated, that if it were ever to be so, the move would have to come from him. And I also knew that as long as Lesser was there, it never would. Dad had given me the clues I needed to make sense of his behaviour. Not, as Dad had admitted, that there was much sense to it, in reality. But it was how Peter saw it, and because of that, he couldn't say the words. Even though they'd be true. And though, as any woman would, I longed to hear those words from him, the way things were it would be no kindness on my part to make him say them.

At last I gave in to the knowledge that I wasn't going back to sleep. I went downstairs to the living room, my feet silent on the soft carpet. I heaved at the heavy sash window, pushing it up as far as it would go. Then I took my usual place on the window seat, my elbows propped on the white paint of the sill, my chin cupped in my hands, feeling the cool flow of the air passing me into the flat, as I watched the sky, listening to the birds in the garden singing in the new day.

Until it was time to get dressed, to go to work. And to mentally prepare myself for the meeting later in the day. At last I would get to meet the man who had sent Peter undercover, with such terrible consequences. The one who kept him on the team, because he hoped that somehow his continued presence would result in Lesser's downfall. And I couldn't help wondering how much of that was for Peter's sake, and how much sheer pragmatism, simply a means to a desired end. Wondering what kind of man he was. Well, in only a few hours I'd find out.

He was already there when Peter ushered me into the meeting room, standing with his back to the door, in conversation with Alan; Ben was seated at the table. Alan saw us, and said something. Laird turned round, and looked at me.

Commander Robert Laird was fifty-two years of age. Not as tall as Alan, he had sandy blond hair and a pair of pale blue eyes capable, I learned, both of a charming smile and a penetrating regard. An almost palpable sense of authority seemed to be an innate component of his physical presence; 'Commander' immediately felt like a more than apt title for him. He came toward me and shook my hand.

"Thank you for coming, Mrs Gregory. It's a pleasure to meet you. I'm only sorry it had to be under these circumstances." He offered the platitude with great charm. His native Edinburgh accent was not overly marked but nevertheless detectable. He took his eyes from me for the brief moment it took him to award a nod of acknowledgement to Peter. I saw Ben watching us.

"I feel much the same," I said, rather dryly.

There was a glint in his eye as he invited me to sit down. He drew out the chair at the near end of the table and seated me, then took his place at the other end. A deliberate strategy, then. He wanted to be able to see my face clearly while the discussion took place. I wondered what was coming.

He waited for Alan and Peter to take their places; Alan next to him, Peter next to me, facing Ben on my left. Then he leaned forward, interlocking his fingers and resting his forearms on the table. Clearly not a man to waste time.

"The first thing I want to do," he began, "is to offer my apologies for the situation in which you find yourself. DCI McLeish has, I know, made it clear to you under what constraints we are operating, and therefore why it's so difficult for us to take effective measures to relieve it for you. I'm grateful for your understanding in the matter, but I do want to assure you that we are taking every step that we can, and will continue to do so, until the matter is resolved."

Of course you will. Thanks for pretending that's on my account, I thought to myself.

"Thank you," I said aloud.

"I'd also like to express my admiration for the way in which you captured your interview" – he smiled briefly – "with Matthew Lesser. I find your quick thinking and courage in such a difficult and stressful situation most commendable."

I contented myself with a nod to convey my thanks this time.

"However, the main purpose of this meeting is to try to determine how to take this matter forward. Under ordinary circumstances" – he glanced round at his colleagues – "Superintendent Salisbury would also have been attending this meeting, but as of two days ago he's had to take sick leave." From the looks on their respective faces, Alan already knew, Peter and Ben didn't, though the latter nodded with an air of *that explains it*. The name meant nothing to me – Peter had never mentioned him – but Ben explained to me later that Salisbury was next in the hierarchy between Alan and Laird, which was why he would normally have been involved.

"So for the moment, in his absence and until further notice, I'm overseeing this matter personally," Laird continued. "DCI McLeish, perhaps you'd refresh my memory by summarising the timeline of encounters between Lesser and Mrs Gregory." He didn't look to me like the kind of man who forgot anything, but doubtless he had a reason for wanting to have the full roll-call of events presented aloud. He smiled along the table at me. "May I call you Jenny? If you don't mind the informality?"

"Please," I concurred.

"The attack on Peter took place in May last year," Alan began, evidently interpreting Laird's suggestion as tacit permission to extend the use of first names to everyone involved. He was using what I thought of as his 'professional' voice. "Jenny didn't actually see Lesser on that occasion, but we infer from the presence of the unidentified footmarks outside the house that he must have seen her, and was therefore able to recognize her subsequently. Her phone and laptop were stolen on that occasion, and we have to assume that Lesser's been able to obtain some measure of personal data from them. There were no further known encounters until April this year, but it seems clear that at some point in the intervening period he somehow came across Jenny again and was able to identify her, without her being aware of this. We also have to assume, from Lesser's subsequent interest in her, that he is aware of her" – he hesitated slightly over the term – "relationship with Peter, and that this accounts for his actions toward her from that time. We believe that the attack on her in Croydon was masterminded by him. If so, that would imply that at the latest he must have identified her so as to give him sufficient time to monitor her movements and plan the attack, making it a matter of weeks or days only. Two weeks later Lesser approached her openly for the first time, though without identifying himself. However, Jenny was able to confirm visual identification from our records. In the first week of July, Jenny was abducted by him but returned unharmed. On that occasion Lesser once again had access to the data on her phone. Three days ago, in the last week of July, Jenny was again attacked; she was threatened but once again left unharmed."

"Only just," Ben muttered under his breath, but audible to everyone. Laird ignored him.

"Three attacks in just over three months," he summarized. "It seems fairly clear that this persecution is likely to continue. Unfortunately, we have a precedent for thinking so." He was looking at Peter as he said it, but didn't even blink. Peter stared back at him without expression. "Equally unfortunately, there's little we can do about it."

"Why can't we put her under surveillance?" Ben asked. "She's clearly at risk." His voice was level but his eyes even harder than Peter's. Laird, I could see, had registered his latent hostility.

"I have to prove that the outcome will justify the commitment of resources," he said. It sounded callous, but later, when Alan explained it to me, I had to concede he had a point. Surveillance doesn't come cheap. Six officers, say; two on duty at any one time, for an indeterminate length of time – and time is money. And when money is short, when budgets are cut on an annual basis and there is less and less with which to try to do more and more, sometimes hard decisions have to be made. My life was on the end of one of those decisions now.

"He was on the point of putting a bullet through her head!" Ben burst out. His hands, on the desk in front of him, both clenched into fists. "How much justification d'you need? Her dead body – that do you? That's how far you let it get with Laura!"

"DS Sullivan, you will kindly moderate your tone!" Laird rapped out. His voice was hard, the anger in his eyes clearly visible. Ben stared back at him mutinously, then slowly sat back, exhaling a long, loud breath. But he didn't retract the challenge of his gaze. It appeared to be all Alan could do, to keep his face impassive. I couldn't even look at Peter. The tension in the room was almost tangible. I felt a desperate urge to try to defuse it.

"What would be really helpful would be if one of Lesser's so-called friends would fall out with him and go and shoot him for us," I heard myself saying.

"That would, indeed, solve a great many things," Laird agreed, his attitude softening slightly as he registered my attempt at levity. "Unfortunately nobody seems to want to be that obliging."

I hardly heard what he said, because Peter had turned his head sharply to look at me; then his eyes unfocused, as if he was looking at something I couldn't see. I don't think Alan had noticed, but I could see Ben had, and so had Laird.

"Do you have something to add, DS McLeish?" he said, looking at him through suddenly narrowed eyes.

Peter came back into focus; he looked down at the table in front of him, and shook his head vigorously, as if waking himself from a bad dream.

"No," he said. "No."

Laird continued to regard him thoughtfully for a moment, then turned to Alan.

"We need to define a plan of action," he said. "What options do we have?"

I felt my stomach clench. I'd been thinking about that myself, and I'd come to a conclusion. One I didn't like. And I knew Peter wasn't going to like it, either.

"Excuse me, but – can I say something?" I interjected. Everyone turned to look at me.

"Please," Laird consented, making a gesture of invitation with one hand.

I swallowed, and took a deep breath.

"Aside from our two – personal encounters, I only know about Lesser what I've been told," I began. "But you've been trying to get him for more than a decade, and he's managed to escape you all this time. So it seems to me that unless something game-changing happens, this is only going to end one way for me." I tried to keep my voice as flat and dispassionate as I could, as if I was talking about someone else. "My only hope is that this time he'll want to string it out as long as possible. Because he knows he won't get another chance like this. He knows Peter will never, ever risk this happening again. And afterwards, once he's concluded that there really is no other way he can hurt Peter any more than he's already done, he'll kill him, too." I couldn't look at him as I said that; I kept my eyes on Laird. "So unless that game-changer happens, you'll end up with two more deaths – two more murders – that you won't have been able to prevent. So – something has to be made to change."

Laird's face was expressionless, but I knew I wasn't saying anything he didn't already know. Even so, I thought I detected in his eyes a gleam of respect for my realism and forthrightness.

"What are you suggesting?" he asked.

"He's already using me to get to Peter," I said flatly, trying to hide my inner turmoil at what I was about to suggest. "So why don't you turn that on its head?"

Laird continued to regard me, his interest caught. He was already following where I led.

"How?" he asked, pointedly.

"Use *me* to get to *him*. Trap him into incriminating himself, somehow. If he's focusing on me, make me the goat to catch the tiger."

"No!" Peter exploded, and shot to his feet. Laird gave him a fierce look and used a sharp hand gesture that ordered him to sit down again. He did, but he was stiff with fury.

"Go on," Laird said, addressing me, but his eyes fixed like steel rods on Peter's face, daring him to speak.

"I don't know how, exactly," I admitted. "But as long as he thinks what he's doing is working on Peter, maybe it'll give you a chance to pin him down in some way. Get him to incriminate himself. Somebody who knows more about these things than me must be able to think of something, surely?"

Peter was obviously bursting to protest, but Laird continued to fix him with that quelling stare.

Alan shifted in his chair, unhappily.

"She may have a point, sir," he said heavily. "Lesser's clearly getting a kick out of persecuting Peter by proxy, through her. If he's so distracted by the pleasure he's getting out of that, he might trip himself up. And it's obvious from the conversation at Kew that Jenny caught his interest by standing up to him. It seems to be what changed his mind about killing her on the spot. Perhaps he now sees her as a challenge in her own right. One that" – he hesitated over the word – "intrigues him. We might be able to make use of that."

"Alan!" Peter could hold himself in no longer. He stared at his cousin aghast. "This is Jenny we're talking about! You *wannae* put her in danger? Use her as – as *bait?*"

"She's already in danger," said Laird bluntly. "You know Lesser's *modus operandi*. Once he's started using someone like this, he doesn't let them go. Not alive."

A sensation of cold crawled over my skin at this flat statement of fact. This was me, my life, he was talking about with such detachment, as if I wasn't there. Me whom Lesser would continue to torment, so as to torment Peter, unless he chose to kill me. Or, rather, until he chose to kill me, because he undoubtedly would do, once he decided that was what would cause Peter the greatest suffering.

"The only other thing we could do to protect her is to send her into hiding. We'd do our best, but how long could we realistically guarantee her safety?" He turned to me. "I'm sorry to be so frank, Jenny, but those are the facts." His slightly less formidable tone was in belated deference to my feelings, which must have been showing clear on my face. "If you're freely volunteering to be used by us as you suggest, it may be the only way out of this."

Peter's eyes had gone huge and dark, as they did when his feelings were at their most intense, silently pleading with me not to consent. I looked back at him with distress. *Think about it, Peter. If they send me into that kind of hiding, you won't be able to be with me. You won't be allowed to contact me. Is that what you want? Is that the kind of life you want me to have? Always afraid he'd find me, sooner or later? Because it isn't what I want. I'd rather do it this way. Resolve it once and for all.*

311

"What else is there to do?" I asked him rhetorically, my voice trembling slightly. "I want you free of him." I looked at Alan, then at Laird. "Work out what you need me to do, then tell me what it is."

Laird nodded.

"We will." He turned to Alan. "But I think that had better be the subject of another discussion. Arrange it, please, DCI McLeish. I want you to give this utmost priority. And" – he turned back to me – "thank you, Jenny. You're being very courageous."

"If this is what 'courageous' feels like, it's overrated," I said, my voice still tremulous.

"Not by me," he said flatly.

There was a short silence.

"We'll work on Jenny's suggestion. Come up with some possible strategies. In the meantime, the situation remains unchanged. She, and we, will continue to exercise all possible caution," Laird said with decision. "Jenny, we'll talk to you again when a course of action has been determined. Thank you, everyone." He rose; the meeting was over. "Alan – a word, if you please?" Alan got up and followed him out of the room.

Ben, Peter and I were left sitting in silence. Then Peter expelled a long breath, and, visibly refraining from all the things he could have said, said instead, "Well, now what do we do?"

"Well, I'll tell you one thing, for starters," said Ben promptly. "We get a CCTV system put in at Jenny's flat. Cover the staircase and the driveway at least. Remind me – those stairs aren't the only way in, are they?"

"No," said Peter quickly. "There's the door from her flat into her parents' part of the house. You'd need to cover the whole front and back, to be sure."

"Then we will," said Ben flatly. "What about the security of the cameras?"

"Pretty good," Peter returned. "We can put them all up high on the walls, where nobody can get to them without a ladder. Run all the cables in through the roof." He turned to me. "Will Richard be all right with that?"

"I think, in the circumstances, he might be persuaded."

"We'll talk to him." Peter was more animated now that there was a positive course of action to be taken.

"Uh – I hate to mention this, but – where's the money going to come from?" I enquired. I had the feeling it wouldn't come cheap.

"Don't worry about it," said Peter bluntly. "From me, if we can't get it through official channels."

"Damned if I'm letting you pay for something Laird should be paying for!" Ben exploded.

Peter shrugged. "If I have to, I have to."

I wanted to protest about him spending his money on me; but, looked at in another light, it would be a kindness to let him. Because it would be a way of assuaging the guilt he felt. I hoped that one day I'd be able to make it up to him, somehow. If I ever got the chance… But whoever paid for it, the ugly truth was that it was necessary.

Unexpectedly, Ben laughed, and we looked at him enquiringly.

"What's so funny?" Peter demanded, slightly irritated; he wasn't in a humorous mood.

"I was just thinking," said Ben. "Some girls get flowers, or chocolates. Some even get diamonds. What does Jenny get? A CCTV system!" He winked at me, grinning.

And I found myself laughing back. After all, there was an incongruity there to be appreciated. And when I looked at Peter, I saw his lips begin to twitch, in spite of himself.

Thank you, Ben. Nicely done.

Chapter 30

Peter spoke to Dad and Mum about the CCTV that evening, and received an endorsement that could hardly be described as enthusiastic, given the reason for its necessity, but was nonetheless sincere. He wasted no time; within a couple of days the system was in and working, and we had all been shown how it operated.

I hoped it would be a protection for Mum and Dad, too. After all, Lesser knew where I lived. The fact that he'd abstained from harming Alan's family gave no guarantee for my parents' safety, if they got in his way. Got between him and me. I didn't say any of that either to Peter or to them, but I knew Dad, at least, was capable of coming to that conclusion without my assistance. Perhaps that had contributed to his readiness to agree to the installation; though he would have been thinking of me in the first instance, I'm sure Mum would have been in his mind, too. But he never referred to it, so I didn't, either.

Even though I was on the alert for it, I never saw anyone overtly watching the house. But someone must have been. Seen the CCTV being installed, and reported back. That became obvious only three days later.

I don't know what arrangement had been agreed by Alan and the team, but Peter seemed to be more and more available to be around at the times when my parents weren't going to be at home. Perhaps Alan was doing as much as he could to make up for the fact that he couldn't give me twenty-four hour protection. This particular day, Dad had taken Mum on a shopping expedition; she wanted a couple of new evening outfits for the cruise, and he'd driven her up to London to find them.

So when, after picking me up from work and helping me do some food shopping, Peter brought me home, we had more of the driveway to ourselves than usual, because Dad's car wasn't there. Peter killed the engine, and we both got out and headed for the back of the car to get the shopping out of the boot. But we didn't get the chance.

The only warning was the sound of loose gravel on the pavement being ground under a heavy boot. Then they appeared; their approach had been masked by the hedge on that side of the drive. Two men, who strode purposefully toward us, so swiftly that we barely had time to react to their presence.

Without a word, one walked straight up to Peter and with a stiff, brutal movement of his arm, punched him viciously in the stomach. Taken by surprise, Peter wasn't able to take any evading action, and it was a true solar plexus blow. He grunted – a horrible, animal sound – as all the air was driven from his lungs by the force of the blow. He doubled over, then fell to his knees, hands clutched to his paralyzed abdomen, struggling even to breathe.

And there was nothing I could do – not even cry out – because the other man had seized me and swung me around so that he was behind me, one hand reaching across me to seize my right wrist, effectively trapping both my right and left arms, and pulling me tight back against him as his other hand gripped the lower half of my face, covering my mouth and savagely muffling my attempts to make any sound at all.

The man who had punched Peter turned to look at me. There was a violence in his eyes so ferocious, and yet so controlled, that it was as if something inside me wizened and froze under its regard.

"Think that camera's gonna help you? *Nowhere* is safe," he said to me, with terrifying intensity. Then he leaned down and grasped a handful of Peter's hair, dragging his head up so he could stare straight into his eyes.

"Got that? *Nowhere*," he said again. Then he thrust Peter's head downward, savagely, so that he collapsed helplessly over onto his side. The other man let go of me, and together they simply walked away, out of sight, as quickly as they had appeared. The whole thing couldn't have taken more than fifteen seconds.

Of course, I didn't try to follow them, or get my camera out and photograph them, or get the number of their car, or any of the things that would have been really useful to do. They'd probably counted on the natural instinct of a woman to go to the aid of her injured man, and I turned out to be entirely predictable on that front, as they'd known I would be.

"Peter! Are you hurt?" I gasped, seizing him by the shoulders. Oh, the sheer stupidity of the questions we ask at times like those! Of course he was hurt! But between us we got him to his feet, and, leaning on me, he was able to stumble up the steps and into the flat. As soon as I'd dumped the contents of my ice tray into a plastic bag and had him holding them against his stomach, I phoned Alan.

But as I waited for him to pick up, my mind was playing back something that had happened down in the driveway. Something Peter had said, and the look on his face when he'd said it.

I'd been trying to help him up, and he'd got as far as hands and knees. Well, not both hands, because his right hand was still clutching at his bruised and pain-racked stomach. As I'd crouched in front of him, ready to support him when he attempted the next stage of the process, he'd brought his head up and looked at me.

I'd nearly recoiled. The look in those blazing eyes! I've never seen such a combination of anger and desperation, and I hope I never do again. It was a look that made me feel as if I, too, had been punched in the gut.

"This has got to stop," he'd said, in such a low, savage voice that it made me shiver afterwards to remember it. "*This — has got — to stop.*"

What he'd said, the way he'd said it, the rage and passion in his body language — they'd frightened me. Had made me afraid of — I didn't know what. But for a moment he'd become a stranger; not Peter — someone else. Then he'd dropped his head again, and groaned, and the moment had passed.

But it had happened. Now I couldn't forget it. I wished I could.

Alan and Ben both came, though of course there was nothing they could do. The two men were long gone, tracelessly.

"But don't worry," I said tremulously. "I'm sure it'll all be there on the CCTV for you." Then the tears started to come. Peter tried to rise from the sofa, but his abused muscles wouldn't let him move quickly enough, and he sank back with a gasp of pain. It was Ben who put his arms round me and hugged me, muttering soothing noises into my ear, the way my father would have done when I was a little girl and had fallen over and skinned my knee.

Peter looked at me, weeping in Ben's arms, and the anguish on his face was clear to see. But as he looked at Ben, and then up at Alan, standing over him, his expression transmuted to one of raw anger and determination. Neither of them said anything. After all, what could they say? What could they do, that they weren't already doing?

"Come on, Jenny," said Ben gently. "Coffee. Come and show me where everything is."

I had a better hold on myself now, and disengaged from him, wiping my eyes. "This way," I said shakily.

He followed me into the kitchen, and we put together a tray of coffee and biscuits. The only words we spoke were commonplaces such as "Where d'you keep the sugar?" and "The biscuit tin's in that cupboard," but his sheer presence — stocky, capable, sympathetic — was both a comfort and a reassurance.

Over the coffee, we told our story again in more detail. Alan suggested our seeing if we could identify either of the men from the database, but Peter dismissed the idea with contempt.

"What's the point?" he said. "It won't get us any closer to *him*. It never does! Anyway, they were just messenger boys. Delivering the lesson for today."

The lesson that I wasn't safe anywhere, not even in my own home, not even with Peter. Oh, yes, we'd been read that one, all right.

Alan was looking as grim as I'd ever seen him.

"I'm going back to Laird," he said, his voice full of suppressed anger.

"With what?" Ben demanded. "This, today? That's not going to prove anything other than what he already knows – and that didn't get any change out of him."

"Well, we've got to do something!" Alan burst out. "We've got to find a way of stopping him!"

"Yeh," Peter agreed quietly. He was staring down at the carpet, as if fascinated by something he could see there. "Or I will."

We all looked at him, and he must have known it, but he continued to stare downwards.

"What d'you mean?" Alan demanded tensely.

"What I said. Find a way to stop him. Or I will." Peter's voice was quieter now, but I felt the same chill I had out on the driveway. "*This has got to stop...*"

"Whatever you're thinking, stop thinking it!" Alan's voice was both angry and anxious. "We'll find a way. We've just got to come up with something. Don't you even *think* about doing anything stupid in the meantime!"

Peter didn't look up, and he didn't answer.

Alan opened his mouth to speak again, but I decided someone had better change the subject, before they got really angry with each other.

"There's something I want everyone to agree to," I said abruptly. His eyes switched automatically from Peter to me.

"What?" he snapped. Then he moderated his tone. "Sorry, Jenny – I'm not angry with you."

I ignored that. "It's about Mum and Dad. I don't want them to know about this," I said flatly.

I'd managed to surprise him. Even Peter looked up.

"You can't hide something like this from them!" Alan protested.

"I can, and I will. And so will you." You'd never have thought I was addressing a Detective Chief Inspector. "Because they're booked on a month's cruise in a couple of weeks or so, and already Dad's fidgety about whether they should still be going. They've been looking forward to it for months. Planning for it for years. They've always been going to do it, ever since Dad started planning to retire. I don't want it spoiled for them," I said decisively. "I want them to go, and I want them to enjoy it. As much as they can, in the circumstances. And if they start wavering again, I need to be able to convince them it'll be all right. So nobody tells them."

"How're you going to convince them?" Ben countered.

"I'm going to tell them Peter's going to stay in my spare room while they're away," I said matter-of-factly. "That should do it." I waited for the suggestion to sink in, then went on, "I'm going to tell them that whether it's true or not." I looked at Peter. "Is it going to be?"

Ben cocked an eyebrow at Peter; something about the way he did it gave me the feeling they'd already had a discussion that had some bearing on my suggestion, but I wasn't going to enquire. In any case, Peter chose to ignore him.

"You sure?" he asked me, frowning.

"It's the only practical way I can see of reassuring them I won't be alone any more than possible," I said pragmatically. "And the best way to keep you from worrying about it, too."

Ben couldn't suppress a smile. Peter looked at him with a degree of irritation, but then, reluctantly, he shrugged. I maintained my attitude of 'well, it's obvious, isn't it?' as I regarded the pair of them. The tension of moments ago was easing.

Alan was the only one not amused. He was looking at me from under lowered brows; it wasn't hard to guess his thoughts. He knew, in the light of today's events, that even Peter's presence couldn't provide any real guarantee of protection. Then he sighed. He knew it was the best that could be done – unless Laird changed his mind. I looked back at him, and we read each other's minds. He gave me a barely perceptible nod.

"She's right, you know," Ben said, with a touch of smugness.

"She's right about too damn many things," said Peter, but without rancour. He sighed. "Okay, you win."

"I'm not sure that 'win' is really the word for this situation," I said. "But thanks anyway."

A couple of days later, Ben rang me, just as I was finishing my lunch.

"I need to talk to you," he said. "Is this a good time for us to come over?"

"Er – yes. Yes, of course. Just out of interest, who's 'us'?" I enquired.

"Me and Andy. That okay?"

"Yes, of course," I repeated. "Am I allowed to know what it's about?"

"We need to have a look at your wardrobe," he said. "Andy wants to do some button counting. See you soon." He rang off, leaving me wondering what on earth he was talking about. My *wardrobe...*?

Not the piece of furniture I kept my clothes in, as it turned out. The clothes themselves. And Andy didn't exactly want to count buttons, but she did want to see what I wore that used buttons. They were going to give me a hidden camera, the sort often used for undercover filming with the lens disguised as a button, and they wanted me to wear it every time I left the house. Also a tracking device, installed in a small gold locket, ditto. When they told me, I almost made a quip about having a bit part in a spy film, but decided against it; neither of them looked as if they were in the mood for joking.

"We've been talking about it," Ben explained, "and we can't see a way to make Lesser go for you. He's got a sixth sense about setups; we've never got him with one yet. So, until we can think of something better, the only thing we can do is wire you up and wait for him to make the next move. Which probably won't be long." Ben dealt in truth with me, as he had throughout, but he didn't like having to say the things he was saying.

The familiar knot in my stomach was back, but I did my best to keep my voice calm and level.

"He generally seems to give you just long enough for it to sink in, then back he comes," I agreed, striving to be objective. I caught the look on Andy's face – she was trying to stay impassive, but her eyes were troubled – and gave her a brief smile. "What it is to be popular, eh?" She tried to smile back, but, as smiles go, it wasn't much of a success.

Ben showed me the camera and explained how it worked, and Andy and I looked through my clothes, identifying the ones that most readily lent themselves to the task. The lens had more than one disguise, and Andy had matching sets of buttons for each. Unfortunately not much that I wore was suitable; in keeping with my income, I didn't have a very extensive wardrobe, and Andy cautioned me that changing the appearance of the clothes I had might act as a tip-off.

"Then get down the High Street with her and buy her some stuff that'll work," Ben ordered gruffly.

"But I can't—" I began to protest, cutting off in front of the word 'afford'. But he understood me.

"Yes, you can," he said. "We'll cover it. This is a surveillance operation; it's a necessary expense." Was that a gleam of humour in his eyes, at last? "Just don't go mad."

"As if!" I pretended indignation, and even Andy had to smile. I directed a look of caricatured sympathy at her. "So, your professional duties require you to hit the clothes shops, then? Aren't you gutted about that?"

"I'll try to take one for the team," she said nobly.

"Good job it's not shoes you need," Ben grunted. "Shoeshop would've been doing her nut if she'd missed out on that."

Peter and I had already told Dad and Mum about his moving into my spare room while they were away; now I told them about the tracking device and the camera. They had a big wobble about whether they should still go, but by being consistently adamant I managed to convince them to go through with it.

"Nothing might happen," I pointed out. "And, to be brutally frank about it, what could you do if it did? You couldn't prevent it. Only be there afterwards. And if something did happen, you'd come straight back and do that anyway, wouldn't you?" A rhetorical question if ever there was one.

"You know we would." Dad, seated in his usual place on the sofa, agreed in his usual calm manner, but I could see he and Mum, seated next to him, were holding each other's hand very tightly.

"Are you really sure about this, darling?" Mum asked unhappily.

"Really sure, Mum," I said firmly. "You've been looking forward to this for so long; I've been looking forward to you going. I want you to go, and have as good a time as you possibly can, and come back with lots of wonderful memories. *Please* don't not go because of me." My voice cracked unexpectedly, but I recovered it, and offered my father the ghost of a grin. "Sorry, Dad, double negative… But I mean it. Please go. I couldn't bear it if you didn't go because of me."

They were silent.

"Besides," I went on brightly, "I'll be in touch every day. The way it's going to work is, I'll tell you I'm all right and nothing's happened to me, and you'll tell me you're having the time of your lives and lots of nice things have happened to you! And you'll take millions of photos and prove to me what a wonderful time you had, when you come back. Because I will be demanding proof, you know!"

Dad sighed, and at that moment I came closer to pure hatred of Matthew Lesser than I had ever done. Dad's chosen self-reward for all those years of public service, all the pleasure of anticipation he'd shared with Mum for so long, and Lesser was ruining it all for them. I was boiling with the injustice of it, while at the same time choked with misery for their spoiled expectations. I think the misery must have been uppermost in my expression, though, because although Dad didn't release his hold on Mum's hand, with his other hand he reached out and took mine.

"Then we will definitely give it to you," he promised. "Will that make you happier?" As if any of us could be happy, in the circumstances. I couldn't get any more words out past the lump in my throat, but I nodded, and gripped his hand more tightly in acknowledgement of his pledge.

And so, a few days later, Peter and I stood in the driveway, watching their luggage being loaded into a taxi. Mum could hardly bring herself to speak, though she did try to smile; she came over to us, and, I think, took Peter somewhat by surprise by embracing him, something she'd never attempted to do before.

"Good luck, Peter," she whispered.

"Thanks," he muttered.

She turned to me and put her arms round me, holding me more tightly than I ever remembered her doing before.

"Bye, darling." She still couldn't speak above a whisper. "I love you, and I'll see you when we get back."

"I love you, Mum," I replied. She let go of me and turned away without looking at me again, and got into the taxi. Dad, who had been watching all this gravely from a couple of paces away, came forward. He took both my hands in his, and smiled at me somewhat crookedly.

"I know you're right, and that there's nothing I could essentially do by not going," he said. "But I still find it difficult to accept that there's nothing I can do."

"But there is," I contradicted him swiftly, "and you're doing it. I need to know that you're doing this. That you're going to enjoy it. As much as you can, in the circumstances… I really need you to do that, Dad. Promise?"

"I promise, darling," he said, and took me into his arms. "I'm fairly sure you know how much I love you, but have you any idea just how proud I am of you?"

My eyes filled, and for long moments we held each other, saying nothing, but at the same time saying everything.

He released me, turned to Peter, and shook his hand. Peter met his eyes with sombre determination.

"I'll look after her, Richard, I promise," he vowed.

"I know it, Peter." Dad put his other hand on their already clasped hands for a moment. "Believe me, I wouldn't trust her to anybody but you."

Peter's lips worked for a moment, but he couldn't speak.

Dad relinquished the handshake, turned and gave me one last brief, fervent embrace, then climbed in beside Mum. They both waved through the back window as the taxi pulled as far as the end of the driveway, its left indicator light blinking on and off as the driver assessed whether he could proceed; then he did. We followed them out as far as the pavement and waved until they were out of sight. Then we went back into the driveway.

Which was as far as I got before I turned blindly toward Peter, and he put his arms around me and held me close, while I utterly soaked the shoulder of his shirt.

"I'm so sorry," he whispered into the top of my head, after a while.

I turned my head so that my cheek rested against his collarbone.

"Peter," I said hoarsely. "What do I say every time you apologize about this?"

There was a pause.

"Shut up…?" he suggested tentatively, as if there was some possibility he'd got it wrong.

"That's the one," I agreed.

After which I took his hand and we went upstairs to the flat, in silence. But I was dripping tears all the way.

Chapter 31

I was pretty keyed up for the next few days. Lesser would undoubtedly know that one of my lines of defence had been removed; on the other hand, he'd also know Peter was with me every minute outside of my work hours. I wondered what his next move would be. But I didn't discuss it with Peter. What was the point? We both knew the score.

So we went on as normal. Except that 'normal' now meant wiring myself up with the hidden camera every day before going to work. I didn't wear it in the library itself, but I did have it installed in my brand new, specially selected coat – specially selected by Andy, that is, so the buttons could be made to match the one concealing the lens. And 'normal' no longer included gratuitous excursions such as sailing lessons. That sort of thing was clearly on hold, as far as Peter was concerned. Which saddened me, in a way, because I grudged Lesser the triumph. But I could see where Peter was coming from on that one; going anywhere public could be putting me unnecessarily at risk. So now we just stayed at home. No going out. Once we did go over to Alan and Jane's, with everyone determinedly trying to behave as if nothing was wrong – even Sophie. Craig, whether consciously or not, displayed an attitude of protectiveness that under other circumstances I might have been amused by; in a good way, mind. But as it was, I found it a source of comfort, and I was touched to the point of tears by it, though not in front of him, fortunately. 'Normal' also now included Peter double-checking every window, every door, and the CCTV, before he and I went to bed in our respective rooms. I don't know how well he slept; better than I did, I hoped. But probably not.

A week passed, and nothing happened. I kept in touch with Dad and Mum every day, as I'd promised, and they with me. But while I remained nothing but positive and cheerful in my communications with them, I couldn't deny to myself that the strain was beginning to get to me. It was wearing that camera every time I had to go out that was doing it, I was sure; it was a constant reminder of my situation, in a way that nothing else had been up to now.

Then it was Monday, and work. After which Peter picked me up to drive me home, as he always did now. As soon as I got into the car, he said brusquely, without any other greeting, "I've got to go in. As soon as I've dropped you off."

I looked at him quickly.

"Why? What's happened?"

"An informant. Says she's got something to tell us, but she'll only talk to me. Apparently."

"Then it's about Lesser?"

"Looks like." His tone was dour, to match his expression.

Silence fell between us. Was this significant? Someone coming forward, despite Lesser's known reputation for retribution for informants? It must be something pretty substantial, if someone was risking that. I wondered, and, for Peter's sake, I hoped.

When we reached home, he didn't bother to pull into the drive, just swung round in the road and stopped in front of the entrance; he evidently didn't want to waste time.

"Go straight inside, lock the door, and don't come out again until I get back," he ordered.

"Of course not," I said patiently. My tone must have registered with him, and he realized how he'd sounded.

"Sorry," he muttered.

"Forget it," I advised him. "Go and talk to your informant. I'll see you later."

As I got out, he suddenly seized my trailing right hand and grasped it tightly. Surprised, I stopped moving and turned to look at him. Just as quickly, he looked away, but briefly squeezed my hand even harder, then abruptly released it. Before I could say anything, he reached across to the passenger door. "Get inside," he said briefly, and slammed it shut. Then he drove off, swerving sharply to avoid the large 4x4 someone had parked only a couple of yards from our driveway entrance.

I watched him go, wondering why he was in such a strange mood. But as I walked slowly over the gravel of the drive, each step causing the stones to crunch and shift irritably, my train of thought was interrupted by a movement in my peripheral vision. Over to my left, the near upstairs window of the house next door was opening, and our neighbour Pam was leaning out, looking down at me over the top of the hedge that separated our driveways, her plump, middle-aged countenance wearing the slightly anxious look that seemed to be her default setting.

"Hello, Pam," I said. "Something up?"

"I just thought you'd want to know," she said. "There's been a power cut, about half an hour ago. The whole road. The electricity board said they'd send someone, but they haven't arrived yet. So I'm afraid everything'll be off when you go in."

"Oh," I said. "Well, thanks for letting me know."

"Well, I happened to see you coming in, so..." She allowed the sentence to trail off unfinished. Relaxed enough to proffer a smile now that she'd delivered her message, she pulled the window closed.

I started mentally reviewing what was at risk in my freezer, and it wasn't until I was halfway up the steps that I realized there were more serious implications. I turned quickly to look up at the CCTV camera. The whole system was hooked up to the mains, so it would be down. Should I bother to tell Peter? No, he'd be busy. But I'd better tell someone, or he'd be furious with me if he found it this had happened and I hadn't said anything. Alan, or Ben? Ben, I decided.

I made the call right there on the steps. When Ben answered, I told him what had happened.

"Only about half an hour ago, so I don't suppose we've missed anything exciting. But I thought I'd better let you know."

He grunted; he was evidently not quite at ease about it.

"Maybe I should come over and check it out," he said. "Even when the power comes back on, it might have scrambled it somehow. You get inside and stay there. I'll be there as quick as I can."

"Okay," I agreed, not comfortable with that tinge of unease in his voice. "See you in a while."

"Yeah," he said, and ended the call.

I climbed the remainder of the steps and let myself in, double-checking the door was locked behind me. In the hallway, I tried the light switch in the forlorn hope that the electricity might have magically been restored by now, but no response. Without waiting to shed my coat, I headed straight for the kitchen, to check that the freezer was all right. It was. Door definitely shut, so hopefully the contents would survive, provided the power came back on before too long.

After which I turned to go into the living room, only to be brought up short in the doorway, momentarily petrified with shock.

"Get inside," Peter had told me. "Get inside," Ben had told me. It had turned out to be the worst advice they could have given me.

Relaxed in my armchair, Matthew Lesser smiled at me pleasantly.

"Hello, Jenny," he said. "Come in, do."

As he took his place on the other side of the table, Peter frowned at the informant. He wasn't sure who he'd been expecting, but certainly not a teenage girl. Though she looked as hard as nails. Pretty, yes, with her long, straight blonde hair and dark blue eyes, pale blue eyeliner on the lids and thickly mascara'd eyelashes, but even so, a tough nut to crack, if you had to attempt it. She wore a very short skirt, and a deep-necked vest top that didn't leave much to the imagination. She glanced up at him from under the thick black lashes, then over at Shoeshop, who'd taken the place of the young female constable standing just inside the door. Then her eyes returned to the tabletop at which she had been gazing when they came in.

Peter studied her for a few moments; then he spoke.

"I'm Detective Sergeant Peter McLeish. That's Detective Constable Angwin." He rested his forearms on the table, and waited for the girl to speak, but she didn't. "I was told you had some information for me," he prompted.

"Yeah, that's right," she agreed in a classic East End accent, flashing another glance at him, but didn't volunteer anything more.

"What's your name?"

"Jade," she said in an impudent tone which clearly announced she had no intention of supplying a surname. Peter let it go.

"Okay, Jade. So what is it you want to tell me?"

"This bloke," she said, leaning forward with a quick movement of her body, as if she'd decided to stop teasing and get on with what she'd come to say. "'E told me to give yer a message. I wasn't to speak to no one else, only you." She smiled in a self-satisfied way. "'E must've wanted yer to 'ave it real bad," she commented. "Didn't arf pay! Easiest money I've made in a long time!"

Peter tensed.

"What bloke? What's his name?"

"Dunno," said the girl, watching him with interest. "Didn' ask. 'E said you'd know 'oo 'e was." She shrugged, carelessly.

Peter sensed the change in Shoeshop's body language behind him, heard the slight movement as she straightened up as if for action. He looked down at his hands, flat on the table in front of him, and swallowed; his throat suddenly felt dry. Then he looked at the girl Jade again.

"And what's the message?" he asked hoarsely.

"'E said to tell yer," the girl recited carefully, "you should never leave yer most precious possession unguarded. Never. *'Not even for something like this.'* That's wot 'e told me to tell yer. Exact words." She was still studying him with that same detached objectivity. It would be interesting to know what the message meant, though she didn't care all that much; she'd already got her money. Whatever it was about, it was clearly pretty devastating for the man across the table. She even felt a momentary twinge of what had used to be her conscience as she saw the look in his eyes. But the sensation didn't last; there wasn't much room for conscience in her world.

Peter sat frozen for a few moments, still staring at her, but no longer seeing her. Then he rose, grabbing for his phone even as he fled from the room. Shoeshop flung one glance at the girl still sitting at the table, regarding her with an expression of mild interest, before she, too, left. The young constable reappeared in the doorway; Jade smiled at her.

"Can I go now?" she enquired brightly.

Alan was annoyed with himself. For some reason he was feeling unaccountably unsettled. And though he didn't know why, he knew it was to do with Jenny. He tried to ignore the feeling, but it wouldn't go away. It got to the point where he went as far as getting out his phone. He hesitated, and nearly put it away again. But he didn't. Some hobgoblin inside was prodding away at him, and it wasn't going to let up. Almost irritably, he called her number. But there was no reply. Peter had told him she didn't use voicemail, because of trying to keep her costs to a minimum, so he couldn't try that. But should he bother to send a text? It was just a feeling, after all… He put the phone down on his desk. But the hobgoblin didn't relent. Almost angrily, he snatched it up again.

Not picking up? Please confirm OK, he sent.

There was a pause of several minutes before his phone signalled the arrival of a text. It was from her.

Gr8. C u l8r.

He stared at it. He should have been reassured, but for some reason he wasn't. If she was using her phone, why had she not answered his call, yet answered his text? And there was something about the message… Whatever had been prodding him before had suddenly gone into overtime, but why? It was a perfectly normal text message…

Then he realized. Not for her, it wasn't. Peter had told him; she never used text-speak. *Never.* So a message spelled like that – either it wasn't her, or else she was doing it deliberately. Trying to send a hidden call for help, because she wasn't free to say what she wanted. Which meant…

But before he could take that line of thought any further, his phone rang. Ben. And as Alan listened to what he had to say, he felt adrenalin surge through him.

Peter burst into the office, Shoeshop hot on his heels. Everyone except Ben was there; they looked up, sensing the atmosphere instantly. Peter ignored them all, heading for Alan.

"I can't get through to Jenny!" he exclaimed. "She's not picking up. The girl – the informant – she was from Lesser! She said—"

Alan cut him off.

"Ben's phoned," he said curtly. "Jenny rang in. Power cut in her road.

He went over to check the CCTV. She's not there. Front door was standing open. I've just told Laird."

They stared at each other, while everyone else stared at them. Andy felt a knot of apprehension in the pit of her stomach. You couldn't fault Lesser on his efficiency. Peter lured into separating from Jenny; the electricity supply sabotaged to enable Lesser to take down the cameras and get into the flat. She felt a sick helplessness as she looked at Peter's face. They'd done everything they could, and it still hadn't been enough.

Brad was busy at the keyboard of his laptop. "Her tracker's working," he announced. "She's on the move."

Alan strode over to see, Peter right behind him; a few seconds was enough. Alan straightened up from the screen.

"Right," he said decisively. "All of you except Chris and Peter – vests and firearms, now. Brad, bring your camera. I want this on record. Andy, get in touch with Ben; make sure he joins up with us *en route*. Chris, you stay here. Coordinate. Keep Commander Laird up to date. Line up an AR unit – my authorisation – and keep them briefed on our location. We may need them in double quick time."

Chris looked outraged. "But, Boss, why can't I—?" he began to protest, but Alan cut across him. "Shut up. Just do it. I am not going to debate my decisions. I don't have the time."

"You mean – *you're* coming, sir?" Abhik ventured incredulously.

"This one, I am," Alan snapped, shutting down any possible argument. Abhik knew – they all knew – DCIs don't engage in field operations. Well, this time the rules were going to get broken. This was Lesser.

"And what will I be doing?" Peter enquired tautly.

Alan had been putting this bit off, but there was no avoiding it now. "In my office," he said briefly, with a jerk of his head. Peter followed him in; Alan shut the door, and turned to face him.

"What will I be doing?" Peter repeated.

Alan looked him in the eye.

"Nothing," he said flatly.

For a moment Peter's eyes were blank with shock. Then incredulity began to surface, swiftly followed by anger.

"You can't leave me out of this! Not when it's Jenny!" The two emotions were fighting for dominance in his voice as well as on his face.

"I have to," said Alan. His mouth was slightly twisted, as if the words were a foul taste on his tongue, but his tone was uncompromising. "The Laird specifically ordered your non-participation. You're too involved, Peter. You can't be a part of this. He doesn't want you having anything to do with it."

Peter looked stunned.

"But – but it's Jenny! What if something happens? What if something goes wrong? I've *got* to be there!"

"You know better than that," Alan said sternly.

"But—"

"Enough!" Alan snapped; Peter recoiled at the violence of his tone. "I haven't got time for this! Get this straight. You are *not* a part of this operation. You cannot *be* a part of this operation. And if you try to get anywhere close to it the Laird won't just throw the book at you, he'll shove it so far down your throat you'll be sitting on it. Damn it, Peter!" Frustration erupted into his voice; he was no longer Peter's senior officer, he was his cousin, his friend. "Don't you think I know what you're feeling? How do you think *I* feel? She's *my* friend, she's *your* girl! Don't you trust me to do everything I possibly can to keep her safe? For you and for me?"

Peter stared at him.

"This was always on the cards. And it had to be done," Alan said, fighting to moderate his emotion. "That's how Jenny saw it. She talked it over with me. She said that if we didn't try something to get Lesser once and for all, it'd just go on and on and on. No end in sight. And she's right. That's why she put herself up for this. The tracker, the camera, all of it. Do you think she's doing this for us? For the general good of society? Like hell, she is! She's doing it for one person, and one person only! And you know it! Because she wants it to end. For *you*. So you think about that. What she's doing. And why. And then you let us get on with the job of doing it so it works and we *get* the son of a bitch!"

There was a long silence as they held each other's eye until, eventually, Peter's gaze fell. His shoulders sagged, and he stared unseeing at the floor for some seconds. Then he dropped into the nearest chair and covered his face with his hands.

Alan let him be for a few moments. Time was short, but he needed the respite himself; despite the official line he'd just been delivering and his objective, professional judgement that this was a correct strategy to attempt, privately and subjectively he was sick with anxiety for Jenny himself. For Jenny, for Peter, for both families, and the risk that was being taken that might have such fundamental consequences for all of them. It was just that he couldn't afford to let his own feelings influence his conduct of the operation. What was it he'd said to Peter, once before? "*Get your act together! Do your job!*" That was what he, as the leader of this team, now had to do himself. *Physician, heal thyself*, he thought, grimly.

He reached down and put a hand on Peter's shoulder.

"I know," he said quietly. "I'm sorry."

For a few moments Peter didn't respond. Then he dropped his hands, drew himself upright, and blew out a long breath. His eyes were suspiciously red-rimmed, but calmer now. He looked up at Alan.

"What do you want me to do?" he asked.

Alan felt an intense sensation of relief. Peter didn't like it, but he was accepting it.

He withdrew his hand.

"Stay away," he said. "We don't want you distracting him in your direction. And if we don't have to worry about what you're doing, we can concentrate on getting Jenny back," he added, meaningfully.

Peter threw him a momentary look from under lowered eyebrows, then nodded.

"Yeh, okay," he acknowledged heavily.

"And trust me," Alan repeated. "I *will* look after her for you."

They looked at each other. Silently. But then, words weren't needed for what they were saying to each other.

"Now stop wasting my time," said Alan, and strode out.

Chapter 32

The passenger seat of the 4x4 was roomy and comfortable, but I was in no state to appreciate it. I was too aware of the pistol wedged between Lesser's thigh and his own seat, ready to hand; the pistol with which he had forced me out of the flat and into his vehicle. The same 4x4 that Peter had had to swerve to avoid when he drove away.

I'd been very conscious of that pistol behind me as I'd gone down the steps, too. Despite it, I'd managed, unobtrusively, to turn on the hidden camera, though my heart had been in my mouth every second; I'd had an irrational feeling that Lesser would somehow be able to see through my body, see what I was doing. But of course he couldn't, and it was operating. Thank heaven I hadn't stopped to take my coat off when I'd gone into the flat…

Now I sat in tense silence, my hands clasped in my lap, staring straight ahead of me. From the corner of my eye I could see Lesser glancing at me from time to time, but so far he, too, had been silent. At last, however, he spoke.

"What are you thinking, Jenny?" he enquired.

What I was thinking was that I hoped to high heaven that somebody had missed me by now, that someone was monitoring the tracking device. That help was on its way. But I was hardly going to say any of that.

"I don't think I should tell you what I'm thinking," I said levelly. "It mightn't be a good idea for me to hurt your feelings."

He looked at me with narrowed, assessing eyes, then laughed aloud.

"Oh, Jenny! Our encounters are such a joy!" His enjoyment seemed genuine, but I knew that the cultured veneer was only that – a veneer – and the monster beneath could always break through at any moment, given the right provocation. I had to tread the line of continuing to engage his interest, in the hope that it would prolong my safety – my life, even – without saying or doing something that would fatally rouse the superficially dormant savage.

"I'm glad you think so."

"And you lie so charmingly." He smiled at me with perverse delight.

"Where are you taking me?" I asked.

"Oh-h-h, nowhere in particular," he shrugged with elaborate carelessness.

"Just for a nice afternoon drive. I enjoyed our last conversation so much, I thought it would be nice to have another. Don't you?"

I said nothing.

"I gather you didn't enjoy it as much as I did, then," he suggested with suppressed amusement. "Alas, poor Jenny. But that's a consequence of becoming a part of Peter McLeish's life, you see. You become of interest to me, when that happens."

"So I gather," I said tightly.

"Come, come," he chided me gently. "How could I not be interested in you, Jenny? When Peter so evidently is? Though, I have to admit, I'm a little surprised at him. I thought he'd know better, but apparently not. Although – having come to know you as I do – I suppose it's not as surprising as all that. Ah, well – spilt milk, water under the bridge, and so on… And, besides, there are some questions I've been meaning to ask you."

I stayed silent. He looked at me obliquely.

"Don't you want to know what they are?" he probed.

I shook my head slightly.

"Well, that's unfortunate," he sighed. "Because I'm going to ask you anyway. But" – he paused for a moment, considering, then went on – "I think perhaps we should stop somewhere. I want to give this conversation my full attention, and there are far too many erratic drivers on the roads nowadays, don't you think? Now, where…? Ah, yes, I know…" He smiled, and fell silent. No small feat for someone who loved the sound of his own voice as much as he did.

His chosen destination turned out to be a small multi-storey car park a couple of miles further on, well off the main road. There was a flat area with quite a number of parking spaces out in the open, in front of the multi-storey part; the roadway threaded through them to the entrance. I was a little surprised by his choice; somehow I'd expected him to choose somewhere more secluded. But perhaps he didn't want to delay this conversation he seemed so eager to have with me, and grudged the time it would have taken to clear the urban sprawl of the town. And while he had the pistol, I wasn't likely to try something as rash as opening the door and screaming for help. As it was, here he could be both public and private with me. He drove calmly up the spiral entrance ramp and onto the first level. No spaces presented themselves until, circling the packed cars as lazily as a shark, he was almost back to the ramp leading to the exit; then, astonishingly, two were free, right next to each other, in a double bay that extended out between two of the building's supporting pillars, almost directly above the entrance by which we'd come in. He pulled in, deliberately taking up the whole bay, so there was no chance of anyone getting near enough to us to deduce that something might be wrong.

"I'm sure I don't need to tell you the consequences of trying to attract anybody's attention, do I?" he asked as he cut the engine. He pulled the pistol out from under his leg and held it carelessly across his left thigh. I shook my head silently.

"Of course not," he smiled, and relaxed back into his seat, turning his body slightly so as to be able to look at me more comfortably. "There! Nice and cosy! Now we can talk."

He regarded me for a couple of seconds, then said, with the slightest of edges in his tone, "And I think I'd like you to look at me while we do it. It's never so satisfactory, not being able to meet the eyes of the person you're talking to, is it?"

Reluctantly I turned my head to look at him. In such close physical proximity, I was aware as never before of the size of him, of a sense of the sheer physical power he could exert against me if he chose. Then I thought about the camera, and shifted my whole body sideways, leaning my right shoulder against the seat, as if finding that a more comfortable position. Perhaps he interpreted it as an indicator of my complete submission; he breathed out a sound of satisfaction at my compliance.

"So tell me, Jenny – how are you and Peter getting along these days?" he enquired, for all the world as though we were friends chatting at some drinks party.

I hesitated; I couldn't think how best to reply, without giving away any more than I had to.

"Too intrusive a question? Come, come! Surely not!" he protested. "But I suppose I didn't really need to ask. All the time he spends with you, all those trips to the sailing club... It's fairly obvious, you know. Such close friendship – it's really quite touching."

He was taking delight in disclosing to me just how closely he had us under observation. I swallowed, and said nothing.

"I can't tell you how pleased I am to see it," he went on.

"I'm sure you are," I said tightly. I knew why he was pleased, and he knew I knew.

"Oh, very much," he assured me suavely. "Though, as I say, quite surprised. I thought I had him better trained than that. Perhaps that's why it took me so long to find out about you."

I couldn't stop myself asking. "How did you find out?"

He smiled, in a way that made me think of a cat with a mouse between its paws. "When you called at his flat, and took him home with you. I was watching. He was ill, wasn't he? Just out of interest, what was the matter with him?"

"Flu."

"And you undertook to nurse him back to health, I suppose. Ah, bless you, Jenny! But something of a giveaway, I fear. Don't you agree? And I just happened to be there to see it. Lady Luck was definitely smiling on me that day! So, thank you for your assistance. Otherwise it might have taken me much longer to find out what was going on."

I said nothing. One of the only two times I ever went there – just the two, in all that time! – and he had to be there just *then*; *that* was when he saw me. Was that *fair…*?

"Of course, that earned you my full attention," he went on. "I must admit, I was quite fascinated to see how far Peter would step over the line I'd gone to so much trouble to draw for him, after he'd been so well behaved for so many years. Which brings me to another question I've been wondering about. How do you find Peter as a lover?"

I stared at him for a moment, struck speechless by the sheer invasiveness of the question, and fighting to keep the profound distaste I felt out of my expression. I wondered if it was voyeurism alone, or whether he had another motive for asking. Probing for another weakness that he could use? Probably. Whatever his reason, the answer was the same.

I looked him straight in the eye, and said matter-of-factly, "I have no idea what he's like as a lover. We haven't."

I had managed to surprise him; momentarily, he looked astonished. But he hadn't got where he was by not being able to determine when someone was telling him the truth.

"Really? How very remarkable," he mused, but not because he didn't believe me. "Why ever not?"

I boiled. What business was it of his? But did I dare not answer…?

He read me, and smiled; there was a very nasty element in that smile.

"Oh, come on, Jenny," he exhorted, simulating a wheedling tone. "You can tell me…" *That is, you'd better tell me, hadn't you?* "So let's have it. The truth." He looked at me with narrowed eyes, and waited.

"Two reasons," I said sullenly. "One, because I don't sleep with anyone I'm not married to, and two—"

"Don't?" he interrupted me, with an incredulity that swiftly metamorphosed into derision. "Oh, Jenny! How prudishly old-fashioned of you! Not even Peter?" Ostensibly teasing me, but not without malice.

"Not even Peter," I agreed, flatly and unsmilingly, then went on, "And even if that wasn't my personal morality, there's the second reason. And that's you. You've hamstrung him, as far as relationships are concerned. I've got to hand it to you; you've done a great job on him. Because he's terrified of the consequences of caring. So he's never going to ask me. Not to sleep with him, not to marry him. Now, is he?" I couldn't suppress a note of challenge in the question. And I was angry. He didn't know it, of course – at least, he didn't appear to know it, and I could only hope that he didn't – but I was being forced to strip my relationship with Peter naked for the scrutiny of anyone who might get to see the film that was being recorded by the hidden camera I was wearing. But I couldn't risk anything but truth with this man; he was too canny, and I wasn't a good liar at the best of times. Which this most definitely was not.

Lesser quirked an eyebrow at me.

"Because of me?" he mused. "Sadly, how true. But take heart, Jenny – it's not going to be an issue for much longer." He saw the flash of alarm in my eyes, and chuckled delightedly.

"Why? What are you going to do?" I asked urgently, forgetting all about trying to get him to incriminate himself on camera. I wanted to know for myself. For Peter. For us.

"Come, come," Lesser said reprovingly. "Don't tell me you're the kind of person who turns straight to the last page of a book to find out what happens! It would be criminal of me to spoil the ending of this particular story, don't you think? Quite criminal!" He smiled at his own wit.

I looked at him with loathing.

"You are such a cruel man," I said flatly. "You use cruelty like – like—"

"Like a surgeon," he interrupted. "A man who uses a scalpel with immense skill to cut through skin and flesh. A specific tool to achieve a specific end. I use cruelty in the same way. An almost scientific approach, if you will. For the things I do, the people I deal with, I have many tools to achieve the outcomes I require. Cruelty is one of them. Not just physical, but mental or emotional, too. Which one I use, the degree to which I use it – like the surgeon deciding where to cut and how deeply – that requires a degree of skill, making that judgement. But when used efficiently, it makes people so much more malleable, so much more ready to conform to the requirements of my employers."

"And harassing Peter for all these years – that's been a requirement of your employers, has it?" I challenged.

He looked at me swiftly, the flash of feeling in his eyes making me aware how close I'd just come to crossing a line.

"No, it hasn't," he said in a soft, dangerous voice. "That's a requirement of my own. Personal to me."

"Doesn't it bother them? You spending so much time on a personal grudge?"

"Ah, but I never allow it to interfere with my professional activities," he demurred. "So they allow it, provided it remains that way. And I enjoy it.

335

Professionally, I strive to make objective judgements about how to use the tools at my disposal, to remain detached. But with *him*" – the note in his voice made me shudder – "I enjoy it. I enjoy the distress and the fear I cause him. I like the power it gives me over him. That's why you are so valuable to me." He smiled at me. "By making you fear, I can make him fear... You do fear me, don't you, Jenny?"

"Yes," I said. "Almost as much as I despise you."

As soon as the words were out of my mouth, I wished I hadn't said them. What if I tipped him over the edge of his forbearance? What might he do to me? I shut my lips in a hard line, lest he see them trembling.

But, to my astonishment, he threw back his head and laughed.

"Oh, Jenny, Jenny, Jenny," he tutted, still chuckling. "You're a positive joy to me! No one talks to me in the terms you do. They're all afraid of the power I wield, so they keep silent. What is it about you, that makes you different to all the rest? On the face of it, you seem so ordinary. A totally ordinary woman, who has lived a totally ordinary life, and done not one extraordinary thing, as such things are usually measured. And yet when you're in my power, still you face up to me and say things like that. I almost wish my conflict with Peter could go on endlessly, so you and I might have more conversations like this."

"Forgive me if I wish differently," I said tightly.

"An entirely understandable reaction," he agreed. But then his voice, and his face, changed. "And a wish that will come true. But not the way you want it to."

Everything he'd said, and he'd still not said anything that would incriminate him beyond doubt. I was scared stiff, but I mustn't fail Peter. Even at risk to myself.

"Are you going to kill Peter?" I asked hoarsely. "The way you tried to in Scotland?"

"One day," he said; flat confirmation. "It was my own fault I didn't succeed in Scotland. I should have been more thorough."

"But you shot Mike."

"Mike Clifford? Yes. Yes, I did. It could just as easily have been Peter driving, but it happened to be Clifford. Not that it made much difference, as I thought. I expected them both to be killed in the crash. But Peter's luck held, and Clifford's ran out. It was something of a blow to my professional pride, but there you are – these things happen. And it meant he lived to fight another day. You should be grateful for my lapse, Jenny. You'd never have got to know him otherwise, would you?" He sounded almost pleased about the outcome.

"And Laura?" I countered instantly. "Was that you, as well? Or just one of your lackeys?"

"No, that was me," he agreed. His voice hardened. "I wanted to teach him a lesson, and I did. Personally. You don't do what he did to me, and get away with it." His tone, the suppressed anger in it, was chilling.

I looked down at my hands, clasped in my lap, and saw how white the knuckles were. I'd done it. I'd got him on record, admitting to Mike Clifford's murder, to Laura's murder, to Peter's attempted murder. Intending to frighten me – or, perhaps, giving in to some perverse urge to impress me? – if that was the right word – he'd finally admitted it. And I was frightened. Because why would he have done that, knowing it made me a witness against him? There was only one answer to that that I could think of. I began to tremble.

A silence fell, as he gauged my reaction, studying my face through narrowed eyes.

"Look at me, Jenny," he said softly.

I didn't want to, but I had to. Slowly I turned my head and looked at him. When he saw the fear in my eyes, read the reason for it, he smiled in a satisfied, leisurely fashion. After only a few seconds I couldn't bear to sustain the regard any longer, and looked away, but he'd learned what he wanted to know, and let me. There was silence in the car.

I don't know how long it was before I realized something about the quality of the silence had changed. But I felt it, and looked at him again. He seemed to have become uneasy about something. He wasn't looking at me anymore; he was staring into the rear view mirror, for no reason that I could see. But his head started to move as if he were a dog that had scented something unidentified, something dangerous. Abruptly he opened the car door and got out, pausing to fix me with an inimical stare.

"*Don't* move," he ordered, in a voice that transfixed me to my seat. Then, leaving the driver's side door open, he walked to the front wall of the bay, overlooking the parking area below, the access road, the little square of grass and trees beyond, lined with houses, scanning it all with radar-like sweeps of his head. He didn't seem to see anything particular, but something was making him very edgy. He came back to the open door and stood there, one hand resting on the top edge, looking around at the silent rows of cars.

"What is it?" I asked, his unease communicating itself to me.

"No movement," he said, more to himself than to me. "No cars in or out. No one here. Something's not right…" His voice trailed off. Then he looked at me, and gestured with his pistol toward the back of the car.

"Get out," he said, a snap in his voice. "Now." I obeyed, quickly.

The pistol was trained on me as we both cleared the back of the car. He pointed with it to a spot about four feet from the back left corner of the vehicle. "Stand there, and don't move," he said. He looked at me for a moment, to make sure I was going to do as he'd told me, then he turned sideways on to me and opened the tailgate. On the floor of the boot I could see a rectangular case of some sort. And I'd seen enough crime dramas on television over the years to be able to identify it.

I didn't dare move my feet to turn round, but I looked around the car park, and he was right. No movement whatever. When under normal circumstances there should be people returning to their cars, driving away, other cars cruising round looking for a space. No wonder his antenna had started to quiver, enough to make him feel that the pistol wasn't sufficient. He had a rifle, and he was making it ready to use. Why do that? Why not just drive away?

Oh! Of course…! Because if what he suspected was true, he probably wouldn't be able to. If nobody was coming in, the chances were that it was because they were being prevented from doing so. Which conversely meant he might not be able to get out. Not without a fight. And if that was the case, the rifle would be a greater deterrent than the pistol.

He put the pistol down, and opened the case. I could see the constituent parts of the weapon, cradled in the specially shaped recesses. I briefly wondered if that was the rifle that had killed Mike Clifford, but only for a moment. Of more immediate concern was the fact that the danger I was already in had just got worse. What should I do? Should I try to make a break for it, while I still had the chance? But I was hamstrung by knowing what he could make that rifle do. I'd never outrun that. Oh, where were they? Where were Alan and Peter and the rest? Why hadn't they come?

"What are you going to do with that?" I asked, my throat muscles tight.

He paused in what he was doing, just long enough to turn his head toward me and give me a most unnerving smile.

"Perhaps I've decided to shoot you, Jenny. Not just some cheap handgun for *you*. Nothing but the best for *you!*" His smile broadened as he saw me flinch. Then he went on, matter-of-factly, "My instincts are telling me I'm going to need this. And I always trust my instincts, Jenny. They've got me this far." Straightforwardly explaining his reasoning to me, as if I was someone he trusted, as if I had a right to his explanation. Then his eyes changed; he dismissed me and returned his attention to what he was doing.

He was intent on the assembling of the rifle. I couldn't see the pistol, but I knew it was there, on the floor of the boot, where he could just put out a hand and pick it up. I bit my lip, wondering what to do. Should I risk making a break for it? Half of me was screaming at me to do it, frantic to escape. The other half of me was terrified of the reaction it might precipitate, the violence he might do to me. I've seldom been so scared as

I was then. I couldn't bring myself to make a choice. And was quite possibly too scared to do anything about it, even if I did.

Then, with startling speed, it was made easy for me.

A movement caught my eye, over by the junction from the parking area into the exit ramp. A head poking cautiously above the top of the wall that separated the parking area from the ramp.

Ben! It was Ben! They'd found me!

Lesser, bent over the rifle case in the boot, couldn't see him, but I could. And Ben could see me. He put a finger to his lips; I nodded, stiffly. He must have seen how scared I was, because even from thirty feet away I could see the muscles round his eyes tighten and his lips compress into a thin line.

I looked at Lesser. He was only seconds away from finishing the assembly of the rifle. It was now or never. I mustn't think about what I was about to do, or I would be too frozen by fear to do it; I must just do it. Now. This instant.

I launched myself forward, planted my hands on the left side of his back, and shoved him forwards and sideways as hard as ever I could. Then I took to my heels. I'm always very proud of the fact that I remembered not to run straight toward Ben, which would have put me between him and Lesser, but alongside the wall, leaving him a clear view of his target. I think I must have taken him by surprise as much as I did Lesser, who had been sent sprawling into the boot, rifle trapped underneath his body. Almost instantly he recovered himself, scrambled upright, and went for the pistol. But by the time he'd got it and begun to turn, Ben had fired at him.

The bullet could only have missed Lesser by inches; as if by magic, a hole with cracks starring out from it appeared in the window glass of the raised tailgate, almost in line with his head. He instinctively ducked, and took cover in the narrow space between the car and the wall. I, meanwhile, had reached the exit to the ramp, and swerved across to take refuge by Ben where he crouched behind the wall. I stumbled at the last instant and went down heavily on my hands and knees, scraping the heels of my hands raw and bloody on the concrete. But I never even noticed at the time. I had only run a few yards, but I was breathing in loud, noisy gasps. Not just because of the strenuous, albeit brief, demands I'd just made on my body, but because I had been – was – so scared, and not only by Lesser; I'd thoroughly scared myself by what I'd just done, when it came right down to it.

"Keep your head down!" Ben snarled at me, his eyes fixed on the parking bay in which Lesser now crouched, hidden from view. He took a careful sight, then fired again. The near back tyre began to slump; I could hear the air hissing out of it. A third shot, and the other tyre was also deflating. Ben got out a walkie-talkie.

"Boss," he said into it.

"Ben, what's happening?" Alan's voice snapped back at him.

"Got Jenny with me," Ben said. "Lesser's pinned down in a parking bay on the outside wall—"

"What was the shooting?" Alan demanded.

"Me. He's got two flat tyres. I want backup. He can't get out without—"

"He's got a rifle!" I interrupted hoarsely. Ben had instinctively started to turn to tell me to keep quiet, but then he took on board what I'd said.

"Jenny says he's got a rifle," he said into the walkie-talkie.

"In the boot," I gasped. "He was just putting it together when—"

Perhaps Lesser could hear our voices; he must have known Ben was partially distracted. Swiftly he leapt up and fired his pistol in our direction. We both instinctively ducked. It gave him long enough to reach into the boot and snatch the rifle. Ben bobbed his head up again just in time to see him diving down into cover again, gripping it in his left hand.

"Boss, need that backup, quick," he said. "He's definitely got a rifle. We can't stay here."

"They're on their way," said Alan. Even as he spoke, we heard the thump of feet coming up the ramp, and several Armed Response officers were running towards us, their weapons black and ominous, held at the ready before them. Ben briefed them swiftly and concisely, then turned to me.

"Come on, Jenny," he said. "Let's get you out of this."

The AR men were deploying themselves as we headed down the slope, Ben's hand gripping my upper arm as if determined to make sure I kept going. But a few yards down I reached out and clutched at him. My face must have been white as a sheet, if the way I was feeling was anything to go by. I tried to speak, but didn't get time, before I had to turn away from him so I could vomit the contents of my stomach onto the concrete.

He put his hands on my shoulders as I stayed bent over, retching. When it became clear it wasn't going to happen again, he pulled me upright and put his arm round me.

"I'm sorry," I mumbled, my mouth sour and my eyes watering. "I'm sorry."

"Forget it," he told me. "Nothing to worry about. Come on."

I clutched at him. "Where's Peter? Is he here?"

"No," he said tersely. I was half relieved, half disappointed, but I don't know which was showing more clearly on my face. "Come on," he said again.

"Ben, the camera – I've got it." For some reason it was very urgent that I tell him now, not wait until I was safely out of there. "His confession. All of it. Mike – Peter – Laura. He told me. I got it."

For a moment his face lit with pleasure, and his arm tightened round my shoulders.

"Good girl!" he approved. Then he coaxed me back into motion. "Come on. Let's get it, and you, out of here and safe."

I don't have a very clear recollection of what happened in the next little while, after they got me clear. I remember Alan, gripping me by the shoulders and asking if I was all right. Someone produced a bottle of water from somewhere, because I was able to swill out my mouth. There seemed to be a lot of activity around me – dark uniforms hurrying past; more AR officers deploying, presumably. Someone – a paramedic? – attending to my damaged hands. Ben relieving me of the camera, telling Alan what I'd told him about Lesser's confession, and the look of savage triumph on Alan's face. Alan telling me Andy was going to take me home, and I was to stay there until he got in touch. Andy escorting me to a car, loading me into it, driving it away. I can't remember if she tried to talk to me on the way home; I can't imagine she got much joy out of it, if she did.

The one thing I do know for sure is that I tried to ring Peter, but he didn't reply. So I texted – *AOK. Ring me?* – but still nothing. I wondered where he was, what he was doing. I asked Andy, but she didn't know. The only thing she did know was that Alan had ordered him to keep clear of the operation. I was relieved. Whatever else was going on back at the multi-storey, at least he wasn't involved. But I felt irrationally frustrated – angry, even – that he wasn't responding to his phone. I wanted – I needed! – to hear his voice, to know that he was all right, to tell him I was all right. So where was he? What the hell was he playing at, not answering me?

After that, I began to shake in reaction. I saw Andy look at me with concern, and speed up slightly.

The next thing I remember clearly was when we got to the steps up to my front door, and I started to thank her for bringing me home, but she needn't come all the way up. She stopped me.

"You're not done with me yet," she said. "Orders. I'm to stay with you 'til the Boss tells me otherwise."

I blinked at her. "Oh…" I said uncertainly. "Well, you'd better come in, then."

We'd hardly got into the living room before her phone sounded. I watched her anxiously as she answered it.

"Shoeshop!" she said. "What's happening? Yes… Yes, we're back at Jenny's. We're fine. What about you?"

She listened intently as Shoeshop briefed her, nodding from time to time, as if she could see her. "Right, I'll tell her," she said at last. "We're—"

She broke off, and her expression changed.

"What's happening? What's going on?" she exclaimed, but it seemed Shoeshop had gone. She lowered the phone slowly, and looked at me, saw the silent demand for answers in my eyes.

"They've got him surrounded," she said; I wondered why she felt she had to pick her words so carefully. "She says it's only a matter of time. But" – she hesitated – "I think something started to kick off just then. She just – went." She bit her lip, then put on a determinedly positive expression. "But don't worry, Jenny. He can't get away. And someone'll get back to us as soon as they can."

I nodded, conscious of the tense knot in my stomach. I was safe, but Alan wasn't, and Ben wasn't. Not while Lesser had that great cannon of a rifle. No one in the vicinity of that car park was safe. But at least Peter wasn't one of them. At least he was out of harm's way.

But I didn't like the way Andy's eyes were so troubled as she looked at me. I wondered if there was any point in asking her why. Probably not. I gave it a try, but it didn't work. She didn't answer, and changed the subject by telling me I needed a hot drink. So I'd been right; no point.

Definitely not. Because even if I had asked her, she was never going to admit to me that what she'd heard, before the call had ended so abruptly, had been Shoeshop screaming, *"Peter! What are you doing...?"*

Chapter 33

It's so strange, the way time telescopes. The perception one has that it does, anyway. Waiting for the next update from someone, anyone, seemed to go on forever. I could hardly ring Alan or Ben in the middle of a siege, but it didn't stop me wanting to do it, or being frustrated that I couldn't. I don't know how many coffees we drank, but probably too many; we tried putting the television on and scanning the news channels, but the media didn't seem to have noticed what was happening yet. Then Andy called me back from the kitchen, where I was making yet another coffee. I dropped what I was doing and bolted back into the living room. She jerked her chin at the screen, and turned the volume up.

"...Where a gunman is believed to be under siege by the police," the newsreader was saying. The screen showed a street cordoned off by the standard blue and white 'Police Do Not Cross' tape, with two uniformed officers standing in front of it, one of them studiously ignoring the camera trained on them, the other eyeing it somewhat balefully. "A number of streets in the area have been sealed off, but there has not yet been any official confirmation of the nature of the incident, although witnesses earlier reported hearing what they believed to be shots coming from the vicinity of the multi-storey car park in—"

With an abruptness that made me jump, Andy put one hand up in a gesture of warning. With the other she stabbed at the 'Off' button and threw the remote down as if it had burned her. Then I could hear it, too. Someone, very quietly, was opening the front door.

We looked at each other. For a moment neither of us moved. Abruptly Andy pulled out her pistol and made a hasty '*stay there*' motion with her free hand. Then she went out into the hallway.

As if I could stay there, not knowing what was happening! I didn't want to face it – whatever or whoever was out there – but an overpowering feeling of compulsion was acting on me. Whether it was the right thing to do or not, I had to follow her, hard on her heels, as she hurried along the hallway until she could look around the corner toward the end of the passageway from the door. When she realized I was right behind her, she grimaced angrily and made another savage gesture at me to go back, but it was too late for that.

There was utter silence. But the amount of light on the walls showed that the door must be open.

I didn't think it was possible for my heart to beat harder than it was already doing, but I was wrong.

Then the quality of the light changed. There was movement. Somebody was there.

Andy visibly readied herself. Then she jumped out into the passageway, arms rigidly straight out in front of her, the pistol trained on whoever was there. Almost instantly, her face changed. Then I saw the pistol sinking downwards. She was staring at whoever was in the doorway, but then she turned her head and looked at me.

"Jenny," was all she said. As I came toward her, mystified and pumping with adrenalin, she put the pistol away into its holster. She looked at me again, and her eyes were bright. Then she walked toward the door, and vanished from my sight. I could hear her tread on the steps outside.

I turned the corner of the passageway, and stood staring. Andy was gone. Forgotten.

Because Peter was standing there, Alan behind him.

Peter's face... I don't know how to describe the expression on it in those first instants. He was pale, his hair disarranged, his eyes red-rimmed in grey pits of stress and exhaustion. There was a wildness in them, a queer kind of aftermath of tragedy; I've never been able to find the words to describe the look in those huge, dark, frantic orbs.

For a moment, he simply stared at me. Then his eyes filled, and his face began to crumple. Instinctively I went toward him, held out my arms. He still didn't move, but then Alan gave him a gentle shove between the shoulder blades. With a gasp, Peter stumbled forward, reaching out for me, the tears already starting to roll down his cheeks. He seized me with a kind of desperate strength and clung to me like a drowning man. A huge, racking sob burst from him. Then another. And now he couldn't stop. His long body quivered and shuddered against mine as if something kept impacting against it. I grasped him to me as tightly as I knew how. I didn't know what had happened, but something had; that much was clear. Lesser! Had Peter been there after all? And was it over? Why else would Alan be here? But how...? What...?

Not now, Jenny. Worry about that later. I looked up, over Peter's shoulder, at Alan, my own eyes swimming. Silently I mouthed, "*Thank you.*"

He nodded, once, then reached forward and pulled the door shut.

Closing us in, and himself and the rest of the world out.

I didn't learn until later the detail of what happened after Andy drove me away from the multi-storey. But a few rules got bent on my behalf once it was all over, so that I got to see the footage Brad had shot of the incident; and Alan and Ben filled me in on what the footage didn't show. Plus I have my own theories about why some of the things that were said and done were said and done as they were.

So although I wasn't there, I'm going to describe it that way – marrying the facts and the surmise, piecing the story together into a coherent whole, the way Craig might edit a series of video shots into a sequence. Truth, or just guesswork? Who's to tell?

And with those caveats, this, as I understand it, is what happened...

"...Two stairwells," said Ben tersely. "We've got men in both, covering the doors. A lift in one of the stairwells. AR are covering the parking bay, but they can't get into a safe position to see directly into it." They had tried, in point of fact, but Lesser had brought his rifle into play. No one had been hit, but they hadn't tried again, just held their positions and kept him pinned down. "He must be in that corner, with his own vehicle for cover."

He and Alan were sheltering behind a large white van, parked sideways on to the entrance into the multi-storey; Alan followed the direction of his pointing finger to the front right-hand side of the bay. The van was one of a number of vehicles in the external parking area through which the road that led to the entrance ramp wound its way. It wasn't a large car park, but a line of eight adjacent bays, all occupied, was giving cover to Abhik, Kevlar and Shoeshop, all crouching there in their ballistic vests, pistols at the ready. As per Alan's orders, Brad, also prudently sheltering behind a car, was positioned a few feet beyond the white van with a camcorder, where he could use wide angle to cover both the line of officers behind the cars on one side of the shot and the parking bay on the other, with the stretch of roadway between the two; making sure that, whatever the outcome, there would be a record of the incident.

"More AR up there," said Ben, indicating a small two-storey office block behind them. "If he stands up, they'll have a pretty clear shot at him."

"What kind of rifle is it?"

"Didn't get time to see, but a pretty heavy duty one. Professional hit type. Probably the same one he used up in Scotland. What we don't know is how much ammo he's got. I didn't see him grab anything except the rifle, but I can't be sure. Or maybe he already had some in his pockets."

"So he could have none, some, or lots. That's helpful," said Alan with heavy sarcasm.

Ben was about to speak again, when Alan's phone sounded. He pulled it out of his pocket and put it to his ear.

"McLeish," he said curtly.

"So it *is* you," said a man's voice, which for a moment he didn't recognize. "I thought it would be. It's quite some time since we last spoke, DCI McLeish. Before my trial, that would have been, I think?"

Now Alan knew who he was speaking to. He swiftly put the phone onto loudspeaker, so Ben could hear the conversation.

"I want you to put that rifle down and give yourself up," he said levelly. "We've got Armed Response covering every exit. You can't get away."

"Oh, you people," Lesser sighed elaborately. "You can't overcome the urge to speak in clichés, can you?" Then his voice changed. "How did you find me?"

"Jenny was carrying a tracker," said Alan. "And a hidden camera."

There was a long pause. He could almost hear the implications sinking in.

"Ah…" said Lesser at last. "Then you have a full record of our conversation?"

"Yes." Alan bit down on the urge to add anything further to that one syllable. There was another long pause.

"But you've got her safely away now." It was a statement, not a question. Evidence secured, witness safe.

"Yes."

"Oh, Jenny… That after all this time, it should be you," Lesser mused, as if she could hear him. "You know, it's strange, but – in a way, I'm glad. That she's safe." That could have been meant to patronize, but Alan had the feeling that, if at no other time, in this Lesser was speaking the truth. There was a quality to the tone of his voice that carried conviction. "It's rather ironic, isn't it? I was going to use her as a means to bring Peter down. And instead it's she who's brought me down. She's quite a woman, isn't she? Tell Peter from me, he's a lucky man." Still he was being honest. "I almost envy him. She's—"

But the conversation never got any further. Because it was at that moment that it happened. The thing that took them all by surprise.

To Shoeshop, crouching behind the line of cars, time felt as if it was moving unnaturally slowly. She seemed to have been there for hours, rather than minutes. She wondered when things would start happening. There was no way Lesser could escape, but how long would he drag out what must be his inevitable surrender? It seemed strangely quiet. There was the background hum of traffic from the surrounding streets, and the occasional low mutter of tense conversation between her colleagues; the rustling of leaves as the breeze thrust through the stand of trees in the square behind them. And, had she been able to hear that too, the controlled, quiet breathing of every armed officer as he concentrated on the corner of that first level parking bay, alert for any hint of movement from the man crouching there. But, so far, there was none.

As she shifted her position slightly she became aware of how physically tense she had become, focused on that same small area on which every weapon in the vicinity was trained. As if she'd see anything from down at ground level that the AR boys wouldn't from their vantage points. She deliberately breathed in deeply, and out again, and consciously tried to relax her body, though she remained poised, down on one knee, her other foot ready to take the weight if she suddenly had to stand up.

It occurred to her that Andy might appreciate an update; and she could confirm she'd got Jenny safely home. Still concentrating on the parking bay, Shoeshop pulled out her phone.

"Shoeshop!" The relief in Andy's voice was almost palpable. "What's happening?"

"Nothing at the moment. You got her home all right, did you?"

"Yes," Andy confirmed. "Yes, we're back at Jenny's. We're fine."

"Good. I'll tell the Boss."

"What about you?"

"He's still there, and he can't get away. It's only a matter of time. Looks like we're just going to have to sit it out till he gives in. Don't know how long that's going to take. But you tell Jenny we're going to get him. He's clever, but he's not so clever he can get past this many of us. And Ben says Jenny got him to admit it. So, one way or the other, we've got him, haven't we? Tell Jenny that, from me."

"Right, I'll tell her," Andy said. "We're—"

As Shoeshop listened, she glanced to her left; Alan and Ben were on their feet behind the white van; Alan had his phone out, and was holding it out in front of him as if he had it on loudspeaker, though she couldn't hear what was being said. Ben, though, was staring at the phone with an intense look on his face. She wondered what was going on, who they were listening to. She glanced to her right; Kevlar, and beyond him Abhik, still both watching the space above the wall, motionless.

So because her head was turned that way for those few instants, she was the first one to see the movement.

Her peripheral vision picked it up first; a swift, decisive motion coming into view from the right, from the direction of the trees in the little square behind the entrance to the car park. Her eyes automatically went to it, to identify it, classify it, react to it. And when her brain had done the first two things, she instinctively did the third. Andy, still in mid-sentence, was forgotten.

"*Peter! What are you doing?*" Shoeshop yelled, dropping the phone from her ear.

Kevlar's and Abhik's heads swivelled instantly toward her. Over by

347

the van, Alan and Ben, distracted from the phone, looked over at her for a split second. Beyond them, Brad, too, was staring at her. Then all of them looked where she was looking, saw what she was staring at. And Brad was getting it all on film.

Peter McLeish was striding out into the open space of the approach to the multi-storey. He was wearing a three-quarter length grey coat, that must have kept him drably anonymous until he chose to break cover. His long hair was disordered, the fringe splaying wildly across his forehead and down into his eyes; those dark eyes fixed so unblinkingly on the bay where Lesser had taken refuge, as if nowhere else in the world existed, and no one except the man who was sheltering there.

"Peter!" Now it was Alan who was yelling, but Peter ignored him, ignored everyone. He strode on out until he was in the centre of the roadway to the multi-storey's entrance. Alan started to run towards Peter, though he hadn't a hope of reaching him in time. Ben stared at the implacable figure walking so steadily into danger. Where had he come from? How had he got here? And who the *hell* had let him through the cordon?

A movement up on the first storey caught Ben's attention. Lesser! He'd heard the shouts; alerted to Peter's presence, he was rising up to see for himself. The top of his head was visible, the barrel of his rifle projecting above the wall, held at the ready.

Peter came a halt, planting his right foot out in front of him so that his body was turned sideways on to the man he'd come to confront. His right arm, which had been hidden by the grey coat until now, came sweeping upwards like a radar scan, locking onto its target. In his hand was his Glock, pointed swiftly and remorselessly in Lesser's direction. As calmly as if he'd been on the practice range, he fired, twice.

Lesser's reaction was instant and instinctive. He leapt to his feet, began to bring the rifle up to his shoulder.

It never got there.

Several shots barked out as the AR officers reacted, so almost instantaneously that they sounded like one single explosion. The figure showing above the wall jerked, then seemed to crumple in on itself. The rifle, released from the hands that had gripped it, clattered forward against the brickwork, teetered for a moment on the top of the wall, then fell to the tarmac below with a final, brief death rattle of metal on stone.

After which there was silence. The tall figure stood alone out in the open space, eyes still fixed on the place where his adversary had been, the hand with the pistol in it slowly sinking back down to his side.

There was something about his stillness that held everyone else motionless for long moments. Then the spell was broken. As Alan and others converged on him, bedlam broke out around the solitary figure in the roadway. But Ben – who remained where he was, watching the commotion – could see he was completely untouched by it; was hardly even aware of it. He was still caught in the instant, staring up at where Lesser had been. Alan seized him by the shoulder, pulling him round to make him meet his eyes, but Ben could see the look on Peter's face; even Alan was hardly real to him at that moment.

"You'll catch it for this, mate, big time," he muttered, as if Peter could hear him. Pretty certainly what had just happened would mean the end of Peter's career in the police. It could just as easily have been the end of his life. Briefly, Ben considered the possibility that Peter hadn't cared if that was the way the situation had ended – at least it would have been over... And if he had been killed, Jenny would have been no further use to Lesser. It would have been one way of securing her safety. And that was what Peter had wanted so desperately.

But, as things had worked out, the way it had happened had secured that anyway. Laird would be incandescent, and Peter was without doubt going to be on the end of some pretty heavy disciplinary proceedings, but Lesser could never hurt Jenny, or him, ever again.

As far as Ben was concerned, that was a result.

He regarded the mayhem around Peter for a few more seconds, then walked toward it. He shouldered his way through the group and grasped Peter's upper arm, making eye contact with Alan as he did so. Alan read him, and nodded tightly.

"Get him to my car," he said. "I'll be there as soon as I can." The words were bitten down on; Alan had had a profound fright, and, experienced professional though he was, he was having trouble dealing with it. He thrust his car keys into Ben's hand with an abrupt gesture. "Get him out of here."

"Come on, Peter," Ben said.

Peter looked at him, and nodded silently.

"We'd better have that." Ben gestured at Peter's pistol, still clasped in his right hand. Peter nodded again, and handed it over to him. Ben made sure the safety was on, then indicated to Shoeshop that she should take it.

"Bag it," he said briefly. Shoeshop instinctively frowned in protest, but recognized the inevitability of the instruction. She hastily dug into a pocket, pulled out an evidence bag, separated the lips, and held it out. Ben gently dropped the pistol into it, and turned away.

He ushered Peter to Alan's car, and unlocked it. Peter got into the front passenger seat, moving like a sleepwalker. Ben slid into the driver's seat, and they sat in silence for a while, Ben studying Peter's face. It was white and set, and he was staring ahead with dilated eyes. Ben got the feeling he wasn't seeing anything around him.

"How did you know where we'd gone?" Ben asked softly, at last. "Did you follow us?"

Peter shook his head. "Andy's laptop," he said, his voice so low it was only just audible.

Ben nodded. Of course. Brad had loaded the tracking software on there so he could train Andy to use it; he remembered it being done. It would have been on her desk, easy for Peter to take.

"She's all right, you know," he said. "Jenny... He didn't hurt her. She was scared at the time, but she'll be all right. Andy took her home."

Peter's eyelids trembled slightly, and there was a minuscule movement of his head.

"She'd done it, you know," Ben said after a pause. "He admitted it to her. Mike and Laura. We'd've had him this time. No question."

The muscles round Peter's eyes tightened momentarily, but there was no other reaction.

"Maybe that was why he tried to shoot. Because he was afraid he wouldn't get another chance at you. Not for years, anyway. Maybe never."

No comment.

"I mean, why else would he do it?" Ben went on, not expecting any response now. "He must've known what would happen if he tried it. Maybe he thought it would be worth it, as long as he got you as well."

Silence. Ben gave up vocalizing his thoughts and went on pursuing his line of reasoning in his mind. But he kept coming back to that very first possibility he'd extrapolated from Peter's behaviour, and it was that, in the end, that compelled him to break the silence.

"You didn't deliberately set out to get yourself killed, did you?" he asked, keeping his voice as expressionless as possible.

Peter didn't look at him, but shook his head slightly.

"Didn't think so," Ben commented. He hesitated, slightly uneasy, but he had to know. "Because... Because you wouldn't have done that to Jenny, would you?" *You wouldn't, would you? Not* Jenny...*!*

Peter's lips moved slightly. There was no sound, but they briefly formed the shape of the word 'No'.

Ben nodded, and was about to speak again. But then he saw the tears leaking out of the outer corner of Peter's right eye and trailing down the side of his face, soaking into his beard. Why? Reaction? Relief? Or something else...?

He didn't ask any more questions. They sat side by side, silent, waiting for Alan.

And that, as far as I've been able to piece it together from various sources, is exactly what happened on the day that Matthew Lesser was shot dead.

Chapter 34

I didn't get to put all the pieces together until later, of course.

At the time, all I was concerned about was Peter, whether he was all right. He didn't say much, and I didn't press him. It didn't take long for me to get him down onto the sofa; I sat alongside him, holding his hand, until he fell asleep. Which also didn't take long.

Then I was able to go out into the hall, where my voice would be safely inaudible to him, and phone Alan.

"How's Peter?" was the first thing he asked.

"Asleep, on my sofa," I said. "Don't worry, he's well out of it. It'd probably take an explosion to wake him right now. He said" – I had to take a deep breath before I could say it – "he said Lesser's dead. Is he?" Not that I doubted it; it was an invitation to expand on the bald fact.

"Yes, he's dead." There was no missing the satisfaction in Alan's tone.

"How did it happen?"

"What's he told you?" he countered.

"Nothing more than the bare fact. Perhaps he will when he comes to. But I want you to tell me, Alan – is there anything I need to know, before he does?"

He sighed. "You won't like it…"

"I don't suppose I will," I agreed flatly, and waited.

So he told me, and my guts clenched within me when he told me about Peter walking into the range of that rifle, completely physically unprotected, and loosing off those two shots. He'd got through the cordon very simply and easily, by flashing his warrant card at some poor uniform who'd probably catch a rocket for it, but couldn't really be blamed because he had no idea that DS Peter McLeish wasn't supposed to be allowed anywhere near; so of course he'd updated him on the situation, and let him through. Alan made no bones about it; if the AR officers hadn't reacted as quickly as they had done, it was a certainty that Lesser would have taken Peter down. Peter wouldn't be lying asleep on my sofa; he'd be lying on a mortuary slab. Dead to the world, quite literally.

"What the hell was he was playing at?" Alan demanded, rhetorically and indignantly. "I mean, what was going on inside his head? You'd think he was deliberately trying to get himself killed!" He didn't really mean that;

he was just upset. Even so, my stomach knotted at the mere suggestion, though instinctively I, too, knew that wasn't it. Desperation, not suicide, had been the driver; I was sure of that.

"No, I wouldn't," was all I said. "Because it won't have been that. Look – try not to worry, Alan. It didn't happen. He's here, he's safe. We can sort out the rest later. I'll look after him for you."

He snorted with sour laughter.

"How ironic," he said. "That's what I said to him about you."

"Then you're a man of your word, aren't you? Here we both are." I offered the comfort, glad he couldn't see the lopsidedness of my smile as I said it.

He snorted dismissively, then said, in a different tone, "Are *you* all right, Jenny?" He'd belatedly realized his focus had been purely on Peter. Now he'd remembered me, too. What had happened, what might have happened.

"I will be," I said. "We all will." Then to forestall anything else he might have said, I added, "Look, I'll be seeing you tomorrow, shan't I?"

"You certainly will," he agreed heavily.

"Let's leave it at that for the moment, then, can we? And, Alan – thanks... Thank you. G'night. Give my love to Jane and the kids." I rang off.

After which I went back and found a blanket to drape over Peter. Then I sat down in the armchair, gathering my feet up under me and folding my arms over my chest so that I was perched in the seat like a little ball, staring at Peter's sleeping face for a long, long time by the light of the one small table lamp I'd left on to keep the darkness at bay. Pointlessly upsetting myself with 'what ifs'. And I won't pretend that there weren't tears trickling down my cheeks on occasion, either.

I'd put my phone into silent mode – I didn't want to risk anything breaking in on Peter's sleep – but I only realized I was still clutching it when it made me jump by vibrating in my hand. A text. From Dad. *Is everything all right? Please ring.* I looked sharply at the clock on the mantelpiece; I hadn't realized how late it was. And he hadn't heard from me today, when I'd promised I'd be in touch every day. He'd be worried sick. They both would.

I got quietly out of the chair, found a piece of paper, wrote briefly, then propped it on the coffee table where Peter would be able to see it if he woke. *Gone downstairs to phone Mum and Dad.* Then I went to my back door, opened it, and went down to the hall.

Dad must have positively pounced on his phone when it sounded. "Jenny?" he almost demanded.

"Hello, Dad," I acknowledged. "I'm using the landline. Hope you don't mind."

"Of course not!" He almost sounded angry; he must have been very worried indeed. "You could have just texted, though. I wouldn't have minded. We only wanted to know you were all right. You are, aren't you?"

"Yes. Yes, I'm all right. Everything's all right. Everything's fine..."

"Darling, what is it? What's the matter?" It was my tone he'd heard, not my words.

"Nothing, Dad. It's over, you see. It's over. They've got him. Lesser. He's dead. He can't hurt Peter, ever again. He's dead!" At which point my throat closed up on me and I broke down into tears.

At least he knew they were tears of relief, not distress; I think he came pretty close to tears of relief himself once or twice, as the conversation went on. I know Mum did; I could hear her, after he passed on what I'd told him. Then he put his phone on loudspeaker so they could both hear the whole story. Which I gave them; as much of it as I knew myself at that point. Though I deliberately glossed over the fact that Lesser had got into the flat despite everything, and only told them that he'd forced me into his car. I'd have to tell them the whole story at some point, of course, but they didn't need to know that particular detail, not yet. They had enough to deal with for now, and I knew how difficult they'd find it to cope with the idea that I hadn't been safe in my own home; in their home. So I kept that back, and gave them the bare bones of what had happened afterwards. Enough to relieve them, and reassure them.

"Hey! I hope you aren't listening to this in the bar, or somewhere," I remarked at a tangent. "I wasn't planning on broadcasting it to the whole ship!"

Dad managed a laugh. "Of course not, darling. We're out on deck, looking up at the most glorious moon. Stars in the sky and on the water. It's very beautiful." He sounded as if it would be even more beautiful, now the load of anxiety, the strain of uncertainty, had been lifted off them.

"Then I'll shut up for now and let you enjoy it. I've got Peter asleep on the sofa upstairs, and I don't want to be away too long, in case he wakes up and I'm not there."

"Of course, darling. And you must be tired. Ring again tomorrow, won't you?"

"I will, I promise. But I don't know when it'll be," I added hastily.

"It doesn't matter," my father retorted. "Not now we know you're both safe. It's enough to know that you will." Lesser could no longer hurt Peter, but Dad's first priority was that he could no longer hurt me, either. "Good night, darling. All our love, both of us. And to Peter, too."

"Thanks, Dad. Good night," I said, and put down the receiver. Then I had to stand for a while with eyes closed, taking deep breaths. When I'd regrouped, I went back upstairs. Peter hadn't so much as stirred. I picked up the unread note and laid it face down on the coffee table. Then I resumed my place in the armchair, and went back to watching his sleeping face.

It was pins and needles in my left forearm that woke me. I was still curled up in the armchair, but the weight of my head propped on my hand must have been too much eventually. I blinked at the early morning light coming in through the window, and started to move. Relieved of the pressure on it, blood raced enthusiastically back into my arm, and the sensation abruptly rose to a pitch of discomfort that made me bite down on a gasp.

It woke Peter. I froze in the act of rubbing my throbbing forearm, and watched his face. Slowly, heavily, his eyes opened. Recorded my presence, acknowledged it. We regarded each other in silence for a while before I spoke.

"You," I remarked, "look like hell."

He emitted a muffled snort of something that was supposed to resemble amusement. As carefully as if he was hung over, he propped himself up on one elbow, stayed there for a few moments; then, with a lurch, made it all the way up to a sitting position, thrusting the blanket aside into an untidy heap. He rubbed his eyes with the heels of his palms. Then he let his hands fall into his lap, and sat looking at me.

"It's over," he said at last.

I nodded, slowly.

"I know."

"You've been watching over my sleep again."

"Yes."

"You keep doing that."

"Yes."

There was another silence. Full of all the things we didn't need to say.

"Coffee?" I enquired at last, practically.

He thought about it, and nodded. "Thanks."

I got to my feet and went out to the kitchen. As the kettle boiled, I heard the bathroom door close and, shortly afterwards, open again. By the time I returned with the coffee he was back on the sofa, but, with washed face and tidied hair, looking considerably better. I told him so as I handed him his mug.

"Do you want any breakfast?" I asked. He shook his head.

"Is there anything else you want me to do?" I persisted. "Anything you want to do?"

He looked bleak.

"I'll have to go in," he said. "There'll be debriefing, paperwork, all the usual stuff. Probably an inquiry, because it was a fatal shooting. Always is. But that'll be later on. Not yet. Nothing to worry about."

"Nothing?" I enquired. "Apart from them throwing the book at you, presumably?"

He looked at me quickly.

"Alan told me what you did," I said levelly.

He returned my regard impassively, and his tone of voice matched mine. "Do I look as if I care? Do you?"

"We're both here, we're both alive," I shrugged. "Whatever they decide to do won't change that." There were a lot of other things I could have said – about what he'd done, what I'd felt, what I'd thought – but none of them would achieve anything useful now, so I let them lie.

"They can do what they like," he agreed. "Won't make any difference to me." He met my eye, and seemed satisfied with what he saw there. "I'd better go, but – see you later?"

"Don't be stupid," I remarked, with scornful tolerance. His mouth twisted in a half-smile.

"Right."

He studied me in silence for some moments after that. "Are you all right?" he asked eventually.

I shrugged with deliberate carelessness. "If you don't count this," I said, and showed him the heels of my palms, still raw from their contact with the concrete of the ramp. He looked at them with distress; not because they were serious in themselves, but because of what they represented.

"Don't, Peter," I said, leaning forward. "I spent half the night on might-have-beens myself, and all it did was upset me to no purpose. Yes, either of us could have been killed, but neither of us was. The point is, we're still here, still alive. And he can't touch us ever again."

"You've been through a lot in the last few weeks," he said sombrely. "You might think you'll get over it easily, now he's out of the way. But you won't. I *know*."

"Easily?" I snorted derision at the concept. "Tell that to the poor council worker who's had to clear up my sick from the car park! I threw up on the way out, you know. Didn't Ben tell you? So don't think I don't know there won't be some after-effects! But the point is, Peter, they'll *pass*. We'll get over them. And especially now you won't be scaring me half to death anymore."

"What d'you mean?" he asked quickly, though I think he knew very well.

"Well, you took a hell of a gamble, you know," I pointed out, trying to make it clear I was only commenting, not criticizing.

He looked at me, and his face was unreadable. Then he said, "Worked, didn't it? And, anyway, you can talk!"

"Meaning?"

"Meaning you did exactly the same, didn't you? Put yourself at risk for my sake. '*Greater love hath no man*,'" he quoted softly.

And when it came down to it, there was only one part of what he'd said that I could argue with.

"I'm not a man," I pointed out.

"No – no, you're not," he agreed, and now, despite everything, there was a catch of laughter in his voice. "Definitely not. I can absolutely vouch for that. Hundred per cent."

We met each other's eyes, and were content. But there was something else I needed to tell him.

"Peter…"

He looked at me, alerted by the carefulness of my tone. "What?"

I hesitated.

"I'm so glad it wasn't you that shot him. For your sake."

His eyes were locked on mine.

"So'm I," he said. "For yours."

I stared at him. *Was that why you did what you did? Because you were thinking about me?*

There was a pause. Then he said, in a quite different tone, "You'll have to go in sometime, too. They'll be wanting you for a statement."

"I suppose they will," I agreed, slowly. Then I began to smile at him. "You were wrong, you know."

He frowned. "About what?"

"About it being over."

The tone I was using must have told him there was no real cause for concern in my words, but even so his voice rose slightly as he demanded, "What d'you mean?"

"I mean," I said, smiling even more broadly, "the demands of British bureaucracy. It won't be over until the paperwork's done!"

He stared at me for a moment. Then he began to laugh. He reached out and clutched me, and, inevitably, within seconds I was laughing, too. Like him, so hard it brought tears to my eyes. In the end, I wasn't sure which we were really doing – laughing or crying. I wasn't sure that it mattered, either.

They did want me in, of course. Alan rang up not long after Peter had left, and asked me to come.

"Of course," I said. "That is, I was about to go in to work. I'm going to be late as it is. Should I call in and tell them I'll be even later? They're beginning to work out something's going on, you know. I'm getting a lot of funny looks and snide remarks."

"No, I don't want to cause you problems. Come in this afternoon, as soon as you can."

"Can I tell them anything? I'd like to tell Elizabeth, at least. She ought to know; she's my line manager, after all."

Alan considered. "Okay," he said at last, "but don't give her anything more than the broad outline for now."

"I won't," I promised. "Thanks! Much more of this and I was worried I was going to find myself out of a job!" I hesitated, then plunged on, "Is that what's going to happen to Peter, do you think?"

He was silent for a few seconds. "Maybe," he conceded heavily. "It's a possibility. He was specifically ordered to stay clear, you know."

"Yes. He told me."

"The Laird just about went ballistic when he heard." That verbal slip – he'd never normally refer to his senior officer as that to me – told me how disturbed he was. "He's called me and Peter in for this afternoon. I'm not looking forward to it, Jenny." His personal anxiety for Peter was clear to be heard.

"Try not to worry about it. I don't think you'll find Peter'll care all that much, whatever happens." Small comfort, perhaps, but the best I could offer him. And it had the merit of being the truth.

He sighed. "You're probably right," he admitted. "But I'm still not looking forward to it." Then his voice changed. "Jenny, one thing I want to know. That text I got. Was that Lesser? Or was it you?"

I blew out a gust of breath to try to relieve the immediate tension the recollection of that episode had created.

"It was me," I admitted. Then I realized why he might be asking. Had he recognized that message for what it was? "Why? Did you—?"

"Peter told me you never used text-speak," Alan explained succinctly.

"He" – Lesser, not Peter, of course – "told me to reply. I assume the fact it came so soon after you tried to call me made him realize he had to try to put you off the track, because I can't think why he wouldn't have just ignored it, otherwise. It was a bit message-in-a-bottle, I know, but I couldn't think what else to do. I suppose I was hoping you'd show it to Peter. Not that there was any reason why you should. But if you did – well, I knew he'd know. Or I hoped he would, anyway. But it was such a long shot, I…" I let the sentence trail off, and shuddered despite myself. "Anyway, he" – that other 'he', again – "he made me show it to him before I sent it, but of course he didn't know. So he thought it was all right, that it'd make you think I was all right."

After which Alan started to say nice things about me having my head screwed on, so I shut him up.

It was the first time for weeks I'd driven myself into work, alone; in a way, it felt quite strange. But no need for a bodyguard, not anymore. Fortunately the traffic was fairly good and in the end I was only a couple of minutes late. And I was able to speak to Elizabeth almost immediately. She was startled, then shocked, and immediately told me to take the rest of the day off. Her concern and offers of support were genuine and appreciated, and I told her so.

"Will you explain to everyone else?" I asked apologetically. "It's been getting a bit awkward, sometimes. But I couldn't really say anything before. I was told not to, you see. If you tell them something along the lines of me having trouble with a stalker? Though it's a bit more complicated than that, but – that might help?"

"Of course I will," she promised warmly, then looked at me more intently as a thought struck her. "That business with Moira – was that something to do with this?"

I nodded, heavily. "I'm afraid so. I wish she hadn't had to get hurt, the way she did. It wasn't her fault; she just got used, that's all. I hope she gets over it soon. She hardly speaks to me now, if she doesn't have to."

"She doesn't blame you, does she?" Elizabeth asked, looking a bit shocked.

"I don't think so. But I can't help being a constant reminder, I suppose. Things've been a bit strained."

"She'll be all right," Elizabeth said consolingly. "Let's face it, it seems pretty much of a calamity to her at the moment, but it won't last; she's not the type. She'll bounce back, no problem. Once you can tell her the full story, I bet she'll start seeing it in a very different light. You know what she's like – you'd have to go quite a way before you'd find somebody better at turning a drama into a crisis than Moira! Or, in this case, a crisis into a drama…"

I felt a sense of relief; Elizabeth is a canny reader of people, and I realized that that insight would turn out to be true. I hoped so, for Moira's sake as well as for my own, and I said so.

"Look, don't worry about it. Off you go for now, and we'll see you tomorrow," Elizabeth said, cheerfully brisk. "Sorry I can't give you a bit more time, but I'd better not push my luck. Or yours! Go on, now, go away!"

I rang Ben as I made my way back to my car.

"Jenny! How are you?" he asked immediately.

"For the purposes of this conversation, let's say I'm fine, shall we?" Which might or might not have been true, but I certainly intended to behave as if it was. "Alan told me I could let them know at work – up to a point, anyway – and I've been told to take the rest of the day off. I was coming in this afternoon anyway, but will it throw you completely if I come in now, instead?"

I took his snort of derision to be an emphatic indication that it most certainly would not, and laughed.

"Okay, be there shortly," I told him, and rang off.

And that was when I got to see the film Brad had taken. Ben showed it to me, after I'd given my statement; he told me of its existence, and I asked him if I could see it. He looked at me for a few moments, then nodded. But though he didn't comment on his reasons, I noticed that he didn't take me into the office to see it, but instead brought a laptop down to the interview room, so it was just the two of us. From which I concluded I'd better not tell too many other people I'd seen it.

It didn't take long to find and watch the bit that mattered. We watched the playback together; when I asked him to rerun some parts of it, and to zoom in to confirm particular details, he did so without comment. When I asked him questions, he answered them all factually and impartially. When we were done, he knew what I knew, and he'd seen what I'd seen. Alan's seen the film, too, of course, and so has Robert Laird; and they're too observant and intelligent not to have come to the same conclusion Ben and I have. I'm sure of that, even though none of us has, as far as I know, ever articulated our thoughts aloud – not in my presence, at least – and I don't suppose we ever will. If no one puts them into words, no one will have to confirm or deny. Or try to prove the truth of them.

"*This has got to stop,*" Peter had said. "*Find a way to stop him. Or I will.*" Had he done just that?

Because what the film shows, to anyone who looks really closely, is that when Peter strides into shot, then halts and takes up his stance, the direction of his eyes and the direction of the pistol don't match. His eyes never leave Lesser's face for an instant. But the pistol is not aiming at Lesser. Extrapolation of the line of his arm and hand show the pistol is aligned above Lesser's head. Indeed, the two bullets Peter fired were both found to have hit the storey above, close to the bottom edge of the brickwork and within a couple of inches of each other. And a man as good with a firearm as Ben confirmed Peter to be, and with his years of experience in pressure situations, isn't panicked into aiming at the wrong place. When you watch the film, you see that the arm that brings the pistol up moves swiftly, but with deliberation, and the hand is steady as a rock. Peter hit exactly what he was aiming at.

But then, it really hadn't mattered whether that pistol was aimed at Lesser or not.

Because Peter must have known from the very beginning that in the circumstances – trapped, armed, desperate – if Lesser caught sight of him, he was likely, whether instinctively or because he knew he might never get a better chance, and even without the goading of a pistol raised in his direction, to take a shot at him. And once Lesser had raised his gun, with all those Armed Response officers training their rifles on him, there was only ever going to be one outcome.

And Peter had known it. He must have. He'd known exactly what would happen, if he did what he did.

It wasn't Peter who shot him, no.

But, for all that, it was Peter who killed him.

I've never asked Peter if that's true, and I never shall. After all, what would it achieve? And after some pretty brutal self-examination – I still find this an extraordinary thing to discover about myself, though I've decided I am being as honest about it as it's possible for me to be, but – the fact is, it doesn't change anything for me; doesn't change the way I feel about him, or the kind of man I perceive him to be.

Human beings, of course, have a capacity for rationalization and self-deception that sometimes borders on the phenomenal, and I'm no different from anyone else. Yet I find I can still only see Peter as a man who was finally driven not just to the limit by desperation, but beyond – well beyond – to do what he did.

And if I'm right? Whose fault? Whose fault does that make it?

Peter's, for not being strong enough after the murder of his wife and child and more than a decade of ceaseless persecution, and faced with the further persecution and violent loss of someone else he cared about?

Robert Laird's, for that operational decision of which he could never have foreseen the consequences, or for subsequently keeping Peter deliberately in the line of fire, where he could be used as an ongoing lure for Lesser?

Mine, for not withdrawing from Peter, not backing off once I understood the potential consequences – for *him* – of being in a relationship with him, but insisting on seeing it through together, despite the obvious risks to both of us?

Society as a whole, for a code of law that had repeatedly shown itself impotent in dealing with Lesser, unable to prevent him doing what he did both to Peter and to others, and thus repeatedly failing Peter to the point where he felt compelled to step outside that code and take action himself?

Or did it all come back to Lesser himself, for initiating, persisting in, and at the end intensifying a campaign of relentless retribution over what essentially came down to an episode of injured pride? Was he, in the final analysis, responsible for his own death?

You answer. I can't.

Chapter 35

When I got home I called Dad again, as I'd promised, and we talked for some time. I also took calls from Jane and from Craig. Jane was concerned and relieved, and urgent with offers of hospitality; Craig was merely jubilant.

"I knew they'd get him!" he crowed, unable to subdue his triumph. "Didn't I tell you so?"

"You did," I agreed, grinning like a madwoman; his excitement was infectious. "You were quite right, and you have my full permission to say so."

"Croydon, here we come!" he whooped. Of course, he wasn't just relieved for Peter, and for me. Lesser's shadow no longer fell over him or Sophie, either, and he was revelling in it. His parents, his sister, he himself; Peter wasn't the only one who'd been released, and Craig knew it.

After he rang off, I looked out of the window. It was a glorious afternoon; the sunlight was pouring down out of a cloudless sky, and I wondered if it was as blue up there as it was where Dad and Mum were. Being in the Mediterranean, they probably shaded it. But the garden suddenly looked irresistible. And I could go outside and sit in it, alone, without fear. My feet hardly touched the steps as I went down them.

I sat on the bench in my usual place, drew my feet up, and clasped my shins, my chin resting on my knees. I was drinking in not just the warmth but the sense of release Craig had awakened in me. I had so much to think about, my head was buzzing with all of it. Mostly about Peter. I wondered what he'd do now. Go on with the sailing lessons, I hoped. Maybe even think about buying himself a yacht, a small one. Even if it was an old one. Doing it up, renovating it, equipping it, sailing in it, would give him something positive to focus on. I wanted those things for him, wanted them fiercely, because I so much wanted him to be happy after all the misery. And whatever else he chose to do, I hoped he'd at least remember my offer of the cottage. If there was anything more I wanted for him now, it was for him to have a haven, a replacement for that horrible, soulless little flat and all that its emotional paucity represented. Even now, I couldn't regret what had happened, if only that could be an outcome.

And me? Us? *Was* there really an 'us'? I so desperately wanted to be with him – wanted *him* – but was it too soon? It couldn't possibly be too soon as far as I was concerned, for myself, but I'd been brought to realize that it might not be the same for Peter, because of something Dad had said to me earlier. I hadn't fully taken in the implications at the time, but now I found myself replaying that part of our conversation in my mind.

"Don't try to rush anything, will you, darling?" he'd said. "You'll need to be careful. And patient."

"What do you mean?" I'd asked, puzzled.

"Because you're feeling euphoric at the moment. Of course you are! But you haven't been living in this situation as long as Peter has. That was his life for the best part of thirteen years. His *life*, Jenny. He was used to it being that way. Now it's all changed. Very suddenly. And even though it's a change for the better, it might still take some getting used to. If you put an animal in a cage it will always be trying to get out. But if it's been caged for long enough, even if you do set it free, it'll sometimes go back into the cage of its own accord. Because that's what it's become used to, that's what it knows. And change can be frightening at first, even good change. So just be careful, Jenny. Peter's whole life is going to be different from now on, and he might – might! – need time to adjust. I know you'll be anxious to do everything you can to make him happy, but you need to let him set the pace. Do you see, darling?"

"I suppose so, yes… Yes. Oh, Dad – what would I do without you?"

"Adjust, of course," he'd said, as if slightly surprised I should need to ask, before adding dryly, "Though I must confess to a rather fervent hope that you won't have to for a good while yet…"

"You and me both," I'd assured him.

I knew he was right. I'd been patient until now, for Peter's sake; for his sake, I might need to go on being patient. Though the way I felt now, so ambitious for whatever might ensure his future happiness, that might be harder for me than I realized. Only time would tell if that was what he needed from me, or whether he'd already made up his mind what he was going to do.

In point of fact, he had. And other people were in the course of discovering it, at that very moment.

Robert Laird leaned forward, his fingers steepled in front of him, and subjected Detective Sergeant Peter McLeish, seated on the other side of the desk alongside his cousin and superior officer, to a particularly basilisk stare. It was a tool he had generally found to be useful in disconcerting the person on the other end of it, but not this time, it seemed. Peter met his eyes steadily, with no change of expression.

"What, exactly," Laird enquired acidly, "did you intend to achieve with the histrionics you displayed yesterday?"

Peter didn't answer, just continued to regard him, unmoving. Laird emitted a short sound of frustration. He threw himself back into his chair and regarded his recalcitrant junior with icy blue eyes.

"You're not helping yourself, DS McLeish," he said crisply, the use of rank and surname emphasizing the official nature of the interview. "You're shortly going to be the subject of disciplinary proceedings; the consequences could be very severe indeed. You disobeyed a direct order from your superior." Alan shifted slightly before relapsing into stillness. "As a result of that disobedience, a suspect we needed to arrest and question as a key witness was instead shot dead. That's not only a setback to our ongoing investigations. It's also going to need a lot of hard work to regain the ground we will have lost as a result. For all those reasons I need you to account for your actions, to give me a comprehensive explanation of why that is the situation we now find ourselves in. So I'm waiting." He raised one eyebrow meaningfully.

There was a short silence. Alan, seated at a slight angle on Peter's side of the desk, didn't have to turn his head much in order to see his cousin's profile, but being able to do so didn't help him glean any useful information. Peter's face was almost completely expressionless. Alan wondered if Laird's tone, his description of what was going to happen, had touched Peter at all. The large, dark eyes had never wavered from Laird's face; there had been no flicker of reaction to anything that had been said.

It was dawning on Robert Laird that he wasn't going to get the explanation he was calling for.

"Have you *nothing* to say?" he demanded, almost incredulously.

Peter shook his head, very slightly. "No, sir," he said, quietly and respectfully, but definitely. "I have nothing to say. Except what I've said in this." His brown eyes held Laird's blue ones as he put a hand into the inside breast pocket of his jacket. From it he extracted a sealed white envelope and leaned forward to place it on the desk in front of Laird, positioning it with almost mathematical exactitude within inches of Laird's fingertips. Alan gave it no more than a glance before returning his gaze to his cousin's face. No need to guess the contents.

"Effective immediately, if you will, sir," Peter said calmly.

Laird stared down at the white rectangle of paper, then raised his eyes to Peter's face. "This won't make any difference," he said. "The disciplinary will still go ahead."

"That's up to you, sir." Peter's face didn't change. "But I agree. It won't make any difference. I'll still have nothing to say. So it's up to you. You can spend the time, the money, the manpower. If you want. Or you can accept that" – he nodded at the envelope, but his eyes never left those of the man

363

opposite him – "and let me go. You can say I had a breakdown. That I'm being discharged on medical grounds. You can say what you like. You can do what you like. I don't care. Either way, I *am* leaving. And I don't care if it's in disgrace, or not." The tone of his voice never changed, the precision with which he was pronouncing his words for emphasis, but now his eyes had hardened. "I've lived through thirteen years of hell. For the sake of the job you needed me to do. I put up with that. My family have had to put up with it, too. Sophie, and Craig. That was bad enough. But once it touched Jenny, that was it. You wanted me to cross a line that I should never have been asked to cross. And nor should she. You wanted Lesser. You wanted him out of operation. Well, now he is. So I'm asking you, sir" – his voice had become very soft, very quiet – "to accept my resignation, and accept it now. I think you owe it to me. Don't you?" His eyes remained fixed on Laird's. "*Sir.*"

There was a prolonged silence after that final syllable, delivered with such deadly respect. Alan looked from one implacable face to the other. Irresistible force, immovable object. He leaned forward; he had a question of his own. And it might be a tiebreaker.

"Sir." He was careful to keep any interpretable intonation out of his voice. "Is it Lesser being out of the way that you're angry about? Or is it only because of the way it happened?"

The blue eyes flashed once in his direction, then back to Peter. Laird didn't speak, but the subtle shift in the muscles of his face was there to be seen. Alan sat back again, his question answered.

Then Laird's eyelashes flickered briefly. Slowly, he picked up the envelope, holding the edges in his two hands, and he nodded, just the once, without speaking.

"Thank you, sir," said Peter calmly. He stood up, pushed his chair back, and walked toward the door.

Alan threw an anxious glance at Laird, and saw the slight sideways gesture of the head telling him to follow his cousin. He acknowledged it with an equally slight nod of thanks, and did so.

Peter's fingers were on the handle of the door when Laird spoke again.

"Peter…" Still the voice of a superior officer whose will has been opposed, but, despite that, there was a detectable shift in tone. Both men turned back to look at him.

"I have my own opinion of what's been done. I am aware of at least some, if not all, of the reasons. And whatever else may or may not happen as a result, I want you to know this. You have still been one of the best officers I have ever had under my command, in spite of the circumstances in which you found yourself. And I agree with Matthew Lesser. You *are* a lucky man. She was – she is – worth fighting for. Whatever my official views are, I think it's entirely possible that had I been in your place, I might have done the same."

Peter's eyes flickered at the admission, and the expression on his face relaxed. Then he nodded, opened the door, and left. Alan, however, paused.

"Sir…" he began.

Laird fixed him with a forbidding look.

"I hope you're not about to thank me, DCI McLeish," he said severely.

"No, sir," said Alan, and left it at that; they'd understood each other. He, too, went out; the door closed behind him.

Robert Laird let the envelope drop on the desk again, and went back to staring at it. But now, now that there was no-one there to see it, there was a gleam of quiet satisfaction in the hooded blue eyes. Triumph, even.

The corridor outside Laird's office was punctuated with large, deep-silled windows. Alan found Peter standing at one of them, his hands spread wide to take his weight as he leaned forward, his head bowed below the level of his shoulders. He straightened up as Alan came and stood beside him, but otherwise didn't move. For a few moments they both stared out of the window. It wasn't much of a view; three other blocks similar to the one they stood in, all enclosing a small paved square, with a shabby-looking bench in it that probably nobody ever sat on. Not inspiring. But then, they weren't really looking at it in any case.

Peter was the first to speak.

"I suppose you're angry with me," he said levelly.

Alan shook his head, still staring out through the window.

"No," he said. "Not about this; not about the rest of it."

"You gave a pretty good impression of it, at the time," Peter commented dryly.

"You'd just given me the biggest scare of my life," Alan pointed out, reasonably. "I thought you were going to get yourself killed. How did you expect me to react?"

"Yeh," Peter acknowledged. It was, after all, a fair point.

Silence.

"What are you going to do now?" Alan asked, at last.

"Start living again," Peter said.

Further silence.

"Maybe hire a small yacht," Peter said after a while. "Take her sailing somewhere. Caledonian Canal, maybe. The Great Glen."

"What about a job?" Alan asked carefully. "Will you be staying in London?"

"Don't know. Doubt it. Don't know what I'm going to do, yet. Don't really care, at the moment." He shrugged. "I'll find something."

"Where are you going to live, then? If you're not staying in London?"

"Hampshire, probably. Jenny owns a cottage there. She rents it out. She said I could live there if I wanted."

Alan cocked an eyebrow at him. "On your own?"

Peter allowed a faint smile to touch his lips.

"Hope not," he said.

There was another pause.

"Should I start practising my best man's speech?" Alan enquired.

"I'll find out," said Peter. He turned and walked away, along the corridor, toward the exit. He had reached the double swing doors when Alan spoke again.

"Peter…"

Peter stopped, his hand flat against a fingerplate, and looked back at him.

"Give her my love, as well as yours," said Alan.

Their eyes locked for a moment. Then Peter smiled, and it was as if the sun had come out from behind a cloud. Like looking at a different man.

A moment later, the door was swinging closed behind him.

It was about half past five when my phone sounded. It was Peter.

"Hi," he said. "Just leaving. Do you need me to stop off and get you anything on the way?"

"Oh! Er… Yes, actually. I could do with some more milk. And a dozen eggs. But I think that's all. Is that all right?"

"Yeh, no problem. Be home soon, okay?"

And he rang off. It was only after he'd gone that what he'd said percolated into my consciousness.

He was coming here, to me, and he'd called it *home*.

I was sitting on the window seat when he arrived, gazing out at the garden. I had the window open because it was such a beautiful, warm evening. Here at the back of the house, the sound of the engine carried so quietly that I wasn't sure I'd really heard it. But then I heard the front door open and close. The hall carpet muffled his footsteps until suddenly he was there, standing in the doorway, two carrier bags in one hand as he put the keys into his jacket pocket with the other.

"I'll just put this stuff in the kitchen, okay?" he said, disdaining any more formal greeting.

"Mm. Thanks," I said.

He came on into the sitting room, went past me into the kitchen. I heard the rustle of the carrier bags as he unpacked them, the fridge door open and close, a cupboard door likewise. I swivelled on the window seat and waited for him to come back. When he did, he took off his jacket and cast it over the back of the sofa. Then he turned round, and we looked at each other.

"I resigned," he said, at last. I nodded, unsurprised.

"Did he put up a fight about it?" I asked calmly. Because if he had, Laird had lost, I could tell that much. The look of satisfaction in Peter's eyes was unmissable.

He shrugged.

"And he's going to let you? Not fire you?"

He shrugged again. "He owed me that much. And he knew it."

"I'm glad," I said softly. He came over and sat beside me, turning his body so that he could lean his elbows on the sill, rest his chin on his hands, looking out. I turned likewise, folding my arms and leaning my weight on them, and studied him. It was like looking at a different man. His body language was completely changed; he was relaxed, calm, completely at ease. It gave me an intense sensation of pleasure just to look at him and see him like that.

We sat quietly for quite some time. There was so much to be said, but now that it could be said, we were in no hurry; it could wait. We knew, both of us, the enormity of it. It was better to keep to the mundane and the domestic for now. And in the meantime we could sit together in the warm evening air, an evening that thought it was still summer and not September, and communicate in other, silent ways.

Eventually Peter shifted slightly, turned his head on his hands to look sideways at me.

"Okay if I have a bath? I could do with one."

I had the feeling that was nothing to do with physical cleanliness, more to do with the symbolism of the act. I smiled.

"Of course you can. That's why I gave you that key in the first place, remember?"

He smiled back. The difference in that smile! The same difference as in the relaxation of his body. I felt a flutter of sensation in the pit of my stomach.

"I won't be long," he promised, as if he needed to.

"Take as long as you like," I said. "You've earned it."

I waited until I heard the water running, and him go upstairs to get some clean clothes to change into afterwards. Then I went into the kitchen, reached into one of the cupboards; my fingers closed around the neck of the bottle I was after. Then I sought out one of my whisky tumblers. Carefully, I poured a three-finger measure into it. As I did so, I heard Peter coming back down the stairs.

He was reaching for the bathroom door when I caught up with him. "Peter…"

He turned, and I held the glass out to him.

"I thought you might like this, while you're soaking," I said.

Slowly he reached out and took it, and while he didn't exactly smile, there was a sort of luminous pleasure on his face that would do very well as a substitute.

"Thanks," was all he said. But not all he meant.

"See you when you're ready," I said, and left him standing by the door.

I was curled up on the window seat again when he returned. He was wearing blue jeans and a white shirt, the sleeves rolled half-way up his forearms, the neck open. His hair was damp at the ends with condensation; his skin was still flushed from the warmth of the bathwater. I wondered if he could tell the effect the sight of him was having on me.

"Are you hungry?" I said almost at random, picking the first thing that came into my head to say.

He shook his head. "Not yet." A pause. "Got a message for you."

"A message? From whom?" I prompted, slightly mystified.

"Ben said to tell you he sent his love."

I shook my head in mock incredulity, my face alight with mischievous laughter. "Doesn't it strike you as funny, the way the investigating officers in this case have veered so much from the professional to the personal? Or does he do that to every woman he comes across during an investigation?"

Peter pretended to consider his answer, screwing up his face slightly as if concentrating. "Well, I've known him for over fifteen years now, and I can honestly tell you, absolutely not."

"Then I'm honoured," I said, with a dip of my head to acknowledge it.

"I think you should be. Mind you, he wasn't the only one. Do you want to know what Alan said?"

"What?"

"He said, '*Give her my love, as well as yours.*'"

I wasn't ready to field that one. "*Let him set the pace,*" Dad had said. He was doing that, all right. Talk about being on the rebound. From all that had happened before, to this.

I stood up. I didn't know why, but I had an overpowering feeling that I should be on my feet to hear what he was going to say. Immediately he came toward me. I had such a sense of something momentous about to happen that I almost felt the air quivering with the imminence of it.

He came to me, reached out toward me, and took both my hands in his.

I didn't know what to do. It wasn't as if he'd never touched me before. But this felt different. This *was* different. These were no longer the hands of a man afraid to care about somebody else because doing so put them in danger. These were the hands of a lover. Clasping my fingers, caressing my wrists.

"I love you, Jenny," he said.

My heart lurched in my chest. After all these months, he finally felt free to say it. Lesser was dead, could never touch either of us again. It was over. Peter was free. *We* were free.

And he loved me. He was finally telling me he loved me. Because now, at last, he could.

"Seems fair," I said; how incredibly strange that my instinctive response should be a slight shrug, as if what he'd said was only to be expected. "I love you, after all." *Obviously. Of course. Did you not know?*

He moved closer, taking me into his arms. A thrill coursed through my entire body at his touch.

"I love you," he said again, his eyes searching my face. Now his tone was different; this was a vow he was making. I ducked my head, failing to cope with the intensity of the moment, but he put his fingers under my chin and gently raised it again. I met his eyes, my nerves taut with emotion, vibrating like harp wires.

"When did you know?" Woman-like, I wanted to fix my reference points.

"The flight down from Inverness. That moment at Gatwick when I walked away from you. Since then."

"What took you so long?" I demanded. "You had me the very first time you smiled at me! All done up in bloody bandages – remember?"

"Not since you took all my clothes off when I wasn't looking, then?" he teased. He was having some trouble keeping his voice steady, but then, so was I. Under the banter, his emotions were rising; he'd suppressed them so long, their turbulence was probably all the greater now he felt free to release them. I couldn't criticize; I was in no better case.

I laughed, feeling strangely shy, and shook my head.

He lifted one hand, and cupped it round my cheek and neck, the thumb caressing my earlobe. Then he bent his head down toward me. I closed my eyes. His lips brushed mine, lightly, and withdrew. Then they returned briefly, with more pressure. He took my lower lip between them and tugged at it gently, delicately. The sensations he was generating were making me tremble uncontrollably; he must have been able to feel it.

He pulled me closer and kissed me again, and kept kissing me for what felt like an eternity of elation. When he stopped, it was to cradle my face into his shoulder, and hold me tightly; then I could feel that he was shaking just as much as I was, and for the same reason. We stood in each other's arms, without speaking, for some time.

"We should go away," he said at last, breaking the silence. "Go somewhere. Unwind, now it's all over."

There was another silence, a brief one.

"Together," I said, eventually. It was a statement, not a question. His arms tightened around me momentarily.

"Of course together. You've watched over my sleep so many times already," he said, talking into my hair. "I want you to go on doing it. So the first thing I see, every morning, is gonnae be you." A pause. When he spoke again, his voice, like the rest of him, had begun to tremble again, ever so slightly, but detectably. "And I know you're gonnae tell me there's a problem with that." As ever, when his feelings were intense, his Scots accent had become very marked.

"The '*not sleeping with anyone I'm not married to*' problem?" I suggested, trying to ignore the sudden surge of adrenalin throughout my body.

"That's the one," he agreed. "But there's a pretty obvious solution, of course."

And I suddenly realized what was making him tremble.

Laughter. He was trembling with laughter.

"So I'm gonnae need your cooperation with that bit," he went on. "You know what I'm asking, don't you?"

I pulled my head back and met his eyes, full on; they were luminous with a combination of earnestness, excitement, and hope.

"Does this come under the heading of helping the police with their enquiries?" I enquired brightly, fighting down my own urge to laugh – to laugh out of sheer, pure joy.

"Oh, yes," he assured me. "And, believe me, said police will be making further extensive and *very* thorough investigations of the witness..." His arms tightened around me, and he bent to kiss me again, then locked those huge dark eyes on mine.

"So – about that cooperation... Will you?"

"You know I will," I said.

On a day almost one month later, he took me to be his wife. That night, in our bed, he took me as his wife. With love, with tenderness, and with a heart-touching hesitancy that betrayed more clearly than anything else how hard it still was for him to believe that he was finally free to love me without fear of consequences.

Afterwards, as we lay body to body, arms around each other, I felt him begin to shake; then he began to cry. I knew why, as I held him close, and he clung to me. It wasn't happiness – not just happiness, anyway. It was relief. He was feeling the lifting of the pressure he'd been under for so many years. No longer hunted, pursued, alone. And because that was true, I wept, too – with happiness for him. And not a little, of course, for myself.

And that was the first day of the rest of our lives, as they say. It won't be entirely straightforward, of course. What relationship is? Happily ever after is neither simple nor effortless; it takes commitment and hard work. You certainly can't go through what he – what we – went through and expect the effects to vanish overnight. We're still living with them, even now.

Because, in a way, Dad was right. In some things, Peter still goes back into his cage of his own accord, even though he isn't always conscious of doing it; but living with Lesser's persecution for so long trained him into certain behaviour patterns that he hasn't overcome, not yet. When we drive somewhere, for instance; when he gets out of the car, he still scans the area around him, as if expecting to find that we've been followed by someone. I'm fairly sure he doesn't even know he's doing it, but he had to for so long that now it's become instinctive, even though it's no longer necessary. Maybe eventually it'll seep into his subconscious that he no longer needs to do it, but perhaps it's still too soon to expect anything different. And sometimes he still screams in his sleep, and I wake him and hold him until he calms down and sinks back into merciful oblivion. But not as often now as he did at first.

The past will always be there, for both of us; of course it will. But hopefully the shadows it casts will get shorter, become more tenuous, as time passes. Leaving me free to go on doing everything in my power to make him happy. Because that's what will make me happy.

No longer on the periphery of his life, but at its heart.

His life. Reclaimed.

The life of Peter McLeish.

Lightning Source UK Ltd.
Milton Keynes UK
UKOW04f2001220115

244929UK00001B/9/P